BOOKS WE LOVE BEST

A Unique Guide to Children's Books

by

San Francisco Bay Area Kids

Foreword by
Marilyn Sachs

A project of the
SAN FRANCISCO BAY AREA BOOK COUNCIL
in cooperation with
Foghorn Press, San Francisco

❤

Dedicated to all the puzzled grandparents, clueless aunts and uncles and frazzled parents, who never know what book to choose for their favorite kids. We hope this helps! —The Junior Publishers

❤

Proceeds from **Books We Love Best** go to the San Francisco Bay Area Book Council Reading Fund, which provides grant monies for literacy programs in the San Francisco Bay Area. Inquiries about the Reading Fund or Book Festival may be addressed to:
THE SAN FRANCISCO BAY AREA BOOK COUNCIL

ISBN 0–935701–01–X
Published in the offices and with the cooperation of
Foghorn Press, San Francisco
Printed by Griffin Printing, California

BOOKS WE LOVE BEST

A Unique Guide to Children's Books

"What an absolute delight! Here's a book that tells it like it is: what kids of all ages read and why. I found the reviews unabashedly honest and oftentimes refreshing in insight—as in the six-year-old reviewer's remarks that a story about a troublesome, tiny ant reminded her of her own year-old baby sister. These junior reviewers give high marks and the lowdown on books that inspire them, make them laugh, make them scared, or give them the answers to troubling questions. As a fiction writer (and a children's book writer), I found **Books We Love Best** to be a real eye opener on what appeals to young readers."

-Amy Tan

"**Books We Love Best** is a marvelous collection of reviews by the readers who really count. Because it was also produced entirely by young people, its publication is truly cause for celebration."

-Yoshiko Uchida

"Here, in this small collection, you will find book reviewers with heart and a page-turning enthusiasum for stories they enjoy. Most writers should be so lucky as to have such astute readers."

-Gary Soto

Foreword

by Marilyn Sachs

This remarkable book, written, edited and published by students from around the Bay Area, includes a selection of book reviews submitted by children 5 to 17. All proceeds from the sale of the book will be used to provide mini grants for a number of teachers developing creative literacy and reading programs in their classrooms.

What better way to promote reading than to celebrate books? And what better critics than the kids themselves? Children who read are children who think. This is "the first book that ever made me cry," writes one young critic. Another says her favorite book "is a great novel for an eight year old, but it's still very pleasurable for adults." "This book," says another, "is about believing in yourself."

Readers are seldom neutral. They can love certain books, and they can hate others. That is their privilege and their reward. A reader doesn't have to agree with any other reader. Sharing a favorite book is a great pleasure, but disagreeing is perhaps just as great a pleasure.

We hope these reviews will help new and old readers find their way to books they enjoy. We want them to come up with their own "Best Books," to discover the pleasure and refuge that books provide, and to speak up in their own reviews about books that they love (or hate).

Illustration by : Tina Lee

Table of Contents

The 1991 Junior Publishers*
Editorial Department:
Sherri Marshall (Oakland) . . . . .Managing Editor
Lauren Bensinger (San Francisco) . . Series Editor Grades K-3
Yasmin Webster-Woog (San Francisco) . . . .
. . . . Series Editor Grades 4-6
Genni Schmidt (San Francisco) . . . Series Editor Grades 4-6
Jessica Escobar (San Francisco) . . . Series Editor Grades 7-9
Mechaka Gardner (Oakland) . . . . Series Editor Grades 10-12
Marketing Department:
Nancy Mendieta (San Francisco) . . . . . . Marketing Director
Aviva Cushner (San Francisco) . Assistant Marketing Director
Rita Ortez (San Francisco) . . . . Publicity/Promotions
Eli Sarnat (Portola Valley) . . . . Promotions
Lily Wong (San Francisco) . . . . .Publicist
Lucy Acerno (San Francisco) . . . . .Publicist
Jesse Adamo (San Francisco) . . . . .Publicist
Production Department:
Saethra Fritscher (San Francisco) . . . . .Production Manager
Cressy Wood (San Francisco) . . . . Art Director
Esther Odekirk (Potter Valley) . . . . .Desktop Publisher
Kysha Davis (Oakland) . . . . Desktop Publisher/Proofreader
With Special Thanks to:
Foghorn Press: Publisher Vicki K. Morgan (Program Developer), and willing Foghorn staff: Annie Hosefros, Gilda Gonzales, Tim Moriarty, Lisa Schiffman, Dave Morgan, and Ann-Marie Brown
Department Leaders: Eric Kettunen, Lonely Planet Publications (Marketing), Kiran Rana, Hunter House, Inc. (Editorial), and Malcolm Barker, Londonborn Publications (Production)
Teacher: Jeannie Brondino
Speakers: Alice Acheson, William Kaufmann, Kermit Boston, Nicky Salan, Darcy Provo, Cindy Fahey, Joan Dahlgren, Carol Muller, Donald Paul, Elgy Gillespie, Jerry George, Suzanne Guyette, Stephanie Kelmar, Ann Duntz, John MacLeod, Roseanne Werges, and Michael Wesley
Donors: (also see back cover), The Gap, Cover to Cover Bookstore, Brittanica Software, Zellerbach Family Fund, Columbia Foundation, Nestle Beverage Co., San Francisco Review of Books, NCBA, NCCBA, and San Francisco Chamber of Commerce

Front cover illustration: Jenny Mac, age 13, winner of the 1991 *Books We Love Best* cover illustration contest
Back cover illustration of world: Jana Martin, age 12
*The Junior Publishers (ages 11-17) spent seven weeks this summer at Foghorn Press learning about book publishing as a part of the San Francisco Bay Area Book Festival year-round literacy program. The result is *Books We Love Best*. To learn more about the program, see the end of this book.

Introduction

With a lot of dedication, the Junior Publishers Program has put together this very special book, filled with reviews from kids ranging from 4-18. We happily present this collection to all the puzzled parents, frazzled grandparents, and desperate aunts and uncles who would like to know (without going through every book on the shelf) which book to get their favorite youngster.

The reviews are grouped by grades into three chapters: kindergarten through 3rd grade, grades 4 through 6, and grades 7 through 12. Within the chapters the reviews are arranged in categories. The basic categories are animal, fantasy/science fiction, mystery, and people. Just as the ages of our reviewers grow, so does maturity. The reviews in K-3 deal more with animals, grades 4-6 deal more with science fiction, aliens, and monsters. Grades 7-12 tend to get more serious: there are more reviews of non-fiction having to do with topics like child abuse and the environment. Also, horror books are popular with older children.

We are proud to say that children are reading at a young age. We even had a 4-year-old send in a review. Our biggest response was from grades 4-6, though we were quite disappointed at the lack of reviews from grades 10-12 and had to combine them with grades 7-9 into what is now 7-12.

Although we have changed a lot of grammar and done a little editing throughout the reviews, we have in no way changed the feeling of how an 8-year-old, for example, would write. We want to keep the voices in each review, to keep their full meaning. Included are reviews of classic books that many adults have read, enjoyed, and remember, which they may still now as adults enjoy reading again.

The reviews for the book were collected through the KQED Action Kids Program and other sources. The cover art along with illustrations used with the reviews were submitted-for the Books We Love Best Contest, and we thank all those who sent in their wonderful, interesting and crazy entries.

It's taken us a lot of teamwork and help from people to do this. Now that it's completed, we take pride in sharing these reviews with you. We hope it will make it easier for you to find a book for your child or a child you know, or even for yourself. —The Junior Publishers

Illustration by: Slava Viner

Grades K-3
(ages 5-8+)

Fascinating tales have brought the chapter to its best. Young children (some even the age of four years old) have written about their favorite book. This is a delightful section filled with many different book reviews from children around the Bay Area in the grades of Kindergarten-3rd.

Animal

Dogs, horses, rabbits, and pigs make this a zoo of book reviews. Explore the wonderful wildlife in an excellent book about fascinating animals.

Little Rabbit's Loose Tooth

Author: Lucy Bate

Publisher: Crown

Reviewed and illustrated by: Reina Aguilar

Little Rabbit's Loose Tooth is about a little rabbit that has a loose tooth. But one day while she was eating pudding her little tooth came right out. Little Rabbit thought what to do to her tooth. One of her thoughts was that she could save it for the Tooth Fairy. But she didn't believe in the Tooth Fairy.

I liked this book very much because I have had it ever since I was 6. This book said a lot about a little rabbit's loose tooth, while I also had a loose tooth. I think kids would like this book for what Little Rabbit does through the book. This book is for all ages. Any kid can like this book.

Old Wattles

Author: Wynelle Catlin

Publisher: Doubleday

Reviewed by: Christina Garcia

Eleanore wants to do her share of the work on the farm. But finding the eggs of the ordinary old turkey hen is just about the worst job she can imagine. Eleanore wakes up and eats breakfast, and goes to the barn, and looks for Old Wattles. Eleanore follows Old Wattles, that's her job.

I like this book because Old Wattles is trying to trick Eleanore. I think kids in second grade would like this book because they could read it themselves.

Henry Huggins

Author: Beverly Cleary

Publisher: Avon

Reviewed by: Bradford C. Lee

Henry was bored because nothing exciting ever happened. Then he found a dog and named him Ribsy. So he asked his mom if he could keep him and he could. Then he tried to take him on the bus three times.

Henry and Ribsy

Author: Beverly Cleary

Publisher: Dell

Reviewed by: Bradford C. Lee

Henry took Ribsy to the pet shop to get a collar and a dog dish. Then he saw a sale for $7.00 for 2 guppies and 1 snail, 1 fish food, and a fish bowl. Henry took Ribsy and the fish back to his house and then the guppies started to have more babies. His mother said that he had to get rid of some of his fish because he had too many fish. So he gave some of the fish to his friend and the rest to the man in the pet shop. The man in the fish shop gave Henry $7.00 to spend in his store. Henry bought a catfish with the tank and heater.

Catundra

Author: Stephen Cosgrove & Robin James

Publisher: Price Stern Sloan

Reviewed by: Marcy Lariz

It is about a cat who ate too much and a mole helped her lose weight. I liked it because I like the authors and I like cats. Other kids my age would like it because the author is great and fun to read.

One Little Kitten

Author: Tane Hoban

Publisher: Greenwillow

Reviewed by: Natalie Abbott

I think that it is a good book because it has photographs instead of drawings. And I think that it is a good book.

Fox Be Nimble

Author: James Marshall

Publisher: Doubleday

Reviewed by: Whitney Boughtonage

I think it's funny because they do silly things. And I like this story because I like wolves.

Christmas at Gumps

Author: Mimi McAllister

Publisher: C. Salway

Reviewed by: Lisa Laurent

I really enjoyed this book *Christmas at Gumps*! I really like the end when the animals leave the place "totally blitzed out." This is what my mom says about my room.

Reviewed by: Lauren Low

I love this book *Christmas at Gumps*. I wish, I wish I can have a book or a picture of *Christmas at Gumps*. I like Snow the Cat and Fred the Dalmation.

The Story of Orange

Author: Vernise Elaine Pelzel

Publisher: H.P.L. Publishing

Reviewed By: Jessica Escobar

The Story of Orange is about believing in yourself. It would be a wonderful book for young children. It is about a young zebra who loves to draw. But when Orange, the zebra, is told that his pictures were no good he stops drawing. It teaches you self-esteem and to have faith in your work.

Henry's Awful Mistake

Author: Robert Quackenbush

Publisher: Parents Magazine

Reviewed by: Chelsea Lake

This story is about a duck and an ant. Henry the duck invited his friend Clara over for supper. Henry saw an ant and was worried Clara would see the ant and tried to catch it. If I was Henry I would just leave it alone because ants are too small to be seen. The ant ran all over the house. Henry saw the ant go into a crack. Henry grabbed a hammer and started to make a hole in the wall. SPLASH the water came running out of the wall. I liked the part when Henry broke the wall and water came running out of the wall because just a little ant made that much trouble. Natalie, my little sister, is just one and makes a lot of trouble.

Marathon and Steve

Author: Mary Rayner

Publisher: E.P. Dutton

Reviewed and illustrated by: Alexandria Flowers

Marathon and Steve is about a dog and his owner. Steve likes to jog but Marathon would rather watch TV. I liked it because it was funny and I used to have a dog like Marathon. I think both older and younger kids would like it.

Reviewed by
Alexandria Flowers
age 9

Caps For Sale

Author: Esphyr Slobodkina

Publisher: HarperCollins

Reviewed by: Rajiv Smith-Mahabir

My favorite book is *Caps For Sale*. I think it should be in *Books We Love Best* because the story is funny and makes me laugh. It is about monkeys which zip all the caps from a peddler's head while the peddler takes a snooze under a tree and put them on their heads. When he asks the naughty monkeys for the caps, they say, "Tsz, tsz, tsz." Then the peddler gives up and throws his own cap down. The monkeys copy him.

Amos and Boris

Author: William Steig

Publisher: Penguin

Reviewed and illustrated by: Timothy Eng

I like the book because it shows how good friends help each other when they are in need. In the story, Amos is a mouse who builds his own ship to sail off to sea while Boris is a very big whale. One day, Boris saves Amos' life. Many years later, Amos saves Boris' life. As good friends Amos and Boris tell

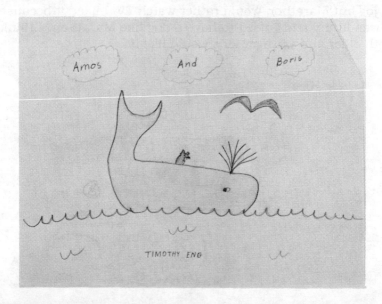

each other about their lives and their secret dreams. Although they go their separate ways, Amos and Boris will remain good friends forever! I am sure that other kids will like this book very much, because it shows that close friends who live apart will always remain together in their hearts.

Max's Dragon Shirt

Author: Rosemary Wells

Publisher: Dial Books For Young Readers

Reviewed and illustrated by: Angelica Flowers

Max is dirty. He needs new overalls. His sister takes him shopping. He wants a dragon shirt but Ruby says "No!"

I like this book because Max is a rabbit and I love rabbits. It is funny. I think it is good for reading if you are 5.

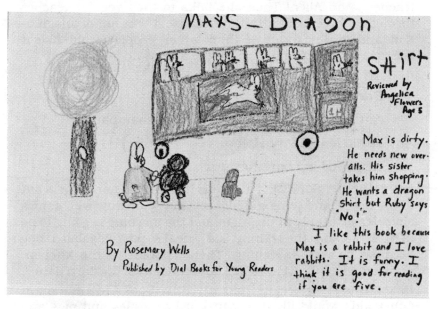

Fantasy/Science Fiction

Do you like to dream? Would you like to have all your wishes come true? Do your hopes soar high? Well come along to Never-ever land where water is purple and the sky is orange. Expand your imagination to somewhere beyond in a fantasy book.

My Teacher is An Alien

Author: Bruce Coville

Publisher: Minstrel

Reviewed by: Zack Mates

It's about a boy named Peter and a girl named Susan. Susan followed their teacher to his house and found out that their teacher is an Alien! Then she talks to their regular teacher through a force field. I liked it because it was full of imagination and it was funny. I think other people would like it because it's very funny. I think the age would be 8 and up.

Barn Dance

Author: Bill Martin, Jr. & John Archambault

Publisher: Henry Holt

Reviewed by: Lars Kosager

In this story a skinny kid awakens in the night and he gets out of his house and joins a fiddle-playing scarecrow who comes alive. Magic is only in the night and the morning is going to be here soon and the skinny kid sneaks past his barn dog because he was stretching. Then he went to the kitchen, grabbed an apple, went to bed, and thought of the barn dance. I liked this story because our Itty Bitty Book Light fits on it. Other kids would like it because it has mules and pigs and cows in it and other animals too.

Space Case

Author: Edward Marshall

Publisher: Dial

Reviewed and illustrated
by: Katie Toker

It is about a little robot that comes from space and it is Halloween. On Halloween there are trick or treaters. I like this book because it is funny and the age is 8.

Elmer and the Dragon

Author: Ruth Stiles Gannett

Publisher: Random House

Reviewed by: Katrina Lake

When you read this book it feels as if you are in Feather Island eating tangerines and tangerine peels with Elmer and the dragon, talking to King Can XI. I liked this book because it has lots of adventures, flying through the storm and sitting inside King Can XI's nest. It had excitement too like when they got to Feather Island and when they heard the "click" of the treasure chest's lock turning. The most beautiful part was when Elmer played the silver harmonica so gracefully. I think 8-year-olds should love this book.

The Magic Fish

Author: Freya Littledale

Publisher: Scholastic

Reviewed by: Leslie Phillips

The book is about a woman who catches a fish and is too greedy. Until the fish said, "No!" and she loses everything. I like this book because it tells you a very good lesson. I think other people would like it because it's a very interesting story. Kids from 5 to 10 would like it.

Cinderella

Author: Walt Disney

Publisher: Smith Publishers

Reviewed by: Christina Garcia

Illustrated by: Carmen Lee

The book is about a girl whose father died. Cinderella lived with her stepmother. She was a servant for the stepmother and the stepsisters. Cinderella worked every day very hard. I liked the part where the mice made Cinderella a beautiful dress. I think other kids would like it because it is like a fantasy. Kids 4-7 would like it because it's great.

The Night After Christmas

Author: James Stevenson

Publisher: Greenwillow

Reviewed by: Paula Galvez

The book is about a doll named Annie and she gets thrown away and a bear too. The doll makes friends with the bear and they meet a dog named Chauncey who finds them a home. It was the night after Christmas. Teddy was in the garbage. "Jingle bells Jingle bells," he sang "Jingle all the way."

Kids ages 5 and 6 would like this book. They will like it because it is a good story. I liked it because it was good, funny, and interesting. I think that other people will like it too.

The Velveteen Rabbit

Author: Margery Williams

Publisher: Doubleday

Illustrated by: Patrick Price (no review)

Mystery

In the misty sky night you can see a castle on top of the hill. People say spooks live there, and a whole collection of mysteries are in the castle's library. So if you are brave enough, walk up the hill to the castle and pick up a mystery book.

Cam Jansen and the
Mystery of the Dinosaur Bones

Author: David A. Adler

Publisher: Dell

Reviewed by: Eve Nettleton

Some dinosaur bones got stolen. Cam and her friend Eric help the museum find them and they get free passes for a year.

Why I like this best: I like mysteries.

The Haunting of Frances Rain

Author: Margaret Buffie

Publisher: Scholastic

Reviewed by: Angela Hamilton

This book is about a girl who found some old glasses in the attic and when she puts them on she sees things from the past! And if you like ghost stories then you will like this book a lot! I think you will like it no matter how old you are!

The Boxcar Children Collection

Author: Gertrude Chandler Warner

Publisher: Albert Whitman

Reviewed by: Jessica Porter

The books are mysteries but not scary mysteries. The main characters are Benny, Violet, Jessie, and Henry. They live with their grandfather. Their grandfather always has something for them to do when they're not in school. But wherever they go, they find a mystery. I liked it because they're fun mysteries. I think other kids would like it because they're interesting. I think that ages 8 and 9 would like them.

The Midnight Mystery

Author: Betty Ren Wright

Publisher: Scholastic

Reviewed by: Naima Walls

Hi! My name is Naima Walls and I like mystery, and if you like mystery you will like this book. It's about a girl whose father has to move away for a new job. In the middle of the night she sees figures in the moonlight and she hears doors slamming, too. She is really scared and she tries to figure it out herself. It's very spooky!

I like this book because I like mystery and it is good for people who like mystery like me.

It's a Spook!

Illustration by: Edmund Lin

People

Strange creatures live all around us, but the strangest are people. These next books don't talk about the future but how different people react and live today.

Starring Sally J. Freedman As Herself

Author: Judy Blume

Publisher: Dell

Reviewed by: Ngoyen Han

I like this book because it is about a girl and the book tells about her life. I like to tell the world about this book because it can take about three days to finish so you can be busy. You will like this book.

The Saddle Club #1: Horse Crazy

Author: Bonnie Bryant

Publisher: Bantam

Reviewed by: Liezel Zapanta

What I think the book is about is making up with friends and getting together. Why I like the book is because it shows how you can make friends and stay together. I think why other kids would like the book is just because it's fun to read. I think the age kids would like the book is from 6 years to 12 years.

Beezus and Ramona

Author: Beverly Cleary

Publisher: Dell

Reviewed by: Bong Ian Dizon

It's about two sisters who sometimes fight because Ramona always gets into things when Beezus is around. Beezus hates Ramona but she realizes that sisters are supposed to love each other. I like this book because it's funny and interesting to read. I think other kids would like it because it's fun to read and you can even read it with your family. Seven and up would like this book.

Mei Li

Author: Thomas Handforth

Publisher: Doubleday

Reviewed and illustrated by: Emily Sweet

I think this book is a neat old book because it teaches you about what Chinese do for Chinese New Year. A girl named Mei Li wants to go to the fair but her mom won't let her so she sneaks out of her house to go to the fair with her brother San Yu and a fortune teller says Mei Li is a princess and says she will rule over a kingdom and her kingdom is her house and everyone who lives there must serve her.

Emily's Runaway Imagination

Author: Beverly Cleary

Publisher: Dell

Reviewed by: Jessica Alberto

This book is about a girl named Emily who has a runaway imagination. Emily is a very courageous girl. She is also very funny. I liked this book because it was very interesting and good. I think other kids will like this book because it's very good and once you start reading it you can't stop. I think kids 7 and up would enjoy this book.

My favorite part of this book is when Emily lets all the pigs out and they're all drunk, from eating rotten apples she fed them.

The Twits

Author: Roald Dahl

Publisher: Puffin

Reviewed by: Martina

Hi, my name is Martina and I just read this funny book called, *The Twits*. It's about a man and a woman who are really twits! The man and woman play tricks and jokes on each other. And they make their monkeys do tricks. I think you should read this book. The End!

Chester's Way

Author: Kevin Henkes

Publisher: Scholastic

Reviewed by: Mallory Portillo

Chester and his best friend Wilson are exactly the same. They like the same things. But then Lilly moved into the neighborhood and things changed.

Me and Katie (the Pest)

Author: Ann M. Martin

Publisher: Holiday House

Reviewed by: Cecilia Y. Chen

This book is about a girl named Wendy who is taking horseback riding lessons. But then Wendy's little sister Katie gets to take them too. This is not when Wendy is going to let the pest be the best because Katie is always winning prizes. I liked the book because it was funny. I think you should read this book.

Five Minutes Peace

Author: Jill Murphy

Publisher: Putnam

Reviewed and illustrated by: Trenton English

A mom wanted five minutes peace. And the kids are making a mess. And they keep bugging her so she can't have five minutes peace. She didn't get it but four minutes and five seconds. Before that all the kids wanted to join her in the bath tub.

It is and they are funny. The little elephant is wet and squirting water while the brother and sister are dry with towels.

Why I think other kids would like it: the pictures are good and they'll like them. What age kids would like it: 4-year-olds, 5-year-olds, 6-year-olds, any kind of olds—any kid.

Harry's Mom

Author: Barbara Ann Porte

Publisher: Dell

Reviewed by: Jerome Wan Dees

Harry's mother passed away when he was one. He asked his aunt and grandparents about his mom. He finds out all kinds of information. I like this book because it's like he is a detective. It's a good book.

Johnny's in the Basement

Author: Louis Sachar

Publisher: Avon

Reviewed by: Racheal Yeager

Do you like a good laugh? If you do, you would probably like this book. The main characters in this story are Johnny, Valerie, Donald, and Christina. The book is about a boy who has the biggest bottle cap collection in the world. Then he has to get rid of his bottle cap collection and doesn't know what to do. I liked it because it was very funny. I think other kids would like it too, because it was very funny. Both boys and girls of all ages would like it.

It's Hard Work Being Bitter

Author: Charles M. Schulz

Publisher: Holt, Rinehart

Reviewed by: Steve Chu

Because it's a fun book to read because I like cartoons and because it's a funny book!

Jelly Belly

Author: Robert Kimmel Smith

Publisher: Dell

Reviewed by: Evan Kuluk

If you'd like a funny book about an overweight kid at camp you'll love *Jelly Belly*. It's a story about an overweight kid whose parents send him off to a camp for fat kids to lose weight. He has lots of adventures and a happy ending. I liked it and I'm sure you'll like it too, no matter how big you are.

Home Alone

Author: Todd Strasser

Publisher: Scholastic

Reviewed by: David J. Standring

The book *Home Alone* is about a boy named Kevin McCallister who wishes that his family will disappear. When his family is going to France the next day at 9:00 sharp they leave Kevin behind!! I think kids will like it because it's a funny book. I like it because the robbers (Marv and Harry) really get beat up. I think kids age 6 and over will enjoy this book.

Momotaro the Peach Boy

Author: George Suyeoka

Publisher: Island Heritage

Reviewed by: Dylan White

Momotaro, a young samurai, defeated the Oni, with his friends a giant dog, monkey and bird. He saved his village and returned the treasures stolen by the Oni. I think 7 to 11-year-olds would like the story. They would learn about bravery, courage and to be kind to others.

Meet Molly, an American Girl

Author: Valerie Tripp

Published by: Pleasant Company

Reviewed by: Debra Mao

This book is about a family during 1944 (during World War II). The main character is Molly McIntire. It tells about Molly's 9-year-old childhood. I like this book because Molly's mother said that there are too many people fighting in the world and she will not allow fighting in her house. I think other kids will like it because they will learn lessons.

The Little House in the Big Woods

Author: Laura Ingalls Wilder

Publisher: HarperCollins

Reviewed by: Randi Ketcher

The book's about Laura as she's growing up in the woods. In her books she has lived in a lot of places. Like the prairie. Kids will like it because maybe they had the same experiences and maybe they like true stories. Mostly kids ages 8 and older will like and understand this book.

Reviewed by: Michi H-Wong

This is a story of life in America long ago when there were no cars, no supermarkets and no electricity. It is a story of a family that lived in a little log house and what their lives were like.

I liked it because it makes me appreciate my life. Life is a lot simpler today. We have medicine, cars, telephones and other things. Sometimes we take those things for granted, but everyone who reads *The Little House in the Big Woods* will appreciate all the wonderful things we have today.

Children around 7-years-old would like it especially because the main character is around that age. But it is a story that children of all ages would like.

The Little House on the Prairie

Author: Laura Ingalls Wilder

Publisher: HarperCollins

Reviewed by: Emily Gibbs

A young girl grows up in Indian territory. She wants to see a papoose (an Indian baby). I like it because it tells you about life back in the 1800's. I think other people would like this because it is a very neat book and you can learn things. Any age would love this book.

Morris and Boris

Author: B. Wiseman

Publisher: Putnam

Reviewed by: Michael Becker

I like *Morris and Boris* by B. Wiseman. I think Morris is funny. I just finished reading *Morris Goes to School*.

I think it's a good idea to read it or have someone else read it to you. Morris gets to go to school. He learns to count, read, and hoof paint. He also learns to use the boys' restroom instead of the girls'. That was funny.

Poetry

Many Luscious Lollipops

Author: Ruth Heller

Publisher: Grosset and Dunlap

Reviewed by: Nikki Esposito

I picked this book because I like the way the adjectives rhyme like: "An ADJECTIVE's terrific when you want to be specific. It easily identifies by number, color or by size. TWELVE LARGE BLUE GORGEOUS butterflies. It describes all things with style and grace . . . "

I think other kids will like this book because of the colors and the decorations in the pictures. This book makes learning fun.

Fox in Socks

Author: Dr. Seuss

Publisher: Random House

Reviewed by: Tony Goldmark

I like this book because it was really funny and had a lot of tongue twisters. It was really very funny. I liked the characters very much. I'm glad this book was by Dr. Seuss because I like him a lot. He does really funny tongue twisters. I think people of every age, even adults should read this book because it's so funny. Thank you and good night.

CDB

Author: William Steig

Publisher: Trumpet Club

Reviewed by: Lodrina Cherne

I like this book because it is not like a regular book. It has lots of pictures and letters instead of words. You read the letters out loud and they sound like words. This is for grades 1 and up.

Miscellaneous

Fables You Shouldn't Pay Any Attention To

Author: Florence Heide

Publisher: Dell

Reviewed by: Chloe Hanna-korpi

I think people should read this book because it is very funny and all aged people can read it. This book is a bunch of little funny stories that I think kids would like.

The Big Book of Peace

Editor: Marilyn Sachs

Publisher: Dutton

Reviewed by: Saethra Fritscher

Illustrated by: Lavell

This is a good book. Its stories are simple, easy to comprehend and perfect for kids ages 6 and up. *The Big Book of Peace* is a great book for teaching children about peace. I highly recommend it to everyone, even the really young children, 6 or younger, for parents to read aloud at bedtime.

Grades 4-6

(ages 9-12)

This chapter is a collection of book reviews and illustrations done by children in grades 4 through 6 from around the San Francisco Bay Area. This chapter is the one we received the most entries for. We feel this happened because this is the point in a child's life when he or she is the most excited about reading and therefore reads as much as possible.

Animal

Animals are a very important part of childhood. Most children are very curious about them. These reviews are all about animals both big and small and their great adventures.

Why Mosquitos Buzz In People's Ears

Author: Verna Aardema

Publisher: Dial

Reviewed By: Dante Gardner

This book is about a mosquito that goes around buzzing in other people's ears. At the end of the book the mosquito is killed by a man, who while the bug was buzzing in his ear, the man slapped his ears and hit the bug. I liked this book because it was funny. Other kids between the ages of 9-11 and maybe older would also like it.

Mr. Popper's Penguins

Author: Richard and Florence Atwater

Publisher: Dell

Reviewed by: Amina

Mr. Popper's Penguins is a good book. I would get it if I were you. It is a funny book. It tells you about the Artic. It's a great book to read. Mr. Popper is a house painter. It tells you how he learned about the Artic. He loved to go to the movies a lot. You would like it a lot. So like I said before, get this book right now. Tell everyone to share this book.

The Mouse and the Motorcycle

Author: Beverly Cleary

Publisher: Dell

Reviewed by: Keir F. Davidson

A mouse named Ralph lived in an old motel off the highway. A family named the Kents were staying there. When Ralph fell in the garbage can Keith (the Kents' son) got him out. They became good friends when Keith trusted Ralph he let him ride a toy motorcycle. I liked this book a lot because of all the adventure in it. I think this is great for children because it was a very fun experience for me. This book is good in these categories: adventure, fun, and laughs. Again, I recommend it to people age 8 through...death.

Ralph S. Mouse

Author: Beverly Clearly

Publisher: Dell

Reviewed and illustrated by: John Ikeda

It is about Ralph the mouse at the school of a boy that is Ralph's friend. I like this book because it has all sorts of adventures in school and more. The part that I liked was when Ralph was put in a jar and the press came and took a picture of him.

The Black Stallion

Author: Walter Farley

Publisher: Random House

Reviewed by: Hannah Mello

The book is about a boy named Alexander and his horse, Black. He is trying to take his horse home in New York City, but his ship gets wrecked. I think it is a great book for all ages to share.

When Hippo Was Hairy

Author: Nick Geaves

Publisher: Barron

Reviewed and illustrated by: Marcy Territo

"The Race That Was Rigged," one story in this book, is a Swazi story, a tale from Africa. I liked it because it is like the tortoise and the hare. It is about a rabbit asking a tortoise if he wanted

a race because he wanted to make fun of the tortoise. Tortoise not only accepted but made the race longer. On the day of the race he had all of his relatives lined up, one after every rise. Tortoise was at the finish line. Rabbit kept on meeting tortoise's relatives until he met Tortoise. So Tortoise beat Rabbit at his own game.

The Wind in the Willows

Author: Kenneth Grahame

Publisher: Dell

Reviewed by: Josh Kline

"The Open Road," a chapter in *The Wind in the Willows* is a fabulous story. I liked it because Rat, Mole, and Toad have such different temperaments yet they are all friends. Water Rat likes poetry, boating, and has a good nature. Mole also likes boating and has a candid nature. Toad is simple, affectionate, and perhaps not so clever. He may be a little boastful and conceited at times but all-in-all good natured.

The Celery Stalks at Midnight

Author: James Howe

Publisher: Avon

Reviewed by: Andy Barnes

The Celery Stalks at Midnight is about four animals. The animals are a dog, cat, puppy, and bunny. The bunny is a vampire. So one day the bunny is not in the cage. The three animals are worried because the bunny might bite someone. So the three animals look all over the town to find the bunny. The bunny bit a vegetable.

I liked this story because there was a lot of action. The book was thrilling and it was chilling. It had a lot of funny parts in the book. The book had a very good ending. The action parts were the best parts in the book. I did not like the book because it did not have enough action in it. Most of the book had boring conversation, like dogs asking other dogs if they have seen the bunny.

Pecos Bill

Author: Steven Kellogg

Publisher: William Morrow

Reviewed and illustrated by: Max Hendin

I chose this book because I liked how Steven Kellogg took the time to put so much detail in his drawings. I also admire his imagination and how he thinks of pictures. I like how he retold the story. It is about a boy that gets raised by coyotes and learns about the wild. He thinks he's a coyote.

The Island of the Blue Dolphins

Author: Scott O'Dell

Publisher: Dell

Reviewed and illustrated by: Sara Mo

It is about a young Indian girl who was stuck on an island alone for 18 years and how she survived by herself and with animals. I liked it because it had a sad beginning and middle and a happy ending. It was the first book that ever made me cry. I think that other kids would like it because it tells what Indians did to survive. I think 9 to 15-year-olds would like it.

Reviewed by: Sabrina Arey

Island of the Blue Dolphins is a true story about an island girl named Karana, who is left behind when her tribe is forced to leave the land. I think other people would like this book because it's exciting and very interesting the way the 12-year-old girl survives alone on the island. It should be included because it's my favorite book and it should be many others'. It's a haunting unusual story, yet beautiful in its own strange way. *Island of the Blue Dolphins* reveals courage, serenity, and the greatness of spirit. It's a moving and unforgettable story.

The Spooky Tail of Prewitt Peacock

Author: Bill Peet

Publisher: Houghton Mifflin

Reviewed by: Karla Kane

I liked this book because it was a great book. It was about a peacock named Prewitt. He was sad because he had an ugly tail. One day he looked at his tail. It had grown a spooky face. The other peacocks were mad at him and they chased him away. But then a tiger saw them. Prewitt's spooky tail scared the tiger away. The other peacocks made Prewitt their leader.

Poems of A. Nonny Mouse

Selected by: Jack Prelutsky

Publisher: Alfred A. Knopf

Reviewed by: Tara Pandeya

My favorite poem in the book was called "The Three Young Rats with Felt Hats." It was about some animals who wanted to put on fancy things to wear. Then they went out for a walk, but it rained. So they all went home again. Another reason why I liked it was because whoever wrote it used a play on words. The way A. Nonny Mouse should be is "anonymous." That means that they do not know who it was written by.

Mrs. Pig Gets Cross

Author: Mary Rayner

Publisher: E.P. Dutton

Reviewed and illustrated by: Jessie Nelson

This was my favorite book because I like to read about pigs. This story was about ten piglets that never pick their toys up. One day Mrs. Pig said she was tired of picking toys up. That night a fox came. He tried to open the door and it opened easily. The fox grabbed Mrs. Pig's jewels and Mr. Pig's wallet. He went back down the stairs and tripped over the toys. The money and jewels went flying. The robber left. The toys saved the day.

Once There was a Stream

Author: Joel Rotleman

Publisher: Scroll

Reviewed by: Kelly Furano

One of my favorite books was called *Once There Was A Stream*. I like this book because it tells how once there was a stream, which was so clean that you could drink out of the water, fish, and even swim. Then it became polluted and the fish soon died out. They could no longer fish in that stream. They couldn't swim in that stream or drink from the water. I think everybody should read this book because it teaches you not to litter and to just take the time to throw litter in the trash can.

The Conversation Club

Author: Diane Stanley

Publisher: Macmillan

Reviewed by: Molly Alliman

This book was about a mouse who was just moving into town. Another mouse came over to greet him. He wanted him to be in his conversation club. He agreed to be in the club. So next Thursday he went to the club. The club members started to talk. It got so loud he couldn't hear anything because they were all talking at once. Then they stopped. The mouse said he had a listening club and they could join. So they went to his club. It was quiet. He was very happy.

The Trumpet of The Swan

Author: E.B. White

Publisher: HarperCollins

Reviewed by: Aaron Tam

The Trumpet of the Swan is about a boy named Sam. He and his father Mr. Beaver built a cabin in Western Canada and went there every three to four months for vacation. On his first trip to Canada he went hiking and exploring and seemed to walk by a nest of trumpeter swans. He will visit the pond where the swans live every morning. One day the female swan laid a couple of eggs called cygnets. Then on one summer day the cygnets hatched and the baby swans were born.

I liked this story because it has a happy ending and because it is a very adventurous story. I recommend this book for all ages, even parents and senior citizens. If you like birds or nature life, this book is for you. You will like this book because it tells about a swan and a boy's lifetime together. This book also has a little romance and is very exciting to see how he escapes from one thing to another. This book is by the famous author E.B. White. He also wrote some famous books named: *Charlotte's Web*, *Stuart Little*, and won lots of awards. If you had read those books before I will guarantee you will like this book too!

Humphrey: The Lost Whale

Author: Wendy Tokuda and Richard Hall

Publisher: Heian International

Reviewed and illustrated by: Zachary Houston

I liked this book because I'm interested in the ocean. I also liked it because I love whales. I think it's a good demonstration of care for the environment. Humphrey had to have lots of courage to try to escape from the bridge that he got caught in.

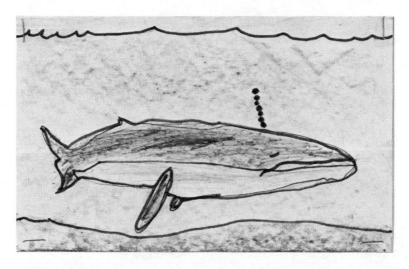

Fantasy/Science Fiction

This section of fantasy contains stories about imaginary people, with creative and exciting lives. Using a vivid imagination, and a strong love for the unbelievable, you will be more than ready to explore the lands of strange castles and many strange creatures, of this section. So use your imagination well, and blast off to a whole new world.

The High King

Author: Lloyd Alexander

Publisher: Dell

Reviewed and illustrated by: Simon Cheung

This story is about a man called Taran and Prince Gwydion. These two men get a whole army to fight a man called Arawn-Death-Lord.

What I like about this book is that it has lots of adventure and lots of monsters, ghouls, and goblins. I would recommend that you read this wonderful book. When you read it you feel like you are inside the story, plus you can read this book when you are bored or when you are doing nothing.

What I don't like about this story is that the evil man (Arawn) got killed so fast. This book does not have enough fighting, but every chapter you read is all packed with adventure and fantasy. This book could be read by any age from 6-2,000,000-years-old.

Tuck Everlasting

Author: Natalie Babbit

Publisher: Farrar, Straus, and Giroux

Reviewed by: Elaine Gee

Tuck Everlasting is about the Tuck family. They drink from a magic spring. The water makes the Tucks live forever. Winnie, a young girl, finds out their secret. She learns that there are some good and bad points about living forever.

I like this book because it made me think about whether or not I'd like to live forever like the Tucks. Kids in the fifth or sixth grade would enjoy *Tuck Everlasting*.

The New Adventures of the Mad Scientist Club

Author: Bertrand Brinkley

Publisher: Scholastic

Reviewed by: Jerrad Pierce

The book is about a group of boys around 12 who are in a club. They use science to do many things.

One time they let go one hundred mini hot air balloons. In the distance they look like UFO's. Which is just what they want.

Rescue Mission

Author: Ben Butterworth & Bill Stockdale

Publisher: Wright

Reviewed by: Prescott Yeung

There was a man named Jim. His mission is to rescue a girl named Anna at the Kozan Castle.

I like Jim very much because he was brave and smart. He

was brave to go to Hozan Castle because there were many soldiers with guns, but the good thing is that he has a watch for emergencies. I think that this is a great story for children. Jim went through lots of adventures and he almost got trapped in Hozan Castle. There were lots of soldiers. That's why it was hard to get out of Hozan Castle.

The Chocolate Touch

Author: Patrick Skene Catling

Publisher: Bantam

Reviewed by: Jennifer Hee

This story is about a boy named John Midas who loves chocolate. He found a weird coin. That's when he found a candy store. He went inside and looked at all the chocolates. When he found a big box of chocolates he gave the man the coin.

John brought the box home and opened it, but there was only one candy in there. He was mad but he ate it. After that everything his mouth touched turned to chocolate.

At first he liked it being all chocolate. Later on, he didn't. He didn't like it because he was very thirsty, his golden trumpet was chocolate, and worst of all, his mother was chocolate!

I like the story because I like chocolate. I wish I had the chocolate until I read this book! The book is really good and interesting. I like this book and so will you!

I didn't like this book because I know that there is no such thing as a special touch, but that is the only thing I didn't like about it. Otherwise, it was a terrific story.

Charlie and the Chocolate Factory

Author: Roald Dahl

Publisher: Alfred A. Knopf

Reviewed by: Shannon Venable

The book is about a boy named Charlie and he goes to a store to buy one candy bar and he sees a contest that say five people will win a chance to go into the chocolate factory. Then a little later Charlie gets the golden ticket and gets to go to the chocolate factory. So he brings his old grandpa there, and everyone gets drowned or eaten or dies except Charlie. So that's when Charlie wins and gets gobs of chocolates and then they live happily ever after.

I liked it because Charlie and his grandpa won and it was the greatest story I've ever read. I think other kids would like it because it's a great story. The ages kids would like it would be age 7 to about age 15.

James and the Giant Peach

Author: Roald Dahl

Publisher: Bantam

Reviewed and illustrated by: Sara Kinsey

This story is about a boy named James. His parents died from a Hippo. The Hippo ate them when they were on their vacation to England. He has to live with his evil aunts. Their peach tree grew a big peach.

I think that other kids would like this book because it is a very weird, funny, and an adventurous book. And it exaggerates a lot. I think that you should put this in your book because I think that a lot of kids would really enjoy this hilarious book.

The Witches

Author: Roald Dahl

Publisher: Puffin

Reviewed by: Roger O'Neal

I like my book because it is funny and interesting. I think you would like it because the book is by Roald Dahl and I think it is one of his best books. Roald Dahl and his books are funny, interesting and are impossible to put down. It is kind of weird too.

Reviewed by: Nicole Gazzo

The book is about the MOST powerful witch in England, named The Grand High Witch, who is mean and vicious and hates children. She also plans to turn all of them in the hotel into mice.

I liked *The Witches* because I could feel the emotions as the author expresses them among the characters. You felt as if you are right there, in the same room where the Grand High Witch and her evil assistants are brewing up deliciously wicked plans to turn all the children they can into mice.

I think other kids will like this magnificent adventure book as well as I did because of funniness and over-all wiseness that this book is offering.

Kids from 8 to 14 will probably enjoy this book on their age level. Whoever reads this book I know will love this supernatural, spookish tale of witchery.

How to Find a Ghost

Author: James M. Deem

Publisher: Houghton Mifflin

Reviewed by: Catherine O'Leary

Have you ever wondered what it would be like to see a ghost? If you have, this is the book for you. Based on a thorough examination of ghosts reported in the United States and Europe, this book will tell you where ghosts come from and what they really look like. It describes six different types of ghosts, from the ghost that dwells in a haunted house to the mischievous poltergeist.

I liked it because it tells you the true facts about ghosts and they also tell true ghost stories through the book. Other kids would like it because the book also tells you how to start a ghost hunt. I think most brave kids would do this.

The age may vary. Only the brave read this book.

The Neverending Story

Author: Michale Ende

Publisher: Penguin

Reviewed by: Hilary Gilmore

The book is about this boy named Bastian and he gets this book from the bookstore and he feels and sees what's happening to Fantasia. Fantasia is falling apart from the nothing and he has to save it. I thought it was great. It made me happy and sad. I think other kids would like it because it's a fantasy. I think all ages would enjoy and be able to read this book.

Hercules

Author: Bernard Evslin

Publisher: Morrow

Reviewed by: Kevin Quan

The story is about the strongest man in the world in Greek mythology. The story is about his life from birth to death.

I liked this book very much. If you like to read adventure books I recommend that you should read *Hercules*. There are many adventures he goes on in this story. He also meets fair maidens and saves them from monsters. This book is fun to read when you are bored and have nothing to do. If you don't like books without pictures you don't have to worry because this book has pictures that are very well detailed. If I were you I'd hurry up and read this book.

The Great Race

Author: Paul Goble

Publisher: Bradbury

Reviewed by: Julia Jozwik

This was an excellent book. I liked it a whole bunch. It was very interesting, but it was not a true story. They said long ago that buffaloes used to eat people, then they had a big race and whoever won got to eat the other one. The birds joined the people and the animals joined the buffalo. The people won the race.

Top Secret

Author: John Reynolds Gardiner

Publisher: Little, Brown

Reviewed by: Yvonne Wang

The book is about a 9-year-old boy named Allen. The science fair is coming up and he wants to do a project on human photosynthesis. Allen decides to mix lots of ingredients to make the formula for human photosynthesis. When he was done mixing, he drank it and later in the story, he turns green. I liked the book because it was adventurous and this story made me read on and on and never stop. I think others will like it because parts of the story are funny and it makes people think what will happen next in the story. I think 9 to about 13-year-old kids will like reading this story.

Rip Van Winkle

Author: Morrell Gipson

Publisher: Doubleday

Reviewed and illustrated by: Mick O'Connell

This was my favorite book because a man named Rip Van Winkle went into an enchanted forest. He saw a little man that

led him to their camp site. There he saw a lot of little men playing a game. Then he fell asleep. When he woke up they all were gone and he was an old man. He went into the village and saw his son. At first they didn't recognize each other. Then they found out they were father and son, and they lived happily ever after.

The Devil With Three Golden Hairs

Author: Jacob Grimm and Wilhelm K. Grimm

Retold by: Nonny Hogrogran

Publisher: Alfred A. Knopf

Reviewed by: Charlie Sarkis

I like this book because it was neat, because a boy gets to get married when he turns 14-years-old. But the king does not want the boy to get married to his daughter. He tells the boy if he can get three golden hairs, he can get married to his daughter. But the golden hairs were on a Devil's head. The Devil's mom turned the boy into an ant to help him. He crawled on her shoulder and she took the golden hairs off the Devil's head. The boy got married to the king's daughter.

The Phantom Tollbooth

Author: Norton Juster

Publisher: Random House

Reviewed by: Irene Luu

The book was about a boy named Milo who did nothing and was always in a hurry back home. He found a Phantom Tollbooth in his room and he went through it. Soon Milo found himself going into strange lands he never went before. Milo made new friends and he was off on a dangerous journey to the Castle in the Air to save Princesses Pure Reason and Sweet Rhyme. At the end they escaped the demons and Milo and his friends had a celebration and Milo went back home.

I think kids would like it because of the exciting adventure. I think all ages would like The Phantom Tollbooth.

The Lion, The Witch, and The Wardrobe

Author: C.S. Lewis

Publisher: Macmillan

Reviewed by: Eunice Lee

This hair-raising extraordinary illustrious book is the most exciting book I've read. This magnificent book has it all — humor, adventures, magic, and a lot more! Every living human should read *The Lion, The Witch and The Wardrobe* whether you are short, tall, fat, or skinny. If you're a fun-loving human being, you're sure to like this. If you already read it, read the other books in this series, *Chronicles of Narnia*.

Reviewed by: Gilbert Martinez

This book is about four kids who had to move in with their ugly old uncle. The kids' names were Peter, Susan, Edmund, and Lucy. One day they played hide-and-seek. Lucy hid in the wardrobe. Then all of a sudden she's in a new world. The new world is Narnia. When all four enter the wardrobe the adventure begins. In Narnia the animals can talk! And their enemy is the wicked, selfish White Witch. The White Witch makes it winter but never Christmas. And she can turn people to stone. Who will save Narnia now?

Other kids will like this book like I do because the book is very descriptive. And because it is very imaginative. For kids age 8-up.

Reviewed by: Camille Combes

I thought it was a very good book. It had a lot of things in it: courage, adventure and a lot more. I think it could be the best book I ever read. My Mom even has it on tape. The other books by C.S. Lewis are good, too.

I think you should run out to your bookstore to buy it and read it. It is the best and you will love it! I just know it. It is the greatest. And it is not that long. It took me four days to finish! Try it.

The Silver Chair

Author: C.S. Lewis

Publisher: Macmillan

Reviewed by: Stacey Sims

I like *The Silver Chair* because it has lions, witches, princesses, soldiers, knights, kings, and queens in it. The main thing that happens is the lion tells Jill to go far away to look for Prince Rilian. The best part is when the wicked witch comes and takes the prince to her underground kingdom and he becomes king. Then the witch puts a magic spell on him and he becomes evil just like her. Jill, Scrubb, and Puddleglum come and Prince Rilian kills the wicked witch. Then Jill, Scrubb, and Puddleglum free the prince from the magic spell. I think kids 7, 8, 9, 10, 11 and 12-years-old would like this book, because it's a fun story.

Robin Hood and the Great Coach Robbery

Author: Ann McGovern

Publisher: Scholastic

Reviewed and illustrated by: Melissa Gibeau

I like this book because Robin Hood always gave to the poor. I always read this book every night when I go to sleep. I think other kids would like it because they might like adventure books. I think all ages should read it, because it's a really nice book.

The Space Ship Under the Apple Tree

Author: Esphyr Slobodkina

Publisher: Macmillan

Reviewed by: Sam De Vore

This story is about a boy named Eddie. Eddie helps his grandfather in his apple orchard. One night Eddie looked in the sky and saw something going down. He thought it looked like a space ship.

In the morning Eddie went in the orchard. He saw a space ship. There was a little man up on a tree. So Eddie and the man met. The man showed Eddie all around his space ship. Eddie took the little man home with him.

I liked this book because it was funny. I liked it when the little man was wearing some of Eddie's blue jeans. You should check this book out. It is full of adventures. It also has more than 100 pages. I also like this book because aliens are my favorite creatures. The reason I checked it out is because the apples on the cover look delicious.

Solomon the Rusty Nail

Author: William Steig

Publisher: Farrar, Straus, and Giroux

Reviewed and illustrated by: Carl Gould

This book interested me because it was all fantasy. Solomon

discovers he can turn into a rusty nail. He decides to keep his ability a secret.

After awhile he forgot about his secret. Butterfly collecting got his attention. One day he almost bagged a rare one when a cat with a knife said, "Hands up and march!" Solomon did just that. Suddenly he realized his life was in danger! He remembered the nail trick and turned into a nail. Then he turned into a rabbit, but it was too soon. The cat took him home as a nail. They had waited too long for him to turn into a rabbit, so they hammered him into the house. There was a fire and he got himself free.

The Hobbit

Author: J.R.R. Tolkien

Publisher: Ballantine

Reviewed by: Felicia Ortez

This book is about a hobbit with the name of Bilbo Baggins. It tells about his adventure with some dwarves, when he takes his chances with spiders, trolls, elves, evil goblins, giants, and a green monster that looks like a frog.

I love this book because I like the way the author had Bilbo show his courage by being able to face all those horrible creatures. And all the magic wonders of the swords, rings, bags of potion, and the shields. I liked the courage and strength of the dwarves and Bilbo because they all survived.

The Lord of the Rings Trilogy

Author: J.R.R. Tolkien

Publisher: Houghton Mifflin

Reviewed by: Ben Lowe

This epic trilogy is beyond imagination. In between Sauron, Saruman, and the orcs, against a wizard and a hobbit bearing the link to doom, and a few allies, who will win? I advise this trilogy for 10 and up.

Mystery

The world is filled with mystery stories and here are just a few of the favorites among 4th through 6th graders. They vary from the Hardy Boys to Nancy Drew and many more. These stories are full of suspense and are all quite thrilling.

The Hardy Boys: The House on the Cliff

Author: Franklin Dixon

Publisher: Grosset & Dunlop

Reviewed by: V. Clare Badillo

The book is about two young super-sleuths who are helping their dad, who is a famous detective, in solving a mystery case. The case was that some professional smugglers are smuggling illegal drugs and are bringing and shipping them through the docks. The Hardy Boys, Joe and Frank, are having a hunch that an abandoned house on the cliff is the smugglers' hiding place.

I like the story because it was action-filled and it's so suspenseful and heart throbbing.

Jamie and the Mystery Quilt

Author: Vicki B. Erwin

Publisher: Scholastic

Reviewed By: Kimi Kan

A girl named Jamie lived with her mom. They lived in an old, wrecked up house. In school one of the boys in her math class was not doing very well, so she helped. She said she'll teach him after school. His name was Kevin. They liked each other a little. Jamie wanted to know him a little bit better anyway. One day they walked to her house to do the math. After a while they both got bored, so they went upstairs to the attic. Jamie's mom was not home but they went up anyway. Jamie didn't know she had so many antiques in her attic. Then she found a 50 year old quilt! It was a whole map of the whole house! There was a little rainbow on the side of the quilt. What did it mean? When her mom came home she wanted to sell the house to a nasty man named Mr. Payne! One day when she left the quilt outside, somebody stole it. She knew it was Mr. Payne! Jamie and Kevin go through a lot of hard things but they find the quilt and know what the rainbow on the quilt meant!

Nancy Drew Files: Into Thin Air; Case #58

Author: Carolyn Keene

Publisher: Pocket Books

Reviewed and illustrated by: Laurel Lynn Snead

Into Thin Air is about Nancy Drew and her friends. I really like this book. Nancy Drew is a very good series. This series is a very good series for kids. I advise everyone to read this book. This book is one of the best in the series. I really adore Nancy Drew, especially in this one book. Everyone should read this book, or any other book from the series. Carolyn Keene is a very good author. I hope you have a chance to read it.

Nancy Drew Files: A Secret in Time; Case #100

Author: Carolyn Keene

Publisher: Pocket Books

Reviewed by: Andrea Choye

In this story Nancy solved a case about a clock. Nancy had an old clock and she displayed it at an antique exposition. The front of the antique clock was open and somebody stole a rose brooch and hid it in the front of the clock and closed it. Then he ran off. The man who stole the brooch tried to run Nancy and her friends off of the bridge. But, Nancy and her friends didn't fall off of the bridge. Then Nancy went home and heard a knock on the door. She opened the door and a knife was stuck to the door with a note on it. Then Nancy got a phone call. On the other line, there was a man that said he kidnapped her friend. If Nancy wanted to see her again, she had to bring him the brooch. So Nancy brought him the brooch and he took Nancy and her friend to a freezer where George was waiting and locked them up. Soon they saw two figures outside the glass door. They were police officers. They opened the door and got Nancy and her friend out.

The Mystery of the Blue Ring

Author: Patricia Reilly Giff

Publisher: Peter Smith

Reviewed by: Danny Lee

The story is about a girl named Emily Arrow. Her blue ring is missing. Now everyone knows that Dawn stole it just because she borrowed it last week for a unicorn. So now with her grandmother's detective kit she's going to find the thief.

The book was o.k. Dawn's kit was funny. Dawn shouldn't have been looking for the ring because Emily and Dawn hate each other. Emily should have remembered that she had taken it off. The good thing was that she didn't get in trouble. She was lucky that she remembered about it. She's also lucky that it might have been even serious.

The Ghost at Dawn's House

Author: Ann M. Martin

Publisher: Scholastic

Reviewed by: Emily Abernathy

Would you like a good scare? Well, if you do this is the right book for you. This book is about a secret passage. It is a surprising book, so if you like mysteries, I suggest you read this book.

Something Queer at the Library

Author: Elizabeth Levy

Publisher: Dell

Reviewed and illustrated by: Thomas Yi

Jill and Gwen try to solve a mystery about a person who cut pictures out of library books of Lhasa Apsos (a dog).

I like the book because it shows details like clues and it's pretty funny. I think other kids will like it for the same reasons I have. I think ages 8-12 should read this book.

Mallory's Mystery Diary

Author: Ann M. Martin

Publisher: Scholastic

Reviewed by: Eileen Tram

There are two parts I liked. I liked how Mallory always felt when she read a part from Sophie's diary. I liked when Buddy finds a paper in the trunk that is a clue. I'll bet mostly all the girls will love it because it makes you want to know what happened to Sophie.

The Egypt Game

Author: Zilpha Keatly Snyder

Publisher: Dell

Reviewed by: Cheryll Del Rosario

This book is about two girls (plus a little brother) who start a game in the backyard of a strange antique shop. Soon the three kids turn to four, four then to six. Suddenly strange things start to happen. Is it the Professor, owner of the antique shop? I like this book because it's exciting up till the very ending. I think kids will like this book because it has a lot of mystery in it. I think kids who are 9-12 will like this book.

The Secret of Gumbo Grove

Author: Eleanora E. Tate

Publisher: Franklin Watts

Reviewed by: Camille Hearst

Who was Alexander Morgan G. Dickson? Why was he dug up from his grave? Raisin Stackhouse discovers this and many other secrets of African-Americans from her town Gumbo Grove, S.C. For instance Gussie Ann Veeren, who died when she was 10-years-old, is kin to 14-year-old Big Boy, who weighs close to 200 pounds. Raisin also discovers her Great-Uncle Jarvis. At one time he was the only African-American to own part of the beach. If you're like me, 10 (or older), and like mystery, history, and adventure, then pick up this book at your local library.

People

Kids like reading about people they can relate to. It's encouraging to read about people who have the same problems as we do and who are able to solve them. It's also fun to read about real people who do great things. Some of the books in this section are light hearted and will make you giggle. Others deal with more serious topics.

Romeo and Juliet Together (and Alive) at Last

Author: Avi

Publisher: Avon

Reviewed by: Tiffany Varek

This book is about two kids in the eighth grade, one is a boy named Pete Salte and the other one is a girl named Anabell Stackpool. Pete has fallen in love with Anabell and she likes him too. But both are much too shy to do anything about it. So Pete's friend Ed Sitrow and the other eighth graders at South Orange River School cook up a scheme to give the budding romance a boost. It's a school production of *Romeo and Juliet* with the bashful pair in the leading roles, everybody's waiting for the kissing scenes. What happens next is the most hilarious and disastrous production of *Romeo and Juliet* ever.

I think kids 9-12 would enjoy this book because it's filled with laughs, romance, disaster, and more action than even Shakespeare imagined. I strongly recommend this book.

Lee Ann: The Story of A Vietnamese-American Girl

Author: Tricia Brown

Publisher: Putnam's Sons

Reviewed by: Maika Onishi

Lee Ann is a story about a Vietnamese-American girl who lived in Vietnam then moved to America. She takes English as a Second Language every day. She does the pledge to the flag.

Her whole life has changed, Vietnamese to American. This is a wonderful book. Any age would like this book.

Reviewed by: Kara Yamagami

Lee Ann is based on a Vietnamese family and their lives. Before Lee Ann was born there was a war. Her family wanted to move so they could have a better life. They went to a refugee camp and waited a year to go to the United States. Lee Ann went to a good school and learned a lot.

I like this because I learned about a Vietnamese family. The picture I like the most is the scene where Lee Ann and her mother were preparing a special dinner for the holiday.

Ages 6-9 would probably like this book.

Someone Special, Just Like You

Author: Tricia Brown

Publisher: Holt, Rinehart

Reviewed by: Austin Furta-Cole

Someone Special Just Like You is based on a nursery school of disabled children. It shows that disabled kids can do the same things as everyone else. It has a meaningful story that really means a lot. It's a good book for kids to read with their parents. Kids learn they shouldn't tease other disabled kids because they're just the same as everyone else. The best age to read this is 7 through 14.

A Little Princess

Author: Frances Hodgson Burnett

Publisher: Dell

Reviewed by: Eileen Hu

My favorite book is called *A Little Princess*. It is about a girl who gets sent to boarding school. Her name is Sara and she is very rich. Miss Minchin, the teacher, hates her, but spoils her, so her father would be pleased with the school. One day Sara's father dies penniless and Sara has to work for the school to pay the bills. I don't want to give away the end so it's up to you to read the book and see what happens to Sara. I like this book because it has a happy ending and it taught me some things about people. I think other kids will like this book because it teaches you what it's like to suffer or be out in the cold. This book is for all ages.

Reviewed and illustrated by: Julia Denning

I liked this fanciful book because books without fantasy are usually dull and uninteresting, but this book surprised you with wonderful, magical occurences, and with horrible, unimaginable experiences. After becoming a maid, things magically and wonderfully began to happen to Sara. Then she met the man from India who lived next door to Miss Minchin's Seminary. I won't tell you anymore about the story, but I will tell you this: I recommend this book to people ages 9 to 100.

Scared Silly

Author: Eth Clifford

Publisher: Scholastic

Reviewed by: Cindy Gonzalez

The book's about when Mary Rose and Jo Beth Onetree and their father see a sign "The Walk-Your-Way-Around-the-World." At first it's very boring, but then it gets exciting because at last they can't find a way out. I think they would like it because it talks about being in a museum and you imagine you were there. All ages would like it.

Matilda

Author: Roald Dahl

Publisher: Viking Penguin

Reviewed by: Gwenn Seemel

Who would think that sweet little Matilda was behind the jokes on Miss Trunchbull that made all the kindergarten students laugh? Was it really Matilda who put superglue in her crooked father's hat? Read how this little genius got revenge on all the bad grown-ups and join in the fun!

Reviewed and illustrated by: Douglas Wong

Matilda is the funniest book ever written! It is filled with comedy and a touch of mystery. I love it so much I couldn't get away from it! Over and over I read it! It's super, fantastic, just great!

In this super story, the girl Matilda is a pure genius. Unfortunately, their empty-headed, no-good parents don't think so. Well they don't think Matilda somehow brilliantly got them back.

This story is good for anyone who wants a huge laugh. I love it, it's super! You've got to read it!

Reviewed by: Stephanie Brenner

Matilda is about a girl, her loving teacher, and her family. Matilda doesn't like her family because they hate to read and love to watch the television.

Matilda is a very good book and it might be my favorite book. It is exciting and funny, all in one book. If I were you I would run to a bookstore and get it. It is only 240 pages, and it only took me four days to read it. Try it! You'll like it! Trust me!

Helen Keller

Author: Margaret Davidson

Publisher: Scholastic

Reviewed by: Justine

The book is a very good book. It tells us about a girl and how blind people live. I adore this book. It tells me how it is to learn things when you're blind. I think a lot of people should read this book because it tells them about how blind people lived. The book is non-fiction, and its true. It is very lovely too. This book is great because, it is about a person's life and how she lived. Helen Keller is my all time favorite!

Now One Foot, Now the Other

Author: Tomie De Paola

Publisher: Putnam

Reviewed by: Paul Acerno

It's about a boy and his grandfather and they are best friends and their favorite thing to do is go and make a tower out of building blocks. But one day grandpa has a stroke and the boy does whatever he could do to get Grandpa better. It's a great story and it helps you understand sad things that happen.

The Great Brain

Author: John D. Fitzgerald

Publisher: Dell

Reviewed by: Terrence Wong

This book is about a very smart boy who gets into a lot of trouble with his "great brain" and money-loving heart. Tom Fitzgerald, alias The Great Brain, outsmarts all the kids in his town by using his Great Brain. After he is done with all the kids, they all are broke.

I love *The Great Brain* because it is unpredictable so it makes you want to read on to see what he does next. The book is also very funny because it's written through the Great Brain's trusting little brother's eyes, who always falls for The Great Brain's pranks.

The Great Brain Reforms

Author: John D. Fitzgerald

Publisher: Dell

Reviewed and illustrated by: Marvin Hong

The Great Brain Reforms is a humorous book for people age 8 and above. I enjoyed this book because it was full of action

and comedy. This book is just full of humorous ways Tom D. Fitzgerald, otherwise known as The Great Brain, swindles every male kid in the city. He even swindled his brothers, Sweyn D., John D., and Frankie. This book is very enjoyable.

The Slave Dancer

Author: Paula Fox

Publisher: Dell

Reviewed and illustrated by: Molly Denning

The Slave Dancer was a wonderful, historical novel. It was a book about how slaves were treated in the 1800's. The book was excellent, it had loads of adventure. I also love to learn about history so this book was fascinating to me.

The main character was a 12-year-old boy named Jessie. Jessie was kidnapped because he could play the fife. He was taken to a slave trading ship to "dance" the slaves. He played the fife so the slaves could dance as an exercise to stay healthy until they were sold. I won't tell you what happened next! Read *The Slave Dancer* to find out!

The Patchwork Quilt

Author: Valerie Flournoy

Publisher: Reading Rainbow Book

Reviewed by: Aimee Mizuno

The book is about a girl named Tanea and her grandmother. Tanea's grandmother is making a quilt. She says it's going to be special. I liked the book because it's filled with family love. I would recommend this book to people all ages (because my mother cries every time she reads it to me).

Blue Willow

Author: Doris Gates

Publisher: Scholastic

Reviewed and illustrated by: Megan Gilkey

I like *Blue Willow* because it's good for 7 year olds and up. And the poor family has hardly anything, but Janey has one willow plate but that willow plate has a story. Janey Larkin loves that plate. When I read that book it made me think that I have so much and I hardly need any of it.

I think it's a great book. It really caught my feelings. Read this book now and it will catch yours.

Stone Fox

Author: John R. Gardiner

Publisher: HarperCollins

Reviewed by: Michael Luu

There was a boy named Willy. He lived with his grandfather and a dog named Searchlight. One day his grandfather did not wake up so Willy called a doctor. His grandfather was sick. Willy needed money to save the potato farm.

I think *Stone Fox* is the best book I've ever read. The book is about believing in yourself. I liked everything in the book. This book is for you. You would like the people in the book. Have fun reading the book.

Thirteen Ways to Sink a Sub

Author: Jamie Gilson

Publisher: Lothrop

Reviewed by: Alicia Louie

Thirteen Ways to Sink a Sub is a story about a boy named Hobie Hanson and his class. His class is a fourth grade class, one of two in Central Elementary School. One day, when their teacher, Mr. Star, who almost never gets sick, gets sick, 4B gets a sub who has never taught before. When they find out they plan to "sink the sub," or to make her cry.

Room 4B tries all these obnoxious things on the sub, boys against girls, but the sub knows more than they do.

I liked this story because it showed what a kid could do if he or she had a new, very new substitute teacher in a very bad, noisy, or just plain terrible class. If a class was left alone with a brand new substitute teacher, no doubt about it, would a class go wild? Yes!

What I didn't like about this story is when they play all these weird tricks that might hurt someone if in reality, they tried. Even so, I liked the story. I think you should read this book.

Fudge

Author: Charlotte Towner Graeber

Publisher: Pocket Books

Reviewed by: Felicia Ortez

This book is about a boy named Chad Abernathy. His best friend Thomas Garcia has a famale dog that is pregnant. She had eleven dark brown puppies. The runt of the litter was Chad's favorite and he named it Fudge. He got his parents to buy it for him.

I love this book because this story is really darling. It has a nice happy ending, Chad gets the dog he wanted and everyone is happy. He takes very good care of Fudge and loves him very much. If the dog ever made a mess he would clean it up. He was very responsible, because he didn't want to lose the dog.

Reviewed by: Emily Ortez

Chad's best friend's dog is having puppies! Chad is so excited when his father makes a deposit on one of the puppies! But then his mother says she's having twins! Will Chad be able to keep Fudge? This book was good because Chad did his best to have Fudge and even after some mistakes, in the end Fudge is his.

Wait Till Helen Comes: A Ghost Story

Author: Mary Downing Hahn

Publisher: Clarion Books

Reviewed by: Kiu Ly (Stacey)

Molly and Michael are going to find out who their spooky, wicked, little stepsister is talking to every day in the graveyard right in their backyard! I like it because I've been Molly sometimes. Read this book! I guarantee you that you'll like it, 12-year-olders!

Though Heather was wicked to Molly, she knew she had to save her life from Helen, and FAST!

Kevin Corbett Eats Flies

Author: Patricia Hermes

Publisher: Pocket Books

Reviewed and illustrated by: Dana Medina

This book is about a boy named Kevin Corbett who eats bugs for money. When Kevin was little his mom died. Ever since, Kevin and his Father have been moving from one place to another. Kevin likes this new place where he just moved. But his father said they are moving again. Kevin doesn't want to move, so he and a girl in his class, Bailey, set a date for Kevin's father and their teacher Miss Holt.

I liked this book because it had a lot of humor and warmth; it even has some risky parts. I think kids would like it because it makes you laugh, and shows how risky things are.

The Best Laid Plans of Jonah Twist

Author: Natalie Honeycutt

Pulisher: Bradbury

Reviewed by: Steven H.

The story is about a boy named Jonah. He doesn't have any friends. When he goes to school, people push him around and play tricks on him. People throw pencils at him. He wants to have a pet snake. He has a sister, mother, father and a dog.

This is a great book. I like it because it is kind of funny. It is about a boy named Jonah and his life suddenly twisted. The only thing I don't like about this book is that it is kind of long. If you like to read books that take place in a school, I recommend that you should read this book. I like this book and so will you.

Bunk Mates

Author: Johanna Hurwitz

Publisher: Scholastic

Reviewed and illustrated by: Carmen Lee

This story is about a boy named Jay Koota. His family is planning to spend two weeks of vacation in Vermont. Jay would rather stay home.

The thing I like about the story is that most of the story is about the two families on their vacation in the woods. The part I like was when Jay was surprised that Mickey would be his buddy, even though Mickey is older than Jay by four years. But, Mickey still plays with him. I think Mickey is a nice and kind boy. The part I didn't like is the first part. Jay was always grouchy. But after the vacation, he became nice.

Autumn Street

Author: Lois Lowry

Publisher: Dell

Reviewed by: Daljit Dhami

Autumn Street was about a girl who moves from New York to Pennsylvania because her father has to go to War with the Japanese. So she goes to her granny's house in Penn. and she meets a black boy and they have lots of adventures. I liked it because it was very thrilling and breathtaking. I think kids around 9 to 13-years-old would like it because it lets you feel what it was like to be a kid when World War II was happening.

The Old Man Who Made the Trees Bloom

Author: Tamizo Shibano

Publisher: Heian International

Reviewed and illustrated by: Mark Hutchinson

This is a very exciting story. The reason I like it is because it's sort of like real life and it also teaches you a lesson. The lesson it teaches you is "It doesn't pay to be greedy." I also liked it because when the greedy old man tried to make the trees bloom like the nice man did, he got ashes all over the emperor. Then the emperor made him go to jail.

With You and Without You

Author: Ann M. Martin

Publisher: Scholastic

Reviewed by: Emily Ortez

Liza has always loved her father but she finally finds out that he is dying! She doesn't know how they were going to survive without her father. When he is gone he showed Liza how to love again.

    This book is a really good book and the O'Haras are a very strong family. Their father showed them that even without him they could survive. He also showed them that it is better to love and lose than not to love at all.

The Baby-Sitters Club Super Special #3
Winter Vacation

Author: Ann Martin

Publisher: Scholastic

Reviewed by: Sandy Ross

Every year Stoneybrook Middle School gets invited to a lodge in Vermont for Winter Fun! They babysit a bunch of little kids. A ghost is discovered, two girls fall in love with French skiers. A winter war between two teams and a girl that can't stand up in her skates, and if it doesn't stop snowing they might be snowbound till spring. They're all the BABY-SITTERS CLUB. 10-13 kids will love it! It's exciting and dreamy!

The Baby-Sitters Club Super Special #6
New York, New York!

Author: Ann M. Martin

Publisher: Scholastic

Reviewed by: Sara Constance

I like this book because it's about baby-sitting and I like to take care of children. It's about the Baby-Sitters Club going to New York. One girl is totally freaked out, two of the girls get to baby-sit and the other four just tour all around the city.

I think other kids will like it because it tells you about some of the places in the city and if you like mysteries you'll find one in here!

Reviewed by: Shelley Gullion

This is a book about seven girls who form a babysitters club in Stoneybrook, Connecticut. One winter, the seven girls decided to spend two weeks in New York City visiting one of the girl's (Stacy's) father. The girls split up and have funny adventures.

I think girls ages 8-11 would enjoy reading about the fun they had on a trip to New York.

The Baby-Sitter's Club #19
Claudia and the Bad Joke

Author: Ann M. Martin

Publisher: Scholastic

Reviewed and illustrated by: Cindy Ly

This book is about a girl named Claudia Kishi. She breaks her leg on a booby-trapped swing. Claudia has to go to the hospital. It tells you about a story of a broken leg and tragedies, the story of being in the hospital for three weeks, and trying to out-joke a practical joke queen named Betsy Sobak.

The Baby-Sitters Club #37

Author: Ann M. Martin

Publisher: Scholastic

Reviewed by: Felicia Ortez

This book is about a girl named Dawn. She falls in love with a 16-year old. And she's only 13. Later she finds out that he's cheating on her, so she gives up on him. Then she meets a boy that's her own age.

I think this book is really interesting. It's worth taking the time to read it. You kind-of learn something from it. And I think that some other children will like this book. I know that my sister and I like it. My friends probably will too.

Stacey's Emergency

Author: Ann M. Martin

Publisher: Scholastic

Reviewed by: Rhonda Richards

This story is another one of those great Baby-Sitters Club books written by the talented Ann M. Martin. This story is about how Stacey finds out that her diabetes is getting worse and she ends up in the hospital. I like this story because it helps you understand how people with diabetes cope with the disease. I think kids would like it for the same reason; but it's not all about diabetes. It's basically based on girls, babysitting and having fun. This book would be best from ages 10-13.

A, My Name is Ami

Author: Norma Fox Mazer

Publisher: Scholastic

Reviewed by: Hsiao Cheer

It's a teenage story of two girls that have been best friends for four years. Everything about them either matches or is opposite. The letters of their names are opposite too! I think you will enjoy it, because there are a lot of interesting parts.

New Kids On The Block Backstage Surprise

Author: Seth McEvoy and Laure Smith

Publisher: Pocket Books

Reviewed by: Lauren Masio

This book is all about the exciting adventures New Kids on the Block have. I like this book because it taught me to never talk to strangers and to never go off by myself. Other kids will like the story because it has all the action they'll love. I think all kids that like adventure will love it. You can be any age.

Anne of Green Gables

Author: Lucy Maud Montgomery

Publisher: Bantam

Reviewed by: Adinah Curtis

Anne is an orphan with a good imagination and an excellent vocabulary. One day Matthew and Marilla Cuthbert adopt Anne by "accident." At first they want to send her back to the orphanage but when they see how charming and talkative Anne is, they just can't imagine life without her. You'll read all about the funny predicaments and serious mistakes Anne gets herself into. I like it because you can get a good laugh out of it and at the same time learn something new. I think other kids would like it because it is very different from life nowadays, but just like life in 1908. I think kids ages 11-14 will like it because they can understand the difficult vocabulary used throughout the book and learn some new words too! It's a classic. You have to read it!

Reviewed by: Ratchel Hemphill

Matthew and Marilla want a boy to help with the farm chores. But when Matthew goes to the train station to pick up the boy it turns out to be a freckle-faced redhead girl. They're in for a lot of suprises. This is a book for all ages. I like this book because it's interesting.

Reviewed by: Holly English

I chose this book because it's funny and interesting. It's about an orphan who no one wanted, until she moved to Green Gables and an elderly brother and sister took her in. She lived there throughout the rest of her growing-up years. A lot of strange and hilarious things happen. I think most 11- year-olds and older would mostly enjoy it. (I even know of some adults who enjoy reading it!)

Reviewed by: Luisina Basilico

I liked the book because it is funny how Anne talks so much and uses big, poetical words. I also liked it because I think it is funny what she does when she gets a bad temper. I think other kids of 10 and up will like this book because it is funny and once you start reading it you can't put it down.

Reviewed and illustrated by: Sherry Yu

Some of the reasons I enjoyed this delightful classic were because Anne was always high-spirited, and thought the best of things. Her lively imagination helped her through both good and bad times, but mostly got her into trouble. *Anne of Green Gables* is a great book that I recommend to people ages 10 and over who seek books full of adventure, excitement and surprises. I hope that others will enjoy reading it just as I did.

Reviewed by: Sandy Yu

Anne of Green Gables is a wonderful classic for all children and adults ages ten and above. Anne Shirley is an imaginative, mischievous, talkative, redhead orphan who comes to Green Gables to live with Marilla and Matthew Cuthbert, who wanted a boy to come and help with the farm chores. Matthew thinks that Anne would be a wonderful help to Marilla, but Marilla thinks that Anne would just bother her and wants to send her back. I enjoy this book a great deal because Anne goes through a whole lot of changes, adventures, and misadventures that I'm sure many others will enjoy.

The Girl Who Owned A City

Author: O.T. Nelson

Publisher: Dell

Reviewed by: Sara Baches

This book is about a disease that kills everyone in the United States over the age of 12. They have to survive with no adults. This is an excellent book. Children and even adults would enjoy this book because it is exciting. Kids the ages of 10-15 would enjoy the best.

Sing Down The Moon

Author: Scott O' Dell

Publisher: Dell

Reviewed and illustrated by: Danielle Pittman

Sing Down the Moon is one of the best books I've ever read. It is a story, told by a young Navajo girl, of the destruction of her village and her people. It tells some of the hardships suffered by the American Indians, during the "Trail of Tears."

I liked this wonderful book because there is a genuine heroine in it. The narrator is not weak, and never waits to be

rescued. I also liked it because the Native Americans are represented in a more positive way than they are in most books. I recommend this book for children 10 years to about 15-years-old.

Don't Make Me Smile

Author: Barbara Park

Publisher: Alfred A. Knopf

Reviewed by: K-Linh Ho

This book is funny and also sad. It's about a boy named Charlie Hickle. His parents get a divorce and he said,"How could they ruin my life like this!" Also he wouldn't go to the school. I like it because it made my sister and me laugh, and should do the same for you.

Sweet Valley Kids

Author: Francine Pascal

Publisher: Bantam

Reviewed by: Emily Pena and Nicole Ogden

Sweet Valley Kids is a series of fun and exciting books. It's about identical twin girls, Jessica and Elizabeth, but not just any twins, these twins have lots of exciting adventures together. (For more on this series, see page 80.)

The Sign in Mendel's Window

Author: Mildred Phillips & Margot Zemach

Publisher: Macmillan

Reviewed by: Wendy Cogan

The reason I like this book so much is because I like stories with little towns in them. I also like it because the characters have funny last names. Also all the houses lean on each other. I like how Molly tricked Mr. Tinker by asking him easy but trick questions. When Mr. Tinker got the two questions wrong he was surprised, and he went to jail instead of Mr. Mendel. That is why I like this book.

My Sister the Meanie

Author: Candice F. Ransom

Publisher: Apple

Reviewed by: Bree Hornbuckle

I like this book because I have a sister who is so PERFECT, and I am a nothing. That is the same way Jackie (the main character) feels. She desperately wants to be popular, and she ends up popular in her own way.

Read this book to find out more.

Annabelle Swift, Kindergartner

Author: Amy Schwartz

Publisher: Orchard Books

Reviewed by: Yvette Cashmere

I like this book because I like the characters a lot. This book is about a little girl, Annabelle, who has a big sister. Annabelle's sister tells her stuff that you would not know in kindergarten. When Annabelle was playing a game with the kindergarten she said all the wrong things. At the end, Annabelle counts up the milk money. She got to be milk monitor and it made her very proud.

Tell Me a Mitzi

Author: Lore Segal

Publisher: Farrar, Straus and Giroux

Reviewed by: Carter Harris

This is the book I liked the most. My favorite chapter was called "Mitzi Takes a Taxi." Mitzi wakes up and gets her brother all dressed and tries to go to her grandma's house. She goes to the elevators and goes down. Then she goes to the street and yells "taxi." A taxi stops in front of her. The man that drives the taxi puts her and her brother in the taxi. He says, "Where to?" Mitzi says, "Grandma's house." He says, "Where is it?" Mitzi says, "I don't know." And she has to go back to her apartment.

Kate's Book

Author: Mary Francis Shura

Publisher: Scholastic

Reviewed by: Janel Boshers

This book is about a girl named Kate. She is traveling to Oregon with her family. She has a friend named Fildy. They have lots of adventures. Like when they saw an Indian, or when they got stuck in a twister. Fildy doesn't have a mother, just a father, and a bunch of brothers. So she learns a lot from Kate and Kate's mom. Kate is sad when Fildy's dad decides to go to California. But there's a happy ending.

I liked this book because it was exciting. I think other kids would like it because its exciting. I think kids 8 and up would like Kate because I read *Kate's Book* when I was 8.

Kate's House

Author: Mary Francis Shura

Publisher: Scholastic

Reviewed by: Veronica

In 1843, Kate Alexander and her family are in Oregon at last, by traveling by the wagon trip. But after sunny Ohio, Kate can't accept the dark woods at home because everything is crumbling, the noise is silent and scary.

I liked Kate because she had courage to be alone in a log cabin. The part that I liked the best is when Kate meets a new friend, Cathy Lawosome. When Kate was heartbroken, she was very sad. Kate and Cathy are cheerful, nice, and caring. When Kate is alone, she was scared. I liked this book very much.

Encyclopedia Brown

Author: Donald J. Sobal

Publisher: Scholastic

Reviewed by: Jesse Cano

Encyclopedia is a boy genius. Anytime Mr. Brown, the cop, Encyclopedia's dad, had a case he could not solve, Encyclopedia came out with the answer. I think all kids like it, I like it, my dad likes it, and little kids too. I think the books of *Encyclopedia Brown* should be in *Books We Love Best*, because it is one of the Books I Love Best!

The Slave Ship

Author: Emma Gelders Sterne

Publisher: Scholastic

Reviewed by: Shani Delaney

The book was about a group of men, women and children who were taken from Africa, and held in chains aboard a ship called the Amistad heading for Cuba. After a struggle with the captain they have control of the ship. But they have no knowledge of how to get home except by following the sun. So at night, two white men still on the ship change course.

The ship is zig-zagging around in the ocean! Finally, they run into America, and the rest is for YOU to find out!

I recommend this book to any child 10 and up. It is an interesting book, and true story. I think most anyone would enjoy it.

Noonday Friends

Author: Mary Stolz

Publisher: HarperCollins

Reviewed by: Stephanie Horn

My report is on two girls that live in New York City in Greenwich Village. It will be an exciting story.

It is about a girl named Franny who has a dream. Her dream is about wanting to be rich and becoming a ballerina. She doesn't get to tell her dream to many friends because she has to baby sit her little brother, Marsh, while her mother works.

My favorite part was when Franny had a dream about her becoming a rich person and becoming a ballerina because I used to be one in second grade.

Sweet Valley Twins, Standing Out

Author: Jamie Suzanne (creator: Francine Pascal)

Publisher: Bantam

Reviewed by: Emily Ortez

Billie's mother is having another baby and she already knows it's a boy because she is older than most mothers. Billie is sad that her brother is taking her name and her body is changing. Also Sally is taking her best friend away from her.

This book is a great book because Billie is strong and she lived through life's little changes. She survived all of it and I think that's the most important in people.

Sweet Valley Twins, the Twin's Little Sister

Author: Jamie Suzanne (Creator: Francine Pascal)

Publisher: Bantam

Reviewed by: Amanda Zaccone

One of my books is part of the Sweet Valley Twins series. I think other kids would like these books because the "twins," (Jessica and Elizabeth Wakefield) get into trouble and I like the way they sort them out. Elizabeth is the more serious one and Jessica is the one that likes to have too much fun all in one short time. This book is about the twins babysitting a spoiled 5-year-old girl named Chrissy. I think that this book should be included in *Books We Love Best* because it is a very good book, so good that I've read it thirty times and I've only had it for a couple of weeks. I guarantee that you will love it too.

Sweet Valley Twins, 1-5 Sneaking Out

Author: Jamie Suzanne (Creator: Francine Pascal)

Publisher: Bantam

Reviewed by: Alyssa Rasmussen

I enjoy the series Sweet Valley High because they have twins in it and they are usually getting along. I also like it because they dress up alike and do their hair the same. Also they both go to dances. I think other kids would enjoy it too because there is always something going on that has to involve them. I think that it should be in *Books We Love Best* because almost any age from 2nd grade and up can read them. And also always at the end it asks a question and if you read the next book you would get the answer. I hope that other people get a chance to read these books because they will enjoy them just like I did.

Follow the Drinking Gourd

Author: Janette Winter

Publisher: Alfred A. Knopf

Reviewed and illustrated by: Nate Baumsteiger

I liked *Follow the Drinking Gourd* because it was outstanding. A man can set free slaves by singing the slaves a song about the drinking gourd. If the slaves follow the drinking gourd north it would lead them to freedom. If the slaves also followed a mark of a footprint on some trees they will finally get to the Ohio River. Then Peg Leg Joe rowed them across the river to freedom.

Grades 7-12
(ages 12-17+)

Because older children tend to read less, the number of reviews vary with grade levels. The 7-9 and 10-12 reviews were combined, and more categories were added, such as politics, poetry, environment, and horror. Unlike the first and second chapters, the 7-12 content changed from a lot of science fiction and fantasy to more serious fiction as well as non-fiction topics like abuse, the environment, rape, politics, and other serious topics. Adolescents in junior and senior high school are reading different types of books than their younger brothers and sisters. Some of these are "the classics"; others are extremely modern.

Animal

Are you overwhelmed by animals, a true animal lover? If you have just answered yes to the above question, then you should try some of these recommended books by animal lovers like yourself.

The Cat Who Came For Christmas

Author: Cleveland Amory

Publisher: Little, Brown

Reviewed by: Saethra Fritscher

This book is very good! It's about a cat and his owner, Mr. Cleveland Amory, who is the founder of an animal safety group called the Fund for Animals. This group, among other things, rescues strays and that's how Mr. Amory came to have his cat. It's a funny, true story that people with a sense of humor between the ages of 12 and 17 would be likely to enjoy.

All Creatures Great and Small

Author: James Herriot

Publisher: Bantam

Reviewed by: Genni Schmidt

All Creatures Great and Small is about the adventures (and misadventures) of a Yorkshire vet. The reason I liked this book was because even the sad parts were told with warmth and humor. I think anyone who likes animals would like this book.

Mossflower

Author: Brian Jaques

Publisher: Avon

Reviewed by: Eli Sarnat

Mossflower is an action packed book about mice, moles, hedgehogs, badgers and more who battle rats and foxes for the right to be free. The author has an incredible ability to stay on three different plots at the same time. The combination of suspense, the detailed fighting and joyous, merry festivals can keep you going for hours. The only bad thing about it is that you can't find time to put it down. There are two other books in the trilogy that are equally good, *Redwall* and *Mattimeo*.

White Fang

Author: Jack London

Publisher: Scholastic

Reviewed by: Saethra Fritscher

In my opinion, Jack London's *White Fang* is one of the best books ever written. London conveys a powerful story about a part wolf, part dog named White Fang. The book makes you laugh and it makes you cry. For anybody ages 10 and up who loves animals and/or Jack London's work, I wholeheartedly recommend this book.

Island of the Blue Dolphins

Author: Scott O'Dell

Publisher: Dell

Reviewed and illustrated by: Helen Shum

Island of the Blue Dolphins is a fantastic book that will make you go on reading and probably make you cry. It would appeal to children ages 9-14. This story talks about an Indian girl named Karana who is left on an island and waits year after year for the ship to come back and get her. While waiting on the Island of the Blue Dolphins, Karana first becomes enemies with a pack of wild dogs then they become friends. I really think you will enjoy this book.

Where the Red Fern Grows

Author: Wilson Rawls

Publisher: Doubleday

Reviewed by: Hedy Lim

A young boy named Billy works hard for two years to earn 50 dollars for a pair of hunting hounds. He names them Old Dan and Little Ann, and he trains them to be the best hunting hounds in the country. Its a heartwarming story filled with love, companionship, and loyalty.

Reviewed by: Elizabeth Dong

Where the Red Fern Grows is the best book I ever read. It was an exciting book about a young boy named Billy who had two dogs. The names of the dogs were Old Dan and Little Ann, who spent their entire lives hunting for raccoon fur. They have many wonderful and daring adventures together that risk their lives. At the end both of the two loving, caring dogs die, the red fern grows over their headstones to form an arch. The red fern symbolizes that the angel passed over them and only the angel can plant that red fern. This book was the best story I read in my sixth grade year. The entire family, mom, dad and the sisters of Billy were sad that the dogs died. Little Ann and Old Dan did not live a very long life, but they both showed everyone a lot of courage.

Reviewed and illustrated by: Natalie J. Chan

Where the Red Fern Grows is the most heartwarming book in the world. This book is a joy for children 11 and up (adults too) because it tells how much a boy and his two dogs love each other. It is about an adventurous boy and how he and his dogs go coon hunting. The boy, Billy, trains his dogs to catch the smartest coons. At the end, Billy has grown to love his hounds more than ever. Finally, one of his hounds die. Heartbroken, Billy buries it. The next day, the other hound dies of loneliness. It uses every ounce left in its body to drag itself up to its companion and dies right next to his grave. The summer Billy moves away, he says goodbye to his hounds, and discovers that a sacred red fern has grown in the shape of a rainbow that connected them. There is an old myth that only an angel could plant the red ferns.

The Cricket in Times Square

Author: George Selden

Publisher: Yearling Books

Reviewed by: Tara Mahoney

This is an excellent book. I didn't just like parts of the book, but the whole book. Here's a preview of the book. Chester, a cricket, arrives in Times Square subway station in a picnic basket from his old home, Connecticut. A little boy from an unwealthy family, named Mario picks him up for a new pet and Chester takes up residence in the Bellinis' newsstand. Chester finds three very good friends: Mario, his best friend, and Broadway mouse named Tucker, and Tucker's friend, a cat named Harry.

Two of his good friends Tucker and Harry taught Chester how to sing classical, rock 'n roll, opera, and even Irish jigs. All of a sudden the newsstand went into a boom. The little cricket still wasn't happy. He left New York and took a train back to his homeland, Connecticut.

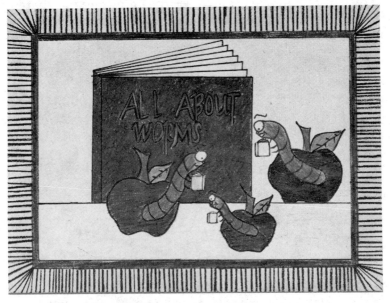

Illustration by: Pillar Teso

Fantasy/Science Fiction

Do you like to imagine things of all kinds? Do you always find yourself drifting into another world? Well, these books will help you in your unforgettable journey. This science fiction and fantasy section will boldly take you where no young man or woman has ever gone before.

Bless Me, Ultima

Author: Rudolfo A. Anaya

Publisher: TQS Rubns

Reviewed: Nancy Mendieta

This is an enchanting book about mystic occurrences in a boy's life after the arrival of Ultima, the town's "good" witch. This is a book that has it all!

Buy it! Pronto! That's Spanish for quick!

Queen Zixi of Ix: Or the Story of the Magic Cloak

Author: L. Frank Baum

Publisher: Dover Publications

Reviewed by: Saethra Fritscher

L. Frank Baum has outdone himself in this book! *Queen Zixi of Ix* is a book that ranks right up there with the *Wizard of Oz* and *Alice in Wonderland*, the all-time favorites of kids around the world. I loved this book because it has Baum's trademark good humor combined with fantastic creatures and silly characters to make up an all-around great book!

The Martian Chronicles

Author: Ray Bradbury

Publisher: Bantam

Reviewed by: Kristan Seemel

What might happen if humankind managed to land on Mars? What if they tried to colonize the red planet? This collection of short stories answers those questions and more in a witty and intriguing way. You don't have to be a science fiction fan to blast-off with this book!

The Mists of Avalon

Author: Marion Zimmer Bradley

Publisher: Del Rey Books

Reviewed by: Esther Odekirk

In my opinion this is a very good book. It's a different view of King Arthur and his time. In this book the readers see Morgaine, Arthur's half sister, as the "good guy" instead of an evil sorceress. It is primarily about two religions, a dying one and a new, prospering one, competing against each other to remain alive in the world. Morgaine is of the dying religion of Avalon, a priestess of the Goddess. Arthur on the other hand is of the new faith, Christianity.

I think of Arthur as a traitor. He broke his vow to Avalon, which was to keep both religions equal, and essentially became a full Christian. His wife, Gwenhyfar, played a big part in his betrayal.

I liked this book because of its originality and its ability to captivate me. I also liked the way the author told the story from a women's point of view. I thought it was a great book. (Most likely for ages 14 and up.)

Max and Me and the Wild West

Author: Gery Greer and Bob Ruddick

Publisher: Harcourt Brace Jovanovich

Reviewed by: Lalit Lakshmanan

I like the book because it is exciting. It tells you about Max and Steve, who bought a time machine for $2.50. They go to the time of the cowboys in the Wild West. Then they are stuck with the game of thieves.

Other people would like it because it gives lots of details of what is happening. The fighting scene looks real.

Playing Beatie Bow

Author: Ruth Park

Publisher: Macmillan

Reviewed by: Amber Fraga

Playing Beatie Bow is about a 12-year-old girl named Abigail Kirk, who gets caught in the past, and cannot return home until she has done the "special something" that she was sent here for. I really liked this book because of its adventure, and think that people of all ages (who can read) would enjoy this book. They will enjoy it because of its many features throughout the book, so as a result, many many people will be attracted to this book.

Alanna— the First Adventure:
Song of the Lioness Quartet

Author: Tamora Pierce

Publisher: Borzoi Sprinters

Reviewed by: Lauren Bensinger

Alanna—the First Adventure is about a girl who wants to become a knight. Read how she manages to stay at the castle where only young knights are allowed. She has trouble keeping her secret and it gets difficult to conceal her womanhood. This is an exciting book that is full of imagination and courage. Girls would love it. It is a lively tale.

Horror

Are you a person who enjoys being scared out of your wits? Do you like books that fill you with HORROR and make you afraid to read each page? Then, this section is for you. Try some of these highly recommended books.

Illustration by: Sherry Uy

Dawn

Author: V.C. Andrews

Reviewed by: Esther Odekirk

Dawn is the beginning of a new series by V.C. Andrews. It is about a young girl who is kidnapped when still an infant and is brought up thinking her kidnappers are her real parents. But at the age of 14 she is found and returned to her natural family. She finds out that her boyfriend is really her brother, and her worst enemy is her younger sister. Her grandmother is as cold as ice and puts her to work as a maid in their luxurious hotel. Her real father is too busy to really care about her needs and her mother is too sickly and weak.

All of the main characters in V.C. Andrews' books have difficulties and obstacles they have to overcome. Oftentimes they don't get what they want and what's best. Things usually turn out for the worst until the very end when at least one good thing happens. This is what I like about her books. Most books that I've read have everything turn out just perfect which, in my opinion, isn't always the case in the real world. I have enjoyed every single one of her books and I hope there are many more to come.

The Silence of the Lambs

Author: Thomas Harris

Publisher: St. Martin's Press

Reviewed by: Aviva Cushner

This is one of those books that you can NEVER put down. If you're in the mood to have a little blood, gore, and discomfort in your life, this is the book for you. Dr. Hannibal Lecter, a famed psychiatrist, a convicted serial killer, clever, brilliant, is knowledgeable about a current murderer on the loose nicknamed Buffalo Bill. FBI agent-in-training, Clarice Starling, must somehow get all the answers about Buffalo Bill's true identity through Dr. Lecter's confusing clues and scheming ways. A truly fascinating book, I highly recommend you read it—but not between the hours of darkness.

Carrie

Author: Stephen King

Publisher: New American Library

Reviewed by: Jessica Escobar

Stephen King has always been my favorite author. I wanted to read another of his stories. *Carrie* is a nicely thought-out book. It was beautifully written, and very scary. Carrie is one very frightened misunderstood character. All his characters seem well planned and his horror books are the best to read if you enjoy being scared. I suggest 14 and up read this book.

Misery

Author: Stephen King

Publisher: Signet Penquin Books

Reviewed by: Monica Villazana

Misery is a compelling novel. Its vividness filled me with horror. Stephen King wrote so descriptively that at times it was overwhelming. I had to close the book. I recuperated from the graphic images. He wrote about something soothing and hopeful. This novel is extremely well-written and much more graphic than the actual movie. I would suggest that you read this novel one day when you are ready to be scared out of your wits. The way Stephen King wrote it just sucked me into the story and I felt the same way Paul Sheldon felt toward Annie Wilkes. I found that this was one of the few novels that I just couldn't put down until I was finished.

Teacher's Pet

Author: Andrew Neiderman

Publisher: Zebra Books

Reviewed by: Jessica Escobar

Teacher's Pet is an interesting book to read. It's about a teacher who has the gift to make his students do anything he wants them to. But somehow the students seem to be more like Mr. Lucky. A very thrilling horror book. Nicely written by Andrew Neiderman. It has nice details and is quite scary.

Remember Me

Author: Christopher Pike

Publisher: Archway Paperback

Reviewed by: Katy Li

This book is about a girl who was murdered at her friend's birthday party. The police thought it was a suicide, but Shari knows better, and she planned to find the murderer and stop him/her from murdering again. In the ghostly world, Shari met an old dead friend who accompanied her while she spied on her friends. Shari even entered their dreams in order to find the murderer.

I like this book because it is very exciting, you never know what's going to happen next. You never know who the murderer is until you finish the book, which made me finish the book in record speed. This book is very creative, and also makes me imagine the scenes in this story.

The Unwanted

Author: John Saul

Publisher: Bantam

Reviewed by: Jesse Adamo

A girl who lost her mother in a car accident gains strange powers that she shares with animals.

It's a thriller and keeps you wide eyed and amazed. The images it creates are incredible, sometimes you even believe there's someone standing there watching you. I recommend it for ages 12 and up.

Illustration by: Brian Ly

Mystery

Wouldn't you like to be the detective who solves the un-solved mystery? Do you often find you're going crazy trying to figure out what will happen in the book, or who killed the millionaire? Was it the maid, the gardener, or was it the butler? If you like mind-boggling books like these, then thumb through this section and find yourself a really mysterious book.

The Grounding of Group Six

Author: Julian F. Thompson

Publisher: Avon Flare Book

Reviewed by: Lily Wong

In this book five students of Coldbrook Country School dis-covered, to their horror, that their parents had hired the organization to murder them because "they had enough of them." The only way the teenagers can outsmart the villains is if they devised a plan of counterattack. But does the group have enough willpower to succeed, now that they know their own "flesh and blood" would rather see them dead? Read this book and find out!

The Grounding of Group Six takes the reader on a roller coaster of fast-paced action from start to finish. The most interesting aspect of the book is that as the group must adapt to this sudden situation, a noticeable, yet gradual maturation occurs in each individual. By the conclusion, each person has uniquely metamorphisized into a responsible young adult.

Locked In Time

Author: Lois Duncan

Publisher: Dell Publishing

Reviewed by: Lily Wong

If you're already a big fan of Lois Duncan's books, you'll LOVE *Locked In Time*, if not you'll become a Duncan zeapt as soon as you read this suspense novel.

As with all of Duncan's stories, *Locked In Time* captures the reader's attention from page one. As soon as the character,

Nore Robbins arrives at Shadow Grove, to spend the summer with her widowed father's new family, her instincts tell her something is wrong.

From that point on, Duncan skillfully builds up the tension in the reader and between the characters as the story reaches its climax. To Nore's horror, she discovers that at Shadow Grove, time stands still—a fact which plays a key role in the mystery.

The reader will find herself *Locked In Time* with the characters as she becomes spellbound with the plot.

Duncan not only manages to end the tale with a dramatic, unexpected conclusion, but also leaves the reader thirsting for more. No wonder I ended up reading the whole Duncan mystery series—they follow the Lay's Potato Chip Slogan: No one can [read] just one!

Nobody Else Can Walk It for You

Author: P.J. Petersen

Publisher: Laurel Leaf Books

Reviewed by: Lily Wong

When 18-year-old Laura decides to lead her group of teenage Y campers deeper into a forest, all she wanted was some peace and quiet. Instead, three rowdy motorcyclists not only relentlessly harass the group, but also set out to stalk the campers as they try to escape them. Now it's no longer just a matter of peace and quiet, but of life and death.

I'd recommend *Nobody Else Can Walk It for You* to anyone who loves nature and seeks adventure. The author, P.J. Petersen, paints the breathtaking scenery of the background vividly through words while reminding the reader that the secluded forest may just as well serve as a perfect place for a murder to occur without anyone's notice.

Thus, as the chase intensifies, so does the theme of the "double-edged sword": that nature can either work for or against you. Only until the very last pages of the book does the reader discover which group fate has sided with.

People

Wouldn't you have liked to be in Paris in the 1700's at the storming of the Bastille, or maybe you would like to live as a young Indian boy who sees the last of his tribe and had to leave his home, where he used to fish and swim. If you love to read about people and their lives, this section is for you.

Go Ask Alice

Author: Anonymous

Publisher: Dell

Reviewed by: Jessica Escobar

Go Ask Alice is not only truthful, but honestly daring and real. Dealing with what most teens deal with—drugs. This is a book for teenagers 12 and up. It's very easy to get lost in Alice's world.

Clan of the Cave Bear

Author: Jean M. Auel

Publisher: Bantam Books

Reviewed by: Sarah Gancher

First in a series of (so far) four books, *Clan of the Cave Bear* is set in prehistoric times, a period of history rarely written about but interesting to imagine. The book is about a Cro-magnon woman being accepted by and growing up with a group of neanderthals. (If you don't know these terms, don't sweat it, you will by the end of the book.) But *Clan of the Cave Bear* isn't just about scientific terms. It's about learning to accept differences as a part of any person.

Jean M. Auel's style attaches you to the main character and makes you care about her. It's also painfully educational, but the story is so great you won't mind. Trust me, you won't be able to put it down. Grades 5-6 and up should really read this book. It's a good first adult novel, about as far from *Sweet Valley Twins* and other "young adult" literature as you can get. You become deeply involved with the book and characters, and I swear I cried at the end.

Reviewed by: Esther Odekirk

This book leads the reader into a world of emotions. The fear of being left alone, the anger and hate from being raped and tortured with words as well as physically, and the sorrow of rejection are only a small part of these emotions. But they aren't all bad, hurtful feelings. There's also the joy of victory and discovery as well as love, peace, hope, and happiness.

This book takes place in the primitive times of cave men. It is about a young girl, who after losing her parents in an earthquake, finds herself part of a strange people, called the Clan. To humans like herself the Clan is considered animalistic, and not as civilized as ordinary men.

Although she knows and practices the ways of the Clan her sick eyes that are always watering, her little outbursts that we call giggles or laughter, and that horrible sneer, considered a smile among us, set her apart from the rest of the Clan. But with all the sorrows and defeats she always seems to get something good out of everything, even in the end ....

This book had me crying one minute, laughing the next. Everybody must read it! (For ages 13 and up.)

The LeBaron Secret

Author: Stephen Birmingham

Publisher: Berkeley Publishing

Reviewed by: Iesha Johnson

This book was about the wife of Peter LeBaron who came to America from Germany. This book had a great scandal of incest which was really the climax of the book. In the end the family grew to be closer and the hostility was resolved.

I love this book because this book was interesting. It kept a lot of suspense throughout the book and it gave me a vivid idea of what the lifestyle of the rich and famous was really like.

It's Not the End of the World

Author: Judy Blume

Publisher: Dell

Reviewed by: Teeunva

This book is about a girl named Karen whose parents are getting a divorce. Karen is having a hard time dealing with the divorce, and she tries many times to get them back together.

I liked the book because I can relate to it, because my parents were never married to each other, they only lived together for eight years. And I now live in California with my mom and stepdad, my real dad still lives in Pennsylvania.

Other kids would like to read this book because if their parents ever get divorced it will help them understand that they're not the only ones who have this problem, and that they can get through it.

Wuthering Heights

Author: Emily Bronte

Publisher: Penguin Classics

Reviewed by: Lauren Bensinger

Wuthering Heights is a wonderful book that talks about the love between two people and the emotions and tragedies that try to keep them apart. I like this book because I feel the emotion of each character. It is beautiful because I can picture the Yorkshire moors and feel like I am walking along them. It is a difficult book but kids will like it because it is a classic and a wonderful piece of art.

The Chocolate War

Author: Robert Cormier

Publisher: Dell

Reviewed by: Sherri Marshall

This is a book about an all boys' school that is having money problems, and to fix the problem they have a chocolate candy sale.

I like this book because it shows the problems of a school and the different little groups that are formed to help the school make its deadline, and not have to merge with the girls' school down the street.

Nectar In a Sieve

Author: Bruce Cutler

Publisher: Juniper Press

Reviewed by: Nancy Mendieta

Nectar in a Sieve is about a poverty stricken Hindu family that strives for survival. The rather large family deals with the hunger and the pain of watching two sons leave in order to find jobs, watching the daughter become a prostitute, and seeing their youngest son die a slow death.

This is a powerful book that combines culture and the hardship of poverty.

Missing: Carrie Phillips, Age 15

Author: Janet Dagon

Publisher: Willowisp Press

Reviewed by: Jessica Escobar

This is a very interesting book. Finally something for those whose older sister or brother has run away. It shows the effect on those who are loved ones left behind.

For those 9-15 years of age, this book can be enjoyed. I believe this book is good mainly because most often runaways have their stories. Now here is a book about the loved ones they leave behind.

A Tale of Two Cities

Author: Charles Dickens

Publisher: Gallery Books

W.H. Smith Publishers Inc.

Reviewed by: Mechaka Gardner

A Tale of Two Cities is an excellent book about the times of the French Revolution and how it came about. It takes place in Paris and London in the 1700's. It began with the storming of the Bastille Prison on July 14, 1789.

I liked this book because when I read the first chapter I didn't understand a word, then when my teacher explained to me the way this book is written and the various contents of the story, I couldn't put the book down.

Other kids would like this book because of the way it was written. It was detailed in a very complex manner, still and yet understandable for youth among the ages of 15 and up.

The Great Gatsby

Author: F. Scott Fitzgerald

Publisher: Macmillan

Reviewed by: Rupert Tagnipes

If a book can ever be chosen based on its flair, originality, and ingenuity, *The Great Gatsby* is the obvious candidate. Fitzgerald deals intelligently with social and ethical issues of that time and prophetically answers the issues of tomorrow.

The main characters in the novel are Jay Gatsby and Nick Calloway. Nick is the narrator and in the early chapters tells of his dislike of the "nouveau riche" Gatsby. Nick soon realizes, however that all the people in New York and perhaps all of the society are truly the demons in this novel. Nick comes to realize that Gatsby is the apparent "good guy," a mere victim in this game of life.

Gatsby is a man who has lived the American Dream, that dream being hard work and labor leading to financial success. Yes, Gatsby has achieved this dream but soon that dream became corrupt. He betrayed the dream for a woman—Nick's cousin Daisy. The money now was dirty, achieved not from hard work but from illicit labor—a needed shortcut; a get-rich-quick scam to achieve his dream of Daisy Buchanan. He chased that dream to the bitter end and the irony of it all was that Daisy wasn't even worth it. Despite Gatsby's secret past and shadowy businesses, Nick soon comes to respect and love him for who he is. Gatsby was killed by his dream and a society that no longer has any dreams nor cares for any who do.

I highly recommend this book for anyone, anywhere who has ever dared to dream.

Nobody's Family is Going to Change

Author: Louise Fitzhugh

Publisher: Dell

Reviewed by: Kysha Davis

This book is about two children, Willie and Emma. Willie is very talented, and always dreamed of being a tap dancer just like his Uncle Dipsey. Emma, being fat and intelligent, wants to be a prosecuting attorney just like her father, but her father is afraid that she will become a better prosecuting attorney than he. So, to avoid this conflict, Emma tells him that she would rather be a doctor, which is not true. William Sheridan, the father, doesn't want his children to become anything but the opposite, but how can a parent take away a child's wildest fantasy?

Emma and Willie are both determined people who basically get what they want, and when they want it. In the long run, Willie ends up receiving private dance lessons given by his Uncle Dipsey without his father's consent and starts dancing on Broadway at the age of eight. Emma kept following her dreams and figured out that as long as she had these dreams and fantasies, no one would take them away from her, not even her father.

I liked this book because of the dreams and fantasies that the children followed upon. The children in this book didn't let anyone put them down and kept striving for their fantasies.

Barrio Boy

Author: Ernesto Galarza

Publisher: U. of Notre Dame Press

Reviewed by: Nancy Mendieta

If you like beautiful imagery and detail, this is the book to buy. It's a story about a Mexican boy, in his "growing" years. Kind of boring. But there's definitely enough description to last for quite a few daydreams.

Julie of the Wolves

Author: Jean Craighead George

Publisher: Harper-Trophy

Reviewed by: Elizabeth Rosseter

Hi my name is Elizabeth Rosseter. I have just finished reading a GREAT book. It's about an Eskimo girl named Miyax who runs away and becomes friends with a pack of wolves.

I loved this book and I just know kids will love this book, too! Know why I really like this book? Cuz it holds you from the start to end, annnnnd it explains things without becoming a textbook and has just the right amount to suspense to keep you reading. The magic holds on for a llooooonnnggg time after you are finished. Plus.....this is what everybody says about a book they really like, I guess.........its GRRREAT!!!! I really mean it. Really mean it.

Julie of the Wolves is a perfect book for 10 years (if they are very mature) to any age but it would be pretty easy for adults, you think? The best thing to do is to go to your library and take it out and read it. I guarantee you will love it,...well, at least, like it.

Cheaper by the Dozen

Author: Frank B. Gilbreth Jr.

                    & Ernestine Gilbreth Carey

Publisher: Bantam

Reviewed by: Lauren Bensinger

Cheaper by the Dozen is a hilarious book that can't be put down. It is about a family with twelve redheaded, freckle faced kids, a father who runs his family like a factory and a mother who agrees on almost everything. I liked this book because it was exciting and made me wonder what would happen when the whole dozen got their tonsils removed. Other kids would like it because it shows them how other families are and they can laugh at America's Best Loved Family.

Can You Teach Me to Pick My Nose?

Author: Martin Godfrey

Publisher: Avon Books

Reviewed by: Melanie Lars

This particular book is about a kid named Jordy Shepard. He is in the seventh grade and very popular. He agreed to a skateboard face-off with a ninth grader named Steve Powell. Steve is the skateboard king. One problem is that Jordy has never been on a skateboard in his whole life. Jordy agreed to the face-off to impress Steve's sister Marissa, whom he likes very much. There's only one person that can save him...a girl named Pamela. The most unpopular kid in school.

I think a lot of other kids would like this book because it's funny and interesting, The age group of kids that would like this book would probably be sixth to eighth grade.

The Friends

Author: Rosa Guy

Publisher: Bantam

Reviewed by: Ly Chang

I really liked this book. I just wish that it had a more interesting title. It wasn't action packed, but it was very interesting. You wanted to keep going on and find out what happens. It is very sad and too many people died. I wanted to know what happened to Edith, and at the end I thought Phyllisia and Ruby were going to be sent away. Right at the last minute there was a sudden change of heart in Calvin and that saved the day.

Tallahassee Higgins

Author: Mary Downing Hahn

Publisher: Houghton Mifflin

Reviewed and illustrated by: Grace Ho

Listen up everybody and hear what I have to say. My favorite book is *Tallahassee Higgins*. The book is about a girl named Tallahassee Higgins. She was sent to live with her Uncle Dan and Aunt Thelma in Hyattsdale, Maryland, while her mother went to California to become a movie star. And while Tallahassee stayed at Hyattsdale, she found out who her father and grandmother is, and she found out her mother's past at Hyattsdale.

This is a book about people living together and cooperating. That's what is important about the book and it's why I liked it, and it's also why I think other kids would like it too. The age that I would recommend this book to is 12 years old.

One Child

Author: Torey Hayden

Publisher: Avon

Reviewed by: Lily Wong

One Child is a heart wrenching non-fiction story about Sheila, a young girl who was the victim of physical and sexual abuse, and how Torey Hayden, part time author and psychologist, struggles to protect her from further abuse while motivating her to persevere.

One Child is more than just a book, it's life. The author forces the reader to realize that reality isn't a bunch of roses and by doing so makes the tragic story all the more poignant. Yet the heart-warming conclusion, on the other hand, serves as a beacon of hope to mankind.

The Sunflower Forest

Author: Torey Hayden

Publisher: Avon

Reviewed By: Lily Wong

The Sunflower Forest is the story of a mother who is haunted by her experiences in Nazi Germany during World War II. Yet all the while she is able to hide this secret part of her past from her 17-year-old daughter, Lesley. That is, until the suppressed memories of the torture she had endured in Germany finally lead her to become mentally disoriented.

This book provides a wealth of insights about Nazi Germany, both historically and psychologically. The quality I love most about this book is that as you read, you'll often find yourself pausing and re-evaluating what democracy really means and where the fine line between liberty and bondage exists.

Next to The Diary of Anne Frank, The Sunflower Forest is a true asset to the accounts of Holocaust survivors. No matter how old you are, as long as you can read, you'll get a taste of the reality of human nature, to say the very least.

To Sail Beyond the Sunset

Author: Robert A. Heinlein

Publisher: Ace Books

Reviewed by: Aviva Cushner

Classified as science fiction, I personally would rate this book as philisophical, in depth, with a very important message to deliver. You watch Maureen Johnson mature from a little girl into the enticing world of adulthood. Born in 1881 in a town in Missouri, Maureen is brought up in a conservative surrounding with liberal parents. We travel with Maureen for 100 years of her life—you know every detail, especially her thoughts, feelings, and quite fascinating emotions that develop as she grows older. As Maureen becomes wise and clever you begin to admire her. As you are reading this book, you will, in a sense, "become" Maureen Johnson, a wonderfully vibrant woman. I totally recommend this book as a necessary part to everyone's life—you can never fully grow up without it.

You Shouldn't Have to Say Good-bye

Author: Patricia Hermes

Publisher: Harcourt Brace

Reviewed: Lily Wong

Patricia Hermes' *You Shouldn't Have to Say Goodbye* will make you smile and cry at the same time. It's an ideal book for anyone 10-years-old and up, especially those experiencing the death of a loved one.

One moment 13-year-old Sarah Morrow is poking fun at her mother, and the next, her mother is diagnosed with an incurable form of cancer. Amid the resulting chaos, Hermes vividly captures the frustration of each character—Sarah's confusion about death, her father's struggle to be a strong, controlled person while being torn up inside by this crisis, and most important, Mrs. Morrow's anger at losing the chance to see her daughter grow.

The story is universal and timelessly captivating because Hermes covers all the bases about what it means to be human, both in a literal and emotional sense.

The Outsiders

Author: S.E. Hinton

Publisher: Dell

Reviewed by: Diana Weiland

This was a difficult assignment because I love books and have read so many—*Moby Dick*, *The Nickel Plated Beauty*, *Light a Single Candle*, etc. I decided on *The Outsiders*.

This book is sad. It is about a boy named "Pony Boy" who is 14. His parents are dead and he and his older brothers (Darry and Soda-Pop) are involved in a gang. If there is any more gang activity, Darry's younger brothers will have to go to the orphanage. Pony Boy and a member of the gang get involved in a murder and ran away. The end is so sad that when I read it I cried. I think other people about my age (11) will enjoy this book. I have recommended it many times to my friends but they never read it because they said they thought gangs were dumb and anyone in them. Maybe so, but this book is about a family who cares to stay together as a related family of friends. Thank you very much.

Ishi, Last of His Tribe

Editor: Theodore Kroeber

Publisher: Parnassus Press

Reviewed: Yasmin Webster - Woog

I found this book moving in a very sad way. He and his way of life. He and his family were one of the last among the tribe. The book follows Ishi through his life: from playing meadow games, to fishing in the rapid-flowing rivers, to sitting on Black Rock and watching the monster (train), making sure he was at a safe distance, to being terrorized by the saldu (white man).

This book made me reflect on my own way of life and actions. The Indians' way of life was so simple; they were content with so little, they planned their whole lives around the seasons and then we destroyed it all so quickly and with such ease. I recently visited the area where Ishi lived (Lake Oroville), since reading this book and it made me so sad. The whole area where Ishi used to fish and swim and gather berries is now gas stations, shopping centers, and fast food chains.

I strongly recommend this book to anybody interested in Native Americans, and their way of life. I am going into the 9th grade, but I recommend it for any age.

If I Should Die Before I Wake

Author: Lurlene McDaniel

Publisher: Willowisp Press

Reviewed by: Mechaka Gardner

This book is about a girl named Deanne who has become a VolunTeen at All Children's Hospital. She met a lot of young people and has become a great friend. Her new friend, Matt, has cancer and he helps her to understand disease and illness. They become close, but Deanne has a problem trying to deal with the effects of Matt's disease. She tells him, "I'll see you in the morning" and he says, (half laughing) "Not if I should die before I wake..."

I love this book because it helped me in the understanding of the disease, cancer, and it was an overall good book. A member of my family has cancer, and this book helped me to get a better understanding of the things they go through.

Sunday's Child

Author: Gudren Mebs

Publisher: Dell

Reviewed by: Kysha Davis

There was once a saying being born on a Sunday means you'll grow up to be a very lucky person. Ten year old Jenny doesn't feel lucky at all. She lives in an orphanage and the other children in the orphanage all have Sunday foster parents and go out with their foster parents every week, but not Jenny, she just waits till everyone comes back.

One day Laura comes to be Jenny's Sunday foster mother. Jenny notices something that every Sunday foster mother has, but not Laura. Laura doesn't have a fur coat, doesn't drive a car, and she isn't even married. But Jenny thinks that is okay as long as she has this attention from a Sunday foster mother. Laura is a lot of fun and talks to Jenny as though she's grown up. It didn't even take long for them to become good friends.

I like this book because dreams can come true and all Jenny ever wanted was to have a Sunday foster mother. This dream has overcome her wildest fantasies with fun and wisdom.

Letters From Prison and Other Essays

Author: Adam Michnik

Publisher: University of California Press

Reviewed by: Doug Schmidt

Upon opening I found many of the book's plots hollow, but I enjoyed the multi-faceted characters for their colorful roles. I think other people would enjoy this book because of the innumerable twists and turns that keep you glued to the pages. This book gives you a hard but clear insight to the way people think when confined to the letter of the law. I even cried when the character in my favorite story died only eleven days short of her seven year sentence.

Secrets Not Meant to be Kept

Author: Gloria D. Miklowitz

Publisher: Dell

Reviewed by: V. Clare Badillo

The book is about a girl named Adri (Adrienne) who has a problem with her boyfriend, Ryan. The problem is that whenever they kiss each other, she just couldn't respond or kiss back. It's just that despite the fact emotions are strong, actions always held her back! What's wrong with her was the only question to ask.

Although things get worse when flashbacks of her forgotten youth are brought back. Phrases like "I'll let you feed the rabbits if . . ." and visualizations of herself naked while playing things at her preschool, (The Treehouse). Looking for answers are very hard she thought until she finds out her little sister Becky, who was deeply troubled with nightmares, can give her all the answers she needed. Answers like sexual abuse was what she got and that Becky is also experiencing the same horrible tragic event in her life. With the help of strong guts and fighting spirit, Adri was able to get enough evidence to bring the preschool to justice, though consequences are as painful as drifting away from her fiancee, Ryan.

For all the years, what did every child try to hide?

I like the book because it was very suspenseful. It is very heartbreaking to see such a tragic experience take over and change the lives of a loved one or at least somebody deeply involved. I think kids from ages 15 to 25 are more to read this kind of book. It is such a great article and that emotions can really carry you within the story.

Cutting Loose

Author: Frances A. Miller

Publisher: Fawcett Juniper

Reviewed by: Sarah Rees

This book is the fourth in a series. It is about a boy named Matt who goes back to his hometown of Craigie, Idaho, where he used to live with his now dead parents and sister. By doing this, he is forced to face the past and get on with his life. I enjoyed reading this book very much, because it depicts a group of teenagers who must decide what to do with their futures, and in order to do this they must evaluate their own morals and values to discover what means the most to them. This is something that everyone must do at some point in their lives, and by reading *Cutting Loose*, I got a better idea of what I want from my future. I recommend this book, as well as the rest of the series to everyone ages 15 to 19.

Bridge to Teribithia

Author: Katherine Paterson

Publisher: HarperCollins

Reviewed by: Nancy Mendieta

This is truly one of the most powerful children's books of all time. It binds fantasy and reality together, to make the friendship in the book the main focus of the story. It deals with the friendship, death, and the boy's love for drawing. Buy this medal-winning book!

Reviewed by: Ly Chang

I really enjoyed reading *Bridge to Teribithia*. I really liked how the author carefully described things so crystal clear and used plenty of her imagination to create such a magical land never even heard of before.

I thought their friendship would last a lifetime. It did ....
just in a different way. After the big storm and terrible accident Jesse begins to understand the true meaning of life and
their friendship. This story will be unforgettable.

I like the book because it is interesting and adventurous.
Other kids would like it because it shows the true meaning of
life. After you read this you'll understand life in a different
perspective. You'll have to deal with death and a relationship
between a boy and girl. You'll feel like Jesse. You can feel the
happiness, sadness, good and bad times. I recommend this
book for people all ages—also people who are grumpy and
miserable all the time.

The Shell Seekers

Author: Rosamunde Pilcher

Publisher: St. Martin's Press

Reviewed by: Aviva Cushner

A drama—the neverending saga of a family torn apart by the
everchanging world around them. Penelope, "the head of it
all," has raised three "different" children. Nancy, very overweight, has married a successful businessman and as a result
of their wealth, two children are very spoiled. Her sister Olivia,
a wild, art gallery director, a fantastically vibrant and overly
protected woman is by far Penelope's favorite. Noel, the
brother, has always been very dependent on other's material
items while still thinking that he is completely independent at
heart. All of them, the Keeling family, are trying to cope with
each other's changing lives. I recommend this book to
anybody with a lot of endurance interested in reading a LONG
book.

The Street

Author: Israel Rabon

Publisher: Schocken

Reviewed by: Sheila Walker

The book is about a woman named Lutie. She was trying to get
out of the ghetto. She had a dream to get out of the ghetto,
with her son and try to find a husband to live with, but instead

she had trouble with her job, and left her son in a home and left the state.

I like this book because it shows the way life is with some people and you learn that it's hard to deal with problems when you let them build up. People should read this book. I recommend this book for ages 16 and up.

The Light in the Forest

Author: Conrad Richter

Publisher: Bantam

Reviewed by: Charles Hammons

There was a boy. He was born in a little town. His name was John. He was captured by an Indians. He was 4-years-old. Then he was an Indian. A great warrior named him. He thinks feels, and fights like an Indian. The Indians make a treaty and agreed to return all white captives to their own people. But this time the boy had learned to dislike white man who were his own people. I like this book because it is fun and cool.

Addie and the King of Hearts

Author: Gail Rock

Publisher: Alfred A. Knopf

Reviewed by: Anne Toohey

This book is about a girl who has a big crush on her seventh grade teacher, Mr. Davenport. Meanwhile, her father was falling in love himself, with a lady named Irene. I liked this story because it was my first love story. I think some kids would enjoy this story because they might be going through a similar situation. The age group that would enjoy this book would be 10 to 15 years of age.

Thunderbird

Author: Marilyn Sachs

Publisher: E.P Dutton

Reviewed by: Mechaka Gardner

This book is about a female car lover by the name of Tina who one day at the library met a guy named Dennis who thought cars were stupid and had a terrible temper. He never heard of a car named Thunderbird and she loved them and dreamed that one day she'd drive her own. They were a terrible couple and fought every time they met.

I liked this book because it started off with them always arguing and fighting and you never would have guessed that they would fall in love. The book in its own special way reminded me of my own life experience with someone I fell in love with. That's why I like it so much and I know others would too.

The Abraham Lincoln Joke Book

Author: Beatrice Schenk de Regniers

Publisher: Random House

Reviewed by: Lalit Lakshmanan

1. I like the book because it has many jokes written by Abraham Lincoln. Some jokes are funny and some jokes are strange.
2. Other people would like it because it is funny.

The Teddy Bear In Your Life

Author: Standifer Shreve

Publisher: Gily Press

Reviewed by: Crystal May

This book should be read because it is about the special friends in your life. It is about sharing your life with a special friend, also about the special friend in your life who cares for you. It's about growing up and needing a special friend to care for you. I do recommend this book.

As you grow older there may be some people in your life who care for you besides your family and friends. You may also love this person too. This person is someone who will bring joy and happiness into your life. This person can be anybody, but this person is special. Being loved is a feeling of happiness. This feeling is a feeling you are sharing with this special person. Knowing that you have this person in your life you can share everything with is wonderful. If this person ever comes into your life, you shouldn't lose him/her for anything in the world.

Circus Shoes

Author: Noel Streatfield

Publisher: Dell

Reviewed by: Genni Schmidt

Circus Shoes is an exciting book about two orphans, Santa and Peter, who live with their Aunt Rebecca. When Rebecca dies, Santa and Peter run away to live with their uncle Gus. Gus is a trapeze artist in a circus. The kids have a great time learning about the circus, but are they really cut out for circus life?

I like this book because it told about Peter and Santa's feelings and adventures in an amusing and interesting way. Ages 10-13 would enjoy this book.

The Joy Luck Club

Author: Amy Tan

Publisher: Putnam

Reviewed by: Aviva Cushner

Amy Tan's *The Joy Luck Club* is a collection of inspirational short stories about a Chinese family trying to overcome the many prejudices the American world has to offer.

If you are a mother or a daughter, if you HAVE a mother or a daughter, the stories will especially touch you in a way no other book can.

You are taken on a journey—a journey of watching a first generation girl try to fit in with American society without interfering with the Chinese culture her parents and older relatives are struggling to keep alive.

As you read these memoirs, you become a part of them. Every time the girl is racially slurred, every time she is hurt — all of these times you feel not only a pang of guilt but a feeling of despair and frustration.

Amy Tan truly deserves all of the acclaim she is receiving. Her stories, vividly warm and sensitive, will make you laugh, cry and feel feelings of joy and luck you never thought possible. You truly become a part of *The Joy Luck Club*.

The Adventures of Tom Sawyer

Author: Mark Twain

Publisher: (many)

Reviewed by: Camila V.

I would definitely recommend this book to any age child. It is a great funny and adventurous book. You can read it over and over again. Each time I can assure you, you will like it more and more. My favorite adventure definitely had to be the one when Tom Sayer and his best friend Huckleberry Finn find a box full of gold. They had been seaching for days and then they finally found the thieves and got to keep the money.

A Jar of Dreams

Author: Yoshiko Uchida

Publisher: Macmillan

Reviewed by: Genni Schmidt

This story is about a girl named Rinko who is living in the heart of the depression. Her family is discriminated against because they are Japanese. Then Rinko's Aunt Waka comes to visit from Japan, and shows Rinko that it is all right to be different and being Japanese is something to be proud of.

I liked this book because it showed firsthand the effects of racism. Rinko's family was courageous and uplifting throughout the whole story, so it was encouraging to read about them. This book is good for ages 10-13.

Homecoming

Author: Cynthia Voigt

Publisher: Random House

Reviewed and illustrated by: Molly McCoy

I have always loved to read, and in my thirteen years I've read many books. My favorite book, *Homecoming*, is about four children whose insane mother left them in a parking lot of a strange town. The oldest child, Dicey, is only thirteen, but she manages to keep her family together. The children decide to try and find their Aunt Cilla, relying on the map that their mother left in the car. On their way, Dicey's family encounters many problems. They need to eat, and food costs money, so they have to find someone who'll give them work and won't turn them in to the authorities. When they finally reach Aunt Cilla, they are met with a terrible shock.

Homecoming is the story of how the Tillerman family find a place to call home, and a parent to call their own.

I think that *Homecoming* is a well-written, entertaining, and touching story. It's challenging, and thought-provoking, for the older reader. I would recommend it for anyone who enjoys reading, and wants to read a great story.

Questions Young People Ask; Answers That Work

Author: Watchtower Bible

and Tract Society of Pennsylvania

Publisher: Watchtower Bible

and Tract Society of New York

Reviewed by: Araceli Ramirez

This wonderful book is about questions and answers youths ask themselves, today like, "Why don't my parents understand me?" "Should I try drugs or alcohol?" "How do I know it's true love?" "What's in my future?" "What about sex before marriage?" Those are a few of the chapter titles in this book. I liked this book because not only it has personal questions in it, but it answers them in easy answers that keep you satisfied. The kids would like it just as myself because a lot of times kids want information, about these basic questions and doubts, and confuse them. Like for example, alcohol.

It can just so happen, that parents do not accept kids to use them, even though parents use them. Magazines and T.V. programs show drinks and alcohol that make you want to take them. Other youths and teens tempt you to take them. So, no wonder kids seem confused about what to do. This book answers those kinds of questions you are wondering. It can benefit all kinds of ages. Starting at 9-? years old. Even adults!!! So, now you know why I love this book. My mother and, I always study it together on Thursdays. We are about half through the book now.

Black Boy

Author: Richard Wright

Publisher: HarperCollins

Reviewed by: Sherri Marshall

This is a true story about the life of Richard Wright, I liked it because it talked a lot about his childhood and all the things he did. It was real funny. I think this is a perfect book for teens because it lets us know it's o.k. to be a little bad; you can still come out on top and become something positive.

Dragonwings

Author: Laurence Yep

Publisher: HarperCollins

Reviewed by: Eli Sarnat

I enjoyed *Dragonwings* because of its different views and thought. The story is told though the eyes of an 8-year old boy going from Japan to the "Land of Gold" or San Francisco during the early 1900's.

The main character, Moon Shadow, must make the sudden and harsh transition into a world of white demons whose tempers lash out at his people. Moon Shadow and his family go through many experiences, good and bad, while battling for a place in their new world.

Poetry, Politics, Environment

This last section of the chapter has reviews that don't fit neatly into the other categories. These books listed below are unique and definitely worth your attention.

Poetry

A Fire in My Hands

Author: Gary Soto

Publisher: Scholastic

Reviewed by: Lauren Bensinger

This book is wonderful if you enjoy poems as much as I do. Gary Soto talks about how you should develop a poem with everyday things in your life. In this book before every poem he has a little paragraph explaining how he got the idea for this particular poem. All his poems are based on his life growing up as a Spanish-American. He loves oranges and the area where they grow. My favorite poem is "Oranges". All the poems have words so descriptive that they are like beautiful pictures.

In his Foreword he explains how he became interested in poetry and he encourages children to write poems not only about fantasy things but their lives. His advice to young poets was "Look to your own lives."

Politics

Animal Farm

Author: George Orwell

Publisher: Harcourt Brace Jovanovich

Reviewed by: Nancy Mendieta

This book is probably one of the more controversial books ever written about the system, about the government. The way this story is told, every official is literally an animal! It's told as a story about animals. This is a beautifully characterized book. Each character seems realistic from the physical to the sounds it makes.

This is a cool book! Great for all ages!

Environment

Economics As If The Earth Really Mattered

Author: Susan Meeker-Lowry

Publisher: New Society Publications

Reviewed by: Airlia

This book is an informative and complete aid to the environmentally conscious economics. It includes intelligent and resourceful alternatives to society's unhealthy and wasteful habits. I learned a lot from this book and believe it could ease many restless consciences. It would be a good book to read if one has any interest in the future of this planet.

Illustration by: Reiko Tanihara

Index by Title

Index By Author

Illustration Credits

Thanks to everyone who submitted artwork for consideration. We would have liked to use it all! Special thanks to Miss Kendra Langer, Art Teacher at Presidio Middle School in San Francisco for giving us such a wonderful selection.

Norman Lai
Lori Hui
Lan To
Abel Lai
Thuc Vong
Tina Lee
Becky Zhang
Corine Scott
Kyoko Nakada
Judy Tan
Slava Viner
Michelle Hom
Rgea Wong
Maggie So
Kol Yim
Aisha Drake
Brian Lee
Bernice Fong
Pillar Teso
Jennifer Lew
Wendy Lau
Philip Chiang
Tania Sheyner
Li Shen
Cathy Zhao
Codi Smith
Loan Chau
Amber Nishimoto
Colleen Tate
Laura Rodshteyn
Emily Wong
Reiko Tanihara
Michael Le
Crystal Ng
Mark Berdichevsky
Johnson Hong

Phillip Lee
Vernon Nq
Jennifer Suil
Jeff Ha
Sara Baik
Hisashi Jmura
Karin Veno
Jennifer Garcia-Lomas
Ninh Tran
Kayo Shibano
Tom Jamgochian
Manuel Timos
Vix Khammounykhoure
Darrin Wong
Janet Kwan
Edmund Lin
Jie Na Zhang
Lap Tran
Jeff Gonzales
Elina Uzin
Jin-Wen Sha
Kenneth Yu
Seav Lim
John Tang
Chai Saelaw
Baya Vuong
Brian Kanoh
Meng Khanthavong
Patti Lee
Jenny Che
Richard Luu
Jenny Lam
Napat Chananudech
Daryl Guidry
Patti Lee
Warren Balint
Stephanie Lim
Karina Tang
Thi Nga Cham
Brian Ly
Jeff Yee
David Ta
Herain Pateh
Tanner Shea
Anna Shapito
Steven Chen
Jamie Lew
Sherry Uy
Minh Lien
Lydia Wu
Michael Kaskey
Jana Martinn
Louie Huang

LaTreace Graham
Andy Tran
Connor Mocsny
David Tran
David Giang
Sonia Martinez
Elina Borotnovich
Tuan Hugh
Muesal To
Van Nuy Chan
Ken Li
Katy Li
Melodye Lee
Ngoc
Ka Man Lok
Jennifer Hee
Steven H.
Kevin Quan
Alicia Louie
Kimi Kan
Amina
Camille Combes
Sherri Tan
Meredith Martinez
Andrea Choye
Carmen Lee
Veronica Lam
Elaine Huang
John Haggerty
Adrianne Barton
Johnathan Gonzales
Brandon Lee
Jeroen Assink-Bastos
Jeannie Hom
Jamal Mashal
Laurel Snead
Justine F.
Andy Barnes
Sam DeVore
Simon Areung
Aaron Tam
Stephanie Brenner
Prescott Yeung
Mitchol
Danny Lee
Stephanie Hom
Jerome
Theresa Leung

Reviewer Credits

Grades K - 3

Reina Aguilar
Christina Garcia
Bradford C. Lee
Marcy Lariz
Natalie Abbott
Whitney Boughtonage
Lisa Lauren
Lauren Low
Jessica Escobar
Chelsea Lake
Rajiv Smith-Mahabir
Timothy Eng
Angelica Flowers
Zach Mates
Katrina Lake
Leslie Phillips
Katie Toker
Lars Kosager
Paula Galvez
Eve Nettleton
Angela Hamilton
Jessica Porter
Naima Walls
Ngoyen Han
Liezel Zapanta
Bong Ian Dizon
Jessica Alberto
Martina
Emily Sweet
Mallory Portillo
Cecilia Y. Chen
Trenton English
Jerome Wandees
Rachel Yeager
Steve Chu
Evan Kuluk
David J. Standring
Dylan White
Deborah Mao
Randi Ketcher
Emily Gibbs
Michael Becker
Nikki Esposito
Tony Goldmark
Lodrina Cherne
Chloe Hanna-Korpi
Saethra Fritscher

Grades 4 - 6

Dante Gardner
Ka Man Loh
Amina
Keir F. Davidson
John Ikeda
Hannah Mello
Marcy Territo
Josh Kline
Andy Barnes
Max Hendon
Sara Mo
Sabrina Arey
Karla Kane
Tara Pandeya
Kelly Furano
Molly Alliman
Zachary Houston
Aaron Tam
Simon Cheung
Elaine Gee
Jerrad Pierce
Phescott Young
Jennifer Hee
Shannon Venable
Sara Kinsey
Roger O'Neal
Nicole Gazzo
Cathrine O'Leary
Hilary Gomore
Kevin Quan
Julia Jozwyk
Yvonne Wang
Mick O'Connel
Charlie Sarkis
Irene Luu
Eunice Lee
Gilbert Martinez
Camille Combes
Stacey Sims
Melissa Gibeau
Sam De Vore
Carl Gould
Felicia Ortez
Ben Lowe
Theresa Leung
V. Clare Badillo
Kimi Kan
Danny Lee
Andrea Choye
Laurel Lynn Snead
Thomas Yi
Emily Abernathy

Eileen Tram
Cheryll Del Rosario
Camille Hearst
Mitchal
Tiffany Varek
Maika Onishi
Austin Furta-Cole
Eileen Hu
Julia Denning
Cindy Gonzalez
Gwenn Seemel
Douglas Wong
Stephanie Brenner
Justine
Terrence Wong
Marvin Hong
Aimee Mizuno
Molly Denning
Michael Luu
Megan Gilkey
Alicia Louie
Felicia Ortez
Emily Ortez
Mary Downing Hahn
Dana Medina
Carmen Lee
Daljit Dhami
Sara Constance
Shelley Gullion
Sandy Ross
Cindy Ly
Rhonda Richards
Hsiao Cheer
Lauren Masio
Adinah Curtis
Ratchel Hemphill
Holly English
Luisina Basilico
Sherry Yu
Sandy Yu
Genni Schmidt
Paul Acerno
Sara Baches
Danielle Pittman
K-linh Ho
Emily Pena
Nicole Ogden
Wendy Cogan
Bree Hornbuckle
Yvette Cashmere
Carter Harris
Janel Boshers
Veronica
Jesse Cano

Shani Delaney
Stephanie Horn
Amanda Zaccone
Alyssa Rasmussen
Nate Baumsteiger
Jamal Mashal
Steven H.

Grades 7 - 12

Saethra Fritscher
Genni Schmidt
Eli Sarnat
Helen Shum
Hedy Lim
Natalie J. Chan
Elizabeth Dong
Tara Mahoney

Nancy Mendieta
Kristan Seemel
Esther Odekirk
Lalit Lakshmanan
Amber Fraga
Lauren Bensinger
Jesse Adamo
Aviva Cushner
Jessica Escobar
Monica Villazana
Katy Li
Lily Wong
Sarah Gancher
Iesha Johnson
Teeunva
Sherri Marshall
Mechaka Gardner
Rupert Tagnipes

Kysha Davis
Elizabeth Rosseter
Melanie Lars
Ly Chang
Grace Ho
Diana Weiland
Yasmin Webster-Woog
Doug Schmidt
Sarah Rees
Sheila Walker
Charles Hammons
Anne Toohey
Crystal May
Camilla V.
Molly McCoy
Araceli Ramirez
Airlia

The Junior Publishers

*From left to right: Front row: **Lauren Bensinger (12), Jesse Adamo(14), Lucy Acerno(11), Aviva Cushner(14), Eli Sarnat (13).** Second row: **Jessica Escobar (14), Genni Schmidt (13), Yasmin Webster-Woog(14), Nancy Mendieta(16), Ester Odekirk(14).** Back row: **Crescent Wood(14), Mechaka Gardner(16), Kysha Davis(16), Tom Woodrow, Sherri Marshall(17).** Far back row: **Saethra Fritscher(14).** Not pictured: **Lily Wong, Rita Ortez.***

About the Program

In the summer of 1991, 17 kids ranging in age from 11 to 17 showed up at Foghorn Press for a seven week San Francisco Bay Area Book Council-sponsored Junior Publishers Program designed to teach them about book publishing. The twist? They would actually produce a book.

In retrospect, the enormity of the obstacles amazes me. Here were 17 kids with no publishing experience. They didn't know each other nor us. They were operating on a condensed seven week publishing schedule. Plus the program took place in the offices of Foghorn Press, a publishing house with its own long list of demands and harried staff.

We immediately organized into a mini publishing company, complete with marketing department (writing press releases and coordinating a publication party), editorial department (reading, sorting and proofing book reviews), and production department (designing and laying out the book). In addition to myself and my staff, local publishers, booksellers and media generously volunteered their time. Three department leaders deserve special recognition: Kiran Rana, Hunter House; Eric Kettunen, Lonely Planet Publications; and Malcolm Barker, Londonborn Publications. We also had teacher Jeannie Brondino to keep on top of the day-to-day demands.

And we did it. What the kids accomplished impressed us from cover design to layout, to obtaining a foreword from Marilyn Sachs and review from Amy Tan — all strong publishing achievements by adult standards. We guided, they decided. It was an amazing process and one that the Foghorn Press and the Book Council are proud to support.

Books We Love Best is a useful and informative guide to the books kids like, featuring the editorial and artistic submissions of kids from nine Bay Area counties. A wonderful book in its own right, proceeds go to the Book Council Reading Fund, a grant program that awards mini-grants to teachers with innovative literacy and reading programs. It's a nice circular touch, I think, that the book completely written and published by kids ends up benefitting them in the classroom.

Vicki K. Morgan, Publisher, Foghorn Press
1992 President, San Francisco Bay Area Book Council

Illustration by: Kyoko Nakada

Blues paced once around the small room, stopping with his back to the two-way mirror, and folded his arms against his chest. "I wasn't there and I didn't kill Jack Cullan."

"I'll be sure to mention that to the judge," Mason said. "You'll be arraigned tomorrow morning in front of an Associate Circuit Court judge who will set bail. I'm guessing bail will be no less than a quarter million and maybe as much as half a million."

Blues said, "The judge won't grant me bail."

"Hey, c'mon. Give me some credit. You'll be out by lunchtime."

"You don't get it, Lou. Charging me with murder one and threatening me with the death penalty is a power play to make me take a deal. Somebody wants me to go down for this, and keeping me in the county jail until trial will be the next card that gets played. Make an ex-cop spend the winter in the general prison population, and see how long it takes him to find religion. If I don't roll over, they hope I'll get shanked before the trial. The last thing I'll hear is, 'Enjoy your stay at the Graybar Inn.'"

"Blues, this isn't the Conspiracy Hour. Cullan was connected to everybody in town, but he would have had to own everybody—the police, the courts, and the mayor— everybody, for you to be right. Plus he's dead. All the IOUs he held have been canceled."

"How are you going to prove I'm innocent?" Blues asked.

"Find out who killed Cullan."

"You'll have to peel the layers off of Cullan's life, read every one of those IOUs."

Mason nodded, grabbing the thread that held Blues's fears together.

"I'll hang every dirty piece of laundry I can find in front of the jury to convince them that someone else did it."

"That's why I won't get bail," Blues said. "Remember something else while you're out there stirring up this shit pot."

"What's that?"

"The killer won't mind killing again to make sure I go down. And no one else will mind either."

BOOK YOUR PLACE ON OUR WEBSITE AND MAKE THE READING CONNECTION!

We've created a customized website just for our very special readers, where you can get the inside scoop on everything that's going on with Zebra, Pinnacle and Kensington books.

When you come online, you'll have the exciting opportunity to:

- View covers of upcoming books
- Read sample chapters
- Learn about our future publishing schedule (listed by publication month *and author*)
- Find out when your favorite authors will be visiting a city near you
- Search for and order backlist books from our online catalog
- Check out author bios and background information
- Send e-mail to your favorite authors
- Meet the Kensington staff online
- Join us in weekly chats with authors, readers and other guests
- Get writing guidelines
- AND MUCH MORE!

**Visit our website at
http://www.kensingtonbooks.com**

THE LAST WITNESS

Joel Goldman

PINNACLE BOOKS
Kensington Publishing Corp.

http://www.kensingtonbooks.com

For Aaron, Danny, and Michele—the greatest kids ever.

ACKNOWLEDGMENTS

Writing is not always a solitary pursuit. Thanks to the folowing people who helped with this book: Stuart Jaffe, my honest reader; Josh Garry and Dan Cofran, my political consultants; John Fraise, my private cop; Karen Haas and Ann LaFarge, my editors at Kensington; and Meredith Bernstein, my agent. Special thanks to my loving wife, Hildy, who keeps my feet on the ground when my head is in the clouds.

Chapter One

Jack Cullan's maid found his body lying facedown on the floor of his study, his cheek glued to the carpet with his own frozen, congealed blood. When she turned the body over, fibers stuck to Cullan's cheek like fungus that grows under a rock. His left eye was open, the shock of his death still registered in the wide aperture of his eyelid. His right eye was gone, pulverized by a .38-caliber bullet that had pierced his pupil and rattled around in his brain like loose change in the seconds before he died.

"Shit," Harry Ryman said as he looked down on the body of the mayor's personal lawyer. "Call the chief," he told his partner, Carl Zimmerman.

Harry knew that Jack Cullan wasn't just Mayor Billy Sunshine's lawyer. He was a social lubricator, a lawyer who spent more time collecting IOUs than a leg-breaking bagman for the mob. For the last twenty years, getting elected in Kansas City had meant getting Cullan's support. Anyone doing serious business with the city had hired him to get their deals done.

Harry guessed that Cullan was in his early sixties, dumpy from years spent avoiding physical exertion in favor of mental manipulation. Harry squatted down to examine Cullan's hands. They were smooth, unlike the man's reputation. Cullan had a Santa Claus build, but Harry knew the man couldn't have played St. Nick without asking for more than he ever would have given.

Harry had been a homicide detective too long to remember ever having been anything else. He knew that the chances of solving a murder dropped like the windchill after the first forty-eight hours. If time weren't a powerful enough incentive, a politically heavy body like Jack Cullan's would push his investigation into warp speed.

He gathered his topcoat around him, fighting off the cold that had invaded the study on the back side of Cullan's house. The windows were open. The maid, Norma Hawkins, said she had found them that way when she arrived for work at eight o'clock that morning, Monday, December 10. The heat had been also been turned off, the maid had added. An early winter blast had locked Kansas City down in a brutal snow-laced assault for the last week. Cullan's house felt like ground zero.

"The chief says to meet him at the mayor's office," Zimmerman said, interrupting Harry's silent survey of the murder scene.

"What for?" Harry asked, annoyed at anything that would slow down the investigation.

"I told the chief that somebody popped the mayor's lawyer. He told me to sit tight, like I was going someplace, right? He calls back two minutes later and says meet him at the mayor's office. You want to discuss it with the chief, you got his number."

Carl Zimmerman had grown up fighting, sometimes over jabs about being a black man with a white man's name, sometimes to find out who could take a punch. He and Harry had been partners for six years without becoming close friends. Harry was older, more experienced, and automatically assumed the lead in their investigations, a batting order he knew that Zimmerman resented. That was Zimmerman's problem, Harry had decided. Zimmerman was a good cop, but Harry was a better one.

Harry wanted to get moving. He wanted to interview the maid, figure out how long Cullan had been dead before she found him, and backtrack Cullan's activities in the hours before he was murdered. He wanted to talk to everyone Cullan had been with during that time. He wanted to search Cullan's home, car, and office for anything that might lead him to the killer. The last thing he wanted to do was run downtown to promise the chief and the mayor that they would solve the crime before dinner. The next-to-last thing he wanted to do was deal with the chip on his partner's shoulder.

"Here," Harry said, tossing the keys to Zimmerman. "You can drive."

Lou Mason read about Jack Cullan's murder in Wednesday morning's *Kansas City Star* while the wind whipped past his office windows overlooking Broadway. In the spring, Mason would open the windows, letting the breeze wrap itself around him like a soft sweatshirt on a cool day. Wednesday morning's wind was more like a garrote twisted around the city's throat by Mother Nature turned Boston Strangler.

The story of Cullan's murder was two days old, but still front-page news. The reporter, Rachel Firestone, wrote that

Cullan had been at the center of an investigation into the decision of the mayor and the Missouri Gaming Commission to approve a license for a riverboat casino called the Dream. The Dream had opened recently, docked on the Missouri River at the limestone landing where nineteenth-century fur traders had first thought to build the trading post that became Kansas City. Cullan's client, Edward Fiora, owned the Dream. Whispers that Cullan had secured the Dream's license with well-orchestrated bribes of Mayor Sunshine and of Beth Harrell, the chair of the Gaming Commission, had circulated like tabloid vapor, titillating but unproved. The reporter had dubbed the brewing scandal the "Nightmare on Dream Street."

Mason put the paper down to answer his phone. "Lou Mason," he said. When he'd first gone into solo practice, he'd answered the phone by saying, "Law Office," until one of his clients had asked to speak to Mr. Office.

"I need you downstairs," Blues said, and hung up.

Blues was Wilson Bluestone, Jr., Mason's landlord, private investigator, and more often than Mason would like, the one person Mason counted on to watch his back. Blues owned the bar on the first floor, Blues on Broadway. He never admitted to needing anything, so Mason took Blues's statement seriously.

Mason double-timed down the lavender carpeted hallway, past the art deco light fixtures spaced evenly on the wall between each office on the second floor. One office belonged to Blues, another to a PR flack, and a third to a CPA. They were all solo acts.

He bounded down the stairs at the end of the hall, bracing one hand on the wobbly rail, his feet just brushing the treads, making a final turn into the kitchen. The cold urgency in Blues's voice propelled him past the grill almost too fast to catch the greasy scent of the Reuben sandwiches cooked there the night before. A sudden burst of broken glass mixed with the crack of overturned furniture and the thick thud of a big man put down.

"Goddammit, Bluestone!" Harry Ryman shouted. Harry hated bars and Blues too much to pay an early morning social call, especially on a day that would freeze your teeth.

Mason picked up his pace, shoved aside the swinging door between the kitchen and the bar, and plunged into a frozen tableau on the edge of disaster. Blues stood in the middle of the room surrounded by Harry Ryman and another detective Mason recognized as Harry's partner, Carl Zimmerman, and a uniformed cop. The beat cop and Zimmerman were aiming their service revolvers at Blues's head. Another uniformed cop was on his knees next to a table lying on its side, surrounded by broken dishes, rubbing a growing welt on his cheek with one hand and holding a pair of handcuffs with the other.

Blues and Harry were squared off in front of each other, heavyweights waiting for the first bell. Harry's dead-eyed cop glare matched Blues's flat street stare. In a tale of the tape, it was hard to pick a favorite. Though half a foot shy of Blues's six-four, Harry had a solid, barreled girth that was tough to rock. Blues was chiseled, lithe, and deadly. Harry carried the cop-worn look of the twenty years he had on Blues.

No one moved. Steam rose off the cops' shoulders as the snow they had carried in melted in the warmth of the bar. The wind beat against the front door, rattling its frame, like someone desperate to get inside. Blues was spring-loaded, never taking his eyes from Harry's.

Mason spoke softly, as if the sound of his voice would detonate the room. "Harry?" Ryman didn't answer.

The uniformed cop on his feet was a skinny kid with droopy eyes and a puckered mouth who'd probably never drawn his gun outside the shooting range and couldn't control the tremor in his extended arms. Carl Zimmerman was a compact middleweight who held his gun as if it were a natural extension of his hand, no hesitation in his trigger finger. His dark face was a calm pool. The solidly built cop Blues had put on the floor had gotten to his feet, his block-cut face flush with embarrassment and anger, anxious to redeem himself and take on Blues again. He took a step toward Blues, and Carl Zimmerman put a hand on his shoulder and held him back.

"You're going down, Bluestone," Harry said.

"I told your boy not to put his hands on me," Blues answered.

"Officer Toland was doing his job and I'm doing mine. Don't make this worse than it already is," Ryman said.

"Harry?" Mason said again.

"This doesn't concern you, Lou," Harry answered, not taking his eyes off Blues.

"That's bullshit, Harry, and you know it," Mason said.

Harry Ryman was the closest thing Mason had to a father. He and Mason's aunt Claire had been together for years, and had been unconventional surrogates for Mason's parents, who had been killed in a car accident when Mason was three years old. Blues had saved Mason's life and was the closest thing Mason had to a brother. Whatever was going down didn't just concern Mason. It threatened to turn his world inside out.

Harry said to Blues, "I'm gonna cuff you. Everybody gets cuffed, even if we have to shoot them first. You remember that much, don't you, Bluestone?"

Blues looked at Mason, silently asking the obvious with the same flat expression. Mason nodded, telling him to go along. Blues slowly turned his back on Harry, disguising his rage with a casual pivot, extending his arms behind him, managing a defiant posture even in surrender. Harry fastened the handcuffs around Blues's wrists and began reciting the cop's mantra.

"You're under arrest. You have the right to remain silent. Anything you say can and will be used against you in a court of law. You have the right to an attorney. If you cannot afford an attorney—"

"I'm his attorney," Mason interrupted. "What's the charge?"

Harry looked at Mason for the first time, a tight smile cutting a thin line across his wide face. Mason saw the satisfaction in Harry's smile and the glow of long-sought vindication in his eyes. Harry had always warned Mason that Blues would cross the line one day and that he would be there to take him down; that the violent, self-styled justice Blues had employed when he was a cop, and since then, was as corrupt as being on the take. As much as Harry may have longed to make that speech again, instead he said it all with one word.

"Murder."

Harry held Mason's astonished gaze. "Murder in the first degree," he added. "You can talk to your client downtown after we book him."

Mason watched as they filed out, first the two uniformed cops, then Carl Zimmerman, then Blues. As Harry reached the door, Mason called to him.

"Who was it, Harry?"

Harry had had the steely satisfaction of the triumphant cop when he'd forced Blues to submit moments ago. Now his face sagged as he looked at Mason, seeing him for the first time as an adversary. Harry thought about the battle that lay ahead between them before responding.

"Jack Cullan. Couldn't have been some punk. It had to be Jack Fucking Cullan." Harry turned away, disappearing into the wind as the door closed behind him.

Chapter Two

Mason scraped the hard crystal snow off the windshield of his Jeep Cherokee. The cast-iron sky hung low enough that Mason half expected to scrape it off the glass as well. His car was parked behind the bar, reminding him that covered parking was the only perk he missed from his days as a downtown lawyer. The Jeep was strictly bad-weather transportation. His TR-6 was hibernating in his garage, waiting impatiently for a top-down day.

Mason drove north on Broadway, a signature street of rising and falling fortunes Kansas City wore like an asphalt ID bracelet. From the lip of the Missouri River on the north edge of downtown to the Country Club Plaza shopping district, forty-seven blocks south, Broadway was high-rise and low-rise, professionals and payday loans, insurance and uninsurable, homes and homeless. The Big Man and the Little Man elbowing each other for position.

As he drove, Mason wondered how Blues had been linked

to Cullan's murder. As far as Mason knew, Blues and Cullan had never even met. Mason wondered whether something had happened between them when Blues was a cop, something that led to Cullan's murder years later. Mason dismissed that as unlikely. Blues didn't carry grudges for years. He settled them or expunged them.

It was possible, Mason thought, that Cullan had surfaced in one of the cases Blues had handled as a private investigator, as either a target or a client. Blues had talked little with Mason about his cases, unless he needed Mason's help.

Before he bought the bar, Blues had taught piano at the Conservatory of Music. Cullan hadn't seemed the type to take up music late in life, and teaching someone the difference between bass clef and treble clef wasn't likely to drive Blues to murder. At his worst, Blues would tell a student to play the radio instead of the piano.

Mason knew that Harry Ryman was right about one thing: Blues had his own system of justice and he didn't hesitate to use violence to enforce it. Violence, Blues had told Mason, was a great equalizer. It leveled the playing field against long odds. Few people would use it, even those who threatened it. The threat without follow-through was weak, a shortcoming Blues couldn't abide. Though Blues wasn't casual about violence. He wielded it with the precision and purpose of a surgeon using a scalpel.

Blues had been Harry's partner when Blues was a cop. Harry was the veteran and Blues was the rookie, a mismatched odd couple. Harry was a by-the-book cop and Blues insisted on writing his own book. Their partnership, and Blues's career as a cop, had ended six years earlier when Blues shot and killed a woman during a drug bust. Internal Affairs gave Blues the choice of quitting or being prosecuted. He quit.

Harry had said little to Mason over the years about his

relationship with Blues, except for warning him that Blues would go down one day and that Harry would be there, waiting. Blues had said less, and both men had refused to talk about the case that had fractured their relationship. The one constant was the tension between them. Mason wouldn't call it hatred. That was too simple. Harry and Blues shared a wound neither man could heal because they both had too much pain. Whenever the three of them were together, Mason felt like the bomb squad trying to guess whether Blues or Harry would go off first.

Mason believed that gatekeepers ruled the world. They were the people who answered the phones, manned the desks, or kept the calendars for the people everyone else needed to see. The ideal gatekeeper was trained from birth in passive-aggressive behavior designed to cause acid reflux in anyone who petitioned for access to the gatekeeper's master. How else to explain the uncanny ability to dodge, defer, and deny Mason's always reasonable requests for access or information? Mason tried being humble, witty, flirtatious, or threatening, depending on what he'd had for breakfast. Sometimes the walls came down and sometimes they got higher.

"I'm Lou Mason," he told the desk sergeant. "Harry Ryman brought in Wilson Bluestone a few minutes ago. I'm Bluestone's lawyer."

The desk sergeant was reading *USA Today*. He wore a name tag that read SGT. PETERSON and had a slack expression that read *who cares?* when he looked at Mason over his half glasses, sighed his resentment at Mason's intrusion, and picked up the phone. "He's here," Peterson said to whoever had picked up on the other end. Peterson traded the phone for his newspaper and resumed ignoring Mason.

A civilian police department employee materialized and escorted Mason to the second-floor detective squad room. She politely pointed him to a hard-backed chair that had been decorated with the carved initials of prior occupants. The squad room reflected the uninspired use of public money—pale walls, faded vanilla tile, and banged-up steel desks covered with the antiseptic details of destroyed lives.

Mason waited while the crosscurrents of cops and their cases flowed around him. He'd been here before, waiting to be questioned and accused. An ambivalent mix of urgency and resignation permeated the place. Cops had a special sweat, born of the need to preserve and protect and the fearful realization that they were too often outnumbered. That sweat was strongest in homicide.

Homicide cops took the darkest confessions of the cruelest impulses. They sweet-talked, cajoled, and deceived the guilty into speaking the unspeakable. The more they heard, the more they were overwhelmed by one simple truth: There were more people willing to kill than they could stop from killing or catch before the bodies were in the ground. Sterile statistics on closed cases couldn't mask the smell of blood and the taste for vengeance that clung to homicide cops like a second skin.

Justice was supposed to cleanse them, but justice was sometimes washed away by the pressure to make an arrest. Even a good cop like Harry Ryman wasn't immune from the pressure or his feelings toward Blues. Mason knew that saving Blues meant slowing down the clock.

Mason also knew that saving Blues meant taking on Harry Ryman. Mason could remember the days when Harry used to pick him up by his belt loops and swing him up over his shoulder like a sack of potatoes. And Mason could remember the day he graduated from law school and Harry bear-hugged him with a father's pride. Easing his grip just enough to see Mason's face, Harry had told him how to navigate the uncertain waters that his clients would take him through.

"Just do the right thing," Harry had told him. "You won't have any trouble knowing what it is. The only hard part is doing it." Life was never more complicated than that for Harry.

Harry interrupted Mason's thoughts. "You can see him now. He's in number three. No one will be watching or listening," Harry said, pointing Mason to the third interrogation room down the hall from where Mason sat. "Don't worry about it, Lou," Harry added. "Just do your job and I'll do mine."

Blues was standing at the far end of the room staring into a mirror that covered most of the wall when Mason opened the door to Interrogation Room No. 3. Blues's burnished, coppery skin, straight black hair, and fiery eyes were muted under the exposed fluorescent tubes that hung from the ceiling.

"You're not that good-looking," Mason told him.

"I get prettier every day," Blues answered. "It's a two-way mirror," he explained, reminding himself and Mason of his previous life as a cop. "Couple of detectives sit on the other side and watch the interrogation. This room is wired for sound."

"Harry said that no one is watching or listening."

"You believe that, Lou?"

"I believe that they aren't that stupid. If they want you for this murder, they aren't going to fuck it up like that. Harry won't, anyway."

Blues took a slow turn around the room as if to measure himself against his surroundings. As he did, Mason thought about his first criminal defense client, Wally Sutherland, a

businessman who had been a client of his last firm, Sullivan & Christenson. Wally's one-thing-led-to-another encounter with a woman he'd met in a bar had ended with his
arrest for attempted forcible rape. When Mason had first
visited Wally in the city jail, he had cried for his wife, his
mother, and God, in that order. Mason had never seen Blues
cry, and didn't expect he ever would. Blues had contained
the coiled anger that rippled through his body when Harry
put the cuffs on him. Mason didn't want to be around when
Blues let that spring unwind.

Mason asked, "They didn't try to question you without
me, did they?"

"Nothing official. Harry tried to make it like old times.
Good old Harry stroking me, telling me how much easier
it would be just to get the whole thing over with. His partner,
Zimmerman, telling him to hold off until you got here. Harry
telling Zimmerman that I was too smart to fall for any tricks,
especially since I had been such a smart cop myself. Saying
that he was just reminding me of what I already knew."

Mason said, "Harry playing good cop with you is—"

"Stupid," Blues said, interrupting. "Ryman's done
everything but put a bounty on my ass, and he thinks he's
gonna talk me into confessing because he's such a damn
nice guy. Bullshit."

"What do they have on you?" Mason asked.

Blues leaned over the oak table that separated him from
Mason, planting both hands firmly on the surface. He was
wearing a black turtleneck sweater and jeans. Mason had a
fleeting image of him in jailhouse orange.

"First things first. Can you do this?" Blues asked.

"What do you mean, can I do this? You've seen the law
license hanging in my office. I'm an official member of the
bar. Murder cases are a walk in the park. Besides, at the

rate I'm charging you, I can't afford to take long to get you off. I'll go broke.''

Blues didn't laugh or smile. His face was a death mask. ''I'm not asking you about the lawyer piece. You're as good as anybody I've ever seen. I want to know, can you do this?''

Mason understood the question. "Harry isn't the issue. He's not looking at the needle. You are.''

"Ryman doesn't just *think* I killed Jack Cullan. He *wants* it to be me. Cops who want somebody found guilty know how to make that happen.''

"Not Harry. He's hard. He probably does want it to be you, but Harry plays it straight. He doesn't know any other way.''

"We get to court, Ryman's on the stand—can you take him on, carve him up, make the jury want to blame him instead of me? Can you tell the jury that Harry Ryman doesn't know his ass from third base and hates his old partner enough to send him to death row even if I'm innocent? Can you go home and tell your aunt Claire when all this is over that it was just business?''

Mason had asked himself the same questions as he drove downtown. Hearing Blues ask them reaffirmed the advice Harry had given him years ago. Knowing the right thing to do was easier than doing it. Since Harry was the lead on the investigation into Cullan's murder, his testimony would have enormous impact on the jury. Blues's life might depend on Mason's ability to turn the case into a trial of Harry and his investigation rather than a trial of Blues's innocence.

Mason realized another troubling aspect of Blues's questions. The criminal justice system was sometimes more about criminals than it was about justice. Innocent people were convicted for any number of reasons. Cops who planted evidence. Lazy defense lawyers. Jurors who believed that only guilty people got arrested, especially if they were black or brown. Being innocent wasn't always enough.

That's why nothing scared Mason more than a client that wasn't guilty. The gang-banger, the embezzler, the jealous spouse turned killer, all knew in their gut that they'd do the time. They knew that after their lawyer turned every technical trick he had, the system would beat them. The odds favored the house.

Innocent people didn't understand any of that. They were just innocent. End of story. Mason carried the burden of their freedom.

Innocent people didn't understand that the government had every edge; that the government didn't have to tell the defense lawyer anything about the government's case. Mason had represented another lawyer who had been charged with accepting kickbacks for settling personal injury cases for inflated amounts. The lawyer had been used to the civil justice system where the rules required both sides to lay all their cards on the table so that there were no surprises at trial. He nearly fainted when Mason had explained to him that most criminal cases were trial by ambush, with the government disclosing as little as possible, even withholding a witness's statement until after the witness had testified.

Mason used to wonder why the rules for fighting over other people's money were so carefully crafted to ensure a level playing field while the rules for saving an innocent person's life were so harsh. He decided it was because the people who wrote the rules were used to fighting over money and took their freedom for granted. He believed in the old joke that a liberal was just a Republican who'd been indicted.

Mason sat down in another hard-backed chair, set the legal pad he was carrying on the table, and wrote the name of the case—*State v. Bluestone*—across the top of the first page.

"If I can prove you're innocent, I'll do it any way I have to. Harry doesn't expect anything less. He won't cut either one of us any slack and he'll get none from me. Now tell me what they've got on you."

Blues hesitated a moment, then nodded and sat down across from Mason.

"Jack Cullan came in the bar last Friday night, about nine o'clock."

Mason asked, "You knew him?"

"He tried to hire me once. He wanted me to take pictures of a dude playing hide the nuts with the wrong squirrel. I took a pass."

"How long ago was that?"

"Not long enough that he didn't recognize me when he came in the bar. When he paid for the drinks, he told me that I should have taken the job since it paid better than bartending. I told him it didn't pay better than bar-owning."

"Was he alone?"

"The absolute opposite of alone. He was with a fine-looking woman, early forties, my guess."

"Did you get her name?"

"Not at first. Before she left, she gave me her card. Her name was Beth Harrell."

Mason said, "As in Beth Harrell, the chair of the Missouri Gaming Commission?"

"Not likely that there's more than one Beth Harrell who'd be out clubbing with Jack Cullan."

"I can't believe she was out anywhere with Cullan," Mason answered. "Cullan and Harrell have been all over the front page of the *Star*. She's got to be out of her mind to be out with that guy."

"Maybe that's why she threw a drink in his face," Blues said.

"Okay," Mason said. "You want to take this from the top or just play catch-the-zinger?"

"You're the one asking the questions. I'm just the defendant."

"Start talking or I'll give you up to the public defender."

"Take it easy, Lou. You've got to work on your jailhouse manner," Blues told him. "I was on the bar. Pete Kirby, Kevin Street, and Ronnie Fivecoat had just started their set. Weather's so bad, the place is dead, but they were killing it, really cooking."

Mason had heard the trio before. Kirby on piano, Street on bass, and Fivecoat on drums. He'd have happily gone anywhere to hear them play.

"So Jack Cullan and Beth Harrell are doing their own jazz-club crawl on one of the worst nights of the year and pick your place to get warm?"

"You ask Beth Harrell why they were there. She didn't confide in me. I served them drinks and didn't pay any more attention to them until she stands up and douses him. Cullan's old and fat, but that old, fat man jumped up and popped her with the back of his hand. Knocked her on the floor."

Mason said, "I assume you didn't just tell them to take it outside so you could listen to Kirby's trio?"

"Would have been the smart play. But I don't like it when fat, old men slap women around. I grabbed Cullan from behind to help him calm down. That little prick scratched me like a cheap whore before I squeezed the air out of him."

Blues held up the backs of his hands so that Mason could see the red claw marks on both of them. "Broke the skin," Blues added.

"Was that it?" Mason asked.

"Almost. I told Beth Harrell that she should press charges against Cullan. She said that wasn't necessary, that they'd just had a misunderstanding. She was very cool about the whole thing. Gave me her business card, like that was some kind of free pass for getting smacked around.''

''And then they left?''

''Yeah. Cullan was breathing again and was very pissed. He promised me that my liquor license would be gone in a week.''

Mason knew that Blues wouldn't have let the threat go unanswered, and he waited for Blues to finish the story. Blues looked at the two-way mirror. ''You sure they aren't listening in on this?''

''Not if they want to see you strapped to that gurney with a needle in your arm. What did you say to Cullan?''

Blues sighed, looked at the mirror again, and then back at Mason. ''I told him that if he tried jacking with my license or ever came in my bar again, I'd twist his head off and stuff it up his ass.''

''Well, that was memorable and stupid. What happened to being the strong silent type?''

''Cullan is used to getting in the last word, shoving people around, pimp-slapping women. No way he walks out of my place like he owned it.''

''Blues's Law,'' Mason said. ''What about afterward? What did you do after you closed the bar?''

''Home, man. By myself.''

Mason stopped writing. ''So you fought with this guy, he threatened you, and you threatened him back. Plus your blood and skin were under Cullan's fingernails when the maid found him. Harry's probably talked to Beth Harrell and Kirby, Street, and Fivecoat. He's got four witnesses to the threat and forensic evidence to go with it. And you don't have an alibi. I'd say he does like you for the murder.''

Mason pushed back from the table and got up. Blues asked, ''Where are you going?''

''Talk to Harry and find out what he's really got.''

"Aren't you forgetting to ask me one thing?" Blues asked.

"What's that?" Mason answered.

"If I did it?"

Mason shook his head and smiled. "Don't have to. You would have told me. Blues's Law."

Blues smiled for the first time. "I guess you can do this, Lou."

"That I can," Mason said.

Chapter Three

Mason found Harry squeezed into his desk chair, talking on the phone and rolling his eyes. "Yes, sir," he said. "I'm glad it's all over too, Mr. Mayor. Good-bye, sir." Harry put the phone down and motioned to Mason to pull up a chair.

"Did you forget to tell the mayor about the trial?" Mason asked as he borrowed a chair from another desk and sat down next to Harry.

Harry was pushing sixty, with half-gray sawdust hair, a soft-squared face, flat on the top and round on the sides. His bulk was more muscle than fat and his hands were like catchers' mitts. His build was constantly at war with his clothes, including the gray suit he'd picked for today. The arms on Harry's chair clamped his midsection like a vise. The police department had not been introduced to ergonomics.

"That's like the next election," Harry said. "Mayor Sunshine will worry about that tomorrow. Today, he'll tell the public that the case has been solved and make it sound like it was his collar.''

Mason said, ''I never saw a politician get so much out of his last name since the Kennedys. Anybody who can campaign on the slogan 'Let the Sunshine in Kansas City' with a straight face wouldn't break a sweat solving a murder.''

Harry freed himself long enough to get two cups of coffee from a machine against the wall. He handed one to Mason as he shoehorned himself back into his chair.

''The people elected him,'' Harry said. ''William 'Billy' Sunshine. His Honor the Asshole.''

Mason sipped and grimaced. He was an occasional coffee drinker, never quite developing an appreciation for the bitter brew.

Harry said, ''Get yourself some cream and sugar. Make it sweet like when you were a kid. You'll like it better.''

Mason set his cup down on Harry's desk. He didn't know whether Harry intended his remark to be a gentle paternal reminder of their long relationship or just idle chatter. Mason realized that he'd eventually have to convince Harry that their relationship was irrelevant to this case. He wasn't looking forward to that moment.

''It's fine,'' Mason told him. ''The mayor been pushing you guys on this case?''

Mason intended the question to sound casual, even innocent—more concerned about Harry than about the implications for the ''rush to judgment'' defense he was already planning for Blues.

Harry gave him a wise smile. ''Lou, I'm going to handle this case like every other one. It doesn't matter to me that Bluestone is the defendant or that you're his lawyer. I'll tell you what you're entitled to know and that's it.''

Mason felt like the little boy again. First Harry told him

how to drink his coffee, and then Harry told him that he's not so clever after all.

"Fair enough," Mason said. "Tell me what I'm entitled to know, but don't leave anything out because it won't be fun for either one of us if I find out some other way."

Harry shuffled through a stack of reports on his desk, humming under his breath until he found the one he wanted. He put on a pair of gold-rimmed glasses and studied the report.

Mason had been on the edge of many of Harry's cases, like a spectator with a front-row seat, listening to Harry's take on the bad guy of the month, his no-good defense lawyer, and the ball-busting judge. The one thing Mason always marveled at was Harry's command of the details, the nitty-gritty. Harry didn't miss much in an investigation, and he forgot even less. Mason had no doubt that Harry knew everything about Cullan's murder by heart and could recite it backward in his sleep. Harry's current display of seeming unfamiliarity was a dodge meant to encourage Mason to underestimate him. Mason figured he was doing it more out of habit than out of any expectation that Mason would take Harry too lightly.

Harry put the papers back on his desk along with his glasses. "Housekeeper found the body when she came to work on Monday morning around eight o'clock. She had a key. The alarm was off, which surprised her. Cullan ate breakfast in Westport every morning with a bunch of his cronies. He was never home when she got there and he always left the alarm on. She figured he was sick and went looking for him."

"Where did she find him?" Mason asked.

"On the floor in his study with a .38-caliber bullet hole in his right eye. Your client was a good shot."

"Or the killer was just lucky," Mason said, not taking the bait. "Did the coroner fix the time of death?"

"That part is a bit tricky. The killer turned the heat off and opened the windows in the study. You could have hung meat in there. The cold temperature makes it tough to determine the time of death. Coroner says that it could have been any time from Friday night to Sunday night."

Mason said, "That's a lot of ground to cover."

"Maybe," Harry said confidently. "But we detectives like clues and we found some good ones."

"Don't make me beg, Harry."

"Too soon for that, Lou. Begging comes during the sentencing phase. Cullan's bed was made, hadn't been slept in. The housekeeper says she made the bed on Friday. The Saturday, Sunday, and Monday newspapers were on the driveway and the Saturday mail was in the box. Cullan was popped on Friday night. Your client wasn't as smart as he thought."

"Any signs of forced entry?" Mason asked, ignoring Harry's jab.

"No."

"How did you get to Blues?"

"We traced Cullan's movements last Friday. His secretary, Shirley Parker, kept his schedule. Shirley says that he was in meetings all day and that she had made reservations for dinner for two at Mancuso's."

"I assume his secretary knew who he was having dinner with," Mason said.

"You assume right. Cullan had dinner with Beth Harrell. She's the one who's head of the Gaming Commission. So we talked with Ms. Harrell. She said that she and Cullan had gone to dinner and then stopped at Blues on Broadway to listen to Pete Kirby's trio. She wasn't real busted up about Cullan."

"She used Kirby's name?"

"Yeah. So what?"

"You've got to be a hard-core local jazz fan to know Pete Kirby's trio. That's all. Did she tell you anything else?"

Harry grinned. "That's all she told us the first time we talked to her. Kirby and his guys gave us a blow-by-blow on the fight she and Cullan had at the club and how Bluestone broke it up. My favorite part was when Bluestone threatened Cullan."

Harry hadn't said anything about the scratches on Blues's hands. Mason didn't know whether Beth Harrell or the musicians hadn't noticed the scratches, or whether Harry was holding out on Mason, waiting for him to raise the subject.

"So you went back to Beth Harrell and jogged her memory?" Mason asked.

"Early morning is a good time to question people. She didn't have her makeup on yet and the bruise Cullan had given her was just turning yellow. She said she didn't tell us about the fight because it was too embarrassing, but she did say that Bluestone scared her more than Cullan."

"Why was that?"

"Because Cullan was old and mean but she could handle him. When Bluestone threatened Cullan, she didn't think anyone could handle him."

Mason said, "None of that places Blues at the scene."

"We're working on that," Harry said. "Try this for starters," he added, tossing the coroner's report in Mason's lap.

Mason scanned the report, his stomach sinking when he found the information he knew would be there. Blood and tissue had been found under Cullan's fingernails. According to Blues's police department personnel file, the blood type found under Cullan's fingernails matched Blues's blood type.

"C'mon, Harry. You talked to four witnesses who saw

Blues grab Cullan from behind to stop him from beating up Beth Harrell. Cullan scratched the backs of Blues's hands. He's still got the marks. You've got to do better than that."

Harry didn't hesitate. "None of the witnesses saw Cullan scratch your client's hands. They only saw *him* squeeze Cullan until his eyes started to bug out."

"That doesn't change a thing, Harry," Mason said. "They just didn't see the scratches. I'll bet none of them told you that they looked at Blues's hands afterward and didn't see any scratches. Because you didn't ask them that question. Did you? Your case sucks without something that puts Blues in Cullan's house Friday night. Tell me what you've got, Harry!"

Harry listened as Mason turned up the volume, his blank expression giving no clue whether Mason's suddenly antagonistic tone bothered him, whether he had the evidence Mason was demanding, or whether he'd even heard a word Mason had said. Harry waited until the silence pressed down as heavily as unspoken bad news.

"I've got enough that the prosecuting attorney was happy to sign the arrest warrant. He says he might ask for the death penalty. Your client's first court appearance is tomorrow morning at nine in Associate Circuit Court."

Mason said, "This isn't a death-penalty case. It's barely a murder-one case. Even if your take on Blues is right— and it's not—you've got him killing Cullan because Cullan pissed him off. That's murder two on a good day. Where are the aggravating circumstances that would make it a death-penalty case?"

"The prosecutor doesn't have to disclose that until he decides whether to ask for the death penalty."

Mason knew that Harry was right, and decided to change subjects. Harry was true to his word. He wasn't going to tell Mason anything he didn't have to tell him. "So who drew the short straw in the prosecutor's office?"

Leonard Campbell, the prosecuting attorney, limited his court appearances to accepting high-profile plea bargains and trying cases with dead-certain guilty verdicts. He was more of a politician and bureaucrat than he was a trial lawyer. Mason assumed that he would assign one of his senior deputies to Blues's case.

"When Campbell signed the arrest warrant, he told me that he would try the case. Nobody here believes that. Campbell may decide to sit at the counsel table, but the lead guy will be Patrick Ortiz."

Mason had dealt with Ortiz several times since he had opened his own practice. Ortiz had a plodding, understated style that often lulled the defense attorney into careless mistakes. Juries responded to him, seeing him as one of them. He was a regular guy who just talked to the jury, making the complex simple, explaining why the alibi was just a lie. He had the highest conviction rate of anyone in the prosecutor's office. Most importantly from Mason's perspective, Patrick Ortiz was always the lead prosecutor in death-penalty cases.

Mason was done visiting. "I've got some other things to go over with Blues. Let me know when I can get a set of the investigative reports."

"I'll have them for you tomorrow morning," Harry said. "In the meantime, I'd like to get a blood and tissue sample from your client so we can do a DNA match with the scrapings the coroner took from Cullan's fingernails."

"Let's see how things go in the morning, Harry."

Harry said, "Today or tomorrow. It doesn't matter to me. We won't have any trouble finding your client. Just tell him that when the judge imposes a sentence, he'll ask us if Bluestone cooperated or made life difficult."

Mason was already tired of Harry's pinprick comments. "Harry, I know you've had a hard-on for Blues since the two of you were partners. Don't use this case to get even. Blues's life is on the line and you're too good of a cop to make it personal."

Harry fired back. "Is that what you think? That this is personal? Well, let me tell you something, Lou. It's damn personal! Your client killed an innocent woman six years ago and walked away. He killed Jack Cullan last Friday, and if he thinks he's walking away this time, he's wrong. Murder is about as personal as crimes get. I take it real personal that I didn't nail the son of a bitch the first time."

Harry's rant attracted the stares of the handful of detectives working at the other desks jammed onto the floor. Mason looked around the room. They all knew about Blues and Harry. Though cops never liked it when one of their own was busted, Blues was an exception. He'd crossed the line six years ago, and none of them thought of Blues as a brother behind the shield any longer. Mason suspected that they had high-fived Harry when he brought Blues in, gleefully reminding one another that paybacks are hell.

"You won't nail him this time either, Harry. I won't let you," Mason said.

Mason returned to the interrogation room, trying not to be obvious when he saw Blues rubbing the scratches on the backs of his hands. Still, the image caught Mason in midstep.

"You don't look like a lawyer who just convinced the cops to let his client go home," Blues told him.

Mason said, "The case Harry told me he has against you doesn't worry me. It's the one he wouldn't tell me about that should worry both of us."

Blues stood and looked down at Mason. Mason had always been impressed at Blues's ability to occupy a room. Though tall and muscular, he wasn't always the biggest man, but when he was backed up, he grew a foot higher and wider with the menace he promised.

"You got something to say, Lou—just say it."

Mason let out a long breath and tossed his legal pad onto the table. "Okay. Blood and tissue were found under Cullan's fingernails. They checked the blood type against the blood type in your police department personnel file and got a match. They want a blood sample for DNA testing to positively match the blood and tissue. Harry says that none of the witnesses in the bar saw Cullan scratch your hands, but they will testify that you threatened Cullan."

"So, I'll testify," Blues said.

"You know what they call a defendant who testifies? Convict," Mason said before Blues could answer. "I told Harry that his case still sucked unless he could put you at the scene."

Blues said, "You told him his case sucked? That's strong. I'll bet he gave up right then."

"Almost. I asked him what he had, and he said it was enough for the prosecuting attorney to consider asking for the death penalty. He said you got away with murder once before and that he's not going to let you get away with it again."

Blues turned away. Mason expected the news to knock Blues back. Instead, Blues gathered himself, straining as if he would break out of the interrogation room by sheer will.

"What do you think?" Blues asked.

"I think a lot of clients hold back information from their lawyer. They want to look their best, their most innocent, especially when they're not. Shit, half of them probably undressed in the dark on their wedding nights so they wouldn't disappoint their spouse.'' Mason paused. ''I think Harry's case sucks unless he can place you at the scene. I need to know if he can.''

Blues paced once around the small room, stopping with his back to the two-way mirror, and folded his arms against his chest. ''I wasn't there and I didn't kill Jack Cullan.''

''I'll be sure to mention that to the judge,'' Mason said. ''You'll be arraigned tomorrow morning in front of an Associate Circuit Court judge who will set bail. I'm guessing bail will be no less than a quarter million and maybe as much as half a million.''

Blues said, ''The judge won't grant me bail.''

''Hey, c'mon. Give me some credit. You've got substantial ties to the community. You're not a threat to anyone else. Carlos Guiterriz will bond you out. The bar will be more than enough collateral. You'll be out by lunchtime.''

''You don't get it, Lou. Charging me with murder one and threatening me with the death penalty is a power play to make me take a deal. Somebody wants me to go down for this, and keeping me in the county jail until trial will be the next card that gets played. Make an ex-cop spend the winter in the general prison population, and see how long it takes him to find religion. If I don't roll over, they hope I'll get shanked before the trial. The last thing I'll hear is, 'Enjoy your stay at the Graybar Inn.' ''

''Harry wouldn't do that,'' Mason said, regretting the words as he spoke them.

''Oh, Harry would do it, except it's not up to Harry. He's just carrying water for the chief, or the prosecuting attorney, or whoever doesn't want my case to go to trial.''

''Blues, this isn't the Conspiracy Hour. Cullan was connected to everybody in town, but he would have had to own everybody—the police, the courts, and the mayor—

everybody for you to be right. Plus he's dead. All the IOUs he held have been canceled.''

"How are you going to prove I'm innocent?'' Blues asked.

"Find out who killed Cullan.''

"You'll have to peel the layers off of Cullan's life, read every one of those IOUs.''

Mason nodded, grabbing the thread that held Blues's fears together. "Cullan was probably killed by someone who wanted to cancel an IOU and won't mind if you take the fall. If Cullan owned half the people the *Star* claims he did, there will be plenty of pressure to keep your case from coming to trial. Otherwise, I'll hang every dirty piece of laundry I can find in front of the jury to convince them that someone else did it.''

"That's why I won't get bail,'' Blues said. "Remember something else while you're out there stirring up this shit pot.''

"What's that?''

"The killer won't mind killing again to make sure I go down. And no one else will mind either.''

Chapter Four

Associate Circuit Court Judge Joe Pistone's courtroom was on the eighth floor of the Jackson County Courthouse, a neoclassical monument to the durability of public-works projects built during the Depression. It was on the East Side of downtown across the street from City Hall, another monument cast from the same mold. Police Headquarters, an uninspired squared fortress, was one block east on Locust. The three buildings, all hewn from Missouri limestone, formed Kansas City's triangle of legislative, judicial, and executive order. The courthouse was eight stories and Police Headquarters was six. City Hall loomed over both of them at thirty stories. The branches of government may have been equal on paper, but the daily grind of governing required considerably more people and space than public safety or justice.

Mason passed through the metal detector in the courthouse rotunda, hurrying up to wait for the elevators. The job of operating the courthouse elevators had been one of the last county patronage jobs to succumb to modern technology. Since the courthouse opened in the 1930s, loyalists at the bottom of the political food chain had been rewarded with the stupefying opportunity to sit for hours at a time on a small stool and bounce the elevators from floor to floor. Over the years, they had perfected a herky-jerky stop-and-go technique that left most passengers gasping when the doors opened at their floor. When the ancient elevators and their equally ancient operators were replaced, the county installed new elevators that ran smoothly, but slowly enough to drive even the most exercise-averse to use the stairs.

Associate Circuit Court was the home of rough justice. Rules of evidence and procedure were loosely applied to hasten the endless passage of collection, landlord-tenant, and traffic cases through the system. Associate Circuit Court judges carried the honorific title of their Circuit Court brethren, though many lawyers treated them behind their backs like minor leaguers. The one exception was the criminal defense attorney whose client stood before the judge seeking bail in an amount the defendant could make. At those moments, the lawyers meant it when they called the judge "Your Honor."

Reporters from the local TV and radio stations had gathered outside the courtroom, creating a media gauntlet for Mason to pass through. Mason ignored the questions they tossed in his path, smiling politely without answering until Rachel Firestone stepped in front of him. Mason recalled her tenacious pursuit of him in the aftermath of the bloody demise of his last law firm, Sullivan & Christenson.

"Listen, Lou," she had told him. "This story is going to be written whether you like it or not. You are the story. Talk to me."

"Not interested," Mason had told her. "Too many people are dead. Let them be."

Rachel had written the story, quoting his refusal. She'd sent him a copy with a note saying she hoped he liked it and asking him to call her. Mason had thrown the note and the article away.

Rachel had short-cropped dark red hair, alabaster skin, and dancing emerald eyes. Her trim, athletic build matched the nervous energy she radiated like a solar flare. Newspaper reporters didn't have to dress for success like their TV counterparts. Rachel put them to shame anyway with a pair of moleskin khakis, lumberjack shirt, bomber jacket, and hiking boots.

"Welcome back to the meat grinder," Rachel said. "Care to talk?"

"No," Mason told her.

"Wrong answer, Lou. I'll give you another chance later," she said before pushing her way into the courtroom and a seat directly behind the prosecutor's table.

Joe Pistone's entire legal career had been spent in Associate Circuit Court, the first twenty-five years as a lawyer and the last fifteen as a judge. He had white hair, a thin face, and shoulders that were hunched like a man who'd spent his life ducking trouble. He rarely looked at the lawyers or the litigants, keeping his head down and the cases moving.

Judge Pistone's courtroom was small enough to be crowded if more than a handful of people were present for a case. When there was a docket call for first appearances in criminal cases, the courtroom shrank as the jury box was filled with defendants dressed in orange jailhouse jumpsuits, their hands and feet shackled. There were two counsel tables, one for the prosecutor and one for the defense. The pews behind the rail that separated the lawyers and judge from the public usually were filled with family members of defendants and victims who divided themselves like the bride's side and the groom's side. Inexperienced lawyers who didn't arrive in time to sit up front wedged themselves into any empty space they could find, while the veterans hung around the judge's bench as if they were at a local bar. Toss in the media pack and the courtroom became standing-room-only.

Mason made certain he was early enough to claim a seat at the defense table so that he could talk with Patrick Ortiz before Blues's case was called. Ortiz arrived at eight forty-five, carrying a stack of files and trailed by two assistants. The other defense lawyers flocked to him like schoolchildren asking for early dismissal. Mason waited while Ortiz listened to their pitches, nodding at some while disappointing others. When the frenzy had subsided, Mason stepped over to the prosecutor's table, buttoning the top two buttons of his three-button gray suit jacket and straightening his black-and-blue-striped tie.

"Morning, Patrick," Mason said, extending his hand.

"Lou, good to see you," Ortiz answered, shaking Mason's hand without conviction.

Mason was six feet tall, with a hard flat body kept in shape on the rugby field and a rowing machine he kept in his dining room. Ortiz was a head shorter than Mason, and had the irregular rounded shape of someone whose diet was limited to those foods that end in the letter O. Mason sat on the edge of the prosecutor's table, a friendly adversary chatting up the opposition.

"I'm here on Wilson Bluestone."

"So I've been told. These are for you," he said, handing Mason a copy of the police reports. "Normally, you wouldn't get these until the preliminary hearing, but Harry Ryman says he promised to give them to you today. Don't ask for any more favors. This is my case now, not Ryman's."

"I'll keep that in mind," Mason answered as he skimmed through the pages.

Ortiz enjoyed taking full advantage of the rules on disclosure of the state's case, and he didn't like the fact that Harry had given up his right to withhold the investigative reports from Mason until the preliminary hearing, which probably wouldn't be scheduled for two weeks. Ortiz rarely granted a favor to the opposition without cashing it in for a bigger favor down the road.

"Sign this," Ortiz said, and slid a single sheet of paper toward Mason.

Mason picked it up. It was a consent form authorizing the State of Missouri to obtain blood, hair, and skin samples from Wilson Bluestone, Jr. Mason signed it and handed it back to Ortiz.

"You want to talk about a plea, come see me this afternoon," Ortiz told him.

"My client's only plea is innocent. I don't expect you to agree to release him without bail. How much are you looking for?"

"No bail. That's what I'm looking for, Lou," Ortiz answered.

Before Mason could respond, three deputy sheriffs led Blues into the jury box. After a night in jail, clad in Day-Glo orange with his hands and feet manacled, even to Mason he looked like a flight risk and a danger to the public.

Mason made eye contact with Blues, who was seated in the middle of the back row. Mason shook his head, telling Blues all he needed to know about the prosecutor's position on bail. Judge Pistone made his entrance as the bailiff called the courtroom to order.

"Good morning, Counsel," the judge began. "We'll take the video arraignments first."

Arraignments for the accused who did not yet have a

lawyer were often conducted by video broadcast from the jail. A projector mounted on the wall directly above the table for defense counsel beamed a six-foot-by-ten-foot image on the opposite wall. The picture was grainy and washed out. The audio was a beat behind the image, and the transmission speed was somewhere between real time and slow motion. The proceedings had the look and feel of justice administered in the middle of a bad dream.

Each defendant appeared on screen, an oversize head shot that magnified every tremor and twitch. The last defendant was a young boy Mason guessed was barely twenty. His blinking eyes tried to retreat from the camera as he nervously patted his thin blond hair. His lips quivered and he tugged at his chin as the judge read the charge and the maximum sentence for the offense.

"You are charged with forcible rape, a Class A felony for which the maximum penalty is life in prison."

The boy whipped his head up at the camera, his mouth gaping at the judge's words.

"Do you have an attorney?" the judge asked. The boy shook his head mutely, robbed of speech. "The public defender will come see you."

Unseen hands pulled the boy offscreen and the picture disappeared. Mason had the feeling the boy was as lost as the image that had been on the wall.

"The next case is *State of Missouri v. Bluestone*," Judge Pistone announced. "State your appearances, Counsel."

Patrick Ortiz stood and announced, "The people of the State of Missouri appear by Patrick Ortiz, deputy chief prosecuting attorney."

Mason followed. "The defendant appears in person and by his counsel, Lou Mason. We're ready to proceed, Your Honor."

"Very well, Counsel," the judge said without looking up. "Will the defendant please rise."

Blues stood from his seat in the jury box. Mason could hear the faint etching sounds of the courtroom artists who were there for the TV stations whose cameras were not allowed in the courtroom.

Judge Pistone continued. "The defendant is charged with the crime of murder in the first degree in the death of Jack Cullan. Does the defendant understand the charges or wish to have them read?"

"We'll waive the reading of the charges, Judge. We'd like to discuss bail," Mason said.

"What's the state's position, Mr. Ortiz?" the judge asked.

"The People oppose bail in this case. The defendant is a former police officer who was forced to resign because of a shooting death that violated departmental rules on the use of deadly force. He has an extensive history of violent conduct. Though we acknowledge his ties to the community, he's both a flight risk and a danger to the public."

"Mr. Mason?" the judge asked.

"Your Honor, my client is entitled to bail. He owns a business that will be shut down if he's not there to run it. Everything he owns is tied up in that business and he's not about to run out on that. Mr. Ortiz is correct that the defendant is a former police officer. He's wrong about the defendant's history. He's never been charged with or convicted of any crime. The state's evidence in this case is as thin as yesterday's soup. While the victim was a high-profile member of the community, the court should reject any pressure to deny my client bail."

As soon as the judge looked up for the first time that morning, Mason knew he'd hit the wrong nerve. "Mr. Mason, if you have any basis for suggesting that someone is attempting to improperly influence this court or that I would be susceptible to such attempts, now is the time to share that with me.''

Mason felt the color rise in his neck. He refused to look at Ortiz, who, he was certain, was smiling wide enough to suck down a bag of Doritos. He couldn't look at Blues. ''I didn't mean any reflection on the court, Your Honor. All I meant that was that the state is pushing a lot harder on my client than they would in any other case with this kind of evidence. Whatever the reason for that, it's not sufficient to deny bail for Mr. Bluestone.''

''You can take that up with the Circuit judge who gets assigned to this case. Bail denied. We're in recess.'' The judge banged his gavel once and left the courtroom.

Mason saw Rachel Firestone shake her head as he walked past. He was beginning to believe that Blues was right. Even though he had roused Joe Pistone's slumbering judicial dignity, the decision on bail had already been made. Mason's gaffe had given the judge all the cover he needed.

Once outside the courtroom, Mason weaved through the media throng, making his way into the hallway that connected to the judge's chambers. It was also the route by which Blues would be taken back to the county jail. He caught up to the sheriff's deputies and Blues just as they were getting onto the elevator.

''Mind if I get a word with my client?'' Mason asked one of the deputies.

''Make it fast. This ain't a parade,'' the deputy said.

Mason pulled Blues by the arm as far from the deputies as he could without getting them too excited.

''Listen, I'm sorry about what happened in there, but I don't think it would have made any difference,'' Mason told him.

''It's cool, man,'' Blues said. ''Like I told you, they're going to try to squeeze me.''

"We'll get another chance in front of the Circuit Court judge. The prosecuting attorney can either ask for a preliminary hearing so that the Circuit judge can bind you over for trial, or take the case to the grand jury for an indictment. I'm betting on the grand jury. That way Ortiz doesn't have to tip his hand. The grand jury meets every other Friday. The next session is a week from tomorrow. Once you're indicted, we can ask the Circuit Court judge to set bail."

"I've got a better idea," Blues said. "Don't ask for bail. If we don't fight for it, they can't hold it over me. Spend your time finding out who killed Cullan, not writing motions the judge is going to turn down anyway."

Mason studied Blues for a moment. "You won't have any friends inside."

Blues gave Mason a broad grin. "You'd be surprised how easy I make friends. There's just two things you need to worry about besides winning my case."

"What are they?"

"First thing is you got to find somebody to run the club. Try Mickey Shanahan. He's the PR guy whose office is next to yours. Mickey's always behind on his rent. Tell him he can work it off."

"Okay. What's the second thing?" Mason asked.

"You're on your own. Don't get dead. They'll throw away the key to my cell."

Chapter Five

Mason didn't wait for the elevator doors to close before he headed back to the courtroom. He found Patrick Ortiz giving last-minute instructions to the more junior assistant prosecutors who would handle the remaining cases when court resumed. They stopped talking when Mason approached, the younger lawyers looking away to hide their smirks.

"Patrick, you were way out of line with that shit about Blues being forced to resign from the police department. You know that there's no way in hell that comes into evidence. Except now it will be the lead on every newscast and plastered on the front page. You must want me to file a motion to move the trial out of town so my client can get a fair trial."

"I'm not going to tell you how to try your case, Lou. Bluestone's record as a cop is relevant. It proves he's already shot one person to death. It may not be admissible to prove he killed Jack Cullan, but it's sure as hell relevant to the sentence he's going to get and whether he should get bail.''

''Forget about the bail. You're lucky that Blues is more patient than I am. He'll take the county up on its offer of hospitality until the trial.''

Ortiz's assistants lost their smirks, but Ortiz maintained his poker face. ''I understand that the food is quite good, though a bit repetitive,'' he said. ''As long as your client is prepared to sit for a while, maybe he'd like to talk about a plea.''

''Is that how you pumped up your conviction record, Patrick? Squeeze the hard cases until they plead and take the chumps to trial? The only plea my client is going to make is innocent. Be sure to tell that to whoever is yanking your chain on this one.''

Mason knocked on the open door to Mickey Shanahan's office as soon as he returned from court. Mickey's office was smaller than Mason's and didn't have any windows. It did have a lot of posters. Mostly from political campaigns. Mickey didn't have a desk. Instead, he had a card table and four chairs. Mason figured that if business was slow, Mickey could always invite people over to play bridge. When Mason knocked, Mickey was straddling one of the card table chairs, his back to the door, while wadding up pages from the morning paper and tossing them at a basketball goal, making the swish sound regardless of whether he made the shot.

Mason had talked to Mickey a few times during the six months Mickey had been a tenant. Mason liked his scrappy attitude, but couldn't figure out how he made a living. Blues told Mason that Mickey had graduated from college a couple of years earlier, worked for a big PR firm in town, and then decided to go it alone. That's when he signed a lease with Blues. Mason had yet to see a client walk into or out of Mickey's office, and wasn't surprised that Mickey was behind on his rent.

"Hey, Mickey. What's going on, man?" Mason asked from the open door.

Mickey glanced over his shoulder, beamed when he saw Mason, and scrambled to his feet.

"You're asking me?" Mickey picked up the front page of the newspaper with the two-inch headline announcing EX-COP ARRESTED FOR MURDER OF POLITICAL BOSS. "I should be asking you what's going on. No, I shouldn't. I should be telling you to hire me to handle the PR on this case. I'm telling you, Lou. This case, win or lose—and don't get me wrong, I'm pulling for you and Blues—this case can make you in this town. Blues too if you win. It's all about spin, my friend."

Mickey had an unruly shock of brown hair that fell across his pale Irish forehead. He could pour nutrition shakes down his throat with a funnel and still be nearly invisible when he turned sideways. He was a five-foot-seven, finger-tapping, pencil-twirling, punch-line machine, all revved up with no place to go.

"I'll keep that in mind," Mason promised. "In the meantime, Blues wants you to run the club for a while. The judge wouldn't let him out on bail. Blues says you can work off the back rent you owe him."

"Outstanding!" Mickey said. He crossed the short distance to the door and shook Mason's hand. "Outstanding!"

"I'll tell Blues you said so," Mason told him. "Do you know what to do?"

"Haven't a fucking clue, man," Mickey said. "But no one will know the difference. That's public relations!"

* * *

Mason took Mickey's word for it and retreated to his own office. Mason's aunt Claire claimed that Mason's office proved her theory of men and their response to available space.

"No matter how much stuff a man has," she told him, "it will fill every available inch of open space. Put him in a smaller office with just as much stuff, and the stuff shrinks to fit. Add a hundred square feet and a man's stuff will spread over it like a rising tide."

Located at the end of the hall, Mason's office spread out on both sides of the door. Bookshelves lined the back wall on either side of the door. Client files were crammed into the shelves on one side and books filled the other. On the right side of the office, more files, a rugby football, and a pair of sweats competed for room on an overstuffed corduroy-covered sofa on which he'd spent more than a few nights. A large brightly colored Miro print hung over the sofa.

A low table and two chairs in front of the sofa created a seating area. Mason dropped his camel-hair topcoat on one chair and his suit coat on the other.

The opposite wall was covered with a four-foot-by-six-foot dry-erase board enclosed by burnished oak doors. The inside panels of the doors were covered in cork. A rolled screen was mounted above the dry-erase surface. Mason was a visual thinker. He kept track of ideas, questions, and answers by writing them in different colors on the dry-erase board. He pinned similar notes written while out of the office onto the cork surface. When a problem was solved, he erased it. He preferred working out difficult cases by studying the notes on his board until order emerged from the chaos.

The exterior wall of the office widened out in a three-sided windowed alcove, the center section of which was occupied by his desk. The desk was flanked on one side by a computer workstation housing a combination printer, fax, scanner, and copier, and a small refrigerator on the other that was usually empty except for a six-pack of Bud. Mason didn't have enough room or business to support a secretary. He gave thanks every day to his eighth-grade typing teacher who had threatened to hold him back if he didn't learn to touch-type.

A faded Persian rug covered the center of the hardwood floor. Mason knew that his aunt Claire was right about men and their stuff. His office was cluttered, but it was a comfortable clutter.

Mason opened the doors to the dry-erase board, picked up a red marker, and began writing. Next to Jack Cullan's name he wrote *victim/fixer* and the questions *Who's afraid of Jack?* and *Who wins if Jack dies?*

Switching to black, he wrote *Blues—at the scene?—connection to Cullan?*

Still using the black marker, he wrote on the next line *Harry—why so certain about Blues? Who's pushing Harry?*

Mason picked up the blue marker and wrote *Beth Harrell—why with Cullan?* His last entry was in red. *Who else?*

Mason was sitting in his desk chair, reading the police reports and deciding what to add to the board, when there was a sharp knock at the door, followed immediately by Rachel Firestone's entrance. She looked first at Mason and then the board before she even said hello. Mason was too far from the board to close the doors and prevent her from reading everything he'd written, so he pretended not to care rather than give her the satisfaction of thinking she'd seen something she shouldn't have.

"I don't suppose there's any point in asking you if you had an appointment," Mason said.

"I don't suppose there was any reason to ask for one since you'd just tell me no," Rachel answered.

"Can't argue with that. How about I just tell you no and you leave?"

"Give it up, Lou. I'm on this story and you're on this case. We can't avoid each other. It won't be that bad. You'll get used to me. You'll probably even get a crush on me, make a stupid pass, and I'll break your heart and make your testicles shrivel like raisins in one fell swoop."

Mason took a good look at her as she posed for him, hands on her hips, her chin punched out at him in a devilish, take-your-best-shot angle. She was luminescent, inviting, and somehow unattainable. Mason felt a surge that had been dormant since he'd broken up with Kelly Holt, the woman who had investigated the murders of his former partners. It was the jolting combination of need, desire, and unexpected opportunity. He'd dated a few women since Kelly, but in each case they'd been using each other to satisfy their needs of the moment, and he hadn't made more than a glandular connection.

"And why would you do that? The testicles part, I mean."

"Can't be helped, Lou. I'm gay. I'm a boots, jeans, flannel-shirt-wearing, short-haired lipstick lesbian. Though I'm a knockout in a simple black dress I keep in my closet for special occasions."

"That would do it," he conceded as his rising sap retreated to its roots. "Thanks for sparing me."

"Not a problem. I like getting that out of the way up front. Fewer complications," she added as she picked up the football and made a place for herself on the sofa. She tossed the ball back and forth between her hands, frowning at its odd feel.

"It's for rugby," Mason explained.

"That's a hard-hitting game. You play?" she asked.

"Not as much as I used to. I'm getting a little old by rugby standards to dive into a bunch of maniacs going after the ball. I'll take you to a game in the spring," he offered without understanding why.

"Great. I'd like that," she said with a smile that filled him with regret. "So Beth Harrell was with Jack Cullan the night he was killed," Rachel said, pointing to Mason's board.

"You heard that too?" Mason asked her.

"Yup. I tried to talk with her, but she keeps her door locked. Any idea why they were out together?"

Mason hesitated. He felt as if he were walking on an active fault line with Rachel that could cleave open and swallow him at any moment. She was beautiful, flirtatious, and completely unavailable. She knew she had him off balance, and was enjoying his disadvantage. He could live with that so long as she didn't take advantage of him in a way that compromised his defense of Blues.

"I think we need some ground rules here," he told her.

"So do I. Here's freedom-of-the-press rule number one. Everything's on the record unless you tell me in advance that it isn't on the record."

Mason shook his head. "Here's defense-lawyer rule number one. Nothing is on the record unless I say so. Rule number two—burn me and I'll cut you off at the knees."

Rachel folded her arms over her chest. "You're just angry about the lesbian thing. Hey, it wasn't my idea. A girl doesn't get to choose. Not that I'm complaining." Mason's only response was to reach for the doors to the board and start to close them. "Okay, okay," she told him. "Nothing is on the record unless you say so."

"Good. I don't know why they were at the bar, but I think she'll tell me."

"Why?"

"First, because I'm not going to print it on the front page

of the newspaper in a story accusing her of being a crook. Second, I can put her under oath and make her tell me, and third, we know each other.''

''How?''

''I took ethics from her when she taught at the law school. I was a first-year student and it was her first semester teaching. We hit it off pretty well, but I've only run into her a few times since I graduated. Alumni functions and that kind of thing.''

Rachel nodded. ''Is your client guilty?''

''No.''

''How do you know?'' she asked him.

Mason said, ''He told me so.''

''That's not good enough for an acquittal,'' Rachel said.

''It's good enough for me. All I have to do is figure out who did kill Jack Cullan. The cops are done looking. Any suggestions?'' he asked her.

Rachel walked over to the dry-erase board, picked up the red marker, and wrote *Cullan's secret files* next to Mason's entry *Who else?*

''I've been chasing after Jack Cullan's shadow for three years,'' she said. ''He was into everything important that happened or didn't happen in this town. Want to get elected? Go see Jack. Want to cut a deal with the city? Need tax increment financing? How about the pay telephone contract at the airport? Go see Jack. He always delivered the goods.''

''How did he do it? Where did he get that kind of influence?''

''Cullan invested in the long term. Long-term relationships. Long-term political IOUs. One day, the city wakes up and peeks out from under its covers. Only the view is from Jack Cullan's back pocket. I kept picking up threads of a rumor that I put together even though I couldn't get anyone to corroborate it. Cullan took a page from J. Edgar

Hoover's playbook. He supposedly had secret files on enough people in town to keep everyone in their place. He liked pulling strings and made certain the strings were tied on very tightly.''

"You said you couldn't corroborate that. How do you know it's true?''

"The same reason you know your client is innocent. I can feel it. I just can't find the files.''

Mason said, "Anyone who was in those files may have had a motive to kill Jack Cullan. The rest of them would give anything to make certain the files stayed secret. The easiest way for that to happen is to make certain Blues is found guilty.''

"I'll make you a deal,'' Rachel said. "You find the files first, I get the exclusive. I find the files first, I'll let you see them before I go public.''

Mason gave her a broad smile. "Deal,'' he told her. "Why so generous?''

"Let's just say that I'm a sucker for a good-looking rugby player,'' Rachel told him. Mason's smile got wider, his hope restored. "In fact, I'm dating one now. She's fabulous. I'll be in touch,'' she said as she left.

Chapter Six

Mason finished studying the police reports without finding any daggers to throw at Harry on cross-examination. Harry had been as thorough as Mason had expected. The crime scene had been hermetically preserved. Photographs were taken from every angle, fingerprints lifted from every surface, and a meticulous search had been made for footprints and fibers that didn't belong. Two separate teams of detectives to check for inconsistencies or forgotten details interviewed every neighbor living in a two-block radius. The maid had passed a polygraph exam. The contents of the house had been inventoried and double-checked against Cullan's homeowner's insurance records. No valuables were missing and there was no sign of forced entry. Cullan had opened the door to someone who had come for one reason— to kill him.

The police and prosecutor had not finished their investigation. Although now their focus had shifted from catching

Cullan's killer to proving that Blues was guilty. Mason had no doubt that the blood and tissue under Cullan's fingernails belonged to Blues. If none of the witnesses saw Cullan scratch Blues's hands at the bar, Blues would have to take the stand in his own defense. No matter how certain he was of Blues's innocence, Mason knew that was a high-stakes gamble. Patrick Ortiz would come in his pants at the prospect of taking on Blues.

There was nothing Mason could do about any of the evidence the prosecutor already had against Blues. He wouldn't make the mistake of trying to win the case on the prosecution's ground. Instead, he'd have to find the killer.

Mason listened to the icy wind as it swarmed over the city, slip-sliding through weak spots in brick and mortar, seeping into cracks and faults, sucking out the warmth. He imagined that Jack Cullan had been that way, wrapping his own cold fingers around the weak spots in other people's hearts until they became brittle and broken in his hands.

There was small comfort in the warmth of Mason's office since he knew that he had to go out into the wind. In the solitude of that moment, Mason conceded that the prosecutor was way out in front. Mason knew that he wouldn't get any help from the people who'd been under Cullan's thumb. Though each of them had probably lit a candle for the killer and asked God to reserve a special place in hell for Cullan, they'd let the wind sweep Blues away.

Mason returned to the dry-erase board and picked up the black marker. Beneath his question *Who else?* and Rachel Firestone's note about Cullan's secret files, he added the names of Ed Fiora, Billy Sunshine, and Beth Harrell. All three were tied to Jack Cullan. It was all he had.

Mason began with what he knew about each of them. Ed Fiora owned the Dream Casino. Though he'd passed the Gaming Commission's background checks, Rachel's newspaper stories had him only a sham corporation or two removed from his leg-breaking days.

Billy Sunshine was a charismatic mayor who'd steal your vote and your wife with equal aplomb. He was glib and charming, a native son with the ethos of a carpetbagger. More than anything else, he was ambitious. He'd been elected by a wide margin to a second term and, by law, couldn't run again. The mayor had all but announced he would challenge Delray Shays, the black incumbent congressman, in the next election. Local wags had it that the casino scandal was the only thing holding up the formal announcement. When last asked about it, the mayor said it was all water off a duck's back and he'd let the people of the fifth congressional district decide.

Beth Harrell was the piece of the puzzle that didn't fit. Ed Fiora was a thug posing as a gaming entrepreneur. Billy Sunshine was the poster boy for mamas not letting their babies grow up to be politicians. Beth Harrell was the good queen.

Mason remembered her from law school. She was only five years older than Mason, having practiced for two years after graduating before becoming a professor. Beth had dark blond hair that dangled above her shoulders, softening her bold walk and magnetic blue eyes. Her body was trim, her lips full, and her look said "authorized personnel only." She carried her beauty with the experience of someone used to taking advantage of it and wary of those who would. All of which made the class she taught the most popular one offered. Mason had resisted the temptation to sit in the front row with his tongue hanging out like his less subtle friends. He'd worked hard in her class, and she'd returned the effort with a good grade and a friendly handshake whenever they'd run into each other over the years.

Beth's reputation as an expert in ethics had brought her

to the attention of the governor. When the previous chair of the Gaming Commission had been convicted of accepting kickbacks from owners of casinos in St. Louis, the governor had turned to Beth to restore credibility to the commission. The license for the Dream Casino was the first major piece of business for the commission after she took over. Mason found it hard to believe that she had stepped over the line.

Mason had learned from Harry that it was much more effective to question a witness when he showed up unexpectedly. Rachel Firestone had proven the point earlier in the day. He'd had great success waiting outside homes, offices, and bars to snag someone with a handful of well-chosen questions.

He doubted that the ambush interview would work with the three people on his list. A layer of muscle that he'd have to cut through would insulate Ed Fiora. The mayor would have a layer of bureaucrats guarding his gate. Mason wasn't certain which layer would be tougher. He doubted that Beth Harrell had a gatekeeper, but he knew better than to just drop by. Even in law school, she demanded that students make an appointment to see her outside of class.

He wasn't surprised when, earlier that day, one of Fiora's assistants had told him that Mr. Fiora would be unavailable until the next millennium, or when the mayor's scheduling secretary had said that he didn't have any openings until after his term expired. Beth Harrell just didn't call him back. It was a refreshing kind of rejection. By the time he'd finished catching up on his other cases, it was nearly eight o'clock.

Mason checked on Mickey Shanahan before leaving for the night. Mickey was behind the bar, gesturing directions to Pete Kirby's trio as they set up for another night. Pete looked at Mickey like he was a blind man directing traffic. Mason decided to take a crack at Kirby's memory.

"Hey, Pete, how you doing, man?" Mason said.

Pete Kirby was a fireplug whose feet barely touched the pedals when he played the piano. He never left home without a black beret that matched his goatee. Kirby moved like a man whose rhythm was always eight to the bar. Mason expected to find his picture in a catalogue of jazz miniatures.

"Everything's cool, Louie my boy. How's my man Blues?" Kirby was the only person who called Mason Louie, a list Mason wasn't anxious to expand.

"He's doing fine, Pete. I understand you were playing Friday night when Jack Cullan came in."

"That's right, I was. Me and the boys wouldn't have stuck around since it was such a shitty night and the joint was empty, but we figured, what the hell, we'll play a set for Blues. Then Cullan comes in with this good-looking broad and the next thing I know, the two of them are playing Frankie and Johnnie."

"Blues tells me he busted up the fight," Mason said.

"That he did. Blues grabbed that old man like he was gonna pile-drive the cat right into the goddamn ground. Don't pay to tussle in Blues's joint," Pete added with a deep laugh. "No, sir, it don't."

"I hear Cullan fought like a cat too. Scratched the hell out of Blues' hands."

Kirby tugged at the corner of his beret and stroked his goatee, measuring his response in a firm meter. "Like I told the detective, I didn't see any of that. Now, you lookin' like your woman just run off with the drummer makes me wish maybe I had, but I just didn't see it. Sorry, Louie."

"Don't worry about it, Pete. It's not important," Mason assured him.

The parking lot behind the bar was covered in old asphalt that had given birth to potholes big enough to swallow women and children. Blues was an easygoing landlord who believed in deferred maintenance. Mason stepped around the craters, afraid that if he fell into one, no one would find him until spring. His car was parked at the back of the lot; the front end aimed at the alley behind the bar. Though there was a curb between the lot and the street, Mason planned to ignore it. Otherwise, he told himself, what's the point of having a Jeep?

The wind had calmed from its all-day shriek to a steady howl, as if it were whining about working overtime. Though the walk to his car was short, it was long enough for the wind to rake tears from the corners of Mason's eyes. Fine crystals of sleet tattooed his face like asteroid dust, whipping around his right arm as he folded it over his face as a shield. Blues's deferred-maintenance program had extended to the parking lot floodlights that had been burnt out since Thanksgiving. The lights were off in the building across the alley, and the sky had been buttoned down with blackout clouds. Moonlight couldn't have found its way to Mason's dark patch even if it had a map.

Mason crunched his nearly closed eyes even tighter when a pair of high-beam headlights opened up on him like lasers as he reached his Jeep. Another car was parked almost nose-to-nose with his, the sound of its engine muffled by the wind. Heavy boots ground sand and salt into the pavement as a man bigger than Mason's Jeep stepped from the shadows and made his way toward Mason.

"Car trouble?" Mason asked, still unable to make out the man's features.

When he didn't get an answer, Mason's internal windchill hit bottom. His new best friend stepped in front of the headlights casting a nightmare's silhouette. He was wearing a full-length topcoat and a fedora jammed low on his brow.

Mason couldn't see the man's face except for the frozen gray breath that leaked from his mouth like poison gas.

Mason reached for his car door, hoping to put some steel between him and the man, but he was too slow. In the next instant, the man grabbed Mason and spun him around, pinning Mason's face flush to the side of the Jeep, the frozen surface burning Mason's jaw. Mason stiffened, trying to leverage his hands against the Jeep and drive his hips and back against the man, but the side of the Jeep was too slick and the man was too huge. He leaned in hard and close to Mason's face. The wet wool of his topcoat smelled like a dog left too long in the rain and his breath tasted of coffee, cigarettes, and licorice. He'd been standing in the storm waiting for Mason.

"You get one chance, you understand that?" the man said.

"Right. Sure. One chance. That's easy enough," Mason answered.

"Your client's gonna get a deal. Make sure he takes it."

"What kind of deal?" Mason asked.

The man jammed his knee into the small of Mason's back. Even partly cushioned by the man's topcoat, it sent a paralyzing jolt through Mason's kidneys. "The only deal that will keep him and you alive. Got that, smart boy?"

"Got it," Mason managed through clenched teeth.

The man released his grip and Mason crumpled to the pavement gasping for air. When he looked up, the man and the car were gone.

Chapter Seven

Mason crawled out of bed Friday morning feeling as if he'd slept in the middle of a rugby scrum. The blow he'd taken to his back had scrambled his internal organs and hardened his soft tissue. He was relieved that there was no blood in his urine. His kidneys had been shaken but not stirred.

Ed Fiora was the only person Mason knew who had been involved with Jack Cullan and had a charge account at Thugs R Us. Mason had called the Dream Casino the day before and asked for Fiora. His call had been immediately transferred to an enthusiastic telemarketer named Dawn.

"This is Dawn. May I make your dream come true today?"

Mason had told her, "Absolutely, Dawn. Just connect me to Ed Fiora."

"We have a fabulous special offer today," Dawn had continued. "I can sign you up for the Dream Casino's free

Super Slot Ultra-Gold New Millennium Frequent Player Bonus Point card. It's personal and confidential.''

"So is my business with Mr. Fiora."

"Just swipe your card through the card reader on any of the Dream's fabulous slot machines and each time you pull the handle, you'll receive, absolutely free, ten bonus points. You can redeem your bonus points for fabulous prizes, beginning with two nights at the Dream's Riverboat Casino Resort in Lake Winston, Mississippi, for only twenty-five thousand points. Isn't that fabulous?''

"No, Dawn, it isn't. Fabulous would be not spending two minutes in Lake Winston, Mississippi. Fabulous would be you putting down your script, listening to me, and connecting me to Mr. Fiora. That would be really fabulous.''

Dawn had started sputtering into the phone, caught somewhere between tears and ticked off. "One moment, please,'' she had managed.

The next voice Mason had heard was all New Jersey bent nose. "Sir, do we have a problem here?''

"Who's this?'' Mason had asked. "One of Frank Nitti's boys?''

"This is Carmine Nucci, guest relations. Who the fuck is this?''

"You're making that up, aren't you, Carmine? I mean your name's not really Carmine and the accent is phony. This is like part of the entertainment. Am I right?'' Mason had asked, though he was certain that none of it was made up. Not Dawn. Not the bonus points, and not the threat laced through Carmine's voice like battery acid.

"Hey, pal. You want to make jokes, call Comedy Central. You want an Ultra Gold slot card, we'll give you one. You want to bust my girl's chops, I'll stick this phone up your ass you come around here.''

"How many bonus points is that?" Mason had asked, and hung up before Carmine could reply.

Mason had called back, this time asking for the business office, identifying himself as a lawyer, and asking to speak with Mr. Fiora concerning a criminal matter. Three underlings later, none of whom sounded as if they'd ever left the Midwest, Mason had spoken with a woman who had identified herself as Margaret. Margaret had explained that she was an assistant to Mr. Fiora.

"My name is Lou Mason. I'm an attorney," Mason had repeated. "It's very important that I speak with Mr. Fiora about a criminal matter."

"May I tell Mr. Fiora what the nature of the matter is?" Margaret had asked.

Mason couldn't tolerate people who didn't take their own calls, who hired other people just to answer the phone calls transferred to them by other people who'd been hired for the same purpose, only to ask the caller the nature of the matter. He had pictured Margaret sitting at her computer, scrolling down the list of criminal matters that would be worthy of Ed Fiora's attention.

"You may tell Mr. Fiora," Mason had said with thin patience, "that the nature of the matter is the murder of his lawyer, Jack Cullan, and what he might know about it."

"I see," Margaret had said with more disappointment in Mason than concern for her boss. "I see," she had repeated as if the words had cured her astigmatism.

"So, if you'll just connect me to Mr. Fiora, I'm sure he'll want to talk with me."

"Oh, I'm so sorry, Mr. Mason," she had said without a trace of regret. "Mr. Fiora is not available."

"And when will he be available, Margaret?"

"I don't believe that he will be available at all, Mr. Mason. I'm so sorry."

"Margaret, you aren't even close to sorry. You aren't in the same zip code as sorry. Sorry would be that Mr. Fiora had a terrible accident on the way to the office, was rushed to the hospital for emergency surgery, but can work me in this afternoon. That would be sorry. This is just a mistake. A big mistake. You tell Mr. Fiora I said so."

"If you insist, Mr. Mason," Margaret had said in a tone that was more gotcha than gracious.

Mason replayed his conversations with Dawn and Margaret as he settled his six-foot frame into his rowing machine and slowly began easing the kinks out of his back. Mason's ropy muscular build was ideal for sports like rowing and rugby. His body was tough, resilient, and he could take a punch better than first appearances suggested.

He set the digital readout for ten thousand meters, and gradually lost himself in the soothing repetitions of the stroke. The rowing seat slid backward with each leg drive and rode forward with each pull of his upper body. He imagined that he was sculling across the freshly poured surface of a lake, the ripple of his lean wake cutting the unbroken water as he slipped unnoticed through the morning's enveloping mist.

A quick look around reminded Mason that he was rowing in the middle of his dining room and that his rowing machine occupied the space that had been home to a table that seated eight. The table, the chairs, and the rest of his worldly possessions had been reduced to a pile of broken legs, glass, and splinters by the Kansas City auxiliary of the Chicago mob. It was their way of saying he shouldn't have taken work home from the offices of Sullivan & Christenson.

The experience had taught him that less was definitely more when it came to home furnishings, proving anew his aunt Claire's theory of men and their stuff. His house had been a gift from his aunt Claire on the occasion of his marriage to Kate. He had grown up in the house under his aunt's watchful, if relaxed, eye. The two of them had decorated it in a combination of early clutter, sixties, retro kitsch, and whatever struck their fancy at neighborhood garage sales. His aunt Claire had moved out when Kate moved in. Kate had tried to bring order, if not taste, to the chaos and failed. Their marriage hadn't fared any better.

Mason had lived for a while on the money his homeowner's insurance company had paid for the loss of his personal possessions, using part of it to pay the expenses for Tommy Douchant's lawsuit. By the time Mason had settled Tommy's case and could afford to refurnish the house, he didn't want to. Instead, he bought only the things he needed, which turned out to be the things he wanted. The rowing machine was docked in the dining room. He had no plans to entertain.

Forty minutes later, he had finished his row. The mist, the lake, and the ache in his body were gone, replaced by the panting exhilaration of a hard row. Plan your row and row your plan was the rower's creed. He hadn't followed that simple rule when he tried to reach Ed Fiora. Instead, he'd smart-assed his way into a one-punch knockdown that underscored what to expect if he insisted on not getting the message.

After downing a bottle of Gatorade, Mason trotted outside for the morning paper. The wind had moved on to punish some other part of the country. A light cover of snow crunched under his feet. The subzero air was bracing after his workout. His dog, Tuffy, a German shepherd–collie mixed breed, joined him on the short walk to the end of his driveway. Her blond and black German shepherd colors were layered through her winter coat in a collie's pattern, complete with a pure white thatch under her chin. Tuffy raced through the front yard, nose to the ground, sniffing for anything interesting. She found nothing, and reluctantly followed Mason back into the house.

Mason wiped the snow off his shoes and Tuffy shook her coat, more for the practice, Mason decided, since her coat was dry. The dog stopped shaking when Mason stopped wiping. She was loyal beyond a fault, for which Mason loved her. He dropped to a knee and scratched her behind her ears, stopping when the phone rang.

Mason picked up the phone in the kitchen, noting that the clock on the microwave oven said it was only six fifty-five and wondering who would call so early in the day.

Mason said, "Hello."

"Lou, it's Rachel. What did you think of the story?"

"What story?"

"Don't tell me you don't get the paper? The story is on the front page, above the fold."

"I just brought the paper in," he said. "Give me a minute."

Mason opened the newspaper and skimmed the story under the headline DEFENSE ATTORNEY CLAIMS PRESSURE TO DENY BAIL. Rachel's story recited Judge Pistone's refusal to grant bail to Blues, and Mason's implied charge that unknown persons were applying pressure to get either a conviction or a plea bargain that would close the case of Jack Cullan's murder as soon as possible. The story summarized Rachel's ongoing investigation into the granting of the Dream Casino's license. It tied Ed Fiora, Mayor Sunshine, and Beth Harrell into a tight circle around Cullan's body, and speculated aloud whether any of them would cooperate with Lou Mason in his defense of Wilson Bluestone, Jr., against a first-degree murder charge and possible death penalty. The article ended by noting that Fiora, Sunshine, and Harrell had refused to comment for the story.

"You left out one thing," he told her.

"What?"

"Off the record," he insisted.

"Fine, fine," she said. "What?"

"I think Fiora commented privately," he said, and explained what had happened the night before.

"Holy shit! Did you call the cops?"

"What for? There were no witnesses. I couldn't ID the guy or the car. Besides, I wouldn't expect to get a sympathetic response. The cops are more likely to look for a cat stranded in a tree than for someone who kicked my ass. And I don't want to read about that in tomorrow's paper. I'll figure some other way to get to Fiora. I don't think he'll respond well to being accused in the paper of ordering someone to assault me."

"My editor would be even less interested in getting sued. Did you have any luck with the mayor or Beth Harrell?"

"Nope. I figure the mayor is the most likely to respond to bad press. I think Beth Harrell will see me because I was an irresistible student."

"Don't sit by the phone. You'll grow old. Listen, the mayor's daily schedule is posted on the city's Web site. He's got several public appearances today. Pick one and show up. It's a free country. The Gaming Commission is holding a public hearing on Monday about problem gamblers during the holidays. That's at the Meridian Hotel."

"Any chance you'll be attending any of these events?"

"You can bet on it, baby."

Chapter Eight

Mason showered and shaved, though he wondered at the wisdom of shaving a beard that was dusky by noon and in full shadow by nightfall. He occasionally thought about surrendering and letting his beard grow, but always ended up scraping his face. He had taken his aunt Claire to dinner after the one time he had given his beard free rein. His aunt was in her late fifties and was a big, rawboned woman with no-nonsense straight-cut hair that had grayed early in life. She wasn't attractive in any classical sense, but her exuberance, self-assured power, and rough take on life had been a siren call for Harry Ryman. The waiter had mistaken Mason for his aunt's husband. Mason had blamed it on the beard, refused to leave a tip, and shaved the moment he'd gotten home.

Making certain that Tuffy's dog door hadn't frozen shut, he patted her on the head and promised to be home for dinner. Tuffy cocked her head, as if to say, *Who are you kidding?* and watched him as he drove off, her paws propped up on the windowsill in the living room that was empty except for the oversize dog bed Mason had bought her.

Mason's first stop was the Jackson County Jail, a study in modern incarceration. Opened several years earlier, it was intended to relieve the overcrowding and lax security in the old jail. The voters were persuaded to fund the new jail after one enterprising inmate tried selling time-shares to prisoners.

The redbrick circular jail was on the east side of Police Headquarters, its exterior perforated by longitudinal rows of rectangular windows. The windows were big enough to satisfy court-mandated quality-of-incarceration living standards, and small enough to make certain the inmates stayed there to enjoy it.

The visitors' entrance resembled the waiting room in a doctor's office, complete with two-year-old magazines and a receptionist who didn't care how long an attorney waited to see his client. She was a civilian employee who wore olive slacks and a pale blue shirt with epaulets on the shoulders to give the ensemble an official uniform appearance. Her bleached blond hair was pulled back tightly enough to raise her chin almost to her lower lip, freezing her mouth in a scowl, though Mason thought she might have just made an awful face as a child and it froze that way. Her face was a washed-out listless shade of artificial light. Mason hesitated a moment when he read the name Margaret on her name tag. He rejected the likelihood of a conspiracy by the World Federation of Margarets to make his life miserable, but clenched his smart-ass impulse just in case.

"Good morning," he told Margaret. "I'm Lou Mason and I'm here to see my client, Wilson Bluestone." Mason handed her his driver's license, Missouri Bar Association membership card, and one of his business cards.

Margaret scanned Mason's card collection like a bouncer

checking for fake IDs. "You didn't sign the back of your bar card. I can't accept it without a signature," she said, handing the bar card back to Mason.

Mason felt the first wave of intemperance ripple through his back and neck. He resisted the urge to vault the counter separating them, and smiled graciously instead.

"Of course. Sorry about that," he said as he signed his name and handed the card back to her.

Margaret held the bar card alongside Mason's driver's license, comparing the two signatures like a Treasury agent looking for counterfeit twenties.

"Bar card is expired," she said. "Can't take an expired bar card. You should have paid your dues," she added, and handed the bar card back to Mason.

Mason gripped the counter with both hands to keep them from Margaret's throat. He decided to appeal to her sense of reason.

"Margaret, consider what you're saying. The bar card only means that I'm a member of the Missouri bar. It's a form of identification. There's nothing in the law that requires me to belong to the bar association or even be a lawyer to visit an inmate. Now, fortunately, I am a lawyer and I have a client who's locked in a cell upstairs who is entitled to the effective representation of his chosen counsel. If he's deprived of that representation because you won't let me see him, the judge will have to dismiss the charges. Now my client happens to have been charged with murder, which most people think is a pretty serious deal. So, why don't you call the prosecuting attorney and tell him that his case is going to get dismissed because you, Margaret, are refusing to let me see my client because my bar card has expired?"

"Jeez," Margaret exhaled. "Are you a tight-ass or what? I'm just doing my job here. Pay your damn dues like everybody else."

"Trust me, Margaret. I've paid my dues. Now open up."

Mason had to pass through a series of security checks that fell one pat-down short of a body-cavity search. He was ushered into a cramped room divided by a narrow countertop that served as a table for both the lawyer and the prisoner. A reinforced double pane of glass cut the room completely in two. A circular metal screen was mounted in the glass that allowed conversation to be heard on both sides.

Mason stood, pacing in the small room until Blues entered through a door on the inmates' side. They looked at each other for a full minute. Mason saw a defiant man, ramrod straight, coal-black hair hanging raggedly over his tawny brow, piercing eyes searching Mason for good news. Blues touched his closed fist to the glass, holding it there as Mason returned the gesture.

"They're going to offer you a deal," Mason said.

"I won't take it," Blues replied.

"I know that."

"How do you know they're going to offer me a deal?"

Mason couldn't tell Blues what had happened in the parking lot. If Blues knew that taking a deal would protect Mason, he might agree to a plea bargain. Mason assumed that whoever had sent him the message was counting on his relationship with Blues as one more source of pressure that would bring this case to a quick conclusion.

"Patrick Ortiz already invited me to his office to talk about it. I turned down the invitation. Are you ready to ride this thing out?"

"All the way, Lou. I'm innocent and I'm not going to let somebody railroad me. Besides, no matter how many of them there are, you and me got them outnumbered."

Mason smiled at the vote of confidence. "Blues, this case is hot and it's going to get hotter. You watch yourself in there."

Blues chuckled. "Man, you forget one thing. All those brothers and white-trash crackers in there are afraid this crazy Indian will scalp 'em in their sleep. No one is going to fuck with me, Lou. Not more than once."

"Be cool, Blues. The case they've got against you isn't worth a shit. Don't give them one they can make in their sleep."

"I hear that," Blues answered. They touched their fists against the glass again, and Mason pushed a button signaling the guard that they had finished their meeting.

There was one message on Mason's answering machine when he got to his office. It was from his aunt Claire telling him to meet her for lunch at the Summit Street Café at noon. It wasn't an invitation. It was an order. His aunt Claire was not much for protocol. Mason assumed that she wanted to talk about Blues's case. If he was caught in the middle between Harry and Blues, she was caught between him and Harry. Though she wouldn't see it that way. She was one of the few people Mason knew who meant it when she said let the chips fall where they may.

Mason booted up his PC, got on-line, and went to the *Kansas City Star*'s Web site. He searched for Rachel Firestone's articles about Jack Cullan's murder, noting that the other murders that had been reported during the same span had been covered with no fanfare and little outrage.

Kansas City knows murder. Any town that began as a river trading post called Old Possum Trot knows killing. Any town that claims Jesse James as a wayward son and commemorates the Valentine's Day Massacre at Union Station knows how to let the lead fly. Any town that has convulsed with riots and raised a generation of hopeless hard cases who expect to die before they're twenty-five knows the sweet agony of death.

Put a million and a half people—white, black, brown, yellow, rich, poor, faithful, faithless, doped, dependent, and demanding—in the rolling river country of the heart of America and they'll find endless ways to kill. Put it in the papers and on the news with candlelight vigils for the funerals of infants. Watch as TV reporters stick microphones in mourners' faces asking how does it feel? and the people will search themselves for shock while keeping a head count, a steady drumbeat of death, ahead or behind last year's pace.

But take the life of a mover and shaker, of one to whom it's not supposed to happen, someone who holds all the cards, someone who gives more dispensations than the pope and holds more markers than the devil. Well, that's showbiz. The mayor grieves the victim and denounces the guilty. The chief of police reassures an anxious community with a quick arrest, and the prosecuting attorney promises justice swift and certain.

Rachel Firestone had reported it all. Her prose was concise, her tone neutral, and her facts straight. Only the headlines above the stories announced an agenda. They painted the crime, the victim, the accused, and the supporting cast with a broad brush dipped in sensational ink to capture mind share and market share in a media-saturated world. KINGPIN MURDERED, screamed the headline in Tuesday's paper. Wednesday's lead promised POLICE CLOSE TO ARREST, and Thursday's paper trumpeted EX-COP ARRESTED FOR MURDER OF POLITICAL BOSS.

None of the stories added to Mason's knowledge of the case. He ran a search for articles on the Dream Casino, printed them, and began reading.

Missouri had been a late entrant in the sweepstakes for gambling dollars. Bible Belt morality had kept the casino interests out of the state for decades, though Kansas City had been a wide-open town from the beginning of the twentieth century through Prohibition. Gambling had flourished in speakeasies all over town, particularly along the Twelfth Street strip from Broadway to City Hall. Tom Pendergast had been the Boss in those years, running his empire of influence and muscle under the guise of a concrete business.

A coalition of clergy, political reformers, and the IRS had brought Pendergast down, and Kansas City had settled into a long quiet period struggling with its lingering reputation as a cow town and unable to compete with the temptations offered on a grander scale by bigger cities.

The gaming people had seen opportunity beneath the blanket of conservatism that lay between the Missouri River on the western border of the state and the Mississippi River that marked the eastern boundary. They sold the Missouri legislature on a scam that would have shamed even Professor Harold Hill with its *Music Man* audacity.

Riverboat cruises reminiscent of Mark Twain's paddleboats were promised. Two-hour cruises with five hundred-dollar loss limits assured that no one would lose the rent money. Funding programs for problem gamblers was good citizenship. Committing the tax revenue from the casinos to education sealed the deal. The legislature doubled down and took the bet, offering the voters an amendment to the state's constitution legalizing riverboat gambling on the Missouri and Mississippi Rivers. The voters couldn't wait to cash in.

The first boat in the Kansas City area came to an unincorporated area north of the city. To the surprise of everyone but its owners, the Army Corps of Engineers ordered that the boat remain docked because of the hazards of navigating the Missouri River. With a sigh of regret heard all the way to their banks, the other casinos built their facilities on huge barges, digging moats around them that were fed by the rivers to meet the legal requirement that the boats be on the river.

The legislative scheme was complex, having been drafted by lawyers with help from the casinos' lobbyists. Like any successful partnership between regulators and those they regulate, the law appeared tough, but was actually more malleable than a politician's oath to tell the truth. The Missouri Gaming Commission was established to oversee and regulate all gaming activity. Each city retained the right to issue licenses to casino operators, subject only to the Gaming Commission's approval of the qualifications of the owners. Rules prohibiting ownership by convicted felons and other unsavory individuals were window dressing to distract attention from the real horse trading that accompanied the grant of licenses.

The competition for Kansas City's license had been fierce. Four casino operators had expressed interest in obtaining a license from the city. Each had put together their own team of local supporters and business partners that had as its singular purpose getting the mayor's blessing. Some had been subtler than others, giving ownership interests to black and Hispanic businessmen who had carried a message of diversity and economic opportunity to the mayor. Others had offered sizable campaign contributions to the mayor and city councilmen.

Mayor Sunshine had announced the appointment of a Blue Ribbon Commission to recommend which of the contenders should receive the sole license Kansas City intended to grant. It had been the mayor's way of remaining above the fray, and gave him plausible deniability of any effort to influence his decision.

Of equal importance to the selection of the casino operator had been the selection of the site for the casino. Kansas

City's river frontage afforded several possible locations, each of them privately owned. The owners of those sites had joined in the free-for-all. They had anguished over whether to choose between aligning with a particular casino operator and waiting to see if their site was selected. The wrong move could cost them millions.

When all the coalitions and alliances had been formed, when all the political contributions had been deposited, and when all the promises that would be broken had been made, the Blue Ribbon Commission had recommended to the mayor that he grant the license to Galaxy Gaming Co. Galaxy was a publicly traded company with casinos in Las Vegas, Atlantic City, and three other states that had approved riverboat gambling. Galaxy had formed a joint venture with three prominent black businessmen and two labor unions whose local presidents were Hispanic. It had pledged $250,000 to the Kansas City chapter of Gamblers Anonymous. Galaxy had signed a ninety-nine-year ground lease, contingent on getting the license, with the owner of the site the Army Corps of Engineers had designated as its first choice for a one-hundred-fifty-thousand-square-foot floating barge. Three city councilmen and Congressman Delray Shays had backed the Galaxy proposal.

The mayor had thanked the commission members for their efforts, had praised their hard work, and then had bestowed the license on the Dream casino. He had then announced that the casino would be docked at the limestone ledge that had once attracted eighteenth-century traders and trappers to pull in and build the trading post that had grown into Kansas City. That site, he had noted, was owned by the city and would be leased to the Dream Casino, turning an unproductive historical footnote into a new source of revenue for the city.

The owners of the losing casinos had shrugged their corporate shoulders, accustomed to the game of chance they played in cities throughout the country. A few local investors in the losing companies had cried foul, more aggrieved by the loss of the money they were convinced they would have made than any misplaced sense of civic outrage. In time, they had let the matter drop and gone in search of the next good deal.

Rachel Firestone, however, hadn't let the story drop. She had dogged the Missouri Gaming Commission, the mayor's office, and the Dream Casino until she found the one thing that tied them all together. It was Jack Cullan. Cullan had represented Ed Fiora and led the behind-the-scenes efforts to win approval of the Dream's application. Before that, he had been treasurer of Billy Sunshine's two successful campaigns for the office of mayor. Though she hadn't found evidence of a direct relationship between Cullan and Beth Harrell, she had cited highly placed confidential sources intimating that Harrell had been improperly influenced in her decision to approve the license for the Dream Casino.

In addition to the conflicts of interest that were Cullan's hallmark, she had traced the flow of money from Ed Fiora to Billy Sunshine. Though her most recent article intimated at a quid pro quo, she fell short of an outright accusation. She had quoted the U.S. attorney as not finding sufficient evidence to take the case to the grand jury, making it sound as if he was part of the cover-up.

Trying to find a connection between Cullan's murder and the Dream Casino reminded Mason of a game of three-card monte. The game was a con, not a game of chance or skill.

The dealer dealt three cards, one of which was the ace of spades. The dealer then turned them facedown, and the gambler bet that he could keep track of the ace as the dealer shuffled the three cards at lightning speed. When the dealer finished shuffling, the gambler pointed to the card he believed was the ace. If the dealer wanted the gambler to win a small pot and keep playing until he lost a big one, the dealer would let the gambler win. The trick was to distract the gambler while the cards were being shuffled so that the dealer could replace the ace with another card, hiding the ace in his clothes.

The dealer worked with a partner who bumped the gambler, offered him a drink, or otherwise pulled his attention away from the dealer just for an instant. Mason looked at the notes on his board, the newspaper stories, and the police report. He wondered who was hiding the ace of spades was and who was trying to keep him from finding it.

Chapter Nine

The Summit Street Café sits at the top of a hill at the intersection of Sixteenth and Summit. When it first opened, it was a vegetarian restaurant whose owner grew her vegetables in a large garden planted in a rocky vacant lot across the street. The restaurant's current owner had added meat to the menu and paved the garden for customer parking. The wood-plank floor was original equipment in the seventy-year-old brownstone that had housed, at various times, a brewery, a pharmacy, a free health clinic, and a tortilla plant. Summit Street was a ski slope that dropped from its peak at Fourteenth Street south to Southwest Boulevard, where it bottomed out in the heart of the predominately Hispanic West Side.

Claire Mason had practiced law by herself for thirty years, waging battles for those who had no one else to fight for them. Whether her battles were hopeless or hopeful, she won enough of them to keep going. Many of the bedrock businesses and institutions in town had been her target at one time or another. One of her favorite tactics was to buy a single share of stock in a company just so she could attend the shareholders' annual meeting. During the question-and-answer session, she would ask the CEO if he preferred that she just file a class-action lawsuit against the company since he was obviously too busy to return her phone calls. One CEO warned her against threatening him, and took her by the arm in a futile attempt to throw her out of the meeting. She responded by serving him with the lawsuit on the spot.

She was already seated at a round, wrought-iron table draped in a red-and-white-checked cloth when Mason arrived a few minutes before noon. The table and chairs were patio furniture that had been recycled as restaurant furnishings. A series of six large paintings of a nude woman plummeting into a black abyss hung on the wall behind Mason. Each one captured a different frame of her descent. Her raven hair flared around her head like a fan, while her arms and legs were splayed akimbo in the imaginary breeze of her descent. Her bemused expression contrasted sharply with the inescapably fatal course she was on. The artist's name and the price of each painting was written in swirling calligraphy on white cards mounted next to each frame.

Claire had draped her heavy winter coat across an empty chair. It was dark olive, impervious to nature's elements, and by Mason's estimation, weighed at least twenty-five pounds. Or so it had seemed to him when he'd carried it for her as a boy. His aunt didn't throw away anything that worked well, and her winter coat was tireless. It helped that she was oblivious of fashion, since the coat looked as if it were designed for a Prussian Cossack. She was wearing a dark brown pantsuit that was equally utilitarian.

Mason's own sense of fashion hovered in a casual comfort zone. He had three dark suits for court, but preferred jeans or khakis. He'd reluctantly dressed for success that morning, choosing a navy pinstripe suit, white shirt, and red-and-navy-striped tie. The mayor was speaking at a fund-raising lunch for the Salvation Army's Holiday fund drive at the Hyatt Hotel in Crown Center. Mason planned on stopping there after his lunch with Claire, and hoped his suit would help him get close enough to the mayor to ask some questions.

"You look like you're dressed for a job interview," she told him as he sat down.

"Interview, not job interview," he told her. "If I get the chance. I need to talk to the mayor about Jack Cullan. His staff won't work me into his schedule, so I'm going to work him into mine. He's giving a speech at the Hyatt. I'm going to try and catch him after he's done."

"When God said let there be light, He didn't mean Billy Sunshine," Claire said.

"Not one of your favorite politicians?" Mason asked her.

"Favorite politician is an oxymoron. Billy Sunshine has the distinction of being both an oxymoron and a regular moron."

"I take it you didn't vote for him," Mason said.

"To the contrary," Claire answered. "The politicians that disappoint me the most are the ones I vote for. I always feel like a sucker afterward. Billy Sunshine was smart, charismatic, and wanted to do all the right things for the right reasons. Revitalize downtown, pump private investment into the East Side, fix the potholes on every street and not just the mayor's. He wanted to unite the people who lived north of the river with the people who lived south of Seventy-fifth Street, neither of whom believed they lived in the same city. He wanted the Hispanics on the West Side to have a bigger role in city government since they were the fastest-growing minority in the city. He wanted to pull the public schools out of the black hole the school board had thrown them into.''

"And you're disappointed he didn't do all of that?'' Mason asked.

"Don't be cute,'' she told him with a smile that appreciated his sarcasm. "Half that stuff is impossible and the rest is just too hard for mere mortals. That's not the point. He made the promises, got the job, and sold out quicker than a whore on Saturday night.''

"Sold out to whom?''

"Anybody with the price of a vote or a sweetheart deal or a zoning variance or whatever else a big campaign contributor was shopping for.''

"Are you saying he took bribes?''

"Maybe. Probably not cash in a brown paper bag. It's usually not done that way. It's more often money that gets funneled to friends or family who get hired by somebody as a favor to somebody who wants a favor. That kind of thing. The mayor ends up with friends who owe him favors and pay him back with big campaign contributions or hidden interests in deals.''

"How do you know all this and why isn't it on the front page of the newspaper?''

"I know it because I represent the people who get screwed in these deals. The business owner whose building gets condemned for some new high-rise, or the schoolchildren who can't read by the time they're in the eighth grade but are smart enough to figure out how to shoplift, sell dope, and get knocked up. And it's not in the newspaper because everyone knows it and no one can prove it.''

"Rachel Firestone thinks she can, at least on the Dream Casino.''

Claire studied Mason over her half glasses. "Since you're short on time, get the lentil soup. They serve it in a bread bowl. It's perfect for a cold day. You probably skipped breakfast, so you need something hearty.''

Mason smiled at his aunt, surprised that she had dodged the subject of the Dream Casino. She had never pretended to replace his mother after her death, though she loved him as well as any parent could have and still worried about him.

''I know you didn't invite me to lunch to make sure I'm eating right,'' Mason told her. ''I figured you wanted to talk about Jack Cullan's murder, not local politics.''

''Good for you. No beating around the bush,'' she answered. ''Solo practice doesn't leave much time for small talk.''

Before Mason could respond, their waitress interrupted with a laconic rendition of the daily specials. She was a lanky white woman, barely out of her teens, whose spiked, violet hair failed to distract from the matching tattoos of elongated suns that ran the length of her arms. Both Claire and Mason ordered the lentil soup. The waitress sniffed the air, gave them a squinty, disdainful look, and scratched their order onto her pad. With a shake of her head, she slowly wandered off as if she'd seen enough and wasn't likely to return.

Mason said, ''Harry and I already talked about it. We'll do our jobs and whatever happens, happens. It'll work out.''

''Don't kid yourself,'' she told him. ''There's not much chance this is going to work out. At least not for us. One of you, or both of you, will end up bloodied by the other. Blues may end up in prison for the rest of his life. Or worse,'' she added in a soft voice he had rarely heard from her. ''No, there's not much that's likely to work out.''

''So what do you want me to do? Walk away? Let somebody else defend Blues?'' Mason asked her.

She glared at him as if he'd forgotten everything she'd

ever taught him. "Sometimes things don't work out. Sometimes they can't. Sometimes those are the things that have to be done no matter what. You'll live with it and move on, but you won't quit. Don't talk to me about the case. Don't apologize or rationalize to me or to yourself about what you have to do. Just do the best damn job."

Mason didn't have an answer, though he had questions. He wanted to ask Claire about Jack Cullan since she must have crossed paths with him more than once. He wanted to ask her if Harry was capable of pushing a bogus case against Blues just to even a score. More than anything, he wanted to ask her what had really happened between Harry and Blues. Instead, he studied her as she pretended to study the paintings on the wall behind him. His aunt never minded silence, believing it preferable to boring conversation. This silence was uneasy.

The waitress returned, depositing their soup in front of them. Mason watched the steam rise from the bowl in front of his aunt and mix with the tears brimming in her eyes. She turned away, red-eyed and red-faced.

"Damn the work we do!" Claire said, shoving the bowl away from her. She stood, grabbed her coat, and left without another word. The waitress gave Mason a withering look that said she blamed him and not the soup. Mason shrugged in reply.

Mason let Claire go, knowing better than to follow or argue. He ate his soup while he thought about her rendition of Billy Sunshine's promises for a diverse city. The Summit Café was on the West Side, the urban West Side, barely south of downtown and slightly west of the revitalized Freight House District where art galleries, coffee shops, and lofts converted to condos were in vogue. West Side meant Mexican restaurants and bakeries and neighborhoods where extended Hispanic families lived in row houses lining an entire block.

Kansas City was dotted with ethnic pockets like the West Side. Decades earlier, Italian immigrants had settled in the North End between the Missouri River and Admiral Boulevard. Though later generations had moved south to the suburbs, enough had stayed to preserve the identity of the area.

The East Side was called the urban core, code words meaning where the black people lived. It had the highest crime rate, the highest unemployment rate, and the worst schools. It was the recipient of the most lip service, campaign promises, and hand-wringing at City Hall.

Midtown was a rough square bounded on the north by the Plaza at Forty-seventh Street, on the east by Holmes Road, on the south by Seventy-fifth Street, and on the west by State Line Road, the divider between Missouri and Kansas. It was home to the city's power elite. Private schools made the dismal public schools irrelevant. Homes in Sunset Hills above the Plaza, where Cullan had lived, and along Ward Parkway fetched seven figures. Fashionably fit white men and women jogged along Ward Parkway, comfortable in the belief that their lives were the ones the city was referring to when it claimed to be the most livable city in America.

His aunt Claire's house, the house Mason had grown up in and later received as a wedding gift from her, was located in the heart of Midtown between Ward Parkway and Wornall Road, two blocks south of Loose Park. Claire had made it one of her missions in life to expose Mason to the entire city lest he grow up thinking that everyone was white and drove a Land Rover. Though they were Jewish, she had taken him to a black Methodist congregation, telling him that no one had the best corner of religious real estate. She took him to the City Union Mission to serve Thanksgiving dinner to the homeless, and then took him on a driving tour of the city's underbelly, where they found those who wouldn't come to the mission and gave them blankets and box dinners.

"You're damn lucky, that's all," she told him after they'd completed their deliveries one particularly cold Thanksgiving when he was ten years old. It had rained all day, the kind of cold, relentless rain that erodes any trace of warmth hidden in the body. Their last stop had been a tar-paper shanty built into the side of a bridge abutment. A man and a woman had lived there, although it was difficult to tell which was which. They both had greasy brown hair plastered to their heads with dirt and rain that had blown into their makeshift shelter. Their eyes were hollow, their cheeks splotched with broken blood vessels, and the few teeth they still had were yellow and rotted.

"Why?" Mason had asked her. "Because we don't live under a bridge?"

"Partly," she had answered. "Mostly because you're an upper-middle-class white male and this country doesn't like anything better than that. Just don't confuse luck with brilliance. Don't think because you were born on third base that you hit a triple. Do something with your life that makes a difference for someone besides yourself. Otherwise, you'll never score. You'll just die on third base."

Mason had envied his aunt for the passion that coursed through her to do the right thing, fight the good fight. He had looked for the same spark in his own practice, first in a small firm that represented injured people, then in a big firm that protected people's money, and now in his own practice, where he just protected people. He'd found the spark. Now he just hoped it wouldn't start a fire that consumed everyone he cared about.

Chapter Ten

Mason was lousy at big social functions. He was no good at being a hail-fellow-well-met, or assuring a new face that he was damn glad to meet him. In a world that ran on networking, he preferred the sidelines. It wasn't that he was shy or unfriendly. He just hated the forced conviviality of events at which new acquaintances looked over his shoulder for a better deal while pretending to be enthralled with their new friendship. Particularly when friendship was the last thing on anyone's agenda. Advantage, fair or otherwise, was the party favor everyone wanted to take home.

He stood at the back of the ballroom at the Hyatt Hotel and listened as Mayor Billy Sunshine thanked each of his dear personal friends who had been so gracious to invite him to this wonderful event at this wonderful time of year. Even from a distance, Mason had to give the mayor his due. The speech had been written for him, but he made the words his own. His DNA was uniquely programmed with a connection gene that linked him to his audience, erasing any suggestion that both he and they were just going through the motions. The mayor may have been tall and handsome, but he made it work for him instead of letting it turn him into a caricature.

Billy Sunshine had been the quarterback for the Kansas City Chiefs for ten years before retiring rather than risk suffering another concussion. Before hanging it up, he had taken the Chiefs to the Promised Land of the Super Bowl, winning the championship on an eighty-yard bootleg as time expired. He had announced his retirement and his candidacy for mayor the day after the ticker-tape parade. He'd been more crowned than elected. Though he wasn't Kansas City's first African-American mayor, he was the first to make teenage girls swoon as if he were a rock star and middle-age white guys tear up when he told football war stories on the campaign trail.

Even his critics, who were few when he took office, conceded that he was more than another pretty face with a Super Bowl ring. He was bright, earnest, charming, and irresistible. Although eight years in office had replaced his cleats with feet of clay, the mayor pretended not to notice. No one else in the ballroom seemed to notice either as he worked yet another football memory into his remarks.

Mason scanned the ballroom, trying to identify the mayor's staff people who would shuttle him to his next meeting after he finished speaking. The ballroom was actually three rooms that could be divided by movable walls, shrinking or expanding the space as attendance required. The Salvation Army's annual luncheon was one of those causes no one could quibble with, and the turnout was huge, at least a thousand people by Mason's estimation. Ten people were crowded around each table, which had a miniature Christmas tree as its centerpiece. Instead of a star at the top of the tree, each one was adorned with the name of the sponsor for that table. The effect was a bit like a political convention where each state's delegation gathered around its banner. Those sponsors who had contributed an additional amount could watch as their names and logos ran across a video loop projected above the head table.

Titanic-sized pear-shaped chandeliers hung from the ceiling, soft yellow light refracting brilliantly through sharply cut crystals, adding an intimate glow to the ballroom. Waiters in short white jackets, ruffled shirts, and tuxedo pants wove in and around tables, deftly serving, pouring, and clearing. Twenty-foot-tall Christmas trees flanked the raised dais, besotted with glistening ornaments and small, twinkling colored lights. A wreath of mistletoe large enough to be a life preserver hung in front of the speaker's podium, and blood-red poinsettias on pedestal planters ringed the room.

Mason was Jewish, and Christmas was a holiday he had always witnessed as a bystander. He didn't consider himself an observant Jew. That didn't matter to him. Whether he believed or didn't believe, whether he was observant or not, he was Jewish and Christmas wasn't his holiday. When he was younger, he'd been envious of his Christian friends, barely able to resist the sweep of the Yuletide season. His aunt Claire had always emphasized the ethical grounding of Judaism, adopting as her personal creed the commandment to heal the world, while discarding the rituals and holidays as little more than historical relics. Mason periodically acknowledged a spiritual itch in the back of his soul, but wasn't certain how to scratch it.

"The gentiles sure know how to throw a party," Rachel Firestone said.

Mason hadn't seen her arrive, though he remembered that she had told him she would be covering the mayor's appearances today. He wondered if she was there to see the mayor or to watch Mason try to see the mayor.

"Let me guess," he told her. "You're a boots, jeans, flannel-shirt-wearing, short-haired, Jewish lipstick lesbian."

"Damn straight! Though I'm certainly not," she added with a grin. "Too bad you can't take me home to your mother."

"More than you know," he answered. "I'm sure she would have wanted me to marry a nice Jewish girl, but not one who also wanted to marry a nice Jewish girl."

Rachel said, "Ooops. A past-tense mother is not a good thing. Sorry."

"Don't worry about it. She and my father were killed in a car wreck when I was three. I grew up with my aunt." He gave Rachel an appraising look. She had upgraded to camel-colored slacks, a deep-teal turtleneck sweater, and black tassel loafers. "Give up on the forest ranger look?"

She dipped her head, blushing slightly. "Business casual, tasteful but serious and boring as hell. What's your plan to get to the mayor?"

"I was thinking of waving a five-dollar bill over my head and whistling. What do you think?"

"That only works with the hookers on Independence Avenue. The mayor's price is higher. See that woman standing over there next to the door to the kitchen?"

Mason followed the aim of Rachel's extended hand, fixing on a dark-haired woman in a severe gray suit standing next to the kitchen door, her arms crossed over her chest, her eyes alternating between the mayor and her watch, her foot tapping impatiently against the thick carpet.

"Who is she?" Mason asked.

"Amy White, the mayor's chief of staff. She ran his last

campaign and is already planning his run for Congress just in case the mayor doesn't get indicted.''

''What's her story?''

Rachel said, ''The usual political prodigy. Savvy, in love with politics, and thinks she's picked a winner who will take her a long way.''

''Savvy enough to keep me from asking the mayor, in front of God and everybody, if he knows who killed Jack Cullan?''

''With one hand tied behind her back. Take your best shot.''

Mason winked at Rachel. ''No time like the present.''

He circled to the far wall of the ballroom, ignoring the murmurs that followed his passage. A little more than a year ago, Mason's picture had been in the newspaper and on television for weeks, accompanied by a media chorus that relentlessly flogged the explosive demise of Sullivan & Christenson. His refusal to participate in his celebrity status had been turned into one more angle, adding to the price of his privacy. He had been relieved when another story had eclipsed his own.

The turned heads and hushed recognition from the crowd proved that Rachel Firestone had been right. His defense of Blues had thrown him back into the mix. His picture was in the paper again and his name was in the news. In her article in the *Star,* Rachel had identified him as Blues's attorney and reminded her readers that he had been called a suspect, a killer, and a hero in the Sullivan & Christenson case.

The mayor had finished his remarks, and a polite ripple of applause washed across the ballroom as the mayor made his way off the stage and headed toward Amy White. Mason was on course to intercept the mayor. The murmurs increased as many in the crowd who had read Rachel's article sensed that something was about to happen that would make their hundred-and-fifty-dollar-a-plate lunch worth the price of admission.

Mason was paying attention to Amy White, figuring she was the first hurdle he had to overcome. As he got closer, they made eye contact, though her piercing slate eyes gave no hint of special recognition. Amy had auburn hair that billowed gently around her head, landing softly against the base of her neck. Her dark-rimmed glasses gave her unlined face a serious cast. The gray suit she wore covered a slender build. She watched as he approached, not flinching and not looking back over her shoulder to gauge the mayor's progress toward her. She knew why Mason was coming, and her intense gaze was more one of curiosity than concern, even as people stood and those closest to the scene surged a few steps closer, not wanting to miss anything.

Billy Sunshine suddenly appeared at Amy's side. The mayor stepped in front of her just as Mason reached them. "Merry Christmas, Lou," the mayor boomed loudly enough to be heard at Santa's North Pole workshop. "Glad you could make it," he added, grasping Lou's right hand with his own while wrapping his left arm around Lou's shoulder. "It's time we talk about that case of yours. I'm sorry we haven't been able to get on your schedule sooner. Thanks for coming down today."

Amy White permitted herself a small smile as Mason glanced back and forth at the two of them. The mayor held on to Mason and his smile until Amy tilted her head slightly toward the doors to the kitchen. The mayor took his cue, realizing that the television cameras had gotten their footage, before leading Mason through the crowd like a lead blocker.

They walked through the kitchen and into an empty hallway that led to a service elevator the mayor had used to reach the ballroom without using the front entrance. Once the three of them were alone, Mason spoke.

"You're as good as people say you are, Mr. Mayor. You saw me coming the whole way."

"A good quarterback has to be able to pick up the blitz, Lou," the mayor said.

Mason nodded at Amy. "It helps to have a good defensive coordinator."

"Best in the business," the mayor said. "You've got five minutes. Don't waste them and don't darken my door again. You do and I'll tell the press that you are harassing me and trying to inject race into the defense of your friend. You can call me to testify at the trial if you think I've got anything to say. You won't hear anything different then from what I'll tell you now."

"It's a little early to play the race card, don't you think, Mr. Mayor?"

The mayor responded with a blank stare, looked at his watch, and said, "Four minutes. I hope you're better in court."

"Try this, Mayor Sunshine. We'll play the two-minute drill. Did Jack Cullan ever represent you?"

"Yes. On private matters that are protected by the attorney-client privilege."

"Did Jack Cullan bribe you to approve the license for the Dream Casino?"

"No. One minute."

"Who killed Jack Cullan?" Mason asked.

"Your client. Thirty seconds. Time for one last play."

"What's in Jack Cullan's secret file on you, Mr. Mayor?"

Amy and the mayor kept their faces turned to Mason, though they couldn't help the involuntary flicker of their eyes toward each other. Billy Sunshine didn't answer. "Maybe you don't know," Mason said. "That could be worse than knowing. I'll make you a deal since you've been so helpful. I'll tell you the next time we talk. I guess that will be in court. Merry Christmas.''

Chapter Eleven

Mason had left his topcoat in his car when he parked on the third level of the Hyatt's covered parking garage. Walking across the wet pavement, he regretted that decision as the bitter wind blew through the open exterior walls of the garage. Melting snow, laced with dirt and debris carried in from the street, mixed with the hot vapor from cooling engines, giving the garage a dank taste like a flooded basement. He slowed his pace, not wanting to be surprised by anyone who might step out of the shadows to deliver more advice on how to handle Blues's case.

Opening his car door, Mason pulled on his topcoat and settled into the Jeep. As Mason turned the key in the ignition, he heard someone rapping a gloved hand on the front passenger window. The sound carried a fleeting jolt of panic to his midsection until he saw Amy White motioning to him to unlock the door. Mason was less startled by Amy's appearance than he was by the Goliath from the night before, but he was getting tired of playing hide-and-seek. He unlocked the door and Amy joined him inside the car.

"If you lost the mayor, don't look at me. I left him with you," he told her.

"Cute. We need to talk."

"I tried that. It didn't work too well." Mason guessed that his closing shot about Jack Cullan's secret files had drained the mayor's Christmas cheer. He assumed that Amy White had followed him to his car to find out what he really knew. He saw no percentage in telling her how little he did know or in alleviating the mayor's anxiety.

"Listen, I'm sorry about what happened in the hotel," she said, "Blame me, not the mayor. I read Rachel Firestone's article in today's paper. She practically accused the mayor of trying to railroad your client onto death row. I had a feeling you might show up at one of the mayor's public appearances since he wouldn't see you at his office. I handled it the only way I could without having another incident."

"Wouldn't it have been a lot easier to make an appointment?"

"The mayor's schedule is so tight I can barely get in to see him."

Mason said, "That's bullshit. You just hoped I didn't have the balls to nail your boss in public. I've got to hand it to you, though. You guys were ready. Made it look like I was at the top of the mayor's Christmas list."

"I can put you there if you want me to," she said.

Mason looked at her. She'd arched an eyebrow and cocked her head to one side. It wasn't exactly a come-hither look. Amy was attractive in a subtle understated way. He had a fleeting image of her throwing off her glasses and letting her hair down, but the image didn't fit with her tightly wound mouth and hard stare. She didn't strike him as the kind of woman who would wet her lower lip with her tongue and open her thighs a provocative inch or two to make an offer he couldn't refuse. The arched-eyebrow-and-cocked-head look was probably her most seductive move. He rested his hands on the steering wheel, feeling the cold leather warm to his touch. He nodded his head, wondering if the quid pro quo would be in his budget. "Of course you can. In return for what? My firstborn male child?"

"Nothing so dramatic. Besides, Rachel Firestone would write a story that the mayor had fathered another child out of wedlock."

"She really gets under your skin, doesn't she?"

Amy said, "Rachel Firestone is the latest in a long line of Woodward and Bernstein wanna-bes. She confuses salacious gossip with news. She doesn't get under my skin. She just creates work for me to do. The mayor has done tremendous things for this city and she can't stand that."

"Save it, Amy. The mayor isn't George Washington or even George Bush. He won the Super Bowl and should have gone to Disney World instead of City Hall. I expected him to be more interested in who really killed Jack Cullan. After all, Cullan was his lawyer and his campaign treasurer. I would think that would buy some loyalty and a small interest in seeing that his killer is caught."

"The mayor believes that the killer has been caught. But he wants to be fair to your client. He's opposed to any rush to judgment."

"You can't possibly believe that and even if you do, you can't possibly expect *me* to believe it. If half of what Rachel Firestone has written about your boss and the Dream Casino is true, the odds are two to one that Cullan's murder is tied to that deal. We both know the best thing that could happen to the mayor is for my client to be convicted or plead guilty before Cullan's secret files end up on the front page of the *Star*."

"Do you have the files?" she asked him.

"What do you think?"

"I think if you did, they would already have been on the front page."

"And you can't let that happen, can you? That's why you followed me to my car. If I keep the mayor out of my case, will he name a street after me?"

"The mayor had nothing to do with Jack Cullan's death. There's no reason to throw mud at him. That won't save your client."

"Finding the killer will save my client. If the mayor wants to stay above the fray, I need his help. I need to know the whole story about the Dream Casino."

"The mayor can't help you. Even if he wanted to, I wouldn't let him. But I'll help you on one condition. If you find Cullan's files—assuming they really exist—I want to see the mayor's file before anyone else. If there's anything in it that will help your client, use it. If there isn't, I get the file and you agree that you never saw it."

Mason considered her offer. Amy knew he wouldn't back off, and she was sufficiently certain that Cullan's secret files were more than a rumor. She was the second person to make him an offer if he found the files. Like the deal he had made with Rachel, this one could also help Blues.

"Okay," he told her. "You've got a deal. Now tell me about the casino."

"Sorry to disappoint you. There's no story there. The casino deal is clean. The U.S. attorney, the prosecuting attorney, and the Gaming Commission have all come to the same conclusion. Ask me something I really can help you with."

Amy was correct that the federal, state, and local law-enforcement agencies had found no basis for an indictment, let alone an investigation. That didn't mean the deal was clean. It only meant that no one was willing to look at it hard enough. He decided to come at it from another direction.

"When was the last time you spoke with Jack Cullan?"

Amy shook her head. "Last Friday night," she said. "But that won't help your client."

Mason leaned toward Amy. "Let me make that decision. Besides, I'd rather know the bad facts now. Finding out in court ruins my day."

Amy pressed her back against the passenger door. She took a deep breath. "Okay. Jack called me at home Friday night. It was late, about midnight. He told me that he wanted a copy of the liquor license for a club called Blues on Broadway and he wanted to know all about the owner."

Mason felt the inside of the Jeep shrink as the case against Blues got a little tighter. "What else did he say?"

"He told me that the owner had roughed him up and that he was going to shut the bar down, teach the owner a lesson he wouldn't forget. I told him that I'd get him the records on Monday morning."

"Is that a service the mayor's office routinely provides?" Mason said with no attempt to hide his sarcasm.

"Favors are what I do," she told him without apology. "It wasn't illegal to provide him with records that are available to anyone who wants to walk into the office of the Director of Liquor Control."

"Do the police know about this?"

"Yes. I told them when they came to see the mayor about Jack. I hadn't had a chance to request the records before we found out that Jack had been killed."

"How did you find out about Cullan?"

"The chief of police called the mayor and said he had something important to discuss. He came to the mayor's office around ten o'clock Monday morning with a couple of detectives."

"Harry Ryman and Carl Zimmerman?"

"That's right. The mayor was very upset. In spite of what you might think about Jack Cullan, he and the mayor were really close. The mayor cross-examined the detectives as if they were on trial. He told them to keep him informed of the progress of the investigation."

"Which means keep you informed?"

Amy nodded. "I'm paid to be his eyes and ears."

Mason was glad to have learned one of the crucial pieces of information Harry and the prosecutor had withheld from him. Amy's story added credibility to Cullan's threat that he would punish Blues for interfering in his fight with Beth Harrell.

"Could Cullan have gotten Blues's bar shut down?"

Amy shrugged. "Depends on what he could have come up with against your client. Jack had a lot of influence but he wasn't the king."

Mason decided to switch gears again. "Do you know Ed Fiora?" he asked her.

Amy gave him a patiently exasperated grimace. "Yes, Lou. I know Ed Fiora. The mayor knows Ed Fiora."

Mason smiled, enjoying her irritation. "Do you know any of the people who work for him?"

Amy hesitated slightly. "A few," she said.

"How about a big guy, roughly the size of New Jersey, with breath that smells like licorice?"

Amy frowned as she silently reviewed the profiles Mason was certain she kept dutifully organized in her mental Palm Pilot. He assumed that she wasn't trying to decide whether she knew whom Mason was talking about. Rather, he figured she was deciding whether to give him up.

"Tony Manzerio," she said at last. "I met him one time at a meeting at Fiora's office. He sits outside Ed's private office like a guard dog. I think Ed gives him licorice instead of dog treats. Why do you ask?''

"Can't tell the players without a program," Mason told her. Her answer was a good-faith down payment on their deal. "I'll let you know if I find the mayor's file."

"I'm counting on you," Amy said as she got out of the Jeep.

Chapter Twelve

The door to Mason's office had a slot in it for mail delivery. He scooped Friday's delivery off the floor, tossed it on the sofa with his topcoat, and opened up the dry-erase board. Using a green marker, he drew a short line down from Ed Fiora's name and added Tony Manzerio's name to the board. He wrote Amy White's name in parentheses next to the mayor's name, and underscored Rachel's reference to Jack Cullan's secret files. His conversation with Amy had convinced him that Cullan's files did exist. He couldn't decide whether the files were the motive for Cullan's murder or the reason for the determined effort to railroad Blues— or both.

The words he'd written on the board didn't suddenly come to life and rearrange themselves into the answers to his questions, even though he gave them a good five minutes to spring into action. It was, he reminded himself, a dry-erase board and not a Ouija board.

Mason picked up the mail from the sofa, sat at his desk, and began sorting through the envelopes. He tossed the junk mail into the trash without a second look. Next he opened the envelopes that looked like they might contain checks from clients. There were a few, but not enough to make him open the envelopes whose return addresses were from companies to whom he owed money. He saved those for the end of the month, hoping by then the checks would catch up with the bills.

Buried in the stack, he found an envelope from the Jackson County Prosecutor's office marked *Hand Delivery*. It contained a motion filed by Patrick Ortiz asking the court to set a preliminary hearing in Blues's case and an order signed by Judge Pistone setting the hearing on January 2. The judge's order was not a surprise. However, Ortiz's motion made as much sense as folding with a full house when no else had placed a bet.

There were a number of steps in the life of a criminal case once a suspect had been arrested. The first was the arraignment, which was to officially inform the defendant of the charges against him and to set bail.

The next step was for the prosecutor to establish that there was probable cause to believe that a crime had been committed and that the defendant had committed it. The prosecutor could meet that burden by presenting the case to the grand jury and asking for an indictment. In the alternative, the prosecutor could ask the Associate Circuit Court judge to hold a preliminary hearing at which the state would present its evidence and ask the judge to bind the defendant over for trial. If the judge found the state's evidence sufficient, the case would be assigned to a Circuit Court judge for trial.

The grand jury met in secret. Witnesses could be subpoenaed to testify and forced to appear without a lawyer to represent them. Taking the Fifth Amendment was the criminal equivalent of a scarlet letter. Hearing only the state's side of the case virtually assured that the grand jury would issue whatever indictments the prosecutor requested.

A preliminary hearing was public. The defendant had the right to attend and listen to the case against him, and his lawyer had the right to cross-examine the state's witnesses and present evidence of his client's innocence. Prosecutors hated preliminary hearings because they were forced to show too many of their cards to the defendant. Secret justice was more certain.

Now, Patrick Ortiz had surrendered the state's right to a secret grand jury. Mason knew that Ortiz wouldn't have made that decision on his own. Leonard Campbell must have told Ortiz what to do, and Mason was certain that Ortiz didn't like it. Ortiz was a career prosecutor who cherished the state's advantages over the accused. He would rather rip out a chamber of his heart than give up the grand jury. Ortiz didn't care about politics or appearances. He fought the battles and let his boss take the credit.

Leonard Cambell was a politician first and a lawyer last. Mason had only one explanation for Campbell's decision. Rachel Firestone's article, and the media frenzy it had launched, had forced the prosecuting attorney to choose a preliminary hearing to defuse Rachel's accusation that Blues was a victim of political expediency. This was one time Mason appreciated the power of the press.

The date of the hearing meant that Mason would be working on New Year's Eve instead of celebrating, though he didn't really mind. He didn't have anyone to kiss at midnight, and now he had an excuse to skip the sloppy embraces of people he didn't know at parties that he didn't want to attend alone.

New Year's Eve held mixed memories for Mason. It

was one of those take-stock moments, demanding an honest appraisal of where he'd been and where he was going.

The best New Year's he'd ever celebrated had been the first one with Kate. They'd been married a month and were still giddy. She'd surprised him with tickets to Grand Cayman, a second honeymoon before they'd finished paying for the first one. The resort Kate had chosen had thrown a party, where they had danced as if they had been possessed, shouted and laughed with strangers, and marveled at the magic in their lives. Shortly before midnight, Kate had led him away from the crowd onto an empty stretch of beach so white it glowed in the dark with the reflection of the moon and stars. They had made love on the beach as the New Year dawned, kept company by the tide washing gently over them.

Three years later, Kate had left him. She had run out of love, she had told him. It was a concept he couldn't understand. Love wasn't like oil, he had told her. You don't wait for the well to run dry and start digging someplace else. Unless you were Kate.

Since then, Mason had done his share of digging, though the relationships he had explored had proved too shallow or fragile to last. He was glad to use work as an excuse to skip New Year's Eve and the annual audit of his personal account.

It was after nine o'clock that night before Mason had finished rowing another ten thousand meters across his dining room. There was nothing smooth about his workout. His strokes were rough, his timing off. He felt as if he were rowing upstream. He blamed it on Blues's case since it was making him feel the same way. The only thing the rowing machine gave him that the case didn't was the opportunity to sweat a bucket, though he expected the case would eventually pull even on that score.

As he neared the end of his workout, his breathing turned ragged, punctuated by a deep grunt each time he hauled the rowing handle deeply into his belly. Tuffy didn't like what she saw, and let Mason know it as she paced back and forth in front of the rowing machine, ears up and tail down until he finished. Mason wondered if his dog had a date for New Year's. That kind of devotion was hard to come by. He was still heaving when the doorbell rang.

Mason staggered to his feet, mopping his face and neck with a towel. His house was fifty years old, and the front door was a massive arched slab of dark mahogany set into an entry vestibule with a limestone floor and deep-burgundy walls. Instead of a peephole, it had a small window that was covered by a door. When he opened the door to see who had rung the bell, his heart rate jumped back to the pace of the final hundred meters of his row.

Beth Harrell was on his front doorstep, facing the door while glancing to her right and then to her left. She kept her head down, sneaking a peek at the window as she bundled herself into her arms to keep warm.

Mason pulled the door open, and for a moment they stared at each other. Mason tried to remember the last time he'd seen her, and the best he could do was to guess between a bar association lunch and a law school alumni dinner. Either way, it had been a couple of years. He was struck by how differently people appeared when they were encountered out of context. Beth Harrell had always carried herself with a born-to-the-manner style that was both regal and relaxed. Her posture was always straight, but there was playfulness in her slender arms and easy smile. She had dressed stylishly while giving an enticing hint of a passionate woman. She had a thing for strong, bold colors—particularly deep blues and reds—accented with a fragrance that lingered after she'd gone.

At the moment as she stood in his doorway, the winter wind buffeting her as she pulled a scarf tightly around her throat, she seemed swept away by more than the weather. She looked at him with searching eyes, trying to gauge his reaction to her unannounced visit and predict what he would say to her when he knew why she had come.

Mason recovered from his surprise, helped along by the prickly sensation of sweat freeze drying against his skin. "Beth," he said. "Come on in before we both freeze to death."

He closed the door behind her and took the heavy down-filled coat she handed to him. In the soft light of the entry hall, the red rubbed into her cheeks by the cold wind rose high in her face. She pulled her gloves off and pressed her long fingers against her cheeks as if to transplant the warmth of her hands to her face.

Folding her arms to her body, she surveyed the empty living room and the rowing/dining room. Tuffy made a pass at Beth, sniffing Beth's feet, nuzzling against Beth's thighs, and brushing her whole body against Beth until she broke down and scratched Tuffy behind the ears. Tuffy immediately sat down, pushing her head against Beth's hand, giving her the unspoken command to keep on scratching. Mason knew that Tuffy was a terrific icebreaker.

"She's beautiful," Beth said.

"She's shameless and will give herself to anyone who scratches her behind her ears," Mason said.

"We should all be so easy," Beth said.

Mason was grateful for the small talk. He assumed that Beth had come to talk with him about Blues's case and that she would get to that subject when she was ready. He didn't mind waiting. He did mind that she looked fabulous even in faded jeans and a bulky cream-colored cable-knit sweater and that he looked like yesterday's dirty laundry in a pair of gym shorts and a sweat-stained Kansas City Rowing Club T-shirt. He knew that he smelled worse than he looked, but he was afraid she'd leave if he told her he was going to take a shower.

"Can I get you something to drink?" he asked her.

Beth answered, "That would be great. Something hot would do the trick."

Mason led her to the kitchen. Tuffy figured out where they were going and raced there ahead of them.

"I've got tea," he said as he searched the pantry. "Never developed a taste for coffee, so I don't keep it in the house."

"Tea would be good, perfect."

Mason boiled a cup of water in the microwave, and a few minutes later they were seated at his kitchen table. Beth stirred her tea, pressing the tea bag against the side of the cup. Mason drank from a long-necked bottle of beer and pressed the cool glass against his neck.

"I read about you in the paper last year. That thing with Sullivan & Christenson," she began. "We didn't teach you that in law school."

"We've both been in the papers," he said. "All things considered, I prefer the comics."

"Amen to that," she said.

The color in her face had evened out to its natural soft, barely tan hue. A slight patchwork of laugh lines had crept into the corners of her mouth and eyes, the unavoidable markers of passing years. Mason decided that the lines looked good on her. He had first met Beth when she was nearly thirty, when her smooth, unlined face was an open invitation full of promise. Then, her beauty lay in her youth. Now, in her early forties, her beauty lay in the fulfillment of that promise, the quiet confidence of things done well and the grace to withstand things gone wrong.

"Was it difficult?" she asked him.

"Was what difficult?"

"Killing that man," she answered, looking at him intently.

Mason paused before answering. He'd come to understand the reluctance of men who'd gone to war to discuss their battles. Heroes, he'd decided, were for bystanders. Soldiers killed so that they could live. He'd done the same thing and found no reason to glory in it.

"It's done," was all he said. "I called you yesterday. You could have just called back. I would have come to your office."

"I was out of town yesterday and today. When I got home I read this morning's paper and saw you and the mayor on the six o'clock news. I decided a house call would be more private. I live at the Alameda Towers and the press has practically camped out in the parking lot."

"How did you get away?"

"Our building is connected to the Windcrest Hotel. I parked in the hotel garage and walked through the hotel. The press can't get past my doorman and they haven't figured out my secret entrance."

"Gee, that's a better setup than having Alfred and the Bat Cave."

Beth laughed. "You were always good at that in law school. I used to watch you with your friends. You were always the one who made everyone laugh."

Mason couldn't hide his surprise. "You watched me?" he asked her, remembering how he had gawked at her when he hoped she wasn't looking.

Beth bit her lower lip and nodded with a grin that nearly took them both back fifteen years. "You were younger than me but not by much. What is it? Five years? I was your teacher, but I wasn't dead.''

"Is it too late for me to ask you for extra credit?"

She answered his question with her own. "Is it too late for me to ask you for help?"

Mason drained the last of his beer and carried it to the sink. He leaned back against the kitchen counter, his hands cupped along its edge, and looked at her. She had drawn him in with a mix of vulnerability and flirtation that he found engaging, flattering, and potentially irresistible. The five years that had separated them when he'd been in law school, and their teacher-student relationship, were insurmountable hurdles to any other relationship. Now the difference in their ages didn't matter. What did matter was that she was a key witness against Blues.

"Beth, you taught ethics. The governor hired you because you were an expert on right and wrong. You know who my client is and why I called you. When this case is over, I could represent you. But not now."

"Lou, I'm not asking you to be my lawyer. I know better than that."

"Then what do you want?"

"I want you to protect me."

"From what or who?"

She rose from her chair, crossed the room to where he was standing, and stopped less than a foot from him. He could almost feel her under her thick sweater. She stood, trembling faintly, silently begging him to hold her.

"Protect you from what?" he repeated. He waited for her answer, not trusting himself to raise his hands from the counter.

She dipped her head, looked away, and then turned her back to him, her arms loose at her sides.

"You're right," she said. "I shouldn't have come here. The office would have been better."

"Beth, if you tell me who or what you're afraid of, I may be able to help you. But you realize the position we're both in here."

She took a deep breath that stiffened her, and shook her head. She walked back to the kitchen table, sat down, and dabbed the corners of her eyes with a napkin. "Let's stick to your business, Lou. I'll take care of mine."

Mason said, "Good enough," though he kept his place at the counter. "Tell me about last Friday night. Why were you out with Jack Cullan?"

"He asked me out. We're both single. He was a very interesting man, well read and charming when he wanted to be."

Mason heard the words but didn't believe them. "You're telling me that in the middle of a scandal that has Cullan bribing you, the two of you decide to go out on a date? Are you nuts?"

Beth leaned back in her chair. "I'm forty-three years old. I've been married and divorced twice and I have no children. I don't even have a damn dog! Most men act like they're afraid of me. I must come across as a blond beauty bitch. Jack Cullan asked and I said yes. There's no crime in that."

"There's no sense in it either."

"We didn't talk about the Dream Casino or any other Gaming Commission business. Rachel Firestone was the only one beating the scandal drum, and no one was listening to her. Until Jack was killed, the rest of the media wasn't paying any attention. We would have had a pleasant evening and no one would have written or said anything about it."

"If it was all so pleasant," Mason asked her, "why did you throw a drink in Cullan's face?"

"I said that Jack could be charming if he wanted to. He

could also be crude when he made certain suggestions. I told him I wasn't interested. He called me a cock-teaser.''

"That's it? He called you a name?''

"He threatened me. He threatened to ruin me.''

"How? I've heard that Cullan collected dirt on his friends and enemies to make certain they did as he asked. Did he have a file on you?''

"He didn't say and I don't know. I haven't led a perfect life, but I never took a bribe. He just said he would do it, that I wouldn't see it coming, and that no one but the two of us would know that it had been him. That was too much. I'd had two husbands who had tried that crap on me, and I wasn't going to put up with it from him.''

"So why didn't you press charges after he hit you?''

"Having dinner with Jack and listening to music afterward was a nonevent. Filing criminal charges against him for assault would have been a media circus. No, thanks. It was better to chalk it up to one more bad judgment about the men whose company I keep.''

Mason moved from the counter to the table, choosing a chair close to hers. "My client is the owner of the bar. His name is Blues and he's my friend. He saved my life and I'm trying to save his. Did you see Jack Cullan scratch the back of Blues's hands when he grabbed Cullan from behind?''

Beth thought for a moment and shook her head slightly. "I'm sorry, Lou,'' she said. "I was pretty upset. I just don't remember.''

Mason waited for her to say more, but she didn't. "Okay. What happened after you left the bar?''

"Jack took me home. He dropped me off. He didn't apologize and I didn't invite him upstairs.''

"Did you stay home the rest of the night?''

The red returned to her face, though not from the cold.

She stood and circled around him, stopping back at her chair. "My God, Lou! You're asking me if I killed him?"

"I'm doing my job, Beth, and you know it. I'm sure the cops asked you the same question."

Beth glared at Mason and headed for the door. He followed her. She jammed her arms into the sleeves of her coat and twisted her scarf around her neck. "I didn't kill him. I'm sorry I went out with the son of a bitch, but I didn't kill him. I'm sorry I came here tonight."

"I'm not sorry," Mason said without thinking. "I don't want it to be you."

Beth's eyes moistened again. She wiped them with her gloves and left him without saying another word.

Mason walked into his living room and sat cross-legged on the hardwood floor next to Tuffy's bed. She trotted onto her pillow, turned three times, scratched at the pillow, and lay down, her head on Mason's leg. He scratched her behind her ears and thought about the last two days.

His working theory was that Cullan's murder was linked to the Dream Casino deal, a theory that led to three suspects—Ed Fiora, Billy Sunshine, and Beth Harrell. Fiora had refused to talk to him but had sent Tony Manzerio to deliver a message. The mayor had played politics and had sent Amy White to plead his case and ask Mason to protect him from whatever was in Cullan's secret files.

Beth Harrell had made a house call and come on to him every way possible without taking her clothes off. Though she was long on motive and short on alibi, Mason had meant it when he had told her that he hoped it wasn't her. He slipped his hand under Tuffy's face and aimed her head at his.

"What do you think? Can I save Blues and still get the girl?"

Tuffy raised her paw and pushed his hand away, then

pawed him again until he resumed scratching behind her ears.

"It's all about you, isn't it?" he asked the dog. "Well, at least you're honest about it. No one else is."

Chapter Thirteen

Patrick Ortiz called Mason on Monday morning and asked if he could meet with him and Leonard Campbell at eleven.

"What's the occasion? You guys ready to surrender, or what?" Mason asked.

"Eleven o'clock," Ortiz answered, and hung up.

Mason didn't think they were ready to surrender. He did think they were ready to negotiate, or at least make the offer that Tony Manzerio had encouraged him to take during their slow dance in the parking lot.

The meeting with Campbell and Ortiz bothered him for a couple of reasons. He knew Blues wouldn't take a plea, and he didn't want to tell Blues that Ed Fiora had threatened to have them both killed if he didn't. Mason would have to tell Blues about the prosecutor's offer. From there, he wasn't certain what he would tell Blues.

He didn't like the prosecutor deciding to oppose bail or summoning him for a meeting to deliver an offer his client wouldn't accept. Mason was glad that he represented the defendant. He just hated being on the defensive. He slapped his hand on his desk, taking his frustration out on an inanimate object that stung his hand in return. *That's solo practice,* he thought to himself. Even his desk gave him a hard time.

The prosecuting attorney's office was located on the first floor of the Jackson County Courthouse. Mason signed in at the receptionist's desk when he arrived, printing his name, address, and telephone number and the name of the person he'd come to see. Four other people were already waiting. Two of them were dressed in lawyer's uniforms and were tapping on their Palm Pilots as if they were sending SOS signals. The other two were an elderly man and woman who both clutched the prosecutor's brochure on how to avoid home-remodeling scams. From their ruined looks, Mason concluded that they had waited too long to take the prosecutor's advice.

The receptionist was a young black woman with big hair that had been styled into heavily gelled ribbons that flipped and curled like a miniature roller coaster from one ear to the other. Her long fingernails were painted bright yellow. She kept her back to him while playing solitaire on her computer screen and talking on her telephone headset. Her conversation was limited to ''Get out!'' and ''You go, girl!'' Had her name been Margaret, he wouldn't have stayed. Fortunately, according to the nameplate on her desk, her name was LaTisha, so Mason decided to gut it out and stand at her desk until she gave in and noticed him.

Their standoff lasted until eleven-fifteen. LaTisha muttered, ''Damn this piece of shit!'' She shook her head. ''Not you, girl," she said into her headset. "This damn computer. Beats me every damn time. I give up."

Mason didn't mind waiting since that meant that Leonard Campbell and Patrick Ortiz were waiting as well. The odds were that they would be more annoyed than he was, since they would assume that he was late. It wouldn't occur to them that the taxpayers were not getting their money's worth from LaTisha.

Mason cleared his throat and LaTisha turned around. "How long you been standing there?" she asked him.

"Just a minute or two," he assured her. "I'm Lou Mason. I've got an appointment with Leonard Campbell and Patrick Ortiz."

LaTisha grabbed the sign-in sheet and saw that Mason had written his arrival time down as eleven o'clock. She gave him a big smile, appreciating that he hadn't given her a hard time for being on the phone. Maybe, Mason thought, she liked keeping Campbell waiting as much as he did.

"He'll be right with you, sir." Mason thought she even meant it.

Moments later, Campbell's secretary, an attractive Hispanic woman with dark hair and a lavender skirt that had been spray-painted onto her tight hips, appeared and told him to follow her. He wanted to tell her to slow down, but didn't think it was a good idea to make Campbell wait any longer. She ushered him into Campbell's office with a small flourish of her hand, and held his eyes as he nodded his thanks.

Patrick Ortiz was seated in a chair on the visitors' side of Campbell's ornate, walnut desk. Campbell stood behind his desk, the phone to his ear. He motioned to Mason to take the chair next to Ortiz and squeezed his thumb and forefinger together to indicate that the conversation would be a short one.

Mason remained standing, smiled at Ortiz, and shook his hand. They didn't speak. Mason had nothing to say, and Ortiz was being deferential to his boss. Mason looked around the office. There were law books on one wall that Mason was confident Leonard Campbell had never opened; pictures of Campbell with various local dignitaries on another; and Campbell's framed law school diploma on a third. Mason examined it closely to be certain that Campbell's degree wasn't from the Columbia School of Broadcasting. He was annoyed to learn that he and Campbell had gone to the same law school, though Campbell had graduated twenty-five years earlier.

Campbell finished his phone call, hung up the phone, and greeted Mason. "Good to see you, Lou!" he exclaimed.

He was a trim, well-kept man nearing retirement, a neat white mustache penciled in above his upper lip. His hair was cut short to the scalp and combed slightly forward to cover more ground without looking too obvious. He was wearing a charcoal-brown suit, bone-colored shirt, a necktie with olive and copper rectangles alternating on a black background, and chocolate-colored suspenders. His suit jacket was carefully draped on a valet standing at one end of the credenza behind his desk. Mason wanted to ask him if his middle name was Dapper.

Campbell reached across his desk and shook Mason's hand with both of his, the left clamped over the right in a firm commitment of fellowship. Mason took it as a sign that Campbell was about to screw his lights out. Mason's aunt Claire had once warned him that the two-handed shake was the male equivalent of a woman's air kiss. It was, she insisted, a gesture of phony intimacy that was nothing more than a warning to be on guard.

Mason withdrew his hand and sat down next to Ortiz. He

smiled politely, waiting for Campbell to tee it up, determined to avoid small talk.

"So, how's your practice these days, Lou? You've got such a high profile, I imagine you've got to use a club to keep the clients away!"

"What do you want, Leonard?" Mason asked. He phrased the question with such a neutral tone, it was impossible for Campbell to be offended or ask him another idiot question. Ortiz stifled a small chuckle with a hand over his mouth, converting it to a cough.

"Very well," Campbell answered. "Let's get to it then, shall we?"

"Let's get to it indeed," Mason concurred.

"Patrick tells me we've got your man dead to rights. No sense in putting the taxpayers through an expensive trial. We've got a proposal for you. Let your client put this whole thing behind him, do his time, and start over while he still has something to look forward to."

Mason thought Campbell was entertaining, but only to a point that had come and gone. "Patrick is too good a lawyer to have told you that you've got my client dead to anything, Leonard. Your case sucks. You've got two guys pissing at each other in a bar. All of your forensics evidence got under Cullan's fingernails when he scratched my client's hands while my client was stopping him from beating up Beth Harrell. That's all you've got. You can't even put my client at the murder scene. The only deal you should be offering me is a dismissal and an apology in return for a promise not to sue your ass."

"We *can* put him at the scene," Ortiz said.

Mason looked at Ortiz, ready to call him a bullshitter, but he stopped when he saw the determined confidence in Ortiz's dark eyes. Ortiz wasn't a dandy. He was a bulldog. He wouldn't bluff Mason with something that Mason could so easily call him on.

"What have you got, Patrick?"

"Your client's fingerprints. On Cullan's desk in the study where the maid found his body. Still think my case sucks?"

Mason refused to be baited. He needed to talk to Blues. "I'm obligated to convey any offer you make to my client. You're still a long way from home on this case and we all know that."

Campbell flashed Mason his most sincere smile. Mason wanted to sew his lips shut.

"We'll accept a plea to second-degree murder and we won't make any recommendation on the sentence. Your man will probably be sentenced to twenty years to life and be paroled in seven years."

"That's not much of a deal. Even with the fingerprints, second degree is the worst that he's likely to be convicted of on your best day in court. This isn't the kind of deal that makes anybody lose any sleep if we turn it down."

Campbell unleashed another smile. "This is our best deal, Lou. It's on the table until the preliminary hearing. After that, it's off the table and there won't be any other deals offered. This deal is in everyone's best interests."

"Does that include your best interests too, Leonard? Why don't you check back with Ed Fiora and ask him if he wants to reconsider? I'll take this to my client but, if I were you, I'd plan on working New Year's."

Twenty minutes later Mason was in a visitors' room at the county jail with Blues.

"They found your fingerprints in Cullan's study. On his desk," Mason told him.

Blues showed no emotion at the news. He didn't curse and he didn't deny.

"Did you hear what I said?" Mason asked him. "Patrick Ortiz told me they found your fingerprints. They can put you in Cullan's house the night he was killed."

"I wasn't there," Blues told Mason.

"Fine. I'll tell them that. I'm sure they'll just throw the fingerprints out. That will take care of everything."

"I wasn't there," Blues repeated.

Mason studied Blues as he spoke. There was no artifice, no subtle tics born of a liar's stress. There never had been with Blues. Mason couldn't think of a single time that Blues had ever lied to him. About anything. Blues knew it would do him no good to lie now. Just as it would do Ortiz no good to lie. They couldn't both be telling the truth.

"Maybe the forensics people just made a mistake. It wouldn't be the first time," Mason said.

"If that's supposed to make me feel better, it doesn't," Blues said. "They want me for this, Lou. They've got to make it be me."

"I don't buy it, Blues. I don't care what happened between you and Harry. I don't buy it."

"Doesn't matter if it is Harry. You've got to go after all of them, Lou. If you don't, I'm a dead man."

Mason sighed deeply, feeling the walls close in on him as if he were the prisoner. "Campbell offered you a deal. Second degree, no recommendation on sentencing, out in seven years."

"No," Blues said without hesitation.

"I know. I told Campbell that was the worst that you would get in a trial. Campbell said it's the best deal you'll get and that it's off the table once the preliminary hearings starts."

"No deals, Lou. Tell Campbell to go fuck himself. Tell

him today—now. I don't want that punk bitch to believe I'm even thinking about it."

"I will, Blues," Mason said.

Mason used his cell phone to call Patrick Ortiz after he left the jail.

"Patrick, it's Lou Mason. My client says he'll take a pass on your deal."

"Have a nice life," Ortiz told him and hung up the phone.

Sure thing, Mason thought to himself. *Whatever is left of it.*

Chapter Fourteen

New Year's Eve fell on a Monday. No one had tried to kill him since Blues had turned down the prosecutor's plea bargain. Mason didn't know whether that was just luck or whether thugs took off the week between Christmas and New Year's.

Mason sat at his desk late in the afternoon gazing out the window onto Broadway. It was a slate-gray day, the sky nearly the same color as the pavement. It was hard to tell where one ended and the other began. Black ice made of frozen slush and grime was pocketed along curbs and buildings the length of Broadway. It hadn't snowed in two weeks, but it hadn't been warm enough to melt the hard-core remnants of the last storm.

There was a strip shopping center across the street and a block south, the edge of which he could see from his window if he leaned forward far enough. Christmas lights had been strung along the outside of the stores in the center. The owner had turned them on even though it wasn't quite dark yet. The lights he could see—red, green, blue, and white—twinkled weakly in the fading light. They needed the night to shine.

There wasn't much traffic. Most people had already gone home to get their game faces on for the night of celebration that lay ahead. The only phone calls he'd had all day had been from Mickey Shanahan, asking Mason's advice for the last-minute preparations for the club. New Year's Eve was the biggest night of the year in the bar business, and Mickey had devoted himself to its success.

Mason had taken Mickey to visit Blues at the county jail so they could discuss Mickey's plans for New Year's Eve. Mason had explained to Mickey that he could go by himself, but Mickey had declined. Jail, he'd told Mason, was a place you should never go without someone who knew how to get you out. They had met Blues in the visiting room separated by the double-paned, bulletproof glass.

"Blues, I've got a terrific idea for New Year's," Mickey had bubbled.

Blues had raised his eyebrows and looked down at Mickey through the glass, doubting whether Mickey was capable of such a thought.

"It's a bar," he had told Mickey. "I've got Pete Kirby's trio booked already. I've lined up extra bar and kitchen help. All you have to do is keep the booze and the food moving."

Mickey had waved both hands in protest. "No, no, no. You've got it all wrong, Blues. This is an opportunity. A huge opportunity. We bill the night as a benefit for your legal defense fund. It'll be a knockout."

He had looked back and forth at Blues and Mason, who both had shaken their heads. "No fund-raiser," Blues had said.

"Not a chance," Mason had added.

"Okay, okay. Plan B. You guys will love this," Mickey had insisted. "We do a murder mystery. You know, hire actors to stage a murder. Involve the people in the bar in solving the crime. Plant clues, stuff like that. Reveal the killer at midnight. I'm telling you guys, it will be fantastic!"

Blues had pressed his hands against the glass like he wanted to reach through and strangle Mickey. "Just say hello to the people when they come in, take their money, and don't fuck it up."

Mickey had overcome his anxiety of going to the jail and had shuttled back and forth, pleading with Blues to approve one scheme after another. Blues had told Mickey that if he came back again, the guards would arrest him.

Mickey had called Mason a dozen times that day with last-minute pleas to approve one off-the-wall idea after another. Mason had said no to the first ten, and hung up on the last two.

He'd spent the rest of the day going over his notes for the preliminary hearing. He didn't think Patrick Ortiz would reveal anything more about his case than was necessary to convince Judge Pistone to bind Blues over for trial. The evidence of Blues's fingerprints at the scene would be more than enough.

Mason had listed the witnesses he expected Ortiz to call on the dry-erase board. The maid would testify that she had found Cullan's body. The coroner would testify to the cause of death. Beth Harrell or Pete Kirby would testify about the fight at the bar and Blues's threat. Harry Ryman would testify about his investigation. A forensics investigator would testify about the fingerprints.

Mason glumly admitted to himself that had no evidence to work with. The last two weeks had yielded nothing that changed the core facts of the case. He had no doubt that Judge Pistone would find probable cause to believe that

Blues had murdered Jack Cullan. The press would have a field day, its monstrous appetite satisfied for the moment. Leonard Campbell would smile into the cameras on the courthouse steps and boast about doing the people's business. The image made Mason want to puke.

The phone rang again. The clock on Mason's computer screen said it was just after five. He let it ring twice before picking it up.

"Listen, Mickey," he said. "Just do it the way Blues told you. It's not a carnival."

Rachel Firestone said, "What's not a carnival? Who's Mickey and what did Blues tell him to do? Are you planning a New Year's Eve jailbreak? Tell me what time and I'll get a photographer over there."

"Shit," Mason said. "I told him not to call me at work. You reporters are too clever. I knew you'd figure it out."

"I'll make certain it's front-page, above the fold," she told him. "All seriousness aside, what's going on?"

"Mickey is a tenant in the building who's running the bar while Blues is on vacation. He wants to turn the bar into the Circus Maximus for New Year's. Since he's the only one who's called me today, I figured it was him."

"Sorry to disappoint you."

"You didn't. What's on your mind?"

"New Year's Eve. What else? You have any plans?"

"It's against my religion. Besides, what happened to your girlfriend the rugby player?"

"Fear of commitment."

"Hers or yours?"

"Mine. I figured you would be the perfect date. I'm on the rebound and I don't like guys. Who could be safer for a girl at the peak of her vulnerability?"

"You make it sound irresistible, but I think I'll pass. I'm not in a party mood."

"I haven't told you about the party yet. You might change your mind."

"Okay, where's the party?"

"The Dream Casino. Invitation only and I've got one. Does your tux still fit?"

Mason perked up. He doubted that Ed Fiora would talk to him about Cullan's murder, but he figured it couldn't hurt to ask. The worst Fiora could say was no. The preliminary hearing was in two days and Mason needed something. He couldn't think of any reason not to try and get it from Fiora, except for Tony Manzerio. Mason didn't think Fiora would whack him in the middle of his casino on New Year's Eve in front of hundreds of witnesses.

"I don't own a tux, but I've still got my bar mitzvah suit. Will that be formal enough?"

"Perfect. I'll pick you up at nine o'clock."

Rachel rang Mason's doorbell at exactly nine. He finished smoothing out the knot in his tie before he opened the door.

"Man, oh, Manishewitz!" Mason said.

Rachel swirled into the house, wearing a full-length mink coat. She slipped one arm effortlessly out of her coat, letting it slide down the other into a pile on the floor, revealing an off-the-shoulder, knee-high black sheath that clung to her body as if she were born with it on. Hands on her hips, she bumped to the right, then grinded to the left, allowing the entry hall light to reflect off the diamond tennis bracelet and diamond stud earrings she was wearing. The heavy gold-braided chain around her neck and the gold and diamond Rolex watch she wore on her other wrist completed her Fort Knox ensemble.

"Am I not fabulous?" she demanded of him.

Mason was wearing a black suit, white shirt, and black tie. Next to Rachel, he felt funereal at best.

"Fabulous doesn't belong in the same sentence as you. You're going to break every heart in the place. The men will die because you won't be interested in them and the women will hate you."

"Only the wrong women, honey. The right ones will know."

"What? You have a secret handshake?"

"Can't tell you. That's what makes it a secret."

"How do you afford all this glory on a reporter's salary?"

"I'm different."

"Why? Because you're gay?"

"No, because I'm rich. Let's go."

Casinos are built on the myth that luck lies in the next roll of the dice; the optimism that prosperity is in the next card and not just around the corner; and the greed of human beings dying to spend the rent money to cash in on something for nothing. Casinos sold euphemisms by the pound. Gambling was gaming. Blackjack dealers were buddies. Losers were high rollers.

Mason knew the truth—the house is not a home. He'd represented a string of people who'd put their faith in hitting on sixteen and hit the skids instead. Some went home and beat their wives and kids. Some stole from their employers to cover their losses. Some went to liquor stores to get drunk and decided to rob them instead.

Mason wasn't naive enough to blame the casinos entirely. No casino ever rounded people up at gunpoint and made them empty their pockets. The casino owners, from the entrepreneurs like Ed Fiora, to the shareholders of the publicly traded companies, knew there was a lot of money to be made in the stuff of dreams. Winning big was the American dream writ large.

The lobby of the Dream Casino was carpeted in deep red and gold, the walls papered in a soothing creamy shade, and the whole area lit by cascading floodlights. Above an arched entryway to the casino, images of demographically correct winners had been plastered on the wall. Three couples— one white, one black, one Hispanic—were locked in ecstatic embraces as poker chips rained over them. The casino's slogan made the point. *Take a Chance! Make Your Dream Come True!*

Mason and Rachel passed under the arch in a crowd of people thick with fur coats and jewels. Mason looked at Rachel. Her eyes glittered more than her diamonds, and her red hair shimmered like woven rubies. Mason was certain that if she'd worn pearls, they would have paled in comparison to her alabaster skin. He shook his head, mourning the loss of Rachel to heterosexual men, himself in particular.

Hidden fog machines spewed white clouds in the path of the partygoers, creating a mystical sensation as they entered the casino. They may not have been walking into a dream, but the effect was like passing into another world.

"Can you believe this?" she asked Mason once they emerged from the clouds into the casino. "It's a hundred and fifty thousand square feet; one of the biggest casino floors outside of Vegas and Atlantic City. Look at the people!"

Thousands were jammed hip-to-elbow as far as Mason could see. Rachel may have had an invitation but, judging from the crowd, Mason figured he was the only person with a pulse in the city who hadn't gotten one. The crowds around the tables were so deep that the players had disappeared from view. The only open areas were in the pits, where pit bosses patrolled under the watchful eyes of the hidden cameras that ran the length and width of the casino.

Mason knew from other cases he'd defended that every person who entered a casino was videotaped from the moment he arrived until the moment he left. The only places that cameras weren't allowed were the bathrooms, and security guards patrolled them on a regular basis.

Rachel said, "I'm going to check my coat and wander. I'll meet you back here at midnight. Have fun."

Mason surveyed the sea of people. There was a bank of slot machines to his right, each one singing out its electronic siren call. Bells and whistles begged the players for more money. Women wearing thousand-dollar designer dresses sat on stools in front of the slots, padded gloves on their right hands to avoid calluses from pulling the handle, plastic buckets in their laps to collect their winnings. They whooped and hollered as the slots paid off.

A casino was one place that welcomed smokers, and a heavy cloud floated above the crowd, turning blue and gray depending on the light that filtered through it. No one seemed to mind. Even the nonsmokers were working too hard at having a good time.

Mason plunged into the crowd. He nodded and smiled at a few familiar faces, and pretended not to notice those who stared at him a little too much. A woman planted herself in his path. Her platinum hair was piled as high as her dress was cut low. The breasts of a well-endowed twenty-year-old practically poured out of her gown. Had the rest of her been as young as her bosom, Mason would have enjoyed the view. As it was, he tried to look away, but the press of other bodies around them made it practically impossible.

"Got 'em for Christmas, so might as well unwrap 'em,"

the woman told Mason as she cupped her hands under her breasts. Her speech was slurred and her stride was unsteady. Mason thought her breasts were the only things keeping her anchored.

"Deck the halls," he told her.

"Deck this, sweetheart," she told him as she grasped his groin, laughed, and moved on to find her next grope.

Mason wedged himself into a blackjack table long enough to win two hundred dollars and give up the chair before it turned cold. He sliced his way through the crowd until he reached a wall of private poker rooms. He leaned with his back against the wall and watched the crowd. A few minutes later, Tony Manzerio, wearing the largest tuxedo ever made, stepped out of the room to Mason's left, forcing the crowd to go around him and cutting off any escape route for Mason.

Mason's throat tightened as if his shirt collar had suddenly lost a size. He wasn't thrilled to see Tony again, but preferred the casino to Blues's parking lot. Mason changed his mind when Tony flashed him the gun tucked in the shoulder harness under his tux jacket. Tony motioned Mason into the poker room.

"Need a fourth for bridge?" Mason asked him.

"Move your ass, wise guy," Tony answered. "Mr. Fiora wants to talk to you."

"Lucky me," Mason said. "I didn't even have an appointment."

Mason walked past Tony, straightening his jacket with a studied nonchalance. Tony shoved Mason between the shoulder blades. Mason spun around, ready to shove back.

"Hey," Tony told him with a shrug. "Your collar was messed up. I was just straightening it."

Mason said, "Perfect. A hood with a sense of humor."

He turned back to the poker room and stepped inside. Tony closed the door behind him, but stayed outside.

The poker room was six-sided. There was a small, well-stocked bar on the back wall and a door that opened into a bathroom on another wall. A poker table shaped the same as the room stood in the center of the floor, covered in green felt. Stacks of hundred-dollar chips surrounded a dealer's shoe filled with four decks of cards. Captain's chairs upholstered in soft brown leather sat in a ring around the table. Wall fixtures provided the only light through frosted-glass shades. Paintings of foxhunts hung on the walls, giving the room the look and feel of an English gentlemen's club.

Mason had seen pictures of Fiora in the newspaper. The head shots were of a man in his forties, slicked-back dark hair, narrow eyes, square chin, and a nose that had been broken more than once. The rest of his body fit the newspaper image of a street fighter. Fiora was little more than five-five, tightly muscled and tightly wound. His tuxedo hung loosely on his slender frame, as if he wanted to avoid being hemmed in by his clothes. He was standing at the bar, pouring himself a scotch, when the door closed behind Mason.

"So, Tony found you."

"Not easy in a crowd like that," Mason said.

"Not hard either. Video cameras picked you up when you came in with that bitch from the newspaper. What's her name? Rachel something?"

"Firestone. Rachel Firestone."

"Yeah, Firestone. You banging that broad? I hear she don't dig guys."

"If you're such a big fan of hers, why did you send her an invitation?"

"You think I made up the list? My PR people did that.

They invited everyone with a pulse but you. You, I didn't invite.''

"I'd hire new PR people. Leaving me off the list could have ruined your party.''

Fiora studied him. ''You're a smart guy, aren't you. Always wising off. Tony told me that you gave him some shit the other night when he tried to talk to you. Offended him. Made him think you weren't listening.''

''Is that why Tony is standing guard outside the door? To make sure I listen?''

''And to make sure nobody bothers us while we're talking.''

''Tony the multitasking marvel. I'm sure his mother would be proud,'' Mason said.

Fiora pulled a cigar from his inside jacket pocket, sniffed it, licked it, and clipped it before burning the end of it with a wooden match he struck against his thumbnail. Mason had smoked cigars years ago, but quit when he got tired of waking up to a mouth that tasted like a garbage truck at the end of its run. He still liked the aroma of a good cigar and Fiora's cigar qualified.

''You don't give up, do you?'' Fiora asked him, pointing his cigar at Mason to underscore his disappointment.

''I don't respond well to structure,'' Mason answered. ''What do you want?''

''I thought you were the one who wanted to ask me questions.''

''You'll just lie to me. I'll wait until you're under oath. Then I'll let you commit perjury.''

''Perjury! Bullshit! I got nothing to lie about.''

''Then why are you trying so hard to make my client plead guilty to something he didn't do?''

''Who says he didn't do it? Him? You? So what? He should take the deal the DA offered him. Everybody will be better off. Including you. Did you explain that to your client?''

''He wasn't moved. He figures if you kill me, he won't have to pay my bill.''

''You keep up the jokes, Mason. Just remember what a good time you had when it's all over.''

''What makes you think Jack Cullan's files will stay hidden just because my client pleads guilty? If those files are so valuable, someone will find them. Then what will you do?''

Fiora set his drink on the bar and walked slowly around the table until he was nearly on top of Mason. Fiora gave up more than half a foot and thirty pounds to Mason, but standing in front of him, eyes blazing, Fiora couldn't have cared less. He knew, as did Blues, that violence leveled all kinds of playing fields.

''Any motherfucker digs up dirt on me, I'll use it to bury him. Got that, wise guy?''

Mason was tired of being pushed and pulled by cops, politicians, and thugs. He said, ''Sure. Now I've got news for you. Any motherfucker who threatens me, my client, or my dog, better have more than an ape guarding his door. Got that, wise guy?''

Fiora ran his tongue over his lips, pushed it around the inside of his mouth, and reached his hand inside his tux jacket. He pulled out a gun and rested the end of the barrel on Mason's chest.

''You got more balls than sense, Mason,'' he told him.

''Helps in my line of work,'' Mason answered, and pushed the gun away. ''Happy New Year.''

Mason pulled the door open and tapped Tony on the shoulder. Tony turned sideways so he could see his boss. Fiora nodded and Tony stepped aside for Mason.

"Hey, Mason," Fiora said. "You find those files, come see me. We'll do some business."

"Not likely," Mason said.

"Don't be stupid, Mason. You'll live longer."

"Doing business with you? Not likely," Mason repeated, and headed back into the crowd.

Chapter Fifteen

Mason retreated to one of the many bars that ringed the gaming tables, ordered a beer, and watched the crowd from his stool, his back to the bar. He added Fiora's name to the list of people who wanted him to find Cullan's files for them. He could live with the deals he'd made with Rachel Firestone and Amy White, but wasn't willing to bet his life on a deal with Fiora.

Not far from where he was sitting, a band of cheerleaders surrounding a craps table screeched as someone ran a hot streak even hotter. The shooter was the celebrity of the moment, mistaking a statistical anomaly for good looks, charm, and wit. Anything was possible while the dice were hot. A collective moan rose from the hangers-on and side-betters when the shooter shot craps. His last reward was a few claps on the back as people shifted their loyalties and hopes to the next shooter, welcoming him with a joy and rapture usually reserved for tent meetings.

Mason caught a glimpse of Rachel now and then. Once she was taking her turn at rolling the dice, basking in the instant adoration of her own good luck. Not long after, he saw her huddled with another woman, a lanky brunette in a black pantsuit and open tuxedo shirt, sharing full-throated laughs and long looks. Mason had assumed that Rachel was on the prowl for a story, not companionship. Instead, he realized, she was using the night to lose herself in the anonymity of the crowd and give free rein to impulse. Tomorrow, no one would remember.

Just after eleven-thirty, Mayor Sunshine arrived and began working the crowd. Amy White hung at his side, whispering the names of contributors who sought him out. She scanned the crowd, looking for opportunities or trouble. Her eyes caught Mason's for a moment, and her calculus was quick as she steered the mayor in the opposite direction. Mason tipped his bottle toward her in a small salute, acknowledging her good call. If she saw his gesture, she ignored it.

Thousands of balloons had been gathered in nets suspended from the cavernous ceiling. Confetti cannons were aimed in a cross-fire pattern to blanket the crowd. Scoreboard-size digital clocks had been mounted throughout the casino to count down the final minutes until midnight. Time was running off the clocks in hours, minutes, seconds, and tenths of seconds. It was eleven forty-five and the clocks were racing to the finish line. Two of the clocks were visible from the bar, and two men seated next to Mason were arguing loudly whether one clock was faster than the other. They decided to settle their dispute by betting which clock would first strike twelve.

Mason set his bottle on the bar and turned to the two gamblers, who were studying the competing clocks with watery-eyed concentration.

"Hey," he whispered to them. "I saw a clock on the

other side of the casino next to the roulette wheels that was a minute ahead of those two.''

"No shit?'' they asked in unison.

"No shit. There's a guy standing under it giving five-to-one odds that it hits midnight first.''

"Damn,'' they said, and left their unfinished drinks to cash in on Mason's tip.

The bar Mason had been sitting at was near the back of the casino. He decided to start making his way to the front to be certain he was there at midnight to meet Rachel. He stood and waited a moment, remembering how to get there. A casino was designed to obliterate all points of reference except for the tables and slots. There were no windows and, except on New Year's Eve, no clocks.

The noise level was rising to near deafening. Slot machines trumpeted new winners with bleating air horns. Piped-in music throbbed overhead with an orgasmic Latin beat. The craps tables erupted in roars as one good throw followed another. Even the blackjack players, notorious for their semicomatose poker faces, were high-fiving one another. The joint was jumping.

A sliver of the crowd parted in front of Mason as a woman cut through their ranks. People peeled away from her path as if pushed aside by her presence, or so it seemed to Mason, when he recognized her.

Beth Harrell, clad in a shimmering silver gown, her head thrown back, was walking toward him. Her left hand was extended over her shoulder, holding on to a mink coat that trailed behind her like a cape. Large, lustrous pearls were roped around her neck. Her diamond earrings and platinum bracelets were lost in the glow of her eyes and the promise of her sly smile. The tops of her breasts swelled gently from her gown as she stopped in front of Mason.

"Happy New Year, Lou,'' she said.

"I'm counting on that," Mason answered, his throat dry.

They stood for a moment, watching each other. She was probing. He was wondering. Mason willed himself to keep his arms at his side. In a room of stunning women, she could have stopped the digital clocks with a single look. Beth handed him her coat and turned her back to him. She pressed herself softly against him as he held her coat and she slipped her arms into the sleeves. The sensation of the fur and her body against his was electric.

Beth faced him again, closer than before. Her perfume was heady, like a full-bodied wine that had to be sipped slowly. "Walk with me," she said.

He followed her through an exit onto the outer deck of the casino. Heaters mounted along the outer wall glowed red, cutting the night's chill as they slowly made their way along the dimly lighted deck.

"Some riverboat," Mason said.

Beth laughed. "It's a barge permanently docked in a moat filled with water from the Missouri River. If the state legislature says it's a riverboat, that's good enough for me."

She slipped her arm through his as naturally as if they'd been doing it all their lives. "I didn't expect to see you here," she said.

"Into the belly of the beast," he told her. "Ed Fiora wouldn't return my phone calls so I decided to come see him."

"Alone?" she asked with a hopeful cast to her question.

"Sort of. I came with a friend but we're not together."

"Good," she said, emphasizing her satisfaction with a slight squeeze of his arm.

"How about you? Are you flying solo too?"

"I'm afraid so," Beth answered. She looked up at him, smiling weakly. "Not many men are anxious to be seen with me, especially since my last date ended up murdered."

"I suppose that would scare some guys away."

They had reached what was, in the mind of a fanciful architect, the prow of the boat. It was an elongated triangle that reached out over the Missouri River. It was at least ten feet wide at its base where it jutted out from the walk, narrowing to a couple of feet at its farthest point. The surface was made of reinforced steel. A wrought-iron rail, fabricated in cross-thatched weave to prevent small children from slipping through, rose four feet to keep adults high and dry as well. Pale blue Christmas lights had been strung along the rail providing the only illumination. They walked out onto the end of the prow, nearly invisible in the darkness, and leaned on the rail as the chill breeze blew off the river.

"How about you, Lou? Are you afraid of me?"

He shook his head. "I don't scare easily."

Beth leaned her shoulder into him and, without intending to, he slipped his arms around her middle and she covered his hands with hers. They stood like that, not talking, until fireworks launched from the casino parking lot announced the arrival of the New Year. Tracers of red and streaks of blue arced high into the sky. Green and white clusters exploded overhead, raining glowing cinders into the swiftly moving current twenty feet below them.

Beth rolled in Mason's arms, her mouth inches below his. "Don't let me scare you," she breathed. She pressed herself fully against him, rose on her toes, and kissed him softly, tentatively.

She barely pulled away, just enough to let him see in her quivering lips how much she wanted him, to let him feel the surge of need in her own body for his.

Mason was lost in the moment, intoxicated with her taste, a series of small shudders building like shifting fault lines in his groin and belly. He saw all that he wanted in her at that split second, and all that he could lose if he took it. He let go his grip, his arms slackened to his sides.

"I'm sorry, Beth. I'm truly sorry. Maybe when this is all over, but not now."

The light went out of her face as swiftly and coldly as the fireworks when they hit the water. She stepped back toward the deck, wiping her mouth with the back of her hand.

"Well, that's one way to start the New Year," she said. "Humiliate myself like a horny middle-aged broad who can't get laid."

"Don't do that to yourself, Beth. You're better than that," Mason told her.

"Am I?" she asked. She didn't wait for Mason's answer, leaving him alone at the end of the prow.

Mason stayed where he was, perched like the lookout on the *Titanic,* staring across the Missouri. The wind was brisk, but compared to the more recent biting cold, he could tolerate it for a few minutes. Besides, he wanted to give Beth time to leave the casino without another embarrassing encounter. He also wanted to let the cold air clear his muddled head.

He wondered whether Beth had sought him out or whether their meeting had been serendipitous. She had been so direct, almost calculating, that he couldn't ascribe it to mere chance. On the other hand, it was unlikely that she knew he was at the casino, let alone precisely where to find him. Someone must have told her. Ed Fiora had reminded Mason how easy it was to find him or anyone else at the casino. They were all being watched all the time. The more intriguing question was why Fiora would want Beth to find him, take him out to the prow of the boat, and seduce him.

The possible answers to that question were more than unsettling, replacing the lingering arousal from Beth's embrace with a dull queasiness. He looked down at the river, noticing for the first time how the end of the prow bobbed and swayed as if the riverboat were churning along with the current. He was surprised at how far out over the black, swirling water the prow extended.

Before he could answer any of the questions running through his mind, a sharp crack, like a stray firecracker, popped behind him as he heard a piercing smack against the railing next to his side. Unwilling to believe what he suspected, he turned around in time to see a muzzle flash from the shadows of the deck at the same instant he heard another pop and another harsh ping into the rail. There was no mistake now. Someone was shooting at him.

Mason realized that he was as exposed as if he were doing back flips naked down Broadway. He crouched and twisted to shrink the shooter's target, but knew there was little safety in the effort. Two more shots careened around him, sending him crashing back and forth in the corner of the prow like a pinball and showering broken Christmas lights at his feet.

The longer he stayed where he was, the more certain it was that he would be hit. The closer he got to the deck, the easier a target he would become. The river was his only option. Crouching as low as he could, he sprang into the air, planting his hands on the rail for added leverage, clearing the rail with his feet, and letting go as a bullet cut through his jacket, singeing his side.

Mason hit the river at an angle, falling forward and slapping his face on the water before being swept under. The water was so cold he felt as if his blood had been drained from his body and replaced with ice. He began to lose feeling in his hands, and struggled to free himself from his jacket, afraid that it would weigh him down as he fought to swim to shore.

Kicking ferociously, he managed to break to the surface, gasping for air and swallowing hard. Looking around wildly and treading water, he tried to get his bearings. The casino was already a hundred yards behind him, grim testimony to the swift current. He was easily the same distance from the bank, having been carried toward the center of the river.

Rather than trying to swim directly across the current, he tried to cut it at an angle. That would keep him in the water longer, but give him a better chance of reaching shore. He refused to think about how long he could stay in the water before hypothermia proved more deadly than gunshots.

Mason pressed one shoe against the other to slip it off and give him a better kick, then used his bare foot to do the same with the other. He guessed that he'd only been in the water a couple of minutes, but his arms and legs already felt heavy and he was getting light-headed as his body temperature dropped. There was no light along the river, and he could no longer judge his location.

An overwhelming weariness, deeper than any he'd ever experienced, crept over him as he realized that in another moment or two he wouldn't be able to lift his arms out of the water or kick his legs to stay afloat. Drowning suddenly had a restful appeal, more irresistible even than Beth Harrell, her breasts pressed against him, her scent filling his heart.

A raspy chopping sound floated over the water, stirring him. It was, he realized, a small motor. At this time and place, it could only be a boat. Flailing around in the water, he waved his arms and cried out for help. A spotlight danced around him, then disappeared as the boat drew closer. Barely able to stay afloat, he tried lying on his back when he heard something hard smack into the water near him and skip to his side. He flopped his hand against it, then grabbed it hard when he realized it was a round buoy that was used to cushion the side of a motor boat against the dock.

Mason rolled over in the water and clutched the buoy with both hands. It was clipped to the end of a rope that drew taut when he took hold of the buoy. He held on, nearly deadweight, as he was pulled to the edge of the boat. He managed to throw his arms over the side of the boat and, with the help of someone else, drag the rest of his body out of the water.

Lying in the bottom of the boat, he looked up, panting and shivering.

"I told you to meet me at midnight, and next time you better not be late," Rachel Firestone told him.

Chapter Sixteen

Mason refused to let Rachel take him to a hospital. "I don't want to explain to an emergency room doc what happened," he said through chattering teeth. "Somebody will call the cops; then the press will get ahold of it."

Rachel had docked the motor boat at the Dream Casino pier, and they were sitting in her car, the heater turned on full blast.

"You'll probably catch pneumonia, ten different diseases from the crap in the river, and it looks like you've been shot," she added, pointing to a red stain on the left side of his soaking tuxedo shirt. "And in case your brain completely froze while you were in the water, I am the press and I've already got ahold of this story."

"You forgot our deal. Everything's off the record unless I say otherwise."

Rachel rolled her eyes in exasperation. "Men are too dumb to live. I'll be right back."

She returned ten minutes later with her mink coat and wrapped it around him. "Take off your clothes," she instructed.

"You mean I've converted you?" he asked. The weakness in his voice robbed the joke of its impact.

"Not in this lifetime. I don't want you to freeze to death in my car. Makes a lousy obituary."

Mason peeled off his tuxedo shirt, wincing from the laceration in his side. Reaching under the fur coat, he pushed his pants down to his ankles and pulled them all the way off with his feet. He was too tired to fool with his socks and too proud to pull off his boxers. The combination of the heater and the insulation of the fur coat was enough to restore the feeling in his hands and feet by the time they reached his house. Mason got another chill when he saw an unfamiliar car parked in front.

"Don't worry," Rachel said. "She's a friend of mine."

Rachel's friend turned out to be a doctor who made house calls before sunrise on New Year's Day. She had short brown hair, round farm-girl features, thick wrists, and a soothing, confident touch as she palpated and prodded Mason. He followed her instructions to take the hottest shower he could stand, after which she dressed the wound in his side, gave him an injection of antibiotic, and left samples of more antibiotics, to take over the next five days.

Mason dressed in sweats and heavy wool socks before coming downstairs to thank her, only to find that she had already left. Rachel was alone in the kitchen, sitting at the table with two large mugs of steaming tea.

"Where's your friend?" Mason asked Rachel. He sat at the table and took a sip from his mug. "I didn't get to thank her."

"I thanked her for you."

"She didn't even tell me her name."

"You didn't need to know it."

"Why? Is that another secret of the sisterhood?"

Rachel slapped her hand on the table, shaking her mug so that tea spilled onto the table. "Damn you, Lou! I drag your ass out of the river before you drown and find you a doctor in the middle of the night on fucking New Year's Eve so that you don't have to go the hospital where you belong, and you've got to crack dyke jokes."

Mason raised his hands in surrender. "I'm sorry. She was terrific. You redefine terrific."

Rachel grabbed a dish towel from the kitchen counter and wiped the tea that had spilled from her mug. "Yeah, well, she is terrific. She's also married and she's gay. That's a tough way to go. She's got bigger secrets to keep than yours and she understands what it means to help someone when they can't go public."

Mason said, "I am suitably humbled. Tell her the door swings both ways. Make sure she knows where to find me if she needs me."

Rachel nodded. "I'll do that. Now tell me what in the hell happened out there."

"Off the record?"

Rachel nodded again. It was a reluctant nod, punctuated by the dish towel that she threw onto the table in surrender. "Off the record," she said.

"It was about a quarter to twelve and I was coming to look for you at the front of the casino. Beth Harrell appeared out of the crowd like Moses parting the Red Sea. She asked me to take a walk with her."

"And since you are cursed with a penis, you had no choice."

"Jealous?"

"Of her? Not a chance. She's not my type."

"You don't give a guy any hope, do you?"

"Get this through your testosterone-drenched brain. No guy has any hope with me."

Mason sighed. "You have made me a believer. So, Beth and I take a walk. We end up out on the end of the prow. She snuggles up, the rockets red glare, and she makes a pass at me."

"A beautiful woman comes on to you and you decide to jump into the river. Are you sure you're not gay?"

"You should live long enough to find out," he told her. "In spite of what you might think about the curse of the penis, I turned her down. It wasn't pretty. She's got a fair dose of self-loathing inside that perfect body. She left and I gave her a good head start. The next thing I know, someone is shooting at me. The river was my only way out. How did you find me?"

"I guess it's time for my little confession," she began. Mason's eyes widened. "No, you moron, I didn't shoot you, but that's starting to look like an attractive option."

"Latent heterophobia?"

"More like overt smart-ass phobia! Fiora sent a bunch of invitations to the newspaper. I took one so that I could ask you to go. I threw you in just so I could watch what happened. I didn't think you could resist going after Fiora. I thought I could get a good story." Rachel looked down and away, a red stain creeping across her checks. She wiped a tear from the corner of her eye. "I'm really sorry," she added in a voice he could barely make out.

Mason exhaled slowly. "Whew," he said. "You didn't make me come with you and you didn't make me go out on that prow with Beth Harrell. But you did save my life and that should balance anybody's books. How did you manage that?"

Rachel looked up. "My God, you are a mess of a human being! You come on to any woman with a pulse, you can't go two minutes without being a smart-ass, and you forgive way too easily.''

''Makes you want me for a brother, doesn't it?''

''Yeah,'' she said softly. ''It really does.'' They sipped from their mugs for a moment. ''I saw Tony Manzerio fetch you for a visit with Fiora,'' she continued. ''I want to hear all about that, by the way. Then I just kept my eye on you. When you went outside with Beth, I went out another exit, figuring I could get close without being seen.''

''You saw what happened?'' Mason asked her.

''I'm in the voyeur business,'' she said with a shrug. ''When Beth left, I was going to hustle back to the front of the casino and wait for you. Then I heard the shots and saw you jump in the water. I'd been at that casino a lot and I knew there was a boat tied up at the pier. There wasn't time to call the Coast Guard. I ran for the dock, which wasn't easy in this body condom I'm wearing. The rest is commentary.''

''Did you see who was shooting at me?''

Rachel shook her head. ''All I know is that it wasn't coming from my side of the deck. Whoever it was couldn't have been much of a shot. It would have been hard to find an easier target.''

''Unless the shooter wasn't trying to hit me. Maybe the idea was to get me to jump, let the river do the rest.''

Rachel said, ''I still don't understand why you wouldn't go to the hospital and let the police take care of this.''

Mason didn't say anything. He drained the rest of his mug and set it down on the table.

''Yes, I do,'' Rachel said. ''I am so dumb sometimes. You don't want to involve Beth Harrell in another scandal. You think she might really have something that you want.''

''I do, but it's not what you think. You were watching me all night. I don't think Beth was. Someone had to tell her where and when to find me. Ed Fiora is the only one who could have told her that. The casino has video cameras everywhere. I'm pretty sure Fiora sent her on her mission. If he got me on videotape making love under the stars with a key witness against my client, I'd be out of this case in a heartbeat. That didn't work, so he went to plan B.''

"Then the whole thing is on videotape. The shooting, everything,'' Rachel said.

"I'll take odds that those tapes are gone by now. I have to find out what's going on between Ed Fiora and Beth Harrell,'' Mason said.

"Of course. You'll drop by, talk about old times, and she'll spill her guts.''

"Something like that.''

"This I've got to see.''

"Sorry. No press. Don't pout. You'll still get your exclusive when it's all over. There is just one thing you may want to think about.''

"What's that?''

"If Fiora saw Beth and me on videotape, he saw you too. I'd be very careful.''

"Happy New Year to me,'' Rachel said.

Beth Harrell lived in Hyde Park, one of the first neighborhoods of Kansas City to have been reclaimed from the scrap heap left by white flight to the suburbs. It had been home to the society swells during the first half of the last century. Many of its Victorian, Georgian, and Dutch Colonial homes had slid into decay, some subdivided into apartments, during the next thirty years. Over the last twenty years, it had become a hip place to live, replacing urban decline with urbane gentrification. Whites were comfortable with the blacks that were their neighbors since many of them had a J.D., M.D., or CPA to go with their BMWs.

Mason stopped in front of Beth's house, a Dutch Colonial whose redbrick had been sandblasted to give it a lighter, brighter cast. The wrought-iron anchors that secured the brick on either side of the front of the house had been recently painted, and the morning sun reflected sharply off the gleaming black paint. Mason liked the sunlight of winter better than other times of the year because the cold air made for cleaner and clearer color. On mornings like this New Year's Day, the sun shot straight through the sky, etching sharp colors and crisp shadows wherever it reached.

He sat in front of her house waiting for some sign of activity inside, knowing what he would ask her and wondering what he would do if she didn't answer truthfully. The harder part, he knew, would be discerning what was true from what was artifice. She had kept him on his heels both times he had been with her in the last two weeks. She was a beautiful, troubled, and vulnerable woman whose traits stoked a dangerous eroticism. That she was a witness, a suspect, and a possible conspirator added a geometric complexity to his feelings about her. Rachel would have told him to leave his penis in the car.

It was nine o'clock. Mason had barely slept, too jazzed by his near-death experience. He hadn't shaved, and the bags under his eyes looked as if they'd been packed for a long trip. Though his body temperature was normal, his skin still had a bluish pallor. Dressed in faded jeans, a navy corduroy shirt, and a Land's End barn jacket, he looked more as if he were getting over a bad hangover than a murder attempt. Though he suspected that Beth might have had a hand in that attempt, he didn't hesitate when he rang her doorbell. Whatever else she may be, he thought, she didn't seem dangerous on her own.

Mason watched through a glass panel on the side of her front door as Beth descended from the second floor. She was wearing a long, white robe, tied loosely at the waist, and as nearly as he could see, very little else. Her hair was tousled from interrupted sleep, and she ran her fingers through it as she approached the door. When she saw Mason's face through the glass, she stutter-stepped, pretended to tighten the belt around her robe, and opened the door.

"It's a beautiful morning, don't you think?" Mason said.

"The best so far this year," she answered.

Beth had recovered from her surprise at finding Mason at her door, and stepped to her side as he walked in. She closed the door and leaned against it. Sunlight washed through the glass side panels, wrapping her in golden ribbons. The front of her robe had slipped open, revealing the swell of her breasts. Her arms hung at her sides, inviting him to look.

She told him, "If you've changed your mind about last night, I'm afraid I have too. I behaved very poorly. I hope you're not too disappointed in me."

It was the most contradictory rejection and apology Mason had ever received. The more he learned about Beth, the less he understood her. The more he saw of her, the more he wanted her.

Mason said, "We need to talk. You should get dressed first."

Beth waited a fraction of a minute, letting him reconsider, then gathered her robe closely to her chest. "Of course. I'll only be a minute." She left a renewed chill behind as she went back upstairs.

The minute she had promised turned into thirty. While he waited, Mason explored the first floor. There was a dining room to the left of the entry hall and a living room to the right. Unlike his, they were furnished. Beth's tastes ran to antiques and oriental rugs, muted taupe and pale burgundy fabrics, and overstuffed pillows.

There was a portrait in the living room of a brooding young girl set in shadow, her long blond hair hanging loosely over a thin white gown, open at the neck. The girl's fingers were wrapped in strands of her hair, her lips half open with wistful longing. Her features were soft, her eyes both dreamy and sad. The artist had captured an ache that reverberated throughout the girl, as if she'd seen her future and wished she could turn from it. Looking more closely, he realized that the girl was Beth.

"I was fifteen. My mother was the artist," Beth said from behind him. "She painted portraits while my father took his secretary on business trips. She told me how he had cheated on her since before I was born but that she couldn't afford to leave him. Then one day, he left her. She said she wanted to paint me while I was still young and no one had crushed my heart like he had crushed hers."

Beth had changed into slightly wrinkled chinos and a plum-colored crew-neck sweater. She had brushed out the kinks in her hair, but wasn't wearing any makeup. She still looked beautiful but, for the first time, she also looked brittle, as if one more jolt would fracture her. The girl in the painting had seen her future.

"You said we needed to talk," she reminded him. "What about?"

"Why did Ed Fiora send you to find me last night?"

"Why do you think?"

"Then he did send you?"

"You won't consider the possibility that I was there alone, that I saw you and wanted to be with you?"

Mason hesitated, choosing his words carefully. "I did consider that. It may be true, but I don't think it's entirely true."

"A concession to your ego and my weakness, Lou?" He didn't answer. "It would be less humiliating if it weren't true at all. Then I'd just be a victim instead of a fool and you might be willing to help me."

"I can't help you if I don't know the truth, and I may not be able to help you even then."

She walked over to where he was standing and studied her painted image. "My mother wasn't exactly a prize either. She was cold and aloof, even toward me. She put her feelings in her paintings, stroking her brushes instead of my father and me. My father needed constant reassurance that he was wonderful and wanted. They made each other's weaknesses worse."

"It's a little late in life to be blaming dear old Mom and Dad, isn't it?"

Beth folded her arms over her chest. "You bet it is. I just got some of the worst from both of them, and I ended up looking for love in all the wrong places."

Mason said, "That song has been covered by a lot of people."

"Listen, this isn't easy. I was so determined not to screw up like they did. I put everything into school and my career. I graduated first in my class, got a job with a top firm, went back to teach law school, got appointed to the Gaming Commission. I was doing everything right publicly, but I made some bad choices privately."

"Including taking a bribe to approve the license for the Dream Casino?"

She shook her head. "No. I really thought Fiora's application was the best one. The key to it was the lease with the city for the location at the landing. It was the best deal for the taxpayers."

"What about Fiora's background?"

"We checked him out every way possible. He's rough

around the edges, but we found no compelling evidence that he was dirty.''

"Then why the scandal?"

Beth looked at Mason, silently judging them both. "Fiora bribed the mayor. Jack Cullan set it up through a secret ownership in the Dream Casino.''

"Can you prove that?"

"I had heard enough whispers that I was going to have the Gaming Commission investigate it. I think we could have made the case.''

"Why didn't you?"

"I was about to until Jack invited me to go out that night. He tried to bribe me during dinner. Not straight up. Just enough subtle hints about what a bad idea it would be if the commission investigated the Dream Casino and that I would be well taken care of if I stayed out of it.''

"You turned him down?"

"I acted like I didn't hear him, like I didn't know what he was talking about. I told him that we couldn't discuss commission business at all. He let it drop until we got to Blues on Broadway. Then he brought it up again. Only this time he threatened me.''

"With what?"

Beth sat down on a sofa, sinking deeply into the cushions. "I told you that I had made some bad choices. One of my husbands was the worst. I let him take some photographs of me." She dipped her head, bit her lip, and looked away. "Doing some things." She rubbed her palms across her eyes. "Jack said that he'd bought the pictures from my ex and had given them to Ed Fiora. He promised to get them back from Fiora if I played ball. That's when I threw my drink in his face.''

Mason paced slowly around the living room, trying to concentrate on the crown molding along the ceiling, the intricate design of the parquet hardwood floor—anything but the person dissolving on the sofa. He didn't know whether he should drop to one knee, take her hand in his, and promise to avenge her honor, or whether he should twist her arm until she agreed to take a polygraph test.

Mason said, ''That doesn't explain last night.''

Beth took another deep breath and sat up straighter. ''No, it doesn't. I was at the grocery and this huge man comes walking down the aisle. He dropped an envelope in my cart. At first, I thought it was an accident. Then I saw my name on the envelope. There was an invitation to the party inside and a photocopy of one of the pictures. Someone had written a note that said Mr. Fiora looks forward to seeing me at the party. So I went.''

''Did you keep the invitation and the picture?''

''No. I almost got sick right there in the grocery store. I burnt them when I got home.''

''What happened when you got to the party?''

''Fiora's moose found me. God only knows how in that crowd. Fiora told me where to find you.''

''And the rest?''

Beth rose from the sofa and walked to the floor-length windows at the front of the room, her hands balled into fists. She banged them against the glass, pressed harder, and turned to face Mason.

''The little prick told me that since I liked being in pictures so much, he wanted to get some of you and me together. He told me to go find you and use my imagination. He said he'd be watching.''

Mason thought about their embrace, her kiss, and his rejection of her. ''What did you do after you left me out on the prow?''

''I got out of there as fast as I could, came home, and got drunk.''

He stared at her, hoping to peel through the layers she was wrapped in and find something or someone he could believe. "Right after you left, someone tried to shoot me. I had to jump into the river to get away. I got shot anyway and nearly drowned."

Beth's hands fluttered to her mouth and she let out a long, low moan as she slid slowly into a heap on the floor. The sunlight poured through the windows behind her, burying her in its brightness. Mason walked over to her and she looked up at him, silently mouthing that she was sorry. She reached for his hand, and he reluctantly took hers as she pulled him down toward her.

"Lou, you've got to believe me. I didn't know. It wasn't me. I'm begging you to help me. Get those pictures for me. I want my life back."

They stayed that way for a time, neither of them saying anything, until Mason's legs started to ache. He stood and left her there without making a promise he didn't know whether he could keep.

Chapter Seventeen

On Wednesday morning Leonard Campbell swept into Judge Pistone's courtroom for the start of the preliminary hearing as if it were the Oscars. He stopped every few feet so that the press could take his picture, giving each reporter and photographer a hearty smile and a thumbs-up. He plopped his thin, cordovan-leather Gucci briefcase on the table reserved for the prosecuting attorney, pulled out an empty legal pad, and placed it neatly on one corner. Planting his hands on his hips, he pivoted slowly, surveying the courtroom as if he were a general trying to decide where to position his snipers. Dressed in a black suit, pale blue shirt with white collar and cuffs, and a subdued gray necktie, he was dressed to kill, if not to convict. He shot his cuffs through the sleeves of his suit jacket and snapped off a crisp nod to the press corps—the little general saluting the folks back home before going off to war.

Patrick Ortiz arrived a few moments later, along with two

assistants; one of whom pushed a two-wheel handcart loaded with bankers' boxes. The other assistant carried two-foot-by-three-foot enlargements of photographs of the murder scene and the victim, the autopsy report, and the results of the tests conducted by the forensics lab. Ortiz and his crew ignored the media, and began methodically emptying their boxes and setting up the files and exhibits they would use throughout the preliminary hearing.

Court was scheduled to begin at nine o'clock. Mason had spent the previous hour locked in a cramped, windowless witness room, little bigger than a walk-in closet, bringing Blues up to date. Armed deputies waited outside the door to take Blues into the courtroom.

"I should have told you sooner about Ed Fiora, but I was afraid you'd try and break out of jail just so you could kick his ass," Mason told him.

"I might have done that," Blues said. "I think you were more worried that I'd take the deal to save your bony white butt."

Mason scribbled a bad sketch of the prow of the Dream Casino and laughed. "Yeah, I suppose that's right."

"Well, guess what? I'm not taking a fall for you or anybody else and you know that. So why are you telling me now?"

"You understand street war strategy better than I do. That's what this is. The trial may only be a side skirmish. I need your help tying all this together. I can't do my job if I keep you in the dark."

"In that case, get me bailed out of here. I can't do either one of us any good inside."

Blues was wearing the one suit he owned. It was brown, worn at the elbows, and too tight across his shoulders, but it was better than the jailhouse jumpsuit.

Mason said, "Pistone is going to bind you over and deny

bail again. Our best chance is with the Circuit Court judge we draw for the trial. In the meantime, I'll try to find you a new suit.''

Mason opened the door, and two beefy deputies on the Dunkin' Donuts diet plan approached Blues cautiously. Blues dropped his right shoulder and gave them a head fake like a running back looking for a seam. Blues cackled when they both grabbed for their guns, blushing like schoolkids when they realized he was pimping them.

"Careful now, boys. I'm a dangerous man," Blues said, sticking the needle in a little deeper.

One deputy cursed under his breath and the other nodded in vigorous agreement. A third officer joined them, and the three of them huddled briefly outside the room while Mason and Blues waited. The largest of the three deputies stepped into the room, flanked by his comrades.

"We're gonna let your little joke go this time, big man. Don't fuck with us again or it's gonna be a rough ride back up in the elevator. Got me?''

Mason said, "Lighten up, Deputy. He was yanking your chain and you just threatened him in front of his lawyer. That elevator gets stuck and you'll be on the other end of a civil rights charge faster than you can sing 'We Shall Overcome.' Got me?''

The deputy turned on Mason, his hand on his nightstick. "You tell your client we don't play games here.''

"Sure. Blues," Mason said, "no games. They'll put you in time-out.''

The deputies surrounded Blues and shepherded him through a side door into the courtroom. Mason followed behind; glad to have avoided the press encamped outside the courtroom. Blues took a seat at the defendant's table, disappointing those in attendance by refusing to turn around. The deputies sat down in a row of chairs directly behind him, while Mason sat down next to Blues. Mason's chair was covered in worn vinyl and the padding had long since surrendered. The chair swiveled and rocked, but Mason couldn't find a comfortable position, making him glad that the preliminary hearing wouldn't last more than a day or two.

The judge's bailiff, a middle-aged black woman with a stern face and a linebacker's build, entered the courtroom through the door to the judge's chambers.

"Judge Pistone says that if he sees a camera in the courtroom, he'll add it to his collection. Pregame festivities are over." Before anyone could grumble, the judge appeared at her shoulder. "All rise!" she barked. "Hear ye, hear ye, hear ye! The Associate Circuit Court of the Sixteenth Judicial District is now in session before the Honorable Joseph Pistone. All persons having business before this court draw nigh and pay attention. Court is now in session." Mason knew that the judge wouldn't need a gavel as long as he had her to keep order.

Everyone stood as Judge Pistone shuffled up the two steps to his seat behind the bench, elevated above the masses to remind them of the power of the court. They all waited for his permission to sit down. Without looking up, he offered a dismissive wave and said, "Be seated."

Mason glanced around the courtroom as the door opened from the hallway. Harry Ryman and Carl Zimmerman slipped inside and leaned against the rear wall. Harry and Lou looked at each other, both trying not to reveal anything. Harry tipped his head at Lou, who responded with the same sparse gesture.

Mason found Rachel standing in the corner on the opposite side of the back wall from Harry and Zimmerman. She was back in uniform, wearing jeans and a green-and-brown plaid flannel shirt over a tan crew-neck T-shirt. They exchanged winks and smiles, comforting gestures that distracted him briefly from the judge's monotone recitation of the name of the case and his instruction for the attorneys to state their appearances.

Leonard Campbell rose majestically from his chair, buttoned his suit coat, and slowly stepped to the podium in the center of the courtroom. "The people of the State of Missouri," he intoned as if it were an invocation, "are represented by Leonard Campbell, prosecuting attorney, and Patrick Ortiz, deputy chief prosecuting attorney. We are ready to proceed at the court's pleasure, Your Honor."

Campbell turned on one heel, struck a confident, serious pose for the crowd, and resumed his seat. Patrick Ortiz hated showboats and adopted Judge Pistone's head-down posture, pleased with the knowledge that Campbell had completed his only assignment in the hearing.

Judge Pistone raised his eyes at Mason, signaling that it was Mason's turn. "Lou Mason for the defendant. We're ready," Mason said as he stood up. "I've got a preliminary matter that I'd like to take up before we get started," he added.

"Proceed," the judge said.

"There are a lot of people in the courtroom, Your Honor. Some of them may be witnesses. I recognize Detectives Ryman and Zimmerman, who investigated this murder, and there may be some others. I'd like to invoke the rule that prohibits a witness from being in the courtroom prior to testifying."

"Mr. Campbell?" Judge Pistone asked.

Patrick Ortiz rose in Campbell's place. "We've got all our witnesses sequestered except for Detective Zimmerman. He's our first witness, and I guess he's just a little anxious to get started."

Ortiz's explanation drew soft laughter from the packed

house, establishing his usual easygoing connection to his audience. There was no jury in a preliminary hearing. Only the judge would make the decision whether to bind Blues over for trial. Ortiz didn't need all the boxes or the blowups to make his case for Judge Pistone. He understood that the reporters in the courtroom would tell everyone who read a paper, listened to the radio, or watched television how overwhelming the state's evidence was. That message would reverberate with the people who would ultimately be the jurors that would decide this case. He also knew that Mason would watch him closely, gauging how his adversary weighed in the lawyer's gamble between trial and plea bargain, between a crapshoot for freedom and a date with a deadly needle. Ortiz felt the connection at his back, like a breeze that filled his sails.

"What about Detective Ryman?" the judge asked Ortiz.

"We don't intend to call Detective Ryman to testify. I don't know what Mr. Mason's plans are."

Mason was surprised at Ortiz's decision to keep Harry off the stand. He wondered if Harry had asked to take a pass to avoid a confrontation with him, or whether it had been Ortiz's idea. Either way, Mason knew Harry wouldn't help his defense of Blues.

Mason said, "I don't intend to call Detective Ryman and I have no objection to his presence in the courtroom."

"Very well, Counsel," the judge said. "The rule is hereby invoked. No witness will be permitted in the courtroom until after he or she has testified. I will expect the lawyers to enforce the rule by keeping a close eye on who comes and goes. Don't expect me to take roll. If you let somebody slip in, it's on you. Any opening statement, Mr. Ortiz?"

"Yes, Your Honor. Even though this is a pretty cut-and-dried case, I'd like to put the evidence in context for the court and let you know who you are going to be hearing from.''

Mason was glad that the state had the burden to prove its case. He understood that was why the prosecutor got to go first at every stage of the preliminary hearing and trial—first to make an opening statement, first to put on witnesses, first to make a closing argument. But Mason couldn't stand going second. Sitting quietly while Patrick Ortiz did his this-defendant-is-so-guilty-why-bother-with-the-trial routine was worse than having a tooth pulled slowly.

"How about you, Mr. Mason?" the judge asked.

"Your Honor," Mason said, "I'm certain that Mr. Ortiz believes that all of his cases are cut-and-dried, that the police only arrest the guilty, and that we could save a lot of tax dollars if we just skipped all this trial stuff. Fortunately, the Founding Fathers decided not to leave it up to Mr. Ortiz, or me or you, to decide innocence or guilt in this case. The jury will make that decision. I'll save my opening statement for the trial."

Mason didn't want to admit that he had nothing to say at this point in the case except that the prosecuting attorney was taking orders from Ed Fiora to offer Blues a plea bargain. He could add that Amy White wanted Mason to find Jack Cullan's secret file on the mayor even though she assured him that it had nothing to do with the murder. He might mention that someone had tried to kill him after he refused to play ball with Ed Fiora. He could describe how Fiora had blackmailed Beth Harrell into trying to seduce him and that she had asked Mason to get back the blackmailer's blackmail so she could seduce him, for her own reasons. None of which, he would have to admit to Judge Pistone, he could prove any more than he could prove that Blues was innocent. So instead, Mason took a shot at Ortiz's understated arrogance and sat down.

"I would suggest that both counsels save their editorial comments for the press, except I'm imposing a gag order. No one connected with this case will discuss it in public outside of this courtroom. When we're done here, this case is going to be assigned to a Circuit Court judge. I don't want the first motion filed by the defendant to be one to move the case out of the county because there's been so much publicity the defendant can't get a fair trial. Now let's get to it. Mr. Ortiz, you may begin."

"Excuse me, Your Honor," Mason interrupted. He stood up slowly and held his hands up, underscoring his regret at delaying the proceedings again. "I'm certain you didn't intend to prejudge this case, but your comments suggest that you've already decided to bind the defendant over for trial. If that's so, I'm compelled to ask that this case be reassigned to another magistrate."

Judge Pistone looked up from the papers in front of him and glared at Mason. "The last time you were before me, Mr. Mason, you practically accused me of being pressured to deny your client bail. I invited you to prove such and you declined. Now you are suggesting that I have prejudged the case against your client. Tell me, is it your desire to be held in contempt by this court? If you are, I shall be happy to oblige you."

"Not at all, Your Honor," Mason answered. "I'm certain that you misspoke when you said a moment ago that this case was going to be assigned to a Circuit Court judge. That will only happen if you bind the defendant over for trial. You can't know until you hear the evidence whether you will make that decision. I didn't want to leave that impression on the record without bringing it to the court's attention. Perhaps you'd like the court reporter to read back your comment."

Mason knew that he was digging a deep hole for himself

with Judge Pistone. He also knew that it didn't matter because Pistone had already made up his mind. Just like Ortiz, Mason knew that he had more than one audience. The judge had just testified on behalf of Blues in the court of public opinion. Mason had given the press a different lead than one about Blues's guilt. They could now write a story about how Mason had trapped the judge with his own words, continuing Rachel Firestone's theme that Blues was getting the bum's rush. The judge wouldn't hold Mason in contempt since that would elevate Mason to martyr status for a wrongfully accused client. Instead, the judge would have to swallow hard.

Judge Pistone, known for his disinterested demeanor, was eye-popping mad at Mason, and gripped the edge of the bench as he fought to keep his self-control. He wouldn't risk asking the court reporter to read his comments aloud. "Thank you for bringing to my attention what was clearly an unintended and unfortunate choice of words. I assure you that I have the highest regard for the presumption of innocence. If you have any doubt on that score, you may request another judge. Is that your desire, Mr. Mason?"

"Not at all, Your Honor. As you said, let's get to it."

Mason knew that taunting Judge Pistone was a high-risk strategy. A defense attorney often made himself a lightning rod, taking hits from the court to deflect attention from his client. The strategy was a don't-confuse-me-with-the-facts ploy that meant one thing: The defense attorney didn't have dick. Mason took no comfort in his strategy as Ortiz ambled to the podium, a slightly rumpled, overweight everyman who knocked back a few brews on the weekend, watched sports, talked about women, and sent men to death row.

"Your Honor," he began, "I agree with Mr. Mason about one thing. It's not his job or mine to judge the facts. It is our job to tell you what the facts are. But don't make the mistake Mr. Mason did. You are the only judge of the facts at this point in this case. Before a jury is asked to decide the defendant's guilt, you are asked to decide whether there is reasonable cause to believe that a crime was committed and that the defendant committed it. If you find that there is probable cause to believe those things, then you must bind the defendant over for trial.

"Mr. Mason seized on an innocent misstatement by the court to suggest that you have prejudged this case, although he knows that you haven't and wouldn't. Mr. Mason has his own reasons for trying to keep our attention away from the facts, away from his client. When the state has finished presenting its evidence, listen closely to hear if Mr. Mason denies any of the facts we present to you. Listen to hear if he offers any other explanation for who shot Jack Cullan in the eye with a .38-caliber handgun. Listen to the silence from Mr. Mason because that's all you will hear.

"I told you that this case was cut-and-dried. Tell me if I'm wrong. Jack Cullan was found murdered on Monday, December tenth, by his housekeeper. He'd been shot to death. Mr. Mason won't deny that. The preceding Friday night, Mr. Cullan and Beth Harrell had been customers at a bar owned by the defendant called Blues on Broadway. Mr. Cullan and Ms. Harrell quarreled. The defendant intervened and fought with Mr. Cullan. Afterward, the defendant threatened Mr. Cullan with physical harm if he interfered with the defendant's liquor license or came back to his bar. Four witnesses, including Ms. Harrell, will testify at trial to the fight and the threat. Mr. Mason won't deny that.

"Blood and tissue belonging to the defendant were found under the fingernails of the murder victim. The defendant's fingerprints were found in the room in which Mr. Cullan died. The defendant has a history of violent conduct, including shooting to death an innocent and unarmed woman while he was a police officer. The defendant has no alibi. Mr. Mason won't deny any of that.

"There is more than enough evidence to bind the defendant over for trial on the charge of murder in the first degree. I call that a cut-and-dried case and make no apology for it. I wonder what Mr. Mason calls it."

Chapter Eighteen

At eleven o'clock that night, Mason was still sitting on the sofa in his office, staring at the notes he had written on the dry-erase board. Patrick Ortiz had presented his evidence in a smooth procession of well-prepared witnesses, finishing at five o'clock. Mason had not called anyone to testify.

Judge Pistone had said that he would deliberate in his chambers and announce his decision shortly. When he had returned fifteen minutes later with renewed pep, Mason had concluded that the judge had used the time to go the bathroom and have a cup of coffee. Resuming the bench, the judge had ordered that Blues stand trial on the charge of first-degree murder in the death of Jack Cullan and that Blues would continue to be held without bail. He had added that the case had been assigned for trial to Judge Vanessa Carter and that Judge Carter had set the case for trial beginning Monday morning, March 4.

True to form, Judge Pistone had kept his head down while

announcing his order. Blues had held his head up, eyes drilling the judge. Blues had remained impassive throughout the long day, occasionally passing Mason a handwritten note in response to a particular bit of testimony. When Dr. Terrence Dawson, chief of the forensics lab, had testified that Blues's fingerprint had been found in Cullan's study, Blues had reached over to Mason's legal pad and written *NO*, pressing hard enough with his pen to have cut through to the next sheet of paper.

Everyone in the courtroom had stood while the judge made his exit. The media had poured from the courtroom; the print reporters had raced to meet deadlines and the broadcasters had bolted for their live feeds from the courthouse steps. Leonard Campbell had clapped Patrick Ortiz and his assistants on their backs, straightened his jacket, and left, looking for the nearest microphone. Ortiz had packed his briefcase and shaken Mason's hand, telling Mason that he'd done a good job. It was the standard empty praise of an adversary who'd won the day, and Mason had grated as Ortiz had delivered the bromide.

Turning around, Mason had seen the three deputies surround Blues again while one of them put the handcuffs back on Blues's wrists. Mason had pressed into their circle and tapped his fists against Blues's balled hands.

"Today was their day, man," Mason had told him. "Tomorrow will be ours."

Blues nodded. "Get 'em," he had said, and left with his escort.

Mason had looked around the empty courtroom. On paper, no one could have found fault with what had happened there. The state had met its burden of proof. Even Mason had conceded that. No appellate court would overturn Judge Pistone's ruling, even though Mason was convinced the judge had decided the case before breakfast. The system had worked, except for one thing: Mason was certain that Blues was innocent. That realization had led him to another conclusion. He would have to find justice for Blues outside the courtroom.

Now, hours later, worn with fatigue and slightly buzzed from a dinner of Budweiser, Mason replayed the few points he'd scored during cross-examination of the prosecution's witnesses, looking for leads. Carl Zimmerman had testified first. He was an experienced witness, directing his answers to the judge, who sat upright in his chair, watching Ortiz and Zimmerman play catch with softball questions. Mason wasn't surprised that Judge Pistone had abandoned his head-down disinterest. Murder had that effect on people.

Ortiz had taken Zimmerman through each step of the investigation, beginning with the call he had received from the dispatcher about a hysterical woman claiming to have found her employer shot to death. The woman turned out to have been Norma Hawkins, the housekeeper. Mason had started his cross-examination with that description.

"Norma Hawkins told the dispatcher that Mr. Cullan had been shot to death. Is that correct, Detective?" Mason had asked.

"Yes, sir," Zimmerman had answered.

"The body was found facedown and hadn't been moved when you arrived at the scene, correct?"

"That's right. The uniformed officers who arrived at the scene first secured the area. The housekeeper said that she hadn't touched anything in the study."

"No gun, bullets, or shell casings were found at the scene, correct?"

"Correct."

"In fact, when you arrived at the scene, you didn't see anything that told you Mr. Cullan had been shot. Isn't that correct, Detective?"

Zimmerman had stiffened as he saw the high hard pitch coming. "I suppose that's correct, Mr. Mason. But, there's no question that Mr. Cullan had been shot."

"Yet, somehow, Norma Hawkins knew that Mr. Cullan had been shot. That's what she told the dispatcher. True?"

"Well," Zimmerman had said, stalling for a better answer than the one he had, "I don't know what she told the dispatcher. I could have heard him wrong."

"There is another explanation, isn't there, Detective?"

"What's that, Mr. Mason?"

"Norma Hawkins shot Mr. Cullan."

"Objection!" Patrick Ortiz had said. "The question calls for speculation. There is no evidence that Norma Hawkins committed this crime. She's an innocent woman who doesn't deserve to be smeared by Mr. Mason."

"The police and the prosecution rushed to judgment in this case," Mason had shot back. "They picked their suspect at the beginning and disregarded any other possibilities."

"Sustained, unless you've got better evidence than that," Judge Pistone had said. Mason didn't.

Norma Hawkins was the next witness. She was a slightly built white woman in her late thirties whose rough hands and sloped shoulders testified to the hard work she did and the hard life she led. Norma spoke slowly and softly, in the upstairs-downstairs tradition of domestic help, describing her daily routine at Jack Cullan's house. Then Ortiz asked her about finding the body.

"What happened when you came to work on Monday morning, December tenth?"

Norma had leaned forward in the witness box and clutched the hem of her dress. "Well, it was like I told the detectives. The alarm wasn't on, so I figured Mr. Cullan was still home. He usually wasn't there when I got to work, so I'd have to turn off the alarm. He gave me the code 'cause he knew he could trust me, you know. I been cleaning people's houses since I was fifteen. Everybody gives me their alarm codes. I never had any trouble till that morning.''

"What did you find when you went inside the house?" Ortiz asked.

"First thing I noticed was that it was freezing in that house. I kept my coat on, it was so cold. I went looking for Mr. Cullan to find out why the furnace wasn't working, and I found him lying facedown on the floor in his study. I turned him over and could see that he was dead. I called 911.''

"Did you know that he'd been shot?"

"I saw blood. I didn't know what else to think.''

Ortiz had placed the enlarged photograph of Jack Cullan's body on an easel. Cullan was lying facedown in the photograph, a dark pool of blood seeping around his head and out into the carpet.

"Does this photograph accurately depict what you saw when you entered the study?" Ortiz asked her.

Norma trembled and turned away, nodding her head. "He was a good man, always treated me fair.''

"No further questions," Ortiz said as he sat down, leaving the photograph on the easel. The buzz from the spectators was like crickets on a summer night.

Norma had explained why she had assumed that Cullan had been shot, and Mason knew he wouldn't get anywhere chasing the slim chance she had killed Cullan. Instead, he walked to the easel, took the photograph, and leaned it, facedown, against the front of the jury box. Ortiz had used it for the press, not Norma Hawkins. Mason waited for Norma to gather herself before probing gently on cross-examination about minor matters, more for the purpose of blunting the emotional impact of the photograph than anything else. Norma admitted that Cullan often forgot to set the alarm. It was a small thing, but Mason knew that credibility was built on a foundation of small things. The more he could chip away at it, the more likely it would crumble.

Pete Kirby, resplendent in a dark green suit and cranberry vest, described the fight in the bar. When he quoted Blues's threatening to tear Cullan's head off and stuff it up his ass, a ripple of laughter cut through the audience, causing Judge Pistone's bailiff to rise and glare the offenders into silence. Kirby admitted on cross-examination that he hadn't taken Blues's threat seriously.

"Yeah, it was jive," Kirby said. "Except with Blues, it was real serious jive. The man was making a very heavy point."

Dr. Terrence Dawson, the forensics examiner, was the last witness. He was a thin man with a sharply angular face who had risen through the ranks of the police laboratory over twenty years to become the director of forensic science. He explained on direct examination how he had matched Blues's blood and tissue samples to those found under Cullan's fingernails, and how he had matched Blues's fingerprints to one that had been lifted from the corner of the desk in Jack Cullan's study.

Mason had not had time to pore over the technical details of Dr. Dawson's report, or to consult with any experts who might poke holes in his analysis. That would have to wait for the trial.

"Dr. Dawson, I assume that other fingerprints were found at the scene besides the ones you claim belonged to Mr. Bluestone?" Mason asked him.

"Yes. That's quite common."

"I'm certain that it is," Mason agreed. "Whose prints did you find?"

"The victim's and the housekeeper's, of course."

"Anyone else's?"

Dr. Dawson glanced at Patrick Ortiz. Mason also looked at Ortiz, who had suddenly become interested in a stack of papers on his table.

"There were a number of fingerprints found throughout the house; most of them were too smudged or incomplete for identification," he said after Ortiz failed to help him by objecting to Mason's question.

"But not all of them, right, Doctor?"

"That's correct. We were able to identify fingerprints belonging to Ed Fiora and Beth Harrell. We matched them with their fingerprints on file with the Missouri Gaming Commission."

"Where in Mr. Cullan's house were those fingerprints found?"

"Mr. Fiora's fingerprints were found in the kitchen. Ms. Harrell's fingerprints were found on the headboard of the bed in Mr. Cullan's bedroom."

His answer made Mason feel like a boxer wearing cement shoes. Patrick Ortiz had spent the entire day dancing around him, landing jabs to his midsection and uppercuts to his chin. Mason had been unable to get out of his way. Dr. Dawson had sucker punched him without knowing it. The press would draw every salacious inference possible about the relationship between Jack Cullan and Beth Harrell. Mason couldn't blame them. The image of Beth in Cullan's bedroom crowded his own memory of the embrace they had shared. He didn't have room for both.

The assignment of Blues's case to Judge Carter had been the last kidney punch of the day. Judge Carter, a former prosecutor, was a conservative Republican with a reputation for harsh treatment of criminal defendants, an African-American woman with ambitions to become a federal judge. Mason was worried that she would use Blues's case as a stepping-stone.

Mason studied the dry-erase board. In the last three weeks it had become a jumbled patchwork of lawyer's graffiti. He drew red circles around the key words and phrases—*Cullan's secret files—pictures of Beth—blackmail by Fiora—Blues' fingerprints—Harry and Blues—why kill me?* He was convinced that the identity of the killer lay within those scraps. The last of them, the question about whether he himself would live or die, shook him more than he cared to admit. Maybe it was the beer. Maybe it was the late hour, or maybe it was just that he was truly alone this time.

Mason went down the hall to Blues's office, using the key to his own office to get in. Blues had told Mason, when he signed the lease, that the locks on their two offices used the same key, and had asked Mason whether he wanted a new lock. Mason had declined, taking comfort in the connection.

Blues's office was furnished in strictly utilitarian metal—bookshelves, file cabinet, and desk. The floor was bare hardwood and the walls were decorated with a calendar. The only concession to emotion was the digital electric piano that sat against one wall. When Blues played, it was like decorating the room with a bucket of rainbow paint.

Mason closed the door behind him and turned on the ceiling light. He pushed the piano away from the wall, and used another key Blues had given him to open a small safe hidden in the floor. As he knelt on the floor, his back blocked the light and cast a deep shadow into the safe. He lingered over the contents of the safe, his hands sweating as he fought with himself. Shivering at the too recent memory of the river's cold grip, he reached into the safe and picked up the gun Blues had given him a little over a year ago.

"It's a .44-caliber semiautomatic with a nine-shot magazine," Blues had told him. "Fits in a holster that goes in the middle of your back. Wear a jacket or a loose shirt over it and no one will notice.''

Missouri had joined the states that had made it legal to carry a concealed weapon. Mason had barely survived the death of his old law firm and, along the way, had shot a hired killer named Jimmie Camaya who was supposed to have added Mason to the law firm's obituary list. Camaya had been arrested, but later escaped. Blues had convinced Mason that he should carry the gun for his own protection. Mason had reluctantly agreed, and Blues had taught him how to handle the gun. After a few months, Mason had returned the gun to Blues.

"I'm not going to spend the rest of my life walking around waiting to shoot it out with someone who's probably forgotten all about me. I'm a lawyer, not a gunslinger.''

"And this isn't Dodge City," Blues had answered. "It's Kansas City, but I'll tell you something, Lou. You've got a real talent for pissing off people who don't know the difference. I'll keep the gun for you. My money says you're going to need it sooner or later.''

Now, alone in his office with his gun and holster sitting on his desk, he wished he had a corner man to patch him up, rub him down, and shove him back into the ring when the bell rang for the next round. Blues was his corner man and Mason needed him. Bone-weary, Mason lay down on his sofa and let it wrap its arms around him.

Chapter Nineteen

Mason awoke to find his aunt Claire sitting in one of the chairs next to the sofa. She was reading the newspaper, and sipping coffee from a stainless-steel mug. The coffee's aroma was strong enough to wake the dead.

"You didn't answer your phone at home last night or this morning, so I thought I might find you here," she said.

Mason sat up slowly, running his tongue over his teeth to brush away the sour remnants of the previous night. Mason enjoyed an hour or two spent sleeping on a sofa while pretending to watch a football game on a dreary winter day. It was time well spent, especially if the Kansas City Chiefs were slogging their way through another mediocre season. Sleeping the entire night on the sofa in his office while doing battle with his demons was worse than no sleep at all. Mason stretched out his arms, and legs in a spread-eagle salute, and then let his limbs flop back onto the sofa, resuming his torso's flaccid posture. He felt trampled.

"You didn't consider the possibility that some beautiful woman had taken me home to comfort her?" Mason asked. He pushed himself off the sofa, stepped around Claire, and stumbled toward the dry-erase board.

"Have you looked in the mirror?" she answered. "Anyone who picked you up would take you to the nearest shelter. Make that the nearest animal shelter. And don't bother with the board. I've been here long enough to read it, and the newspaper."

Mason changed course for the refrigerator next to his desk. He was surprised to find a bottle of orange juice.

Without looking up from her newspaper, Claire said, "You're welcome. By the way, the next time you decide to sleep in your office, lock the door, and don't leave a gun sitting on your desk. Put it under your pillow like all the other action heroes. Just don't shoot yourself in your sleep. That would be pathetic."

Mason settled into his desk chair, shook the bottle of orange juice, opened it, and gulped half of it before taking a breath.

"Any more advice?" he asked her.

"Sorry, I'm fresh out."

Claire read the newspaper, and Mason looked out the window, his back to her. His window faced west, and he could see the morning sun glancing brightly off the windows on the building across the street. The sun was still in the east, behind his building, a cold reminder that his was not the sunny side of the street.

"So," Claire said with as much neutrality as she could muster, "someone is trying to kill you again. That's why you have a gun. Who is it this time?"

She folded the newspaper, slapped it against her thighs to smooth out any wrinkles, and dropped it on the table in front of the sofa. The headline shouted back at her EX-COP

BOUND OVER FOR MURDER. Mason swiveled around in his chair, drained the last of his orange juice, and banked the empty bottle off the wall, and into the wastebasket.

"Don't know," Mason answered.

Mason had often been amazed at his aunt's capacity to listen to the most outrageous stories of abuse told to her by her clients without betraying a hint of her own outrage. She had explained to Mason that her clients had enough emotion invested in their problems without seeing their lawyer lit up as well. He was glad that she employed the same detached interest as he told her about his New Year's Eve swim in the Missouri River.

"You could talk to Harry," she offered when he'd finished.

"Not this time," he told her. "You were right. It's too complicated."

"Can I help?"

Mason considered her offer. His love for her was as unconditional as hers was for him. She had been his anchor, his reality check. She had never waited for him to ask for her advice or help. She had given it whether he wanted it or not. That she had come to check on him, not demanded that he call Harry, not called Harry herself, and only gently berated him, underscored how delicate the situation was.

"There's too much going on here that I don't understand, and I don't want to be the last one to figure it out," he said. "The key players are connected as if they've been inbred. You could fill in one branch of the family tree for me. Tell me what happened between Harry and Blues."

"Why is that so important?" she asked.

"Harry thinks Blues got away with murder six years ago. He's using this case as payback. I think somebody knows that, and is using Harry to make sure Blues is convicted. I can't go to Harry unless I know what happened."

Claire studied the headline in the newspaper. It was a silent sound bite, incapable of telling the whole story. Yet it was enough for most people, and all that many would read or remember.

"Harry and Blues had been partners for a couple of years," she began. "Harry had taught Blues at the Academy, helped him along when he first got on the street, and recommended him for detective when Blues took the exam. Harry always said that Blues had the best instincts of any detective he'd ever seen, but that he also had one of the worst weaknesses."

"He used violence too easily?" Mason asked.

"It wasn't just that," Claire answered. "The violence came too easily to Blues. He didn't get worked up or enraged. He just did it, and went on. Harry didn't know why. He worried that Blues had a dead spot that made it too easy to kill. It scared Harry because he didn't want Blues to get it wrong. Someone would die."

"So why didn't Harry wash him out at the Academy? Why promote his career, and take him on as his partner?"

"I met Harry for the first time at the Nelson Art Gallery. He was sitting on a bench in the Chinese Temple in front of the statue of the Water and Moon Bodhisattva. The Bodhisattva was a Buddhist god that was supposed to protect the faithful from catastrophe. That's what Harry does. That's why he volunteered to go to Vietnam. That's why he became a cop. That's why he took Blues as his partner. He'd seen and done some pretty awful things in Vietnam. Things he barely talked about; just said that they had happened. He'd seen men who had that dead spot, and he thought he could keep it from happening to Blues."

"That doesn't explain what happened with the shooting."

"It was a drug bust. They had an informant who claimed that some Colombians had brought in a substantial quantity of cocaine, and were setting up shop on the East Side. Blues was the first one through the door of the apartment. The Colombians were waiting for them. Blues and Harry both would have been dead if they hadn't been wearing Kevlar vests. Two of the Colombians were killed.''

"I remember when it happened. Harry wouldn't talk about it, but it was all over the newspaper. The woman Blues shot was a prostitute who had a gun," Mason said.

"She was in the back of the apartment. Blues went room to room. He heard a noise. It was Harry's nightmare come true. Blues said he thought the girl had a gun, but she didn't, though she wasn't innocent either."

"Who was she?"

"She wasn't a prostitute. She was the daughter of a very wealthy man who'd used her father's money as seed capital for her drug business. She had hired the Colombians to bring in the cocaine. The father settled for Blues's badge rather than have the story made public. And there was some question about whether the father knew where his money was going."

"That's a pretty tough story to cover up."

"Not if your lawyer was Jack Cullan."

Mason came out of his chair. "Harry and Blues went along with the cover-up?"

"They didn't know. She didn't have any ID on her. Later, Harry and Blues were fed the prostitute story. The Internal Affairs investigation was kept quiet. Blues was given a choice to resign or be prosecuted. It was a bluff that worked because no one wanted to hang the department's dirty laundry in public, including Harry and Blues. Blues took the deal."

"How do you know what happened if Harry and Blues don't know?"

Claire gathered her coat, finished her coffee, and stood

up, facing Mason. "I represented the wife when she divorced her husband six months later. He'd told her what had happened, and she couldn't spend another moment under his roof. She told me."

"What she told you was confidential. Why are you telling me?"

"The purpose of the attorney-client privilege is to protect the client. My client committed suicide last month. The privilege didn't do her much good."

"Did you tell Harry?"

"Yes. I told him this morning. I should have told both of you sooner. I'm sorry."

"What did Harry say when you told him?"

"He thinks Blues found out that Jack Cullan had cost him his badge and had been waiting for a chance to get even. He thinks Blues used the incident at the bar with Beth Harrell as cover."

"That makes no sense. Blues has been charged with the murder, not Beth."

"Harry says that Blues got careless when he left a fingerprint in Cullan's study. Otherwise, Beth Harrell would have been the number-one suspect. Harry thinks Blues is using you to get him off. Harry says that you'll try to convince the jury that Beth Harrell killed Cullan."

"That's a hell of a risk for Blues to take."

"Harry says that a man with a dead spot takes risks no one else would consider."

"Does Harry know that you've told me all of this?"

"He asked me to tell you. He's afraid that Blues will take you down with him. He wants you to convince Blues to take a plea."

"I'm Blues's lawyer, not his coconspirator. How can Blues take me anywhere except to the poorhouse when he doesn't pay my fee?"

Claire walked over to Mason's board, picked up the black marker, and drew a large circle around Mason's question *why kill me?* "Someone knows the answer to that question, Lou. Don't take too long to find out."

Chapter Twenty

Mason decided it was time to connect the dots instead of waiting for someone else to draw the picture for him. He'd spent the last three weeks scrambling to get ready for the preliminary hearing even though the outcome was a foregone conclusion. The trial was in sixty days, and he would have to use that time to make something happen.

Getting Blues released on bail was one thing he had to make happen. He called Judge Carter's chambers to request a bail hearing. He was surprised when the judge's secretary informed him that Judge Carter was sending out an order that day setting a hearing for the following Monday, January 7, at eight o'clock. Shortly after he hung up, his fax machine rang and whirred as the judge's order arrived. He was reading the order when Mickey Shanahan knocked at his open door.

"This is not a good look for you, Lou," Mickey told him. "You've got to be perma-pressed and lightly starched, wrinkle-free, know what I mean, man? No worries. Everything is cool. That's what the people expect. This I-spent-the-night-in-a-Dumpster look isn't going to cut it. Listen to me. It's all about image.''

"Turn around," Mason told him. Mickey hesitated. "Turn around now," Mason repeated.

Mickey saw the gun on Mason's desk, blanched, and did a quick pivot. "I'm just trying to help, for chrissakes. That's no reason to go ballistic, man.''

Mason walked over to the dry-erase board and closed the cabinet doors. He was tired of people walking in and reading his mind.

Returning to his desk, he picked up the gun, balanced it in his palm, and shoved it into the holster. It felt like a prop, not a part of him. He couldn't decide whether to put it away or put it on. The fear he'd felt the night before had receded as he hid the attempt on his life behind the closed cabinet doors. He shook his head at the image of himself as a heat-packing action hero. Carrying a concealed weapon was the road to Palookaville, the punch line to a bad joke. He put the gun in a desk drawer, slamming the drawer shut loudly enough to make Mickey jitterbug in the doorway.

"For chrissakes," Mickey protested again. "Give a guy some warning that you're gonna make him piss his pants for saying hello.''

"At ease," Mason told him. "About face.''

Mickey looked cautiously over his shoulder at Mason, taking care to look for the gun, before turning completely around. "Hey, you still look like shit. You know that, man. That's not good, not good," he added, warming back up.

"What do you know about the Internet?" Mason asked him.

Mickey brightened as if he'd just added a thousand giga-bytes to his game. "That's where it's happening, Lou. A

Web site is just what you guys need. I can have it up for you by the end of the day.''

"I don't want a Web site, Mickey. I want research on Ed Fiora. Every word ever printed. Can you do that?''

Mickey locked his fingers together and stretched his arms out. "My six-year-old nephew can do that in his sleep. I can do better than that.''

"How much better?''

"Asset search, bank accounts, anything you want. There are no secrets anymore. Everyone's life is floating in cyberspace, waiting to be bought or sold.''

"Use my computer,'' Mason told him as he wrote his password on a Post-It note. "Don't look at my board or I'll break both your legs above the knee.''

"Does this mean I'm on the team?'' Mickey asked.

Mason thought for a moment, hoping he wasn't making the wrong choice for Mickey. "Sure,'' he told him.

"Do I get a T-shirt?'' Mickey asked.

"Only if we win,'' Mason said.

A shower and a shave later, Mason parked his car on the curb in front of the old People's Savings & Loan Building at Twentieth and Main. The bank had owned the six-story building, occupying the first floor, until it went under during the thrift crisis in the 1990s. Jack Cullan, whose office had been on the second floor for twenty-five years, had bought the building from the government.

The former S&L space was now occupied by a twenty-four-hour copying company, and the other floors were Class "C" office space. Class "A" space could be had in the newest office towers downtown, on the Plaza, or in the suburbs. Class "B" space was a generation older, but still offered decent amenities and a respectable letterhead for tenants. Class "C" was space reserved for those tenants who didn't care or couldn't afford to care about their address as long as the lights worked and they could pay the rent.

Mason climbed the stairs to the second floor and found the door to Cullan's office. Many law firms spent lavishly on impressive entrances to their offices with carefully designed logos, nameplates, and eye-catching art. Mason knew of one local firm whose lobby had been used to film scenes for a cable movie based on a wildly popular legal thriller. Another firm bragged to its clients that the paneling in its office had been made from a rare tree found only in the Amazon rain forest. As Mason reached for the handle to Cullan's plain oak door, he appreciated the simple inscription that had been painted on it years before—JACK CULLAN, ATTORNEY. Stepping inside, he knew that Cullan's simple tastes were the only things the two of them had in common.

Shirley Parker looked up from her desk as Mason closed the door behind him. She had a buoyant, upswept hairstyle that had been fashionable decades ago, but was now a silvery-blue-tinted artifact. Though she was working for a dead man whose clients were unlikely to have appointments, she was immaculately dressed in a high-throated, deep-navy dress accented with a modest string of pearls. Her makeup was robust, adding an unnatural rose to her cheeks. She was a stout woman with stiff posture and disbelieving eyes, going through the motions because she didn't know what else to do.

"Yes, may I help you?" she asked.

"My name is Lou Mason," he said, as if that would be explanation enough.

"My name is Shirley Parker. I'm Mr. Cullan's secretary," she replied, not offering any more information than he had provided.

Mason wasn't certain where to start. Shirley had the look

of a woman who had been the secretary for the same man for so many years, it was almost as if they were married. She would have known Cullan's secrets, helped keep them, and wouldn't easily surrender a single one.

"I'm the attorney for Wilson Bluestone."

"Yes. I know who you are." Her face gave no hint whether she cared who he was, or whether she resented him as she must have hated his client.

"I'm sorry for your loss," Mason offered. It was a clumsy gesture, and Mason regretted he hadn't been more sincere, though Shirley accepted it graciously.

"That's very kind of you."

Mason looked around, nodding. The furniture in the outer office was nearly as old as he was, though it had fewer nicks and scratches. Framed prints from a Monet exhibit hung on the walls. A stack of unread magazines sat on a corner table at the junction of a short couch and a chair.

"It must be difficult closing up a law practice under these circumstances," Mason said. "I imagine you've been going nuts trying to get clients placed with new lawyers, files transferred, and all those other things."

"Yes," was all she said in a neutral tone, not agreeing or disagreeing.

There were only a handful of papers on Shirley's desk, no more than would have come in the mail on an ordinary day. Her computer screen was on CNN's home page. The phone hadn't rung since Mason had arrived. Looking around again, Mason realized that there were no storage cabinets, no places to keep the files of clients who needed new lawyers, or the secret files about people who didn't know they needed a lawyer in the first place. Maybe, he thought, Shirley had already transferred the clients and their files, and was just coming in each day to open the mail until there was no more mail.

"It looks like you've pretty much cleaned things up. You must have already shipped out the client files," Mason said.

Shirley didn't respond. She simply sat back in her chair and waited for Mason to say something that warranted another polite acknowledgment.

Mason nodded some more as he opened the door to Cullan's private office. He was through the door before Shirley Parker could try to stop him.

"You can't go in there," she said, and was on his heels before he could turn on the light.

Cullan's office faced west, just as Mason's did, though now the sun was up far enough to light the office. Dust mites floated lazily in the shafts of sunlight, the only occupants of the office. Mason was struck by the similarity between the layout of his office and Cullan's. They both had oversize sofas. A pair of shoes and a wadded dress shirt had been abandoned beneath Cullan's, suggesting to Mason that Cullan had spent more than a few nights on the sofa. Cullan also had a refrigerator. The office was cluttered, undisturbed from the last time Cullan had left it. Papers were scattered on his desk, though Mason was confident that Shirley had removed anything confidential, leaving the rest in the empty hope that Cullan would return. The walls were covered with framed photographs of Cullan shaking hands with dignitaries and celebrities from Harry Truman to George W. Bush, from Elvis Presley to Elton John.

Shirley was standing in the doorway, her arms folded across her chest. Mason took a step toward her. She didn't back up as he flicked on the light switch by her shoulder and began a tour of Cullan's photographic souvenirs.

"Where are they, Shirley?" Mason asked.

"Where are what?"

"Your boss's secret files. The dirty pictures and other trash he collected all these years. Now don't tell me you didn't know about that, Shirley. How long did you work for Jack? Twenty years, thirty years? You had to know about the files and you had to know where he kept them.''

''I'll have to ask you to leave, Mr. Mason.''

''Of course you do, Shirley. That's your job even though your boss isn't here to tell you. Maybe you didn't know what he was up to. Maybe he liked you well enough not to make you an accessory to blackmail, extortion, and racketeering. All things considered, you'd be better off helping me now than answering all these questions in court, under oath.''

''I don't know what you're talking about, Mr. Mason. Please leave now.''

Mason stopped in front of a black-and-white photograph of an old man and a young boy. They were shaking hands in front of a barbershop, the barber's pole framed between their outstretched hands.

''Who's that?'' Mason asked.

Shirley expelled an exasperated sigh. ''I'm going to call the police if you don't leave now.''

Mason raised his hands in protest. ''Okay, I'm convinced. Just tell me who's in the picture and I'll leave. That can't be a state secret.''

''Very well,'' she said. ''The young boy is Mr. Cullan. The other gentleman is Tom Pendergast. Now please leave.''

''No kidding,'' Mason said, taking another look at the photograph. ''When was this taken? Last question, I promise.''

''I'll tell you on your way out,'' Shirley said, and turned off the light. She followed Mason out of Cullan's office, locked the door behind them, and ushered him out into the hallway. ''Nineteen forty-five,'' she said, and slammed the outer door tightly shut.

* * *

Mason stepped out onto the sidewalk and looked back up at the window to Cullan's office. For an instant, he thought he saw Shirley Parker lingering in the shadows, then dismissed the image as a trick of the sun against the glass and his own creeping paranoia. Sitting in his car, he turned on the engine and began a U-turn to go back south on Main. As he did so, he had a head-on view of the building across the street from Cullan's office. A barber pole was bolted to the wall of 2010 Main Street. The barbershop, and the rest of the block, was vacant, but Mason suddenly remembered it from the stories told him by his grandfather.

Tom Pendergast had run Kansas City with a velvet hammer Cullan must have envied. Mason's grandfather, Mike, had gotten his start in the wrecking business when Pendergast had given his blessing to his grandfather's plan to salvage the scrap from the construction of Bagnel Dam at the Lake of the Ozarks and sell it. Afterward, his grandfather had gone to Pendergast's office to pay his respects and a cut of the profits to Pendergast. Pendergast had accepted the gratitude but not the cash, and Mason's grandfather had been on his way. Mason's grandfather had always told his grandson how strange it was that such a powerful man who could have had an office bigger than the president's chose to do business from an office above a barbershop on Main Street.

By 1945, when the picture had been taken, Pendergast had been released from jail and his organization lay in ruins. Maybe the young Jack Cullan didn't know or care about Pendergast's background. Maybe he did and respected Pendergast for coming back to his old turf. Maybe it was pure coincidence that Cullan had shaken hands that day with the man whose career he would emulate. Mason didn't believe in coincidences or the ability of people to change their fundamental nature. Cullan's picture reminded Mason of the photograph of a youthful Bill Clinton shaking hands with his idol, President John Kennedy. He wondered whether people picked the footsteps they followed, or whether the path was already laid out.

There was a small diner, another relic from pre-fast-food times, a block south on Main. It was the last building on the east side of the street and offered a handful of parking spaces in a lot on the south side of the building. Mason pulled into the parking lot and called Mickey Shanahan from his cell phone.

"Law offices of Lou Mason. To whom may I direct your call?" Mickey said.

"Are you auditioning for a job as a receptionist too?" Mason asked.

"No job too small, no duty too great. Pay me soon, it's been a week since I ate," Mickey recited.

"I'm not surprised. Your shtick is from hunger," Mason replied. "While you're cruising the Internet, go to the county's Web site and check property ownership records for 2010 Main. In fact, check the ownership records for that entire block. The west side of Main between Twentieth and Twenty-first. Call me back on my cell phone," Mason said, and gave him the number.

Mason took his phone and went inside the diner, noting its name for the first time. The Egg House Diner was a twenty-four-hour restaurant with a counter that seated eight and a row of booths along the front window, none of which were occupied when Mason sat down shortly before noon. A man of indeterminate age, wearing layers of soiled clothing and a strong odor, sat at the counter, stirring a cup of coffee. A large, black plastic bag, stuffed to its limit, lay on the floor at his feet. The booths were empty. Mason knew that a diner that was dead at lunch was not living off its reputation for fine food.

He chose a booth that gave him a clear view of the barbershop, and picked up a menu that had more stains than entrées. A few moments later, a flat-faced woman with dull eyes and thin hair, wearing a lime-green-and-white-striped waitress uniform, brought him a glass of water and took his order for a turkey sandwich. He'd taken his first bite when his cell phone rang. Mason's caller ID displayed his office phone number.

"What do you have for me, Mickey?" Mason asked.

"The whole block is owned by New Century Redevelopment Corporation except for 2010 Main. Shirley Parker owns that building. Her name mean anything to you?"

"It means everything," Mason answered. "I'll probably be out the rest of the day, but you can reach me on my cell phone."

Mason spent the rest of the afternoon in the booth at the Egg House Diner. The man sitting at the counter did the same. The waitress, apparently used to customers who spent little, talked less, and stayed forever, left him alone. He watched the traffic on Main Street, waiting for Shirley Parker to jaywalk from the People's Savings Building to the barbershop across the street.

Mason wasn't good at sitting and waiting. He lacked the patience for a stakeout and wasn't certain whether sitting in a restaurant qualified for that description. He figured a real stakeout meant sitting in a dark car, drinking cold coffee, peeing in a bottle, and scrunching down in the front seat whenever someone drove by. He was just killing time in a dumpy diner, kept company by people who had no place else to go.

After a while, he retrieved a yellow legal pad from his car and tried to reproduce the notes from his dry-erase board.

He wrote the names and the questions again, adding order and precision to the notes without finding any new answers. He drummed his pen against the pad until the vagrant at the counter silenced him with an annoyed look. No one else came into the diner. At three o'clock, Mason ordered a slice of apple pie and a cup of coffee to be polite. He picked at the pie and stirred the coffee, then told the waitress to give it to his counter companion. The man gave him another annoyed look, but didn't send the snack back to Mason's booth.

By five o'clock, clouds had moved in, hastening the transition from dusk to dark. Headlights blinked on, slicing the gloom on Main Street as people began making their way home. As if on cue, the man at the counter grunted at the waitress, hoisted his plastic bag over his shoulder, and left, giving Mason a final silent stab on his way out the door.

A pair of city buses, one northbound, the other southbound, stopped at the corner of Twentieth and Main, momentarily blocking his view. When the buses pulled away, he saw Shirley Parker jostling the lock on the door to the building that housed the barbershop. He waited until she was inside before leaving the diner, trying to remember when he'd had his last haircut.

Chapter
Twenty-one

The door opened into a long, dark, narrow hallway that led to the back of the building. Bare wooden stairs that led down from the second floor nearly to the entrance further narrowed the passage to the rear.

Another door to Mason's right would have opened into the barbershop had the door not been lying on its side, propped against the wall as an afterthought. The shop was nearly empty, having been looted years before. An ancient barber's chair planted in the center of the floor, and stretched into the reclining position used to wash and shave, was the last relic of the brisk trade in grooming and gossip that had once flourished there. Even the sink the barber had used had been uprooted. Steel bars had been bolted to the storefront window frame; a stark concession to the uneasy plight of an abandoned building made too late to save anything but memories.

A naked lightbulb at the top of the stairs cast uneasy

shadows at Mason's feet. He could hear Shirley Parker's shoes scraping overhead against the floor of Tom Pendergast's old office.

Mason had spent the afternoon betting that Jack Cullan had hidden his secret files in Pendergast's office. He was certain that Cullan couldn't have resisted the delicious irony of using his hero's headquarters as his own hideaway. Putting the ownership of the building in Shirley Parker's name was a thin dodge, arrogance mistaken for cleverness—a common weakness of bad guys. Mason was certain that Superman never would have put Jimmy Olson's name on the deed to the Fortress of Solitude.

Mason had also bet that Shirley Parker would make the short trip across the street to be certain that the files were undisturbed. He hoped that his questions had unnerved her, compelling her to conduct her own stakeout of the barbershop from the vantage of Cullan's office just to confirm that Mason didn't try to break in and steal the files. Having spent her day watching the barbershop, she wouldn't be able to resist the compulsion to make sure he hadn't somehow sneaked past her.

Breaking, and entering was a Class D felony, not an upward career move for most lawyers. As he walked from the diner to the barbershop, Mason convinced himself that he was neither breaking nor entering; he was simply making a business visit knowing that Shirley was inside. Besides, he had no intent to commit any crime on the premises, at least not at that moment. He just wanted to talk with Shirley Parker.

Mason's careful rationalization evaporated along with his chilled breath the moment he stepped inside. Shirley Parker had refused to answer his questions in Cullan's office during normal business hours. Popping up like the Pillsbury Doughboy in Pendergast's office after hours wouldn't loosen her tongue. She would make good on her threat to call the police, and the files, if they were upstairs, would disappear overnight.

Mason had a sudden insight into the curious reasoning that frequently landed his clients in jail. It was a mix of overstated need, selfish justification, and unfounded optimism that he could pull off the plan that he had just conceived in a larcenous epiphany. He walked to the end of the hallway, confident that it really was a good idea to hide there until Shirley left the building, then search Pendergast's office until he found the files. Tomorrow morning, he would serve Shirley with a subpoena for the files, and then sit back and watch Patrick Ortiz marvel at his resourcefulness.

His eyes adjusted to the dark as he felt his way along the hallway, soon coming to the backside of the stairway, where he found a door that he assumed led to the basement. Taking care not to aggravate squeaky hinges, he gently nursed the handle until he felt it release, then eased the door open just enough to slip through. Probing the black space with one foot, he confirmed his guess about a basement and stepped down onto the first stair, pulling the door closed behind him. He was sweating inside his jacket in spite of the cold that crept up the stairs from the unheated basement.

Twenty minutes passed, made longer and slower by the stiffness that seeped from his neck downward and his feet upward, merging into an electrified knot in the small of his back. The sound of Shirley's footsteps coming down the stairs drowned out the protests his body was filing with his brain. He opened the basement door a crack to make certain he would hear the front door opening and closing. He took comfort in Shirley's unhurried gait and unbroken march down the stairs and out the door. She didn't hesitate, as she would have if she had heard or sensed his presence.

Mason waited another five minutes after Shirley left

before heading upstairs. Shirley had turned off the light at the top of the stairs, and Mason didn't want to take the chance that she was watching from across the street for a light to come on. The glow from the streetlight and passing headlights scarcely permeated the frame of the front door, leaving him to feel his way along the wall with his hands. If he could have seen his feet, he would have kicked himself for having failed to bring a flashlight.

Still using his hands as his eyes, Mason located the door to Pendergast's office and was relieved that Shirley had left it unlocked. The office was darker even than the stairwell, as if it had been sealed. Recalling that there was a double window overlooking Main Street, and that he'd seen blinds on that window when he'd looked up from his car, Mason felt his way to the street side of the room to peek through the blinds. When his fingers found smooth drywall all along that surface, he became disoriented, so uncertain of direction that he circled the room twice as his mouth dried up in a blind man's panic.

On his second pass, just beyond the door, his knuckles brushed against a switch, flicking it on and blinding himself a second time, though with light rather than darkness. He leaned against the wall, squinting until his pupils stopped dilating. The double window had been covered, the blinds still in place, so that the outside world would see the window, unchanged and unopened—but a window nonetheless. Inside, the light was captive, unable to illuminate the secrets behind the walls.

The room was empty. Mason imagined Pendergast sitting behind a desk, dispensing favors or broken legs, as the moment required. He envisioned a couple of overfed cronies in snap-brimmed fedoras, smoking sour cigars, giving witness and protection to Pendergast's patronage practice. He thought of his grandfather, genuflecting with a humble

"Thank you, Mr. Pendergast." There were no reminders of those times, no photographs on the walls, not even outlines in the dust on the floor where the furniture once sat.

There was a sliding panel that had been built into the wall Mason guessed would have been behind Pendergast's desk. It was the wall that would have afforded Pendergast a straight-on view of each supplicant or sucker who crossed his threshold. A circular groove had been cut at one end of the panel into a finger hold with which to pull the panel open. A lock had been added directly above the groove. Mason tried it without success; not surprised when it didn't yield.

There were no lock picks or crowbars lying on the floor, so Mason used his shoulder to loosen the lock. It gave on the third try, splintering the wood that housed the bolt. He shoved the panel back along its track and stepped into a walk-in closet lined with wooden file cabinets. Expecting the drawers to also be locked, Mason yanked on the nearest one, almost falling over when it easily spilled into his arms. The names on the files should have read *Pay Dirt*. Instead, the files were labeled with the names of the rich and powerful. Skimming the names, Mason found Cullan's files on Billy Sunshine, Ed Fiora, and Beth Harrell. He almost had time to read them before his career as a second-story man ended like a scene from a late-night rerun.

"Freeze, mister! Put your hands where I can see them and turn around real slow!"

Mason left the drawer gaping open and did as he was told. A police officer aimed his service revolver at Mason from the doorway. Mason could see Shirley Parker peering around the cop, her eyes drawn in beady satisfaction.

"I'm unarmed," Mason said. He didn't think there was any point in telling the cop that this was all a misunderstanding; that he hadn't really done what he'd so clearly done. He expected to be arrested, and was more interested in not getting shot.

"Up against the wall, legs and arms spread wide," the cop instructed.

Mason complied again, flinching as the cop ran one hand down his sides, up his legs to his crotch, under his jacket, and around his middle.

Satisfied, the cop said, "Okay. You can turn around now."

The cop was tall, square-shouldered, and vaguely familiar until Mason read the name beneath his badge. Blues had decked Officer James Toland when Toland had tried to put cuffs on him. Mason understood Blues's impulse as Toland looked him over. Mason waited for Toland to pull out his handcuffs, read him his rights, and end his career. None of which happened.

Shirley Parker stepped past them and into the closet, conducting a quick inventory.

Toland broke the silence. "Do you want to press charges, Miss Parker?"

"There doesn't seem to be anything missing," she said. "You can let Mr. Mason go," she answered from inside the closet.

Toland looked like a kid whose Christmas had been canceled. "Must be your lucky day, Counselor," Toland told him.

Mason felt his blood start circulating again as he realized why Shirley had granted him a reprieve. He may have been guilty of breaking and entering, but she was sitting on the mother lode of blackmail that would make her the next front-page defendant. Whatever Shirley intended to do with the files, exposing their existence wasn't an option.

Shirley stepped back into the room, her face suddenly bleak and ashen. She knew she was in over her head. Mason imagined that she had gone through life doing what Jack

Cullan had told her to do, maybe nursing a quiet love that was never noticed or returned, resigned to her life at his side, loyal and lonely. She'd been angry enough at Mason's intrusion to call the cops, summoning righteous indignation, wielding the authority her boss had carried. Now she'd outsmarted herself and could only let him go.

Mason had more questions for her that he was certain she wouldn't answer, but he couldn't resist the most obvious.

"How did you know I was here?" he asked her.

Shirley faced him. "There's a motion detector on the stairs. Satisfied, Mr. Mason?"

"Completely," Mason answered. "I'll be back in the morning with a subpoena for those files, so take very good care of them tonight. You've got enough problems without adding a charge for obstruction of justice."

Mason hurried back up the street to the Egg House Diner, checking over his shoulder to see when Shirley Parker and Toland left the building. He'd just slid into his booth when they emerged. Shirley locked the door, pulling a steel bar across it that he hadn't noticed before.

Toland watched her cross the street back to the People's Savings Building before climbing into his squad car and driving away. Mason waved as Toland passed the diner, pleased with his escape and happy for Toland to know that he was still keeping his eye on the files.

Mason looked around the diner. A second shift had come on duty during his absence. A waiter had replaced the waitress, and a homeless woman seated at the counter had taken the place of the homeless man. Though he couldn't be certain, Mason suspected that the waitress and the homeless man had simply traded places. The waiter's pale skin looked even paler against his two-day growth of beard when he shoved a glass of water across Mason's table. Not wanting to push his luck, Mason ordered another turkey sandwich. The woman huddled inside her tattered overcoat and scarves as if she were in a cocoon for the winter.

"Give her some dinner and put it on my check," he told the waiter.

The waiter returned to the counter, leaned over to the woman, and spoke too softly for Mason to hear. A moment later, the woman shuffled off the stool, gave Mason a poisonous glare, and disappeared down Main Street. The waiter shook his head as if cursing himself for not knowing any better. Mason had tried taking a page from his aunt Claire's book, only to realize that it was now a different book titled *No Good Deed Goes Unpunished*.

Mason didn't trust Shirley Parker to leave Cullan's files where they were until he showed up with a subpoena the next morning. He didn't know whether there was another entrance to the barbershop, and he couldn't watch both Shirley and the barbershop all night. Nor was Mason thrilled at the prospect of spending the night in the diner, pissing off homeless people. The simplest solution was to make a deal with the prosecutor. Mason would tell Ortiz about the files in return for Ortiz's promise to share the contents with him. Ortiz would track down Judge Carter and get a search warrant before Shirley Parker had a chance to come up with plan B.

Mason's deal with Ortiz for Cullan's files would cancel the ones he'd made with Rachel and Amy and more than disappoint Fiora. Mason dialed Patrick Ortiz's direct-dial number on his cell phone, not surprised that Ortiz was still working long after most county employees had gone home.

"Ortiz," he said, answering on the second ring.

"Patrick, it's Lou Mason. I've got a great deal for you."

"Too late," Ortiz said. "I told you the plea bargain was off the table if we went to the preliminary hearing."

"Forget the plea bargain. I'm going to make you the hero in this case. Jack Cullan was blackmailing Beth Harrell and a lot of other people, maybe including the mayor. I've found the files he kept on those people."

"So you're calling to report a crime committed by a dead man?"

"I'm calling to tell you to get a search warrant for those files so you can prevent them from disappearing. Those files are evidence in Cullan's murder. The killer is probably someone whom Cullan was blackmailing."

"Your client is the killer, Lou. Did Cullan have a file on him?"

"No. Listen, Patrick. Cullan's secretary has those files squirreled away in Tom Pendergast's old office on Main Street. She's an accessory to Cullan's blackmail. She knows that I know about the files and if you don't get a search warrant for them tonight, they'll be in a shredder before sunrise."

"Sorry, Lou. I'm not going to bother Judge Carter tonight on a bullshit story like that. You want to take it up with the judge tomorrow, give me a call. I've got work to do."

Mason wanted to throw his phone across the room when Ortiz hung up on him. Instead, he called the homicide division, hoping that Harry Ryman was working late. Carl Zimmerman answered instead.

"Carl, it's Lou Mason. Is Harry around?"

"Nope. He had to go see a witness; a guy he's been chasing for a couple of weeks. What's up?"

Mason hesitated. He intended to tell Harry the entire story and ask him to help baby-sit Cullan's files until Mason could talk to the judge in the morning. He even hoped that Harry would send a couple of uniformed cops to sit outside the barbershop all night. Mason didn't know Zimmerman well enough to ask for a favor like that, but he didn't have another choice. He decided to keep his story simple to convince Zimmerman that there was a good reason to help him out.

"Jack Cullan was blackmailing Beth Harrell. He kept secret files on her, the mayor, and Ed Fiora, plus a lot of other people. I've found Cullan's files but I can't get to them. The prosecutor won't ask Judge Carter for a search warrant tonight. If we wait until tomorrow, the files could be gone. I know you're convinced that my client killed Cullan, but there's a good chance something in those files will prove he didn't. I need your help to make sure nothing happens to them."

"Where are the files?" Zimmerman asked.

"In Tom Pendergast's old office above the barbershop at Twentieth and Main."

"Anybody there now?"

"No."

"Who else knows about the files?"

"Cullan's secretary, Shirley Parker. A cop named Toland, who was with you when you arrested Blues, knows that there's something in that office, but I don't think he knows what it is."

"Where are you now?"

"In a diner up the street from the barbershop."

"Sit tight, Lou. I just got hit with a call on a dead body in Swope Park. I'll meet you when I'm done with that. It may take me a couple of hours, but it's the best I can do."

"Thanks," Mason said.

A couple of hours passed and then another. Mason tried Harry's number again without any luck. He called the dispatcher, asking her to contact Harry and tell him to call Mason. When Harry didn't call, he left the same message for Zimmerman. He called his aunt Claire, who told him that she hadn't spoken to Harry all day. The waiter was eyeing Mason like he should start charging him rent for the booth when Mason's cell phone rang.

"Harry?" Mason asked.

"It's Zimmerman. What's going on?"

"I'm growing old in this diner. I think the waiter is about to add me to the menu."

"Leave him a big tip. I'm stuck in the park. Stay where you are and wait for me."

"Right," Mason said, having decided in the same instant that he couldn't wait any longer.

Mason left a ten-dollar tip for a five-dollar meal, and went to his car. His ex-wife had once given him a tool kit to keep in the trunk of his car. It was one of the first indications that they didn't know each other as well as their glands would have liked. Mason's tool of choice to fix anything was a hammer he could use to beat whatever was broken into submission. The rest of the tools were for guys who knew the difference between a flat head, and a Phillips head. Mason found the small flashlight at the bottom of the kit, and grinned when the batteries still worked. Grabbing the hammer and the flashlight, he closed the trunk and got ready to commit a felony for a second time that night.

Chapter
Twenty-two

Mason walked south to Twenty-first and turned west, then north at an alley that ran behind the block that included the barbershop. He was looking for a back door or a window that he could open with his hammer. If he tripped the motion detector on the stairs, he'd have to be faster than the cops. As he clung to the shadows in the alley, he realized that Shirley Parker could have already taken Cullan's files out the back door, sticking him with a great case of he-said-she-said.

That possibility left Mason with a thin sweat and a twisted gut by the time he reached the rear of the barbershop. Sweeping the flashlight across the wall, he heaved a deep breath mixed with relief and frustration when he discovered there was no rear door, or rear window on the first floor. There was, however, a second-story window next to which a fire escape was embedded into the brick wall. The catwalk of the fire escape ran beneath the window to a ladder that descended halfway to the ground, just beyond Mason's reach.

Mason retrieved a commercial trash Dumpster he had passed in the alley, shoving it across the uneven pavement until it was directly beneath the ladder. Climbing on top of the Dumpster, he reached for the ladder, finding himself a foot shy of the bottom rung. Mason took off his jacket, stuffed the flashlight and the hammer into his belt, and backed up to the edge of the dumpster. Measuring the short step to the wall, his left leg bent forward, his right leg planted on his heel, he launched himself at the ladder with a quick burst.

The cold iron of the bottom rung froze against Mason's hands as he held on, gaining purchase with his feet against the brick wall. Mason pulled himself up each rung, his breath coming in sharp gasps more from the stinging iron than the effort, until his feet found the bottom rung. A moment later he was on the catwalk beneath the window, certain that he was about to be caught in a cross fire of searchlights while some cop demanded that he throw down his hammer before they opened up on him.

Mason tried the window without success. It had been locked or nailed shut too long and too well to surrender to a few tugs. He shined his flashlight through the glass, and could make out the top of the stairs outside the entrance to Pendergast's office. Unlike the window that had been boarded up from the inside, this window would let him in. He hoped the motion detector was at the bottom of the stairs and not at the top.

Mason pulled off his sweater and wrapped it around the hammer to muffle the sound as he broke the window. The glass splintered into several large shards that fell to the floor. Mason climbed through, crunching broken glass beneath his feet. He assumed that he had set off the motion detector, and began counting the seconds he had to grab the files, get out, and make up an alibi.

He left the ceiling light in Pendergast's office turned off, feeling less exposed in the darkness. The beam from Mason's flashlight glanced off something shiny in the center of the floor that Mason didn't remember seeing a few hours earlier. Dropping to one knee, he picked up a white, quarter-sized campaign button with the words *Truman for Senator* in blue. Tom Pendergast had been Harry Truman's political godfather.

Mason aimed his flashlight at the panel door to the walk-in closet, certain that someone had dropped the button on the floor while removing other more current political souvenirs. He traced the flashlight beam up to the lock he had broken when he was flattened by a blast that shattered the panel door, opened the floor like an earthquake, and dropped him into the barbershop.

He slammed into the outstretched barber chair, bounced off onto the floor, and crawled beneath the chair while fire and debris rained from overhead. The explosion was loud enough to scramble the eggs at the Egg House Diner, but Mason was deafened by the blast before his brain could register the sound. Though he was stunned, he understood how life turned on such small moments as bending down to pick up a button. Had he been standing, the panel door would have cut him in two when it blew out from the wall.

Mason ran his hands over his scalp and face, checking for wounds too fresh to hurt. He found a trickle of blood from a cut above one ear that was clotting in his thick hair. He pulled off his shirt to cover his mouth and nose against the acrid smoke that had enveloped him.

The initial wave of debris had settled into fiery heaps that fed flames as they raced up the walls to finish the work begun by the explosion. Mason staggered to his feet, giving a quick and futile pull to the steel bars covering the barbershop window. The glass had blown out into the street and the cold air tasted sweet even as it fueled the fire. Cars stopped on Main Street, and passersby stood in front of the People's Savings Building, pointing and screaming at him to get out in voices that he imagined more than heard. He agreed with their advice even if he couldn't find a way to take it.

The flames were on the verge of engulfing the outer walls of the building. Mason glanced up through the hole in the floor above and saw that the fire had eaten through the roof, obliterating the stars with billowing smoke. He could feel his clothes heating up as if they were about to spontaneously combust.

Gagging into his shirt, he made his way to the front door, cursing Shirley Parker and the bar that she had locked into place like a coffin nail. Any thought of escaping out the window the way he had come in vanished with the stairs that were crackling like seasoned kindling as the fire roared down on him.

Ducking to stay as close to the ground as possible, he stumbled down the hallway to the basement door. Covering the door handle with his shirt, he pulled the door open, yanked it closed behind him, and bolted down the stairs, grateful for the pocket of cool air in the basement. He leaned against the rough cement wall and slid down to the floor gasping and wondering how long it would take the fire to burn through the first floor and bury him.

His question was answered a moment later. The stairs to the second floor were directly overhead and collapsed into the basement, carrying the fire with it.

Mason jumped to his feet, looking around at blank walls that now glowed with a deadly orange like one of Dante's chambers. Smoke rolled across the ceiling, shrinking the empty basement that had been stripped of its contents like the other floors. In the far corner, he saw a half-open chest-high door and raced over to it.

Shirley Parker's body lay inside the entrance to a tunnel, propping the door open. Mason knelt alongside her, feeling for a pulse in her neck and wrist. Her eyes were open, unseeing and untroubled by the smoke. A dark stain above her left breast was still damp with blood. Mason now understood Norma Hawkins's certainty that Jack Cullan had been shot.

Crouching under the low ceiling, Mason felt his way through the unlit tunnel, counting his steps to gauge the distance. Fifty paces later, the tunnel ended against a locked door. Bracing his arms against the walls of the narrow shaft, Mason kicked at the door until its hinges surrendered. Mason stood up inside another basement where the lights had been left on.

Mason took a few deep breaths and went back into the tunnel, bent over and trotting until he reached Shirley's body. The heat and smoke from the fire rolled through the tunnel, though Mason hoped the flames wouldn't follow. He reached under Shirley's arms and pulled her body back to the other basement, closing her eyes and laying her down gently against the floor. There was no peace in her soft features.

The basement was filled with framed and unframed paintings, stacked against the walls. There were two stairways, one that led to the first floor and another that led to a door with a small window in its center. Mason walked wearily up the second stairway, and opened the door into the alley behind the barbershop. It took him a moment to realize that the tunnel had passed beneath the alley.

Looking to his left, he saw firemen running up the alley from Twentieth Street, carrying a hose. A fire engine blocked the entrance to the alley, its red and white lights cascading across the pavement. Two paramedics raced toward him from the south end of the alley, waving and calling to him. Reaching him, one put her arms around him to hold him up while another peered into his eyes.

"Hey, buddy!" one of the paramedics mouthed. "Are you all right?"

Mason answered, "Yeah," wondering whether the paramedic could hear him if he couldn't hear the paramedic. "There's a woman's body down there," he added, not certain whether he was whispering or shouting.

He opened the door and pointed down the stairs. The paramedic who had been holding him up led him toward an ambulance while her partner went to find Shirley Parker.

The police had blocked off traffic on Main Street except for emergency vehicles. The spectators who'd been first in line in front of the People's Savings Building had been herded a safe distance away. Two fire department pumper trucks were pouring heavy streams of water into the burnt-out shell that had been Pendergast's office. Local television stations had dispatched live crews to the scene. Cops, firefighters, reporters, and rescuers did their dance.

No one noticed Mason and his paramedic escort when they first emerged from the alley and made their way to an ambulance parked half a block south of the barbershop. By the time the paramedic had persuaded Mason to sit down inside the ambulance so she could examine him, he'd been picked up on the media's radar. Reporters clustered around the ambulance jostling for an angle. Rachel Firestone squeezed through and sat down next to him. The paramedic started to order her to get out, but Mason said she could stay.

Mason's hearing was gradually coming back, first a dull roar of unfiltered noise, then a steady ringing like a flat-lined heart monitor, and then voices.

"I let you out of my sight for five minutes and you get into trouble!" Rachel told him. "Look at you. You're a mess!"

"I forget," Mason said. "Are you my big sister or little sister?"

"I'm just a sister, and you're still a mess. What in the hell happened?"

Before he could answer, Carl Zimmerman waded through the throng of reporters, trailed by a uniformed cop and the police department's director of media relations, who politely but firmly ordered the reporters back behind the police line.

"You too, Miss Firestone," Zimmerman told her. "You'll get your shot at him if there's anything left worth having, but we get to go first."

"Detective, do I look the kind of girl who'd settle for sloppy seconds?"

"I wouldn't know that," Zimmerman answered without a trace of humor.

Rachel gave Mason a peck on his ash-stained cheek. "Save some for me," she told Mason, and left to enjoy the jealousy of her colleagues.

Zimmerman stood outside the ambulance. "You are one dumb-assed motherfucker, you know that, Mason? I don't know whether to arrest you or just throw you back into that fire and save Harry Ryman the trouble of kicking your tail into next week."

"You hold him down and I'll kick him," Harry said as he joined his partner.

Mason looked at both men and then at the paramedic. "Am I in any shape to have my ass kicked?" he asked her.

"You're so beat up already you probably won't even notice. I say give them a shot. Just don't call me. I'm not interested in repeat business," she said. Turning to the detectives, she added, "He'll be black and blue and shitting soot for a week, but he's all yours."

Mason climbed out of the ambulance as Harry and Zimmerman each took him by an arm.

"Am I under arrest?" Mason asked.

Harry answered. "Not until we figure out all the things to charge you with. Let's get a cup of coffee first."

Mason groaned as they led him to the Egg House Diner. "Too bad this place didn't blow up," Mason said.

The waiter gave Mason his I'm-not-surprised look as the two detectives slid into one side of Mason's booth while Mason returned to his now-familiar seat. The homeless woman was back at the counter, and giggled into her coffee cup as she exchanged a wink with the waiter. Mason caught his reflection in the window of the diner. His face was camouflaged with soot, his hair spiked with blood, his clothes were blackened and torn. He understood the homeless woman's laughter. She looked better than he did. He wondered if she would offer to buy him dinner.

The waiter brought them three glasses of water. "Turkey sandwich?" he asked.

"Two coffees, black," Harry said. "What do you want, Lou?"

"Nothing. I've had enough."

"Why didn't you wait for me, like I told you?" Zimmerman asked.

Mason had an answer that was good enough for him, though he doubted it would satisfy Harry and Zimmerman. "Cullan's files were the key to his murder. If I couldn't get my hands on them I couldn't prove you guys were wrong about Blues. Ortiz hung up on me when I asked him to get a search warrant. The two of you were fighting crime. I waited too long. The files are gone. Someone either blew them up or stole them and made it look like they were blown up.''

''You better rethink that bullshit when the judge asks you to show remorse,'' Zimmerman said.

''For what? Breaking and entering?'' Mason asked.

''That's chump change,'' Zimmerman said. ''I suppose you're going to tell us that Shirley Parker invited you down into that basement so you could pop her?''

Mason looked at Harry, not believing what he was hearing. ''Get real. You can't possibly think I shot Shirley Parker.''

''Who said she was shot?'' Zimmerman asked him, enjoying the role reversal from Mason's cross-examination.

''Good for you, Carl,'' Mason said. ''I had that coming. Maybe the killer just threw the bullet at her.''

Harry interrupted. ''Lou, this is serious. Officer Toland reported that he caught you inside that building earlier tonight, but that Shirley Parker refused to press charges. He says that you threatened her. Carl tells you to sit tight, which for you is not possible. You and Shirley are the only ones inside that building when it blows up, and you are the only one who comes out alive. Only Shirley is shot to death, not blown up. How does all that look to you?''

''It looks like head-up-your-ass police work that is a lot easier than figuring out what really happened. Like figuring out who blew up the damn building, who knew about the tunnel to get the files out before they blew up the building, and who would kill Shirley Parker to make sure nobody found out what was in those files.''

''You'd been sitting on that building all day,'' Zimmerman said. ''You could have found the tunnel, found the files, and been caught again by Shirley Parker. Only this time, you had to whack her.''

''You left out that I also decided to blow my ass up along with the building to hide the evidence of my crime,'' Mason said. "Harry, if you guys are really looking at me for this, take me downtown, book me, and let's go see a judge. I'll crucify you in court and the media will pick at what's left."

Harry said, "You keep up this cowboy shit, and you won't leave us any choice. Same as Bluestone."

"Okay, I'll be a good boy. But do your job. Check out the slug that killed Shirley Parker. Odds are that the same gun was used to kill Jack Cullan. That will clear Blues."

"We don't need you to tell us how to do our job, Counselor," Zimmerman said. "If you killed Shirley Parker, I'll see to it that you share the needle with your client."

"Carl, you know that it's not safe to share needles," Mason said. "Pay the waiter on your way out."

Rachel was waiting for Mason when he got to his car. He stood there shivering in his undershirt as she leaned against the driver's door, warm in her parka, her green eyes and winter-pinched cheeks alive with promise.

"No," he told her.

"No, what?" she protested.

"No, I'm not letting you take me home, patch me up, and put me to bed again unless you're in it, and that ain't likely."

"You need to learn to value a woman's friendship beyond her vagina, Lou. It would broaden your horizons immeasurably."

Mason opened the door to his car and slid past her. Rachel came around to the other side and let herself into the passenger's seat. "How about if you take me home, I wait for you to patch yourself up, and then you tell me what happened? After which, you can go to bed by yourself."

"Rachel, you need to learn to value a man's friendship

beyond the stories you can squeeze out of him. It would broaden your horizons immeasurably.''

''I don't know,'' she said. ''Men have so little to offer otherwise.''

Chapter
Twenty-three

Mason was slow getting out of the house on Friday morning. The paramedic had been right about the epidermal color scheme he would be sporting for a while. Standing naked in front of his bathroom mirror, his body looked as if he'd been tattooed with a Rorschach test. The stitches in his side had held, though there was an angry red ribbon around them. He walked creakily around his house like the Tin Man in search of a lube job, trailed by Tuffy, whose whining and yelping Mason mistook for sympathy until he realized that the dog just wanted to be fed. He tried rowing, but gave up when the rowing machine started to sink. A shower hot enough to parboil his skin loosened the kinks in his muscles and joints.

Rachel had followed him home the night before, and had stayed long enough to extract information she agreed to attribute only to a source close to the investigation. Her story in the morning paper ran alongside a color photograph of him clutching the bars on the barbershop window while flames danced a pirouette around him. A spectator had taken the photograph and sold it to a wire service, turning a quick profit on tragedy. Mason held the picture up for a closer look as he searched for a trace of courage in his bugged-out eyes and gaping mouth.

Rachel's article wove the Pendergast angle into the facts, giving the story a gangland flavor that linked two twenty-first-century murders with a long-dead twentieth-century kingpin. Rachel related the rumored existence of Cullan's confidential files and the suspicion that they contained embarrassing information on the city's leaders. She speculated on whether the files had been destroyed in the fire or whether the fire had been set to cover their theft. She described Shirley Parker as a never-married woman with no survivors whose only known employment had been for Jack Cullan. Mason decided that there was more tragedy in Shirley's epitaph than in her death.

As for him, Rachel played it straight. The caption under the photograph identified him as Blues's lawyer. The article offered no explanation for his presence in the barbershop, noting that he had declined to comment on the record, as had Harry Ryman when she had asked him whether Mason was a suspect in Shirley Parker's murder.

Off the record, Mason had told her the story, not wanting her to think he was a killer.

"I don't," she had told him when he had finished explaining what had happened. "A lousy burglar, yes, but a killer? I don't think so."

"Thanks for the endorsement," he had told her.

"So who did it? Who killed Cullan, blew up the barbershop, and killed Shirley Parker? And what happened to the files?"

"Like G.I. Joe says, knowing is half the battle," Mason

had answered. "The other half is proving it. Ed Fiora is the leader in the clubhouse. Fiora may have been happy for Cullan to work his magic on the license for the Dream Casino. But who wants a lawyer with a file that could send him to the federal penitentiary? Plus he's got the muscle. Tony Manzerio probably gets his rocks off blowing stuff up. Fiora killed Cullan—or had him killed—to preserve the attorney-client privilege. Then, he sends Tony to talk to Shirley and she gives up the files. Tony snatches the files and kills Shirley."

Rachel had chewed on Mason's theory. "Yeah, but killing Shirley is too messy. Threaten her, buy her off, and send her out of town—which would have made sense. Killing her turns up the heat hotter than the fire. Fiora isn't that stupid."

"No plan ever goes down the way it's written. Something went wrong and Tony popped Shirley."

"So Fiora has the files?" Rachel had asked.

"They ain't at the public library."

"So how do you prove it?"

"Beats the hell out of me," Mason had answered.

Mickey Shanahan was sitting in Mason's desk chair, his feet propped on Mason's desk, drinking from a bottle of fresh orange juice, when Mason arrived just before ten o'clock.

"Is that my orange juice?" Mason asked him.

"Sorry, Lou," Mickey told him, wiping his mouth with the back of his hand. "This woman dropped it off a while ago. Said she was your aunt. Said you should call her so she could chew your ass. Whatever you did, she's like totally pissed, man. What's goin' on?"

"First, that is my orange juice. Second, my aunt is probably upset that I got trapped in a burning barbershop with a dead body. Third, when did you move into my office?''

''Sorry, again, boss,'' Mickey said, this time taking his feet off of Mason's desk. ''I give on the OJ. But you've got to tell me about the barbershop and the body. That is too much! And you're the one who hired me to use your computer to check out Ed Fiora. That was yesterday. You left me here without the key. I didn't want to leave the place unlocked and I didn't know when you were coming back, so I stayed.''

''All night?''

''That sofa's not bad. And the orange juice is pretty good.''

Mickey was wearing the same faded jeans and denim shirt under a black crew-neck sweater as he had worn the day before. He had scruffy stubble on his chin and above his lip, though his cheeks were smooth and his unwashed hair looked like it had been finger-combed.

''Mickey, where do you live?''

Mickey brushed his sweater as if to freshen his dignity. ''I've got a place not far from here.''

''What about clients? I haven't seen a single client in or out of your office in six months. What's up with that?''

''It's been a little slow,'' Mickey said. ''I'm expecting things to pick up. This case will be a big boost.''

Mason got a quick picture of a kid barely off the street who thought he had scammed Blues on the office lease and had probably been living at the bar ever since. Mason doubted that Mickey had fooled Blues from the moment he'd said hello. Mason reached into his wallet and took out a twenty.

''I haven't had breakfast. Would you mind picking something up for me? Get yourself something too if you want.''

"Hey, no problem, boss. I'll probably stop at home and get cleaned up if that's okay."

"You bet. Did you find anything out about Fiora?"

"A lot of smoke, not much fire. It's all here in a report I did for you."

"Give me the highlights."

"I've covered the public-record stuff, property ownership, lawsuits, stuff like that. The Gaming Commission files could be the real bonanza."

"Why?"

"I found two things in those records that are the keys to the information universe. Fiora's Social Security number and bank accounts. It will take some time, but I'll eventually be able to follow the money."

"Is that legal?"

"Hey, you're the lawyer. Do you really want to know?"

"No, I really don't. What's the bottom line?"

"Fiora is a big football fan. Just like the mayor. I did some checking on him too."

Mickey handed him a typed report with printouts from the Internet attached. Mason thumbed through it, impressed by the level of detail and organization. He reached into his wallet again and handed Mickey two fifties.

"We haven't talked salary yet. This will cover yesterday until we have time to work out the details."

Mickey folded the fifties and stuck them in his pocket with a nonchalance that clashed with the hunger in his eyes. "Works for me. I'll have to see where I'm at on my other clients before I can commit to anything full-time."

"Sure. I understand. Check your schedule and let me know. I'm probably going to need somebody at least until Blues's case is over. If you're not available, I'll have to run an ad. That's always a pain in the ass."

Mickey pursed his lips and nodded, realizing that they

were playing each other. "So, what's the story on the barbershop and the body?"

"Buy yourself a newspaper and read all about it. Come to work for me full-time and we'll talk."

Mickey smiled and said, "Catch you later, boss."

Mason, certain that he would, settled into his desk chair, checked out the traffic on Broadway, and read Mickey's report.

The relationship between Fiora and the mayor was more complicated than a backwoods family tree and was, in the end, filled with enough smoke that there had to be a fire somewhere. The Dream Casino bought a wide array of goods and services to make dreams come true for its customers, including food, laundry, carpets, paint, security equipment, slot machines, lighting, liquor, and beer. The Dream had an exclusive contract with a local beer distributor owned by Donovan Jenkins.

Jenkins, a former wide receiver for the Kansas City Chiefs, had been Billy Sunshine's favorite target. Jenkins had retired from football a year after the mayor had quit, and bought the beer distributorship. He'd been a steady political supporter of his old quarterback, making modest campaign contributions. A month after Jenkins had inked the exclusive deal with Fiora, mayor Sunshine had refinanced the $250,000 mortgage on his house. The mayor's new lender was Donovan Jenkins. Mickey speculated at the end of his report that the mayor wasn't making house payments like regular folks.

Mason picked up his phone and dialed Rachel Firestone's number at the *Star*. "What do you know about the mortgage on Mayor Sunshine's house?" he asked her.

"Good morning to you too. Nice of you to call and you're welcome for last night," she added.

"I'm sure it was as good for you as it was for me."

"As good as it gets," she assured him. "How did you find out about the mortgage?"

"You aren't my only source," he told her. "What do you know about the relationship between Fiora, Donovan Jenkins, and the mayor?"

"Fiora made Jenkins his exclusive beer supplier. Jenkins loaned the mayor a quarter of a million bucks. It's dirty, it sucks, but it's legal. I've talked to the U.S. attorney about it. Jenkins's loan is a matter of public record. Amy White, the mayor's chief of staff, showed me canceled checks for the monthly house payment Mayor Sunshine makes to Jenkins. The interest rate is a market rate. End of story, but I've got something you might be interested in on that tunnel you found in the basement of the barbershop."

"Should I sit up and beg?" Mason asked.

"Not over the phone. I can't tell if you're really sitting up. I checked the paper's archives. During Prohibition, Pendergast owned a speakeasy that was on the other side of the alley from the barbershop. He built the tunnel so his boys could escape in case the feds raided the joint."

"Who owns the building?" Mason asked.

"Donovan Jenkins. He bought it from Jack Cullan a year ago."

Mason said, "That's handy. Who does Jenkins lease the space to?"

"An art gallery. They had a big opening last month. It was vacant a long time before that. Care to guess who the last tenant was before the art gallery?"

"And rob you of the pleasure of telling me? Never," Mason told her.

"You are so thoughtful. Would you believe it was the Committee to Reelect Billy Sunshine?"

"Get out!"

"Get in and get in deep!" Rachel said.

"Man, is there anybody in this whole mess who isn't in bed with one another?"

"Just you and me, babe. Just you and me," Rachel told him.

Mason didn't know what to say. He couldn't tell if Rachel was flirting with him, and if she was, he didn't know how to flirt with a lesbian. "By the way, thanks for last night," he told her.

"It was nothing. Keep in touch," she added before hanging up.

Mason knew that it wasn't nothing, although he hadn't figured out quite what it was. His relationship with Rachel wasn't sexual or romantic and never would be, despite his complete willingness to overlook her gender preference if only she would. Mason reluctantly conceded that it was easier to make love to a woman than to just make friends with her. That this particular woman spent every waking moment gunning for a page-one headline above the fold didn't make the calculus any easier.

With Cullan's files either destroyed or stolen, Mason was back at the bottom of the hill, still trying to push the boulder to the top. He would let Mickey continue plowing fields in cyberspace while he dug at ground level.

Mason logged on to the county's civil-lawsuit database and punched in Beth Harrell's name. Both of her divorce cases showed up. Husband number one was Baker McKenzie. Mason recognized his name. He was the senior partner in the McKenzie, Strachan law firm. Husband number two was Al Douglas, a name Mason didn't recognize. According to Beth, one of her ex-husbands had snapped nasty pics of her and had given them to Jack Cullan. Mason's best idea of the day was to find the exes and ask which one of them was the shit bag. It wasn't noon yet, but Mason hoped he'd have a better idea before the sun set.

Chapter
Twenty-four

Mason didn't want to ask Beth which of her ex-husbands was the shit bag. He wasn't entirely convinced that she was telling the truth in the first place. If Beth knew he was checking out her story and she was lying, she would back-pedal or find some way to distract him, and he wasn't up to being distracted. If she was telling the truth, she would start crowding Ed Fiora's pole position on the suspect track.

Mason called the clerk of the Circuit Court to locate Beth's divorce files. The voice-mail system cast him into a menu of choices that he accepted and rejected until a human being answered. When the woman said her name was Margaret, he didn't believe her when she asked if she could help him.

"My name is Lou Mason. I'm a lawyer and I'm trying to locate two divorce files," he said.

"Are they on-site or off-site?" she asked him.

Mason swallowed. "I don't know. I was hoping you could tell me."

"If they are on-site, they might only be available on microfilm. That would mean that we shipped the hard copy off-site. If the files are off-site and you want the hard copy, it will take one to three business days to retrieve the files from off-site storage. Hold, please," she added before he could respond.

Mason imagined dozens of different torture scenarios for bureaucrats named Margaret during the three minutes and twenty-seven seconds she left him on hold. Mason timed her.

"This is Margaret. May I help you?" she asked when she returned to his call.

"Margaret, this is Lou Mason. We've already met. I'm looking for two divorce files and I know the on-site, off-site drill. Let me give you the case numbers so you can find out where they are."

"We can't give that information out over the phone. You'll have to come to the clerk's office and sign a form."

Mason took a deep breath. "Should I ask for you, Margaret?"

"Yes. I'll be at lunch."

Mason hung up, confident that Margaret would keep a lookout for him and run out the back door for lunch the instant he crossed the threshold of the clerk's office.

Thirty minutes later, Mason cautiously approached the court clerk's office. He was less concerned that Margaret would actually be at lunch than he was that she would be there and he'd end up a suspect in another homicide. Mason passed through double glass doors, above which CLERK OF THE JACKSON COUNTY CIRCUIT COURT had been embossed in gold-filigree letters on the dark-walnut-paneled wall. A long white counter laminated with Formica separated Mason from women working at desks, processing the county's civil and criminal cases.

He had concluded from past experiences that they had been trained not to look up unless it was at the clock. It was ten minutes to noon when Mason rang the bell on the counter under the sign that read RING FOR SERVICE. The woman at the nearest desk looked up, the resentment at his interruption shot through her glare. He asked for Margaret.

The woman picked up her phone, speaking softly and furtively stealing glances at him until Mason was certain that she'd called the sheriff's office. She hung up the phone, put the cap on her pen, and disappeared to the back of the office. He didn't know where she had gone, only that she was gone.

Mason waited. There was a large clock on the wall to his right. He watched the second hand sweep around the dial and the incremental march of the minute hand to twelve o'clock high. The other women in the office, as if in response to an inner clock, rose in turn from their desks, vanishing into the far depths of the clerk's office.

One woman remained. She was of an indistinct age and build that spoke of middle years without further precision. She wore a tan pantsuit and a flat expression across her wide face. She walked slowly to the counter, eyeing the clock, timing her advance.

"My name is Margaret," she said, this time not offering to help him.

"I'm Lou Mason. We spoke on the phone. You said I had to fill out a form to request a couple of divorce files."

Margaret reached into a drawer on her side of the counter and handed Mason two forms, one for each file. He filled them out and flashed her his best smile when he handed them back to her. He followed her gaze to the clock.

"It's noon. I'm on my lunch break now. Come back at one o'clock," she said.

Mason watched helplessly as Margaret carried the forms back to her desk, dropping them on her chair as she walked past, never looking back.

He returned exactly sixty minutes later. Seventy minutes later, Margaret presented him with both files, neither of which had been off-site or on microfilm. He filled out additional forms to check out the files, which meant that he could take them into a small adjoining room and look at them. He would have to fill out another form to request copies, and he could not under any circumstances, Margaret explained in the severest of tones, remove the files from the clerk's office.

Mason read Beth's divorce files, filling in some of the statistical blanks in her life. The files were one-dimensional ledgers of dates and dollars, the final accounting of dead relationships. He thought about his own marriage, about the passion and pain that had swept both him and Kate along for three years until Kate called it quits, depriving him of the choice to fight or surrender. There was no exuberance in the dry recitation of the dates of Beth's marriages, and no regret in the hollow entries of the decrees of divorce. It was history without humanity. Irreconcilable differences were the code words for hearts empty and broken.

Beth Harrell had married Baker McKenzie shortly after graduating from law school. She was twenty-five and he was twenty-five years her senior. They had met when Beth worked at McKenzie's firm during the summers while she was in law school. The file was thin, the grounds the ubiquitous irreconcilable differences. The marriage had lasted two years. There had been no children, and she hadn't sought alimony or any of his property. He had wanted out, and she had settled for the restoration of her maiden name.

She had waited five years before marrying Al Douglas, an architect fifteen years older than Beth. She had kept her maiden name, and they had signed a prenuptial agreement that prohibited either of them from seeking any monetary settlement from the other in the event of a divorce, with the exception of child support if they had a family. Irreconcilable differences had again been diagnosed, like a recurring cancer. The court had entered the decree of divorce on their fourth wedding anniversary.

It was impossible to draw any conclusions about Beth's marriages from the information that had been presented to the court other than that they had had a beginning and an ending. What had taken place in the middle was not a matter of public record. Mason would have to ask Baker McKenzie and Al Douglas to find out which one of them was the shit bag.

Mason had learned one thing about celebrity. It cleared a lot of scheduling conflicts. Both Baker McKenzie and Al Douglas agreed to see him that afternoon. He started with McKenzie.

Baker McKenzie was the third generation of McKenzies in the firm his grandfather and Matthew Strachan had founded seventy-five years earlier. None of Strachan's heirs had followed their ancestor in the law, though no later generations of interloping partners had suggested removing the Strachan name from the door. McKenzie & Strachan was the oldest, and largest law firm in the city, its bloodlines were the bluest, and its stockings were woven of the finest silk.

Baker McKenzie sat comfortably at the top of the firm, worrying more about his putting stroke than the firm's clients. He had hidden mediocre legal skills and a civil service work ethic beneath the legacy of his grandfather and father. Mason had run across him once or twice in cases where the client had expected the name partner to show his face. McKenzie had shown it just long enough to make certain he didn't get it dirty before begging off because of pressing matters in the case of *Tee v. Green*. He was a society-page regular who never left home without a beautiful woman on his arm, though not one so beautiful as to detract from his own shining countenance.

McKenzie greeted Mason as if they were asshole buddies. "My God, man! How the hell are you? I swear to Jesus that you are turning our profession into one dangerous contact sport."

McKenzie gleamed as if he'd just been washed and waxed. His artificially whitened teeth sparkled, as did his blond hair and silvery temples. His eyes glistened, making Mason wonder if McKenzie was wearing special contact lenses. Even his skin had a ruddy, glowing patina, as if a shoeshine man had just spit-shined his forehead and chin. McKenzie was Mason's height, though broad where Mason was lean. His suit was Italian and cost at least two grand. McKenzie was fit for his age or any other, and shook Mason's hand vigorously enough to make that point.

McKenzie led Mason back to his private office on the forty-first floor of the Citadel Building, the tallest office building in Kansas City. McKenzie & Strachan occupied fifteen floors in the building. McKenzie's office was on the top floor, and had windows on three sides that offered panoramic views of the city.

"You've got a helluva view, Baker," Mason said.

"Hell, I can see from here to next week," Baker answered, permitting himself a hearty chuckle even though he'd obviously used the line a thousand times. "It's really something at night, especially during a lightning storm. I'm telling you, Lou, it's like standing next to Zeus throwing thunderbolts. It electrifies women of a certain erotic sensibility, like their nerve endings get supercharged and they've just got to plug something into all that current.''

"I'll bet you know how to throw the switch," Mason said to humor him.

"I could light up a Christmas tree, my friend."

McKenzie's desk was an oval of smoky glass, devoid of a single piece of paper. A bold, brilliantly colored abstract painting hung on the wall behind his desk. Two sleek, low-backed chairs were paired with a small table in front of one wall of floor-to-ceiling windows. A sofa adorned with plush pillows and bathed in soft light beckoned only a few feet from a well-stocked bar that also housed a Bose sound system. The door to a private bathroom was barely discernible against the mahogany-paneled walls. Mason thought it was more fuck pad than law office.

"I'll bet those are some moments to remember," Mason said.

"Indeed they are. Indeed they are," McKenzie repeated to be certain that Mason knew what he was missing.

Mason said, "All that excitement, it must be hard to remember one woman from another. You ever keep any souvenirs?"

McKenzie's boasting gave way to suspicion. "You didn't really tell me why you wanted to see me, Lou. I'm sure it wasn't to hear about my love life. What's on your mind?"

It had taken Mason only a few minutes to bait Baker McKenzie and less time to hate him. McKenzie was, Mason decided, the kind of man who would mistake diplomacy for deference. Mason was not good at either.

"Beth Harrell says she was being blackmailed with some dirty pictures either you or her other ex-husband took and later gave to Jack Cullan. If that's true, she's a murder suspect and the ex-husband is a shit bag, although there's no law against being a shit bag. I need to know if the pictures are real, and I need to know if you're the shit bag, Baker.''

McKenzie was standing next to the center panel of glass, six steps from Mason. He looked out over the horizon for a moment before turning toward Mason, his face besotted with angry blood. Without saying a word, McKenzie closed the distance between them before Mason realized that he wasn't coming to shake his hand again, and launched a right cross at Mason's chin. Mason couldn't get out of the way, and he spun around once before toppling at McKenzie's feet.

"Dartmouth boxing team, light-heavyweight division,'' McKenzie said as he stepped over a stunned but conscious Mason and opened the door to his office. "Call maintenance," McKenzie said to his secretary. "Tell them to clean up the shit bag on my floor.''

After showing himself out, Mason stopped at a convenience store, where he bought plastic bags and ice to apply to his chin. Al Douglas's office was in a suburban office park surrounded by woods and ringed by a bike path. Banners hung from light poles in the parking lot, depicting festive winter scenes that clashed with the barren trees. Mason sat in his car for half an hour, ministering to his chin and his ego, before going inside.

He was prepared to take a more temperate approach to husband number two when Al Douglas looked up at him from a drafting table a short time later. Douglas worked in an office without walls where no one had a private office. Mason assumed that the design was intended to build camaraderie, but judging from the beehive hum that greeted him, it bred whispers and rumors.

"You must be Lou Mason," Douglas said, extending his hand. "Baker called me. He said he'd already taken out your chin, but that I could have the rest of your face unless I was the shit bag you were looking for. Let's talk someplace quiet."

Douglas's handshake was flaccid and damp. He slid off his drafting stool and looked up at Mason from a distance of at least six inches before he led Mason into a break room where two other people were huddled over a crossword puzzle. Douglas cleared his throat and waited. The puzzle people took their cue and left, closing the door behind them.

Douglas was round-shouldered, thin on top and thick around the middle. He wore half glasses that had slid two thirds of the way down his nose. He took off the glasses, letting them drop to his chest, where they dangled from a thin chain that looped around his neck.

"He really tagged you, didn't he?" Douglas said. "The sucker punch is Baker's specialty. He tried it once with me, but he misjudged how short I am. If he misses the first punch, he's finished."

Douglas's story about Baker McKenzie was a verbal sucker punch; showing up Mason by telling Mason that he had ducked the same punch that had decked Mason. Though Douglas looked like the only thing he'd ever thrown in anger was a fit, Mason realized he had his own way of sneaking up on the opposition. Mason flashed on an image of Douglas hanging around an elementary school offering kids a ride home. Mason already disliked him.

Mason gently rubbed his tender jaw, feeling a knot beginning to swell beneath the skin. "I'll try to remember that when we have the rematch."

"You really should put some ice on that before you grow a second chin," Douglas suggested.

Mason said, "I'll do that. No offense, but you and Baker are not exactly cut from the same cloth. Baker has two last names and you have two first names. Other than that, I can't see the connection. How did both of you end up married to Beth Harrell?"

"She's a woman of extremes, and Baker and I are at the opposite end of several masculine scales. She tried both ends. The next guy will probably be in the middle. Strong, tough, but likes sunsets. I suppose you want to know about the pictures."

"If you don't mind," Mason said. "Do the pictures really exist?"

Douglas poured a cup of coffee and took a chilled bottle of water from a refrigerator. "Here," he said, handing the bottle to Mason. "Put that on your chin. Yes," he continued, "the pictures are real."

Mason rolled the bottle across his chin, increasingly wary of the soft predator look in Douglas's eyes. He was tempted to offer Douglas a drink just to be sure the water wasn't poisoned. "Did Baker take the pictures?" Mason asked. Douglas shook his head. "You?" Mason asked.

"Neither one of us took them. Beth did. She put her camera on a tripod and used a timer. We were both into adult entertainment and she wanted to shock me, stir me up in some different way. I won't lie to you. It worked. She's a beautiful woman and the pictures were quite graphic. I hadn't gotten off like that since my first chat room."

"Did she do the same thing with Baker?"

"I don't know, but I doubt it. Beth always said that Baker screwed around, but only in the missionary position."

"You sound awfully philosophical for a guy who got dumped. You don't even sound angry with her."

"Guys like me never end up with women like Beth for very long. When she left me, it was like the clock struck midnight and I was back to being Al, the invisible man with the boffo porn collection. Except I had the pictures. So, I didn't get mad, I got off and then got even."

Douglas was blasé enough about his relationship with Beth that Mason pegged him for a sociopath interested only in his own needs and indifferent to anyone else. His casual, unemotional vengeance was creepy. "You gave the pictures to Jack Cullan?"

Douglas shook his head again, permitting himself a smug satisfaction. "I sold them. I guess that really makes me the shit bag."

Mason resisted the impulse to shove Douglas's chalky face into the back of his skull. He swallowed hard and forced the next question. "When did you sell the pictures to Cullan?"

"You want to hit me. I can tell from the way your jugular vein is throbbing. But you won't do it. I can tell that too. You're stuck with your conventional ethics. That's why people like me are able to do the things we do."

Mason measured his breathing. Douglas was a gut-sucking parasite with a sunny disposition. He bellied up to Douglas, crowding him into a corner. Douglas backed up, his hands suddenly shaking, causing him to spill his coffee on the front of his pants.

"You don't know me, Douglas, so don't assume too much. When did you sell the pictures to Cullan?"

"Okay, okay," Douglas said, holding up his hand in protest. "I sold him the pictures a couple of months ago. Satisfied?"

"Barely. If I find out you kept any copies of those pictures, or sold them or gave them away or posted them on the Internet, I'll come back here and turn you inside out."

Douglas found more courage when he realized Mason wasn't going to smack him. "I'd be more worried about Beth, if I were you. I kept the pictures, but she kept the gun."

Mason couldn't tell if Douglas was pimping him or not, but he couldn't resist the next question. "What gun?"

"Baker gave her a present when they got divorced since she wouldn't take any money or property. He told her she should use it with her next husband to get a better settlement. I settled very cheaply."

"Do you know what kind of gun it was?"

"A .38-caliber pistol," he answered with a grin that said he'd just gotten even with Beth all over again.

Chapter
Twenty-five

Mason's new theory was that Fiora, the mayor, and Beth Harrell had all killed Jack Cullan, drawing straws to see who would hold him down while one of them shot him. They had such a good time that they played their game again with Shirley Parker. As a theory, it sucked, but it was easier than trying to pick a favorite.

Returning to his car, Mason called his office, curious whether Mickey had ever come back.

"Lou Mason and Associates," Mickey said.

"Associates are young lawyers who are overpaid and underworked. I don't recall hiring any associates. I'm sure I would have remembered," Mason told him.

"Chill out, boss. It's branding, like Coke or Kleenex. Gives the name some flair. Tells people we're going places."

"I catch you playing lawyer, I'll give you some real branding. Understood?"

"No problemo, man. Hey, you got a call from Judge

Carter's administrative assistant, reminding you that she wants to see you and Ortiz first thing Monday morning, eight o'clock.''

"The judge's assistant wasn't named Margaret, was she?" Mason asked.

"She didn't say. Why, do you think you know her?"

"Only if her name is Margaret. Are you still following Fiora's money trail?"

"Inside and outside, boss. I may have something for you tonight."

Mason stopped at the jail to talk with Blues. The sheriff's deputy who brought Blues into the visiting attorney room pointed his thumb and forefinger at Mason, dropped the hammer on his imaginary gun, and told Mason he was saving a cell for him.

Blues spoke first. "Talk inside is that the cops are looking at you for the Shirley Parker thing."

"They can look all they want. Harry knows I didn't do it."

"Who did?"

"Tony Manzerio is my choice." Mason briefed Blues about Cullan's files, the fire, and Shirley Parker. He told Blues about Donovan Jenkins's contract with Ed Fiora and Jenkins's loan to the mayor. He finished up with his visits to Baker McKenzie and Al Douglas.

"You think the same person killed Cullan and Parker?" Blues asked.

"Makes sense," Mason answered. "If the ballistics tests show that the bullets were shot from the same gun, you'll be out of here with a refund. I'll check with Harry as soon as I can."

Blues nodded silently, got up from his seat, and knocked

on the door, signaling the guard that he was ready to return to his cell. He cocked his fist at his side, making imaginary contact with Mason, who returned the gesture.

Mason worried as the door closed behind Blues. Blues's face never betrayed what he was thinking or what he might do. That unpredictability made him particularly dangerous. Even a rattlesnake rattled before it struck.

Blues had been in jail for over three weeks, charged with a murder that could take his own life. Mason had looked for signs that Blues was bending to the grind of incarceration. He had seen none; no tic at the corner of Blues's eyes, no tightening of his mouth, no tremor in his hands. Yet Mason knew that Blues's rage simmered just beneath the surface and that Blues would make someone pay for putting him behind bars. Harry would be Blues's most likely target. Mason worried that getting Blues out of jail might just be the first step down a path that brought him back to the same place.

December's subzero wind chills and snowstorms had given way to a steadily raw January. Each day brought a thin mist or a thicker sleet that whipped and whirled into every body pore and open space. The sun was being held hostage behind a perpetually slate-gray sky that pressed closer to ground with night's early onset. It was the kind of weather that kept heads down and chins tucked against chests. By spring, the entire city would need a chiropractor just to stand up straight.

Mason had parked in a public lot across from the jail. His cell phone rang as he sat down behind the wheel of the Jeep, rubbing his hands against the cold.

"Lou Mason," he said, his breath vaporizing before disappearing.

"I didn't think you would answer." It was Beth Harrell. She sounded slightly breathless, a bit shaky.

"That makes us even. I didn't think you would call."

It was a small lie. Mason had expected that one of Beth's ex-husbands, or both, would tell her about his visits. She was the kind of woman who kept a hold on a man long after the last kiss. He'd expected her to call or reach out to him some other way, but decided that there was no reason to tell her so.

Mason wondered which ex-husband had called Beth. Baker McKenzie would call to brag about decking him. Al Douglas would call so that he could witness her anguish.

"I'm sorry," she said. "Calling you was an impulse, another bad one, I guess."

Her voice triggered a crotch-centered impulse in Mason that he knew was bad. Beth was a dangerous woman under the best of circumstances, and they were a long way from that relatively stable ground. Still, she managed to reach inside him. "Don't apologize. What's on your mind?"

"I'm practically a prisoner in my apartment. If I go out, the press won't leave me alone. I guess I was just feeling lonely and I couldn't think of anyone else to call." She hesitated, waiting for Mason to reply. He didn't. "Bad idea, huh?" she asked in a low, throaty, bad-girl voice.

"Not the best, but I haven't heard many good ideas lately," he told her. "The last guy you went out with on a Friday night ended up with a bullet in his eye. I don't want to make page one again any time soon."

"Neither do I. Although I don't think we could top your picture in this morning's paper unless we were caught having sex on Main Street."

Mason laughed, disarmed by her earthy humor. "You haven't seen my good side," he told her.

"Show me," she teased. "I'll make us dinner. You can

park at the hotel and take the walkway across to my building. No one will see you. You'll be safe.''

''Give me an hour,'' he told her.

Mason had a hard time using the words *safe* and *Beth* in the same sentence, but he had to talk to her about the pictures and about the gun.

Mason stopped at home, showered, shaved, fed the dog, and listened to his messages. His aunt Claire had called again, demanding that he call her. He promised the answering machine that he would. He left the lights on so that Tuffy wouldn't spend the evening in the dark, and drove to the Windcrest Hotel on the Plaza.

There were two entrances to the hotel's parking garage, one on the north side along Ward Parkway, and one on the east side on Wornall Road. Beth's apartment was in a highrise on the south side of the Windcrest. Mason chose the north entrance to the parking garage to minimize the chance that some reporter staking out Beth's apartment would see him.

It took Mason longer than he expected to find the walkway that connected the hotel and the apartment building, and it was past seven o'clock when he knocked on Beth's door. He heard the sharp clack of heels on hardwood as Beth walked hurriedly to the door, opening it with a sigh mixed equally with relief and anticipation.

Mason stood in the doorway, deciding whether to cross her threshold. Beth waited, one hand on the door, the other on her hip. She was wearing black linen slacks with a blood-red silk shirt, untucked at her waist and unbuttoned at her breasts. A sly smile creased her cheeks. She looked like a woman who'd never known trouble she hadn't asked for and who was ready to ask again.

"Come on in, Lou. I won't bite," she teased him.

"Hardly worth the effort then," he said as he walked past her.

Beth's apartment was compact. The entrance hall opened into a living room with a wall of glass that faced north, looking over the top of the Windcrest Hotel to the Plaza fifteen stories below, its eight square blocks of shops sparkling in a quarter of a million Christmas lights. The walls were papered in cream cloth, the hardwood floors softened with rugs in warm colors with dark borders. The furniture was more traditional than he had expected, the sort of chairs and sofas one inherited rather than bought. The lighting was indirect, casting shadows. Long, tapered candles lit with perfect ovals of yellow flame beckoned from the dining room table. Mellow jazz filled the corners from hidden speakers.

Beth followed behind him as he surveyed before stopping to look down at the Plaza. She nestled against his back and put her hands on his shoulders, drawing his coat halfway off. He turned toward her and she pushed his coat onto the floor, resting her hands on his chest. He held her arms, not trusting his hands. "We're alone, if you were wondering," she said.

"That's what worries me," he told her as he took her by the wrists and dropped her hands at her sides. "Get your coat."

Her face reddened as if he had slapped her. "Why?" she demanded.

"We need to talk, and the chances of keeping our clothes on while we do it are much better outside than inside."

She backed up a few steps, hugging herself. "You are the master of the mixed message," she said. "I'm at the end of my rope and you take advantage of me every time we're together. I can't keep playing these games with you."

"That's good, Beth. That's very good. The best defense

is a good offense. Let's stay on task. If I can prove that both you and Blues are innocent, you'll only get one message from me. In the meantime, I don't trust either one of us unless we're standing up with our clothes on and it's too cold to take them off.''

"I won't go with you," she said, adopting a pout. "You can't make me."

"Would you prefer your own front-page story? I don't have a photograph to go with it yet, but sometimes it's better for the reader to create his own picture. Especially when it's a story of a woman taking nude pictures of herself, then claiming a dead man was blackmailing her with the pictures."

"You wouldn't!" she said, wheeling around, her hands planted defiantly on her hips.

"Without pleasure and with regret, I assure you, but I will do it the moment I walk out of here. Rachel Firestone would love to have the story."

"I saw you with her on New Year's Eve. I don't know what you see in a woman like that! She can't love you!" Tears pooled at the corners of her eyes, spilling down past her nose and tracing a wet line along her lips. "Damn you!" she said as she stood crying, her arms limp, her shoulders heaving.

Mason was stunned at Beth's vehemence. Her world was collapsing around her and he was pushing her right up to the edge. Each time she reached out her hand, he was afraid to take it because he didn't know if he could pull her back or if he would be forced to throw her over.

He wrapped his arms around her and she muffled her cries against his chest. He held her while she slowly gathered herself, wiping his sweater with her sleeve, then her eyes and nose.

"God, I'm a mess," she said.

"Not if you like mascara streaks. I understand that's how KISS got the idea for their makeup."

"Screw you," she said, regaining a measure of playfulness.

He said, "Let's go for a drive instead."

"Okay. Let me change."

Beth chose corduroy jeans, ankle-high boots, and a heavy red woolen sweater. She had washed her face and tied her hair back with a bandanna. Not bothering with more makeup, she was scrubbed clean and fresh, indifferent to the crow's-feet and laugh lines that she'd left uncovered. Relieved of the burdens of tears and seduction, she had a fresh vulnerability that pierced Mason's heart. She pulled on her parka, grabbed her purse, and marched to the door while he remained locked in place.

"Let's go," she said. "I'm not going to spend my whole life waiting for you."

Mason pulled the Jeep out onto Ward Parkway, did a lap under the Plaza lights, and headed south. Neither of them spoke. When they'd left the city limits in the distance and the headlights ahead and behind them dwindled to a few, curiosity overcame her.

"Do we keep going until you run out of gas?" she asked him.

"Not much farther," he promised.

A few minutes later, they pulled into the driveway of a farmhouse. Mason got a swift shot of paranoia until a car that had seemed to be following them continued on past the driveway. He got out of the car and walked to the end of the driveway, looking to his west as the car's taillights disappeared over the next hill.

He got back into the Jeep and drove around the farmhouse,

down a rutted path, and into a small clearing in the woods. "Let's go for a walk," he told her.

"Are you nuts? In the dark? In this cold?"

"It's invigorating. The Swedish do it all the time. If we had snow, we'd take our clothes off and roll around in it."

Mason grabbed his flashlight from the glove compartment and got out, followed reluctantly by Beth. He led her through the woods, back toward the farmhouse, quieting her with hand signals whenever she started to ask a question. Mason could make out the shape of the farmhouse when a pair of high-beam headlights bounced off the front windows and splashed back into the front yard. Mason turned off his flashlight and pulled Beth down to the ground.

Mason watched as Tony Manzerio, silhouetted by the headlights, took a quick tour of the grounds. Sound travels farther at night, and in the cold stillness he heard Manzerio invoke ghosts and godfathers in frustration at having lost them.

Mason, and Beth waited in the woods until Manzerio drove away, and another twenty minutes to make certain he wasn't coming back.

"Okay," Mason said. "Let's go." He helped her up and began walking toward the farmhouse.

"Wait a minute," Beth said. "The car is back the other way."

"We're not going to the car. We're spending the night here."

Mason walked to the back door of the farmhouse and knelt at the stoop, where he found a porcelain jug. He twisted the top off the jug and removed a key. He unlocked the door and returned the key to the jug.

"Lou Mason, international man of mystery," Beth said as they stepped inside. "Whose place is this?"

"It belonged to a former partner of mine who was killed

when he got in over his head in a money-laundering scheme. He used to invite me out here. He was a nice man, gentle but weak, and it got him killed. I kind of look after the place for his family, who live on the West Coast. They're waiting for suburbia to get here before they sell it.''

''And you feel safer spending the night with me in an abandoned farmhouse in the middle of nowhere than in my nice, warm apartment on the Plaza where we can actually order room service from the Windcrest Hotel? Don't tell me what you're taking because I don't want any of it.''

''I didn't intend to come here, but it looked like we were being followed. I'm not much good at playing hide-and-seek in traffic, so I tried a little misdirection and it worked. I don't know if Manzerio was following both of us or just one of us. There's no point in finding out by going back to either of our places tonight. No one will bother us here.''

''What about keeping our clothes on?''

''Don't worry. There's no heat or electricity,'' he told her.

Chapter
Twenty-six

"I am not spending the night in a freezing-cold abandoned farmhouse!" Beth said.

"It's a long way to anywhere from here," Mason told her. They were in the kitchen and he shined the flashlight around the room, spotlighting a worn butcher-block table and two vinyl-upholstered chairs. "Let's talk first. Then we can decide about spending the night."

Beth stepped toward the back door. Mason cut her off, aiming the beam of his flashlight at the chairs.

"Oh, please!" Beth said. "You aren't really going to hold me hostage here until I talk. Don't you remember anything from law school? Like kidnapping is against the law? Like coerced confessions are inadmissible?"

"I'm not kidnapping you. You're free to go, but it is a long walk. Just tell me the truth about you, Jack Cullan, your pictures, and his files, and then I'll take you home."

Mason held the flashlight in front of him, pointing the

beam at the ceiling like a torch, illuminating their faces as if they were sitting at the edge of a campfire. Beth looked at him across the beam, her mouth clamped shut, her eyes narrowed, waiting for Mason to call off his parlor game. He tipped his head at the table and raised his eyebrows as if to say he wasn't kidding.

Beth slipped her purse off her shoulder and walked to the table, her back to him. Mason waited for her to sit down, then turned off the flashlight and joined her at the other side of the table.

"We'll do this in the dark," he told her. "Just in case Manzerio comes back. I don't want him to see the light." Moonlight sneaked through a break in the clouds and trickled in the window, a ghostly glow that outlined their faces.

"Turn your flashlight on one more time," Beth told him. "I've got a surprise for you."

"You were supposed to keep your clothes on," he said. He aimed the beam at her chest. She pointed a gun at his. "Does that count as a mixed message?" he asked her.

"Give me the keys to your car," she told him.

"Is that the .38 Baker McKenzie gave you?"

"Give me the goddamn car keys!"

"Or you'll shoot me like you shot Jack Cullan and Shirley Parker?"

Before Beth could answer, Tony Manzerio kicked in the back door, carrying a flashlight bigger than Mason's and a gun bigger than Beth's. Mason jumped to his feet.

"Steady, Batman," Manzerio told him. "I like you a lot better sitting down." Mason hesitated, weighing his chances. "Do it!" Manzerio demanded.

Mason sat down, noticing that Beth was no longer pointing her gun at him. She wasn't pointing it at Manzerio either. Mason didn't know what she had done with her gun or whom she was likely to point it at next.

He heard the front door knocked off its hinges, and tried to guess how much more company they were about to have. Ed Fiora and two men only slightly smaller than Manzerio made their way in the dark to the kitchen.

"Hey, Mason," Fiora said as his two goons flanked him. "It must be hard to tell who your friends are these days."

The goons laughed and pointed their flashlights and guns at him. Mason held his hands up to shade his eyes from the glare.

"Can't tell the players without a program," Mason said.

"You are right about that," Fiora answered.

"Why were you following me?" Mason asked.

"I got something for you that you been looking for," Fiora said. "I wanted to give it to you so maybe you'd get off my back. I sent Tony here to deliver it, only he couldn't catch up to you. You gave him the drop, but I figured you stayed at the farmhouse when we didn't see any other cars on the road."

One of the goons handed Fiora a large envelope. He held it in one hand, tapped it against his other, and tossed it onto the table. "Go ahead, open it. Use your flashlight."

Mason picked up the envelope, guessing at its contents. Beth hung her head, looking away. He put the envelope back on the table. "Not interested," Mason said.

"That's not what I hear. Tony," Fiora said to Manzerio. "Mason's dick has gone limp. Open that envelope for him."

Manzerio stuffed his gun in his pocket and his flashlight under his arm. He ripped the envelope open and fanned out pictures of Beth Harrell across the table. Mason kept his eyes on Fiora. Manzerio gripped the back of Mason's head like a melon, pushing his face at the pictures.

Beth was nude in each photograph, legs spread, squeezing and probing her body with her hands in some pictures, using a dildo in others. Her closed eyes and open mouth mimed a staged rapture that looked stag-film phony.

"Not bad for amateur stuff," Fiora said, nodding at Manzerio, who released his grip on Mason's head.

"What do you want?" Mason asked him.

"Like I told you, I want you to back off. You think I'm blackmailing this bitch with these pictures. Cullan gave me the pictures after I got my license. I never used them except to make sure she came to my New Year's Eve party."

"So forcing her to come on to me while you watched on closed-circuit TV is just taking one of those edges you need every now and then? Is that it? Plus now I'm supposed to believe that you didn't have Cullan whacked so you could get rid of his file on you?" Mason asked.

"I knew all about Cullan's files. They didn't mean squat to me. Cullan couldn't take me down without taking himself down. Hell, I've got my own files. Everybody has files on everybody else. It's like nuclear bombs. Everyone wants them, but none of us can afford to use them."

"Then who killed Jack Cullan?" Mason asked him.

"I don't know and I don't care," Fiora said. "It wasn't me or my boys. I may rough some chump up that tries to stiff me on a tab at the casino, but I got too good a thing going to whack my own lawyer or anybody else."

"What about Shirley Parker?"

"Not my problem. Not my hit."

"If you are so uninterested in Cullan's files, why did you make me that offer on New Year's Eve if I found them first?"

"That offer still stands. I knew who I was dealing with when Cullan had his files. I don't know who or what I'm dealing with if somebody else gets them. I got one more tip for you, Counselor."

"What's that?"

"Cut out all that computer shit your wiseass gofer has been doing. I don't understand that shit, but my people tell me that anyone tries to get in my computer records leaves electronic footprints that lead right back to them. I had a little talk with that kid tonight. What's his name? Mickey something or other. By the way, I think you're going to need a new computer."

"You hurt that kid and I'll—"

"You'll what, Mr. Big Shot? Kill me? Give it a rest. Like I told you, I might rough somebody up but I don't whack anybody. I'm a businessman and I'm done doing business with you. Let's go, boys."

As Fiora turned to leave, Beth whipped her gun from inside her coat and aimed at Fiora. Mason lunged across the table, shoving her gun hand high just as she fired. The bullet lodged in the ceiling.

"Don't shoot! Don't shoot!" Mason screamed as he tumbled on top of Beth and wrestled the gun from her.

Manzerio and the other two goons showered their flashlights on Mason and Beth as they lay in a tangle on the floor. Beth wept as Mason covered her body with his, looking over his shoulder at Fiora and his men.

"I owe you, Mason," Fiora conceded, "but I wouldn't turn my back on that crazy bitch if I was you."

Before they left the farmhouse, Mason emptied the bullets from Beth's gun into one pocket of his coat and put the gun in another pocket. He slid the photographs back in the envelope and offered them to Beth. She shook her head, saying that it didn't matter anymore. She didn't speak during the drive back to the Plaza. Mason tried a couple of times to draw her out with lame jokes or offers to stop for dinner.

She just kept staring out the window, wiping away an occasional tear.

Beth's gun was a .45-caliber Beretta auto pistol, not the .38 Baker McKenzie had given her and not the .38 used to kill Jack Cullan. Mason still didn't know what kind of gun had been used to kill Shirley Parker. He decided to wait until he found that out before deciding what to do with Beth's gun.

Mason tried calling Mickey from the car, but there was no answer in his office. He called Harry at home and asked him to check out a possible break-in at his office, and promised to meet him there as soon as possible.

He parked in the garage at the Windcrest Hotel and turned off the ignition. Beth made no move to get out of the car. Mason wasn't certain she could move at all.

"I'll take you upstairs," he offered.

Beth got out of the car and started walking. He caught up to her, cupping her elbow with his hand. She gave no sign of noticing his presence. He followed her inside her apartment, turning on lights. She plopped down in a soft-cushioned chair. Mason took off his parka and sat down across from her in a matching chair.

He didn't know what to think or feel about her. He didn't understand why she would have taken the pictures. He did understand why she tried to kill Ed Fiora, and wondered if the same thing had happened with Jack Cullan, only no one was there to ruin her aim. Whatever the answers were, he was afraid to leave her alone, but he had to find Mickey.

"Don't worry," she said, sensing his concern. "I don't need to kill myself. I'm already dead."

"Self-pity is a luxury for someone in your shoes, Beth."

She lifted her chin from her chest, focusing her blank eyes on him. "What do you suggest?"

"Start with the truth. How did your fingerprints end up in Cullan's bedroom?"

Beth looked away as she bit her lower lip. "You want me to tell you that I was holding on to the headboard while he fucked me doggie-style?"

"I don't care if the two of you got naked and howled at the moon. Just once, I'd like the truth. Did you take those pictures?"

"Yes," she said with the same flat tone.

"Why?"

"My therapist said I have a self-destructive tape playing in my head because I had an abusive father and a disinterested mother, so I do crazy things to punish myself."

"Do you believe that?"

"I don't believe anything. That's all an excuse. I did it because I wanted to, not because I know why I wanted to."

"Then why ask me to get them back?"

"After Jack was killed, I was afraid the police would think I did it because of the pictures. I had to get them back."

"Where's the gun Baker McKenzie gave you?"

"I got rid of it after Jack was killed. The paper said he was shot with a .38-caliber gun. My gun was a .38. I thought it would look bad. I liked having a gun for protection, so I bought the Berretta."

"The police could have run ballistics tests on your gun and ruled it out as the murder weapon," Mason said.

Beth got up and paced around the living room, finding renewed energy. "I admit I wasn't setting records for clear thinking. I just wanted to get the pictures back and get rid of the gun. I wanted to be a good girl again." She stopped in front of Mason and looped her fingers into the collar of his sweater, pulling him up. "I wanted to be a good girl for you," she said.

She wrapped her arms around his neck, pressed her breasts hard against his chest, and ground her pelvis against his crotch. "You saved me," she murmured as she felt him grow hard.

Mason pushed her away. "What are you?" he asked.

"I'm just a girl who can't say no."

"I'm not asking you to say yes."

Mason picked up his coat and left her standing in her living room.

Chapter
Twenty-seven

Friday nights were usually big nights at Blues on Broadway, but business had slowed considerably since New Year's Eve, and the joint was nearly dead when Mason arrived shortly before midnight. Mickey had turned out to be a lousy bartender, and Blues had hired a temp who wasn't much better. Pete Kirby's trio had taken a gig on the road, and Blues hadn't found anyone to take their place. Jazz musicians were used to oddball gigs, but working for someone sitting in jail on a murder rap hadn't proved to be very attractive.

Mason recognized Harry's off-duty car, an old Crown Victoria that had done time as an on-duty detective's ride. Mason made his way through the bar, where three customers were nursing flat beers while the bartender cleaned glasses, a cigarette dangling from the corner of his mouth, dribbling ashes into the soapy sink water.

He took the stairs two at a time, his concern for Mickey quickening his pace. Fiora was in the casino business, but he didn't strike Mason as a man who bluffed very often. Mason took Fiora at his word when he said that he'd paid Mickey a visit. Mason knew enough about computers to read his e-mail. He had no idea that an amateur hacker like Mickey would leave an electronic trail that could lead to a beating. Mason was mentally calculating Mickey's Worker's Compensation benefits when he saw Mickey standing in the hall with Harry and his aunt Claire.

"Harry," Mason said, "is everything all right?"

Harry was wearing a warm-up suit and athletic shoes underneath an open trench coat. Claire was also wearing a warm-up suit under her made-for-the-tundra topcoat. It took Mason a minute to realize that they were wearing identical warm-up suits, and that his aunt was wearing house slippers and that her car was not also parked outside. Both of them had a slightly rumpled, just-rousted-out-of-bed look. Mason wasn't certain, but he thought he saw a small hickey on Harry's neck. Mason flushed with a queasy jolt, like a teenager who'd walked in on his parents while they were doing it.

"No, everything is not all right!" Claire snapped. "Someone broke into your office and smashed your computer."

Mason stepped into his office. His computer tower was crumpled as if it had been in a head-on collision, and the top was peeled back as if it had been operated on with a can opener. His monitor was shattered. He looked around the rest of his office, confirmed that there wasn't any other damage, and came back out into the hallway.

"Thanks for coming over, Harry," Mason said.

"Is that all you've got to say?" Claire demanded. "Every time I turn around, you're this close to getting killed or robbed," she said, pinching her fingers together. "I won't have it!"

Mason hadn't seen his aunt this angry in years. "I'm sorry," he told her. "I didn't mean to upset you."

"Well, you have and so has he!" she said, jabbing her thumb at Harry. "It's time you two started working together on this case instead of against each other." Harry and Mason both studied their feet, waiting for Claire's outburst to subside. "I'll wait in your office," she said.

Mickey was grinning so widely that Mason practically forgot to ask if he was hurt. "I would not piss off that woman anymore if I was you," Mickey said.

Mason put his hand under Mickey's chin, tilting his head upward. "You look good with a black eye, Mickey. It gives you that mature look."

Harry referred to the notepad he always carried. "Your neighbor here, Mr. Shanahan, says he was asleep in his office when he heard a commotion next door. He jumped up to see what was going on, and ran into his door and knocked himself out. By the time he came to, whoever had broken into your office was gone. That still your story, Mr. Shanahan?" Harry asked with no effort to disguise his disbelief.

"Yes, sir, Detective. That's my story and I'm sticking to it."

Harry turned to Mason. "Are you satisfied with that story, Lou?"

"It'll do for now," Lou answered.

"Good, 'cause it's bullshit and we both know it, but if you don't care, I don't care. At least we don't need anything else from Mr. Shanahan. Let's you and me go have a talk in your office before your aunt makes us take turns walking into the door and knocking ourselves out."

"Don't think for one second that I'm going to clean up that mess for you," Claire said as Mason closed the door behind him.

Mason raised both hands in surrender, knowing better than to get in her way while she still had a head of steam going. Harry picked up the computer tower and peered inside.

"The hard drive is gone," he told Mason. "You back up your stuff?"

"Not in the last six months."

"How long you had this computer?" Harry asked.

"Six months."

"You're screwed."

"Is that a professional opinion?" Mason asked.

"Worth every cent of the tax dollars you paid for it. Who did it?"

"Ed Fiora."

"Why?"

"He objected to me checking out his personal affairs."

"Hacking? You couldn't hack yourself. That kid, Shanahan—he do the hacking for you?"

"Yup."

"Fiora probably has somebody who runs security for his computer systems, picked up the hacking, traced it back to your computer. Fiora values his privacy. So why does Shanahan give me that crap about running into his door?"

"He's like all law-abiding citizens. He doesn't trust the cops and he thinks he's doing me a favor."

"Why were you investigating Fiora?"

Mason took two bottles of Budweiser out of his refrigerator and handed one to Harry. Claire gave him a long, threatening look, and he handed her the other bottle, then grabbed another one for himself. He threw his parka over his desk chair, sat down on the sofa, and put his feet up on the low table in front of it. Harry and Claire dumped their coats on top of his, and each took a chair at either end of the table.

They all swallowed heavily from their bottles. Claire drank the deepest.

"Cullan's murder, Shirley Parker's murder, and the fire at the barbershop were all about one thing—the secret files Jack Cullan kept on his friends and enemies," Mason said. "Though I suspect he had a difficult time telling one from the other. I was looking for a link, something that would tie Fiora to the files and the murders, or at least the other suspects."

"And who might the other suspects be? Assuming, of course, that we don't count your client?" Harry asked.

Mason tipped his bottle at Harry. "You assume correctly. His Honor the mayor is on the take. He made at least one sweetheart deal with Fiora that lined the pockets of his old wide receiver Donovan Jenkins. Jenkins paid the mayor back by refinancing his house. That deal may have actually been legal, but I think there's more. That's what Mickey was looking for."

"Who else?" Harry asked.

Mason hesitated, swirling the beer in the bottle, concluding that he had only one client, not two. "Beth Harrell. She gets the Head Case of the Year award. On the outside, she's a superachiever public servant. On the inside, she's a bad girl who owned a .38-caliber pistol. She threw it away after Cullan was killed because she thought it would look bad. Especially since Cullan was blackmailing her with dirty pictures."

"Where'd did Cullan get the pictures?" Harry asked.

"She took them herself and gave them to her ex-husband. He sold them to Cullan."

"What kind of a woman would do that?" Claire asked.

"A severely messed-up one," Mason answered. "Beth claims she voted to give the license to the Dream Casino because it was the right thing to do. Then she got suspicious that Fiora had bribed the mayor. She was about to start an investigation when Cullan threatened her with the pictures."

"What makes you think she's telling the truth?" Claire asked.

Mason got up from the sofa and retrieved the envelope of pictures from an inside pocket in his parka. He dropped them on the table in front of Harry and Claire. "I've seen the pictures. Fiora gave them to me tonight. He was trying to convince me that he wasn't blackmailing Beth and that he had nothing to do with Cullan's or Shirley Parker's deaths."

Harry reached for the envelope, but Claire snatched it and opened it first. "I am never surprised what we will do to get even with ourselves," she said before passing the photographs to Harry.

Harry looked at the photographs without betraying any reaction. He returned them to the envelope and said, "Shirley Parker was killed with a .38-caliber bullet, but it was fired from a different gun than the one that was used to kill Jack Cullan. It sure would have been nice to have a look at Harrell's gun. Where does all this leave Ed Fiora?"

"Fiora says he wasn't worried about Cullan's files because Cullan couldn't take Fiora down without taking himself down. That makes sense. Fiora wants his file before it winds up with someone he can't do business with. That makes sense. He tried to hire me to find the file for him. That makes sense too. Killing Cullan and Shirley Parker doesn't make sense."

"What about the mayor?" Claire asked.

"Yeah," Mason said to Harry. "Did you ask the mayor if he had an alibi for the time of Cullan's murder?"

"Sure," Harry replied. "Right after we asked him for semen samples so we could clear up some open rape cases."

Mason finished his beer in a final swallow. "All I've

done in this case is chase my tail. I'm getting absolutely nowhere.''

"Maybe you're just digging up a lot of dirt but no killers because your client is guilty," Harry said.

"Maybe. And maybe you and Zimmerman and the prosecuting attorney and the mayor are sweeping a lot of dirt under the rug because you want Blues to be guilty. It's obvious that the mayor was pressuring you to make a quick arrest."

"Sure he wanted a quick arrest. He also wanted a conviction, not a botched case."

"When did you first talk to the mayor about Cullan's murder?" Mason asked.

"Right after we identified Cullan's body. I called the chief and the chief called the mayor. The mayor told the chief he wanted to meet with me and Carl, which really frosted the chief."

"Because that made the chief look like he wasn't running the investigation?" Claire asked.

"Exactly. There's more politics in the police department than the Catholic Church," Harry said. "The mayor told me and Carl that he wanted daily reports on the case until the son of a bitch who killed his lawyer was found guilty."

"So you've been on the phone with the mayor every day?" Mason asked.

"Not me and not the mayor. Carl is the politician. The mayor told Carl to report to his chief of staff, Amy White. She told Carl he was on twenty-four call and his cell phone better be on all the time." Harry laughed before continuing. "She's driving Carl crazy."

"There's one thing I don't get," Claire said. "Where did Cullan get all his dirt? I doubt that everyone was as stupid as Beth Harrell. Maybe whoever was supplying Cullan with information decided to go into business for himself—or herself—which meant putting Cullan out of business.''

Mason and Harry stared at Claire, slack-jawed at her insight. Claire smiled, careful not to smile too much, and set her empty bottle on the table. ''I love both of you, but sometimes you are thick as fence posts. Let's go home, Harry, before that beer drowns out what little spark I've got left.''

Mickey walked into Mason's office as soon as Harry and Claire hit the street. ''Hey, boss,'' he said before Mason cut him off with a raised hand.

Claire had come at the case from a completely different angle than Mason or Harry. Both of them had made the mistake of focusing on the explanations that best suited their bias. Harry wanted it to be Blues. Mason wanted it to be someone Cullan was blackmailing. They both wanted it to be easy, and the truth was seldom that easy.

Mason opened the doors to the dry-erase board, wiped out a week's worth of now meaningless notes, wrote *Cullan's source for dirt* in large red letters on the board, and sat down in his desk chair. He rocked and swiveled, steepled his fingers beneath his chin, rubbed his temples, and thumped his desk with the palms of his hands.

Mickey tried again, ''Lou, I've got—''

''It'll have to wait,'' Mason said. ''Have a seat.'' Mason shuffled through the papers on his desk until he found the initial police report on Cullan's murder. The dispatcher had recorded the call from Cullan's maid, Norma Hawkins, at 8:03 A.M. Mason remembered that the first cop on the scene had been a uniformed patrol officer. Mason scanned the report for his name, finding it at the bottom of the report.

Officer James Toland had arrived at the scene at 8:10 A.M. Harry and Carl Zimmerman had arrived at 8:27 A.M.

Mason was beginning to think that Toland was like the guy who showed up at every major sporting event wearing a rainbow wig and holding a sign that said JOHN 3:16. Toland had been first on the murder scene; he'd been at the bar to arrest Blues; and he'd busted Mason in Pendergast's office just in time to prevent Mason from reading Cullan's files. Nobody had timing that good. Not without help.

Mason picked up the phone and dialed Rachel Firestone's home number. He tapped a pencil on his knee while the phone rang five times.

"What?" Rachel said, her voice thick with sleep.

"It's me, Lou."

"Whoopee," she said.

"I need you to do something for me. It's important."

"I hope it's important enough to die for because I'm going to kill you if it isn't."

"I want you to check for any reports of a body found in Swope Park on Thursday evening any time in the three hours before the fire at the barbershop."

"Of course. Then I'll run a check for Jimmy Hoffa when I'm done."

"This is serious, Rachel."

"This is the middle of the night. Call me tomorrow," she said, and hung up.

Mason was jazzed. He had a hunch that felt so right it had to be wrong, and if he was right, it could still go down very wrong. He smacked his hands together. "Okay, Mickey. What have you got?"

"This," Mickey said, holding up a floppy disk.

"And that is?" Mason asked.

"A copy of the bank records of Ed Fiora and the mayor, plus a few dozen money-laundering stops in between that show a steady stream of cash from Fiora to the mayor. The total is around a hundred and fifty thousand bucks. It began a month before Fiora got his casino license and goes right up to last week. I backed up the hard drive onto the disk just before Fiora and his trolls did a tap dance on my face. I stuffed it down my pants when they busted in here.''

Mason jumped out of his chair, pulled Mickey up, and embraced him. ''I love you, man,'' Mason said, punch-drunk from the whirlwind of the last two days.

''Don't go there, Lou. I'm telling you, man,'' Mickey said, shoving Mason away and dusting himself off. ''Now what?'' he asked Mason.

''First of all, you're hired. Second of all, we work weekends. Tomorrow night, we're going to the Dream Casino.''

''We gamble on the job?''

''Only for high stakes,'' Mason told him.

Chapter
Twenty-eight

Mason had been so wired when he got home the night before that he had rowed three sprints of two thousand meters each just to wind down. By the time he'd taken a shower, he was barely able to crawl into bed. The last thing he saw was his clock telling him it was four in the morning.

He was sleeping the sleep of the nearly comatose when his phone rang on Saturday morning. He let it ring until the answering machine came on.

"Pick up, Lou. The sun is up and you'd better be," Rachel said.

Mason fumbled for the phone, trying to clear his throat while squinting at the clock. It was eight o'clock. "I'm here," he groaned.

"Good. Paybacks are hell," she told him. "Why do you want to know about a body in Swope Park?"

"Can't tell you," he said, pulling himself up in his bed before collapsing back against his pillows.

"Why not?"

"I may be wrong about something. If I am, no one needs to know. If I'm right, you'll get the story," he told her.

"It had better be a good story," she said. "I talked to one of the dispatchers who's a friend of mine."

"You mean an anonymous source who gets a turkey at Thanksgiving?"

"I don't bribe people. The paper is too cheap. She's a kindred spirit."

"A member of the lesbian underground?"

"We're everywhere. She said there were no reports of a body being reported or found in Swope Park on Thursday night or any night for the last six months. What does that tell you?"

"That you may get a hell of a story if I don't get killed," he told her.

"Then don't get killed," she said. "I need all the good stories I can get."

"That's it? No Thanksgiving turkey?"

"I'd miss you. How's that?"

"Nice," he told her, and hung up.

Mason rolled over and tried to go back to sleep. He tossed and turned with the uneasy confirmation of his suspicions. He gave up when Tuffy stuck her nose in his face, reminding him that she wasn't operating on his schedule. Her whimper said she was overdue for breakfast and her morning ablutions in the backyard.

While Tuffy was in the backyard, Mason took another shower, hoping that the pulsating hot water would trick his body into feeling fresh and renewed instead of tired and abused. After pulling on faded jeans, a washed-out green sweatshirt, and sneakers, he let the dog inside and poured himself into a chair at his kitchen table. He'd have to make his own breakfast.

Cooking was not one of Mason's skills. He wasn't the kind of man who could scour his pantry for a few disparate leftovers and whip up a tantalizing omelet while whistling classical music and puzzling over what wine works best with bagel and cream cheese. He relied too heavily on fast food, once prompting his aunt Claire to warn him that one day he would be able to drive through any McDonald's in the city and the cashier would greet him by asking, ''The usual, Mr. Mason?''

Tuffy was pacing nervously around the kitchen, poking her head into nooks and crannies she'd explored countless times, before stopping in front of Mason and pawing his thigh. He gazed down at her, raising an eyebrow as if to ask, what now? She yelped once and trotted to the back door, repeating the ritual she observed whenever she wanted to go on a walk.

''Why not?'' Mason muttered. ''Maybe we'll find some roadkill for breakfast.''

He put on his coat, grabbed a ball cap that he yanked low on his brow, and hooked Tuffy's collar to the leash he kept on a hook by the door. The leash had a twenty-five-foot retractable cord that allowed Tuffy to run relatively free while dragging Mason behind her.

The morning amazed Mason. He hadn't paid attention to the day until Tuffy took him outside. The sun had blasted away the grim bedrock of slate-colored clouds that had covered the city like a fossil layer for weeks. The temperature had climbed into the forties, but felt even warmer in comparison to recent days. The air was crisp and clear and hit him like a shot of adrenaline. The next thing he knew, he was jogging alongside Tuffy, his jacket unzipped and a thin sheen of sweat lining his forehead. He grinned at his dog, who grinned back before sprinting after a squirrel.

Tuffy led Mason to Loose Park, the city's second-largest

park, which was only a couple of blocks from his house. They stopped at the large pond along Wornall Road. Long enough for Tuffy to say hello to the other dogs that were walking their owners. Tuffy sniffed enough dog butts to last a lifetime. Mason was about to introduce himself to a good-looking woman with a white fur-ball of a dog that resembled a dust mop with legs when Tuffy sniffed the dog once and peed all over it. Horrified, the woman scooped up her dog, gave Mason the finger, and marched off in a huff.

A few minutes later, Mason and Tuffy power-walked past Beth Harrell's apartment building. He craned his neck skyward, shielding his eyes from the sun, wondering which windows were hers and what she was doing behind her drawn shades. Tuffy wasn't interested in the answer, and tugged him along the last few blocks to the Plaza.

Mason tied her leash to a traffic sign outside Starbucks while he went inside for a blueberry muffin and a bottle of water. He shared both with Tuffy, pouring the water into a plastic bowl he'd borrowed from the cashier.

On the way back, they stopped at the waterfall in front of the Windcrest Hotel. The waterfall plunged two stories from the pool deck to street level at the intersection of Ward Parkway and Wornall Road. The fountain had been turned off for the winter, but a heavy layer of ice had built up during the storms of the previous weeks. The sun bore down on the irregular slags of ice, reflecting and refracting across their faults, forecasting the coming meltdown.

From his vantage point, Mason could see west to the entrance to the hotel's parking garage on Ward Parkway. He could also see south, up Wornall Road, to Beth's building, which towered over the roof of the hotel. The juxtaposition of both views crystallized something that had lurked in the jumble of details that this case had become.

He remembered Beth telling him that Cullan had taken

her home after the incident at Blues on Broadway the night Cullan was killed. She had said that Cullan had dropped her at the door and that she had stayed inside the rest of the night. Later, she had told Mason that she had begun using the hotel's parking garage to avoid the press, taking advantage of the walkway between the hotel and her apartment building so that she wouldn't be seen coming or going.

Mason guessed that the security system in her apartment building included video monitoring of the apartment garage. Had Beth gone out again that night, or any night, her departure and return would have been recorded. If she'd used the hotel exit strategy, she could have left undetected.

That scenario, Mason realized, would have left her on foot. He doubted that she would have called a cab to take her to Cullan's house and told the driver to wait outside while she murdered Cullan. Cullan lived in Sunset Hills, an exclusive area just south and west of the Plaza. The hills were real hills by Kansas City standards, making the round-trip walk from the hotel to Cullan's house a punishing one of several miles. He realized that Beth could have hiked to Cullan's house, killed him, and walked back.

Mason shook his head at the possibility. The night Cullan was murdered had been brutal, with a lacerating windchill and hard-driven snow. Even a cold-blooded killer wouldn't have made that hike. Unless, he conceded, the killer was convinced that no one else would think she might have done exactly that.

By the time Mason and Tuffy returned home, the prospect that Beth Harrell had covered the murder of Jack Cullan under a blanket of snow had robbed him of his enthusiasm for the beautiful morning. It also didn't jibe with his growing suspicion that James Toland and Carl Zimmerman had been dirt gofers for Cullan, and might have killed Cullan to go into business on their own, as his aunt Claire had theorized.

When Mason had called Zimmerman to ask for his help to preserve Cullan's files, Zimmerman had put him off with a lie about working a case involving a dead body in Swope Park. The lie had only one purpose—to keep Mason away from the files until Zimmerman and Toland could steal the ones they wanted and rig the bomb that would destroy the rest.

It was possible that Zimmerman and Toland hadn't known where the files were kept until Mason tipped Zimmerman. Although Shirley Parker had not hesitated to let Toland into Pendergast's office so he could kick Mason out of it. Maybe Mason's phone call tipped Zimmerman, or maybe they had known all along, and Mason's call forced them to move the files. Maybe Shirley Parker made one last visit to check on the files, and they killed her when she tried to stop them. There were too many maybes, but none of them made Toland and Zimmerman look clean to Mason.

Neither did Mason's suspicions prove anything. Mason knew it would be difficult and dangerous to try to make a case against two cops, particularly when one of the cops was Harry's partner. Over the years, Mason had gathered from Harry and Claire that it was a good partnership, though neither man had embraced the other as a blood brother. Still, they were cops and they were partners, and that was a stronger bond than most marriages.

Mason didn't even know where to begin. He couldn't talk to Harry, who would dismiss his theory as a malicious red herring Mason had fantasized to cast doubt on Blues's guilt. Even worse, Harry would consider it an unholy attempt to drive a wedge between Harry and Zimmerman and an unethical pitch to discredit their investigation. Mason couldn't go after Zimmerman without painting Harry with the same brush.

Mason's best and only idea was to keep an eye on Zimmerman. Mason had been to Zimmerman's house once before to pick up Harry. Zimmerman lived in Red Bridge, a suburban subdivision in south Kansas City. Mason wouldn't stake out Zimmerman's house. That's what cops and PIs did, not lawyers. Besides, Mason didn't want to pee into a bottle on a cold day, even if the sun was shining.

All the same, a drive-by couldn't hurt. Mason looked at Tuffy. "Want to go for a ride?" he asked her.

Tuffy practically ran him over racing to the garage. Mason opened the door to his TR-6, and Tuffy vaulted the stick shift, landing in the passenger seat. It wasn't a top-down day, but it was close enough.

Chapter
Twenty-nine

Mason believed that the TR-6 was the last great sports car ever built. He didn't believe it in the squishy way that some people believe that black is a slimming color, or that all good things come to those who wait. He believed it with the same bedrock certainty as the cinematic heavyweight Rocky Balboa when he told Mrs. Balboa that a man's got to do what a man's got to do.

In Mason's world, BMW, Porsche, and Audi roadsters were for cash-heavy baby boomers willing to overpay for the thrill of the wheel. The Corvette was a contender, but with its powerful engine and oversize tires, it was in another weight class. He conceded that those cars could outperform the TR-6, but they couldn't out-cool it. The brand name, Triumph, said it all for Mason. The TR-6's raw lines and hard look had captivated Mason the first time he had seen the car. By then, British Leyland had inexplicably abandoned the model, turning each of the 94,000 TR-6's it had made from 1969 to 1976 into instant classics.

Mason had never been much of a car guy. He'd always driven whatever he could afford until he couldn't afford to keep it running. He'd never gotten sweaty at the sight of a muscle car, nor had his head been turned by a sleek import. The TR-6 was different. It had snagged his automotive heart, lingering there unrequited until he'd succumbed years later, taking advantage of a neighbor's divorce to buy his dream car. It was a British racing-green, four-speed, six-cylinder real live ragtop trip.

Tuffy loved the car more than Mason, delighting in the endless scents that sped past her when the top was down and her nose was in the wind. Sitting in his garage, Mason resisted his dog's pleading, doleful eyes to put the top down. A man and his dog both blowing in the wind on a cold winter morning would garner too much attention, no matter how brightly the sun was shining.

Not that Mason was trying to be covert. The truth was, he didn't know what he was trying to be or how he was going to try to be it. As he drove toward Carl Zimmerman's neighborhood, he had a throat-tightening epiphany. He was in over his head in a death-penalty case that was as likely to cost his life as it was his client's. He needed help, and the one person who could help him the most was sitting in the county lockup. Mason tapped the clutch, downshifted, and opened the throttle. The burst of growling speed came at the same moment as did a crazy idea how he could get Blues out of jail.

Mason circled Zimmerman's block once, quietly relieved that there were no signs of life in the split-level, brick-front house. He circled again, this time parking at the curb on the street that intersected Zimmerman's. A minivan parked in front of him gave him added cover. Mason had a right-angle view of Zimmerman's house, which was in the middle of the block. He turned off his engine, and hoped that no one would notice the only classic sports car within miles even though a sign at the corner read NEIGHBORHOOD WATCH! WE CALL THE POLICE!

Tuffy pawed at her window, and Mason cranked the engine so he could put it down for her. She leaned the upper third of her body out the window and wagged her tail in Mason's face.

Mason knew a bad idea when he had one and said as much to the dog. "This is nuts. We're out of here."

Before Mason could put the car in gear, a lumbering black Chevy Suburban turned onto the street he was on. Mason blanched when he looked in his rearview mirror and saw Carl Zimmerman behind the wheel. Mason scrunched down in his seat while he racked his memory for any mention that he might have ever made to Zimmerman about owning the TR-6.

The Suburban slowly rolled past him toward the stop sign at the corner. Mason didn't look up, even though the driver's seat in the Suburban was considerably higher above the ground than the TR-6's, making it doubtful that Zimmerman could see Mason's face. Mason peeked at the Suburban, and saw a collection of young faces pressed against the passenger-side windows, mouths agape at the TR-6 and the dog riding shotgun, hanging out the window.

Mason watched as Zimmerman pulled into his driveway and a half dozen young boys dressed in Cub Scout uniforms piled out of the Suburban, some of them staring and pointing at his car parked half a block away. Carl Zimmerman herded them toward the front door, taking a long look at Mason's car before following his troop into the house.

"Brilliant," Mason told Tuffy. "Carl Zimmerman—

homicide detective, Cub Scout leader, and murderer. That's the ticket!''

Tuffy ignored him and pointed her snout into the breeze as Mason headed for home.

Mason picked Mickey up at nine o'clock that night in front of Blues on Broadway. He was still driving the TR-6, counting on the cool to carry into the casino. Mickey had told Mason that he was working crowd control at the bar and that Mason should pick him up there instead of at his apartment. Mason was pretty certain that Mickey's apartment was also his office above the bar, but saw no reason to tell Mickey. At least, Mason figured, he'd always know where to find him.

Mickey was waiting on the sidewalk when Mason pulled up. "Is there a crowd inside that needs to be controlled?" Mason asked.

"Not unless you count three guys who don't have four teeth among them," Mickey answered. "If Blues doesn't get out soon, I doubt that any PR campaign will save this joint. It's going to shrivel up and blow away before spring."

"Did you do what I told you?" Mason asked as he pulled into the light traffic on Main Street.

"Piece of cake. I used a computer at the public library to print out a hard copy of Fiora's bank records, and I put it in your desk just like you told me."

"And what about the rest?" Mason asked.

"That's the part I don't understand," Mickey answered. "I e-mailed the file to Rachel Firestone just like you told me, but I delayed the actual transmission until ten o'clock Monday morning. What's up with that?"

"It's an insurance policy. We're going to trade the disk to Fiora. He'll suspect that we kept another copy of the disk or a hard copy of the records, and he'll send someone back to search my office. Hopefully, when he finds the copy you put in my desk, he'll be satisfied. If he doesn't hold up his end of the deal I'm going to make with him, Rachel will get the e-mail with the records. If Fiora comes through, we'll cancel the e-mail.''

"And if he tries anything rough, we can tell him about the e-mail," Mickey said.

"That is a very bad idea. If he knows about the e-mail, he can force us to tell him how to cancel it."

"How?" Mickey asked. Mason pointed to Mickey's black eye. "Oh, yeah," Mickey said. "I forgot. So what do we do if he tries anything rough?"

"Duck," Mason said.

"I'll try to remember that. Does Fiora know we're coming?"

"Yeah. I called the casino this afternoon and left a message. I think we'll get the VIP treatment."

Mason used valet parking to give Fiora the added comfort of holding his car keys. Mason wanted Fiora to think the odds were all with the house on the game they were about to play. Mason had to press, but not too hard, take risks, but not too large.

Tony Manzerio was waiting for them when they walked in. He didn't speak, settling for the universal sign language of goons everywhere—a nod of the head that meant follow me and keep your mouth shut.

Mason and Mickey did as they were nodded to do, trailing a respectful five steps behind Manzerio. People moved out of Manzerio's way without being told or nodded. The man was large enough and his eyes were dead enough to trigger the flight side of the survival impulse in most people. Mason caught the there-but-for-the-grace-of-God-go-I expressions on the faces of many they passed.

The route to Fiora's office took them on an elevator marked PRIVATE, through a door marked AUTHORIZED PERSONNEL ONLY, and down a corridor marked SECURE AREA. None of which made Mason feel any safer.

Manzerio knocked at an unmarked door, opened it, and led Mason and Mickey inside Fiora's office. The office was plain, almost spartan, a sharp contrast to the extravagance of the casino. The brown carpet, cream-colored painted walls, and unpretentious functional furniture looked more governmental than gaming. A window looked out over the Missouri River, a black view without dimension or detail.

Fiora sat at a poker table playing solitaire. "Did you search them?" he asked Manzerio without looking up.

Manzerio didn't answer. Instead, he ran his porterhouse-sized hands up and down their sides, torsos, legs, and arms. "Nothin'," he said.

"Good. Wait outside," Fiora told him.

Fiora turned over the cards that were still facedown until he found the one he wanted. Smiling, he ran through the rest of the cards and declared, "How about that! I won again."

"Odds always favor the house," Mason said. "Cheating takes the suspense out of it."

"I'm a businessman, Mason, not a gambler. The crap table is for suckers. I need an edge, I take it. I don't make business a game of chance."

"I like to think of it as supply and demand. The market moves buyers and sellers to the middle where they can make a deal," Mason said.

"Your message said you wanted to make a trade. What do I have that you would want?"

"My law practice," Mason said.

"How could I possibly have your law practice, Mason?"

"It's on the hard drive you ripped out of my computer

last night. Client files, my receivables, my payables. The works.''

"That must be inconvenient for you. What's the matter? Didn't you back your stuff up? I don't know much, but I know that much. I got people working for me that don't do nothing but back shit up.''

"Actually, I did back up one thing,'' Mason said. He reached into his coat pocket and pulled out the disk. "It's not much really. Just some bank records you might be interested in.''

Fiora's eyes hardened. "You are taking a hell of a risk coming to my place offering to trade my records to me. Why don't I just have Tony come in here and take that disk and throw your ass in the river?''

Mason didn't flinch. "You said it yourself, Ed. You're a businessman. Buy, sell, trade, but don't take chances. I'm the same way. I was out of line meddling in your business and I'm sorry. Last night, you convinced me that you had nothing to do with Jack Cullan's murder. I don't need to clutter up the defense of my client with extraneous bullshit that the judge won't let me get into evidence anyway. I'm offering you this disk in good faith, the same way you gave me the pictures of Beth Harrell. All I want is my hard drive. You can delete your bank records.''

"And I'm supposed to believe that you don't have another copy of this stashed someplace?'' Fiora asked.

"I can't help it if you're not a believer. I'm a lawyer, not a rabbi.''

Fiora studied Mason for a minute. "Come over here, Rabbi Mason. I want to show you something.''

Mason joined Fiora at the window. The light from inside the office and the lack of light outside made the view opaque.

"Is there something I should be looking at?'' Mason asked.

"You might find this interesting," Fiora said. There were two switches next to the window. Fiora hit one, and the office went dark. He hit the other, and the prow of the boat where Mason had celebrated New Year's Eve was bathed in a spotlight. "Nice view, don't you think, Mason?"

Mason repressed an involuntary shudder. "It's terrific. What's your point?"

"Every public area of this boat is under constant video surveillance. Even if the state didn't require it, I'd do it. I want to know everything that happens on my boat. That prow is a very popular spot. Lovers like to make out there. Losers like to jump off. We got to watch it all the time."

"It must be tough to video in the dark," Mason said.

"Nah! We got these nighttime cameras make it practically like your living room. The technology is fantastic. This case of yours works out okay, you come back and we'll watch some home movies. What do you say?"

Fiora was giving Mason a mixed message. He was telling Mason that he knew what had happened on New Year's Eve and still had the proof. Maybe it was an offer to tell him who had tried to kill him, and maybe it was a not-so-subtle threat.

"You serve popcorn?"

Fiora laughed once without conviction. "You're good with the jokes. Don't be too funny, Rabbi Mason. You and your altar boy here, have a seat, make yourselves comfortable. I got to check with my computer people and see what they've done with your hard drive. It may be they already wiped it clean. In the meantime, why don't you give me that disk of yours so I can check it out?"

Mason grinned at Fiora and tossed the disk to him. "This one is blank. Bring me the hard drive and a desktop computer. Mickey will check out the hard drive. If everything is on it but your records, Mickey will get you the real disk."

Fiora chuckled. "Careful you don't hit on sixteen and go bust, Mason."

He left Mason and Mickey in his office. Mason picked up the deck of cards Fiora had been using and looked at Mickey.

"Gin rummy. A buck a point," Mason told him. "I'll charge your losses as an advance against your salary."

"That's really generous of you, Lou. I haven't played cards since I was a kid. You'll have to remind me of the rules."

Mason sat down in the chair Fiora had been using and motioned Mickey to the one across the table, all the time wondering how many scams Mickey could run at one time. "Am I about to get cleaned out?"

"Right down to your socks, boss," Mickey said. "Deal."

By the time Fiora and Manzerio returned an hour later, Mason was down 250 dollars. They watched as Mickey shuffled the cards as if he'd been born with them in his hands, fanning them, making bridges, palming top cards, bottom cards, and marking the corners of other cards with his thumbnail.

"Hey, kid," Fiora told him, "you get tired of working for this stiff, I got a place for you at one of our tables."

"He can't quit," Mason said. "He's got to give me a chance to win my money back."

"Those words are the secret of my success," Fiora told him. "That, and never trusting anybody, especially a schmuck lawyer who thinks he can come into my place and flimflam me like I was a refugee from a Shriners convention."

Mason matched Fiora's sudden intensity with his own self-righteousness. "I told you the disk was blank and that I'd get you the real one. I'm not trying to con you."

"Then you are a dumber cocksucker than I gave you

credit for.'' Fiora stuck his hand out to Manzerio, who gave him a stack of papers. ''Tony took another tour of your office. Seems you forgot to mention the copy of my bank records you printed out, you stupid fuck! I ought to have Tony beat you right up to the limit!''

Fiora's face turned purple as he bit off each word, casting flecks of spittle like confetti at a parade. Mason hung his head sheepishly, letting Fiora's outburst pass.

''Well, what the fuck do you have to tell me now, Rabbi Bullshit?'' Fiora demanded.

''Look, I'm sorry,'' Mason began. ''I'm out of my league here. It was my insurance policy, but that's it. You've got everything now. Let's finish our business and I'll get out of here.''

''You'll be carried out of here! Why should I trade you anything but your fucking life?''

''Because you don't kill people, that's why. You said so yourself. I've got to have my files back or I'm out of business. You need your files back or you're out of business. It's not very complicated.''

Fiora's natural color slowly seeped back into his face as he rolled the papers into a cylinder and thumped it against his palm. ''Don't fuck with me, Mason. I'm telling you, don't fuck with me. You got that, Rabbi?'' he asked, smacking the side of Mason's head with the rolled papers.

Mason grabbed Fiora's wrist and pulled his arm down to the table. Fiora winced, as much in shock as in pain. Manzerio took a step toward Mason, who released his grip. Fiora yanked his wrist from Mason's hand while motioning Manzerio to stay where he was with his other.

''I got it, Ed,'' Mason said so softly that Manzerio couldn't hear him. ''Now you get this. You hit me again, and you can spend the rest of your fucking life wondering who's going to end up with that disk.''

Fiora held Mason's sharp stare and quietly answered him. "You got balls, Mason. I give you that," Fiora told him. "I give you that. Tony," he said in a street-loud voice, "have that four-eyed geek bring the computer in here. Let's get this over with."

A short time later, Mickey booted up the computer and searched the hard drive for its contents. "It's got everything but the bank records, boss," he told Mason. "You want me to remove the hard drive?"

Mason said, "Give Fiora our other disk first, and let him see what's on it."

Mickey untucked his shirt and reached behind his back, where he had taped the disk. He popped it into the computer and stood back as Fiora's bank accounts flashed across the screen.

"Good enough?" Mason asked.

"Good enough," Fiora said. "You can pull the hard drive out. Tony, give the kid the tools."

Mason said, "I'm glad we were able to work this out."

"Don't press your luck," Fiora told him.

"There is one other thing," Mason said.

"It better not be another disk."

"It's not. It's a favor. The one you said you owed me."

Fiora pulled at his chin until Mason thought he would pull it off. "Mason, you are too much. You bust my balls on this bank account shit, and then you got even more balls to ask me for a favor."

"I saved your life last night. That was a favor. This was business. You owe me the favor."

Fiora sighed, trapped by his own curious ethics. "What is it?"

"I want my client released on bail."

"Sorry, I can't do it."

"I don't believe you. You're wired into the prosecutor's

office. That's how you knew they were going to offer Blues a plea bargain. Hell, it may have been your idea to begin with. I think I may know who has Cullan's files. I can't get to them myself and it's just as risky for you. Blues can get them. If there's nothing in your file that links you to Cullan's murder, you can have it. No copies and no questions. My client is innocent. I need those files to prove it.''

"You aren't asking for much, are you?'' Fiora asked him.

"I need an edge, I take it,'' Mason said. "The assistant prosecutor and I are meeting with Judge Carter on Monday morning at eight o'clock. I want Blues released on bail before ten. Make it happen.''

Chapter
Thirty

Mickey said, "That was extremely cool, Lou."

They had just pulled away from the curb at the casino, and Mickey was practically high-fiving himself as he fiddled with the radio, looking for some celebration tunes.

"Maybe. I just conspired with Ed Fiora to improperly influence an elected official to get Blues out on bail. Fiora probably has the whole thing on audio and videotape. That doesn't sound so cool to me."

"Then why did you make the play?"

"It's the only one I had."

"That's bad public relations, man."

"What's that supposed to mean?" Mason asked him.

"Let me tell you a story, Lou. I was conceived on the Fourth of July under a lucky star. My mother, Libby, spotted it over my father's shoulder from the backseat of his ragtop Firebird."

"I like the car better than the story," Mason interrupted.

"Chill and pay attention. My mother said the star was Altair and that it was found in the wing of the constellation Aquila the Eagle. Aquila was the mythical bird who helped Jupiter crush the Titans and seize control of the universe."

"So you're Aquila and I'm Jupiter?"

"You tell me. Anyway, Altair was a shepherd in love with another star, Vega, who was stranded on the western side of the Milky Way. Once a year, on the seventh night of the seventh moon, the lovers united across the heavens."

"So are you the son of a shepherd or the son of a star?"

"Libby was always a little vague about whether Altair started out as an eagle's wing and ended up a shepherd or vice versa. I figured he was an early cross-dresser, kind of a mythological Ru Paul."

"No doubt the kind of role model that made you what you are today," Mason said.

"My mother told me the story the first time I asked about my father. I may have been a kid, but I knew the difference between an answer and a story. So I asked again. She told me I had two choices. Either my mother got knocked up in the backseat of a Firebird on a hot July night sticky enough to melt bugs together, and my father, who had great shoulders but no spine, ran out on us. Or I was conceived under a lucky star and I was destined for great deeds and greater love."

"Which one did you choose?"

"Adventure and babes. Either you just conspired with Ed Fiora to improperly influence a public official to get Blues out of jail, or you simply asked a friend if he'd put in a good word with the prosecutor to consider a reasonable bail for Blues. That's public relations."

Mason shook his head. "Don't ever run for office, Mickey."

"Why not, man?"

"You just might win."

Monday morning was bleak. The sun's weekend cameo appearance had not been renewed for an extended run. Heavy clouds, thick and dusky with nature's burden, had rolled in from the north overnight, limiting the day's light to the perpetual gray of dawn. The cold front that had delivered the clouds swept along at ground level with a gnawing, eroding wind.

Mason huddled in his Jeep, waiting for a stoplight to change and wondering whether the heater would kick in before he got to the courthouse. The day matched his mood of dark desperation. He'd spent the rest of the weekend chewing over his fall from grace at the feet of Ed Fiora.

Mickey's flexible ethic hadn't soothed his own wounded conscience. He knew where the line was drawn between zealous advocacy for his client and the dark side. Even so, he'd stepped over it. It wasn't a movable line, one that could be redrawn in the sand or one over which he could hop back and forth with a moral pogo stick.

He'd replayed Blues's case a thousand times in the last thirty-six hours, and each time come to the same fork in the road, and each time he'd made the same choice. Not that it gave him much comfort. Neither did the replays that he often watched with his mind's eye of the man he'd killed over a year ago. Then he'd been cornered, left without a choice. This time, there may have been another way out, but he hadn't been able to find it.

Mason knew that Ed Fiora wouldn't treat Mason's favor as a balancing of the books. Instead, he would record it as an investment, the rate of return only slightly less than that of a loan shark. Fiora would come to collect one day unless Mason could wipe the ledger clean once and for all.

Icy pellets peppered Mason's windshield as he parked in the lot across the street from the courthouse. He cursed the weather and his own weakness as he cautiously made his way on the newly slick pavement.

Patrick Ortiz was waiting in the hallway outside Judge Carter's chambers when Mason arrived. Ortiz was sipping from a cup of coffee, studying handwritten notes on his legal pad. Mason had decided to let Ortiz raise the issue of bail, not wanting to be too obvious with his knowledge that the fix was in. He knew that Ortiz wouldn't be happy, and he didn't want to rub his face in it.

"Morning, Patrick," Mason said.

"Morning, Lou." Ortiz greeted him with equal neutrality.

They stood like two commuters waiting for the train, strangers avoiding eye contact and conversation, until the outer door to the judge's chambers opened and her secretary summoned them inside.

Judge Carter was waiting for them in her private office, seated behind her massive walnut desk, signing orders from the previous day's hearings. Her black robe was hanging on a coat hook on the back of the door the secretary closed as she left them alone. A half-eaten bagel and a plastic container of yogurt sat on the edge of her desk next to an empty coffee cup.

Mason had appeared in Judge Carter's court a number of times in the last year. She was a fastidious judge in appearance and demeanor, impatient with the unprepared and notoriously unsympathetic to the guilty. Female African-American judges were no longer a novelty. A conservative, Republican female African-American state court judge who was on a short list for appointment to the federal bench was a rarer phenomenon.

Judge Carter's straight black hair, which she normally wore pulled back in a tight skullcap, hung loosely above her shoulders, several strands out of place as if she'd been twisting them while contemplating her rulings. She had dark circles under her eyes, made darker by the contrast with her own rich coffee-colored skin. Mason had the sense that she'd either worked late the night before or gotten an early start this morning. Either way, she didn't look like she was having a good day and he didn't expect a warm reception.

"Sit down, Counselors," she instructed, waving them into the leather chairs opposite her desk. Floor-to-ceiling bookshelves crammed with statutes, appellate decisions, and treatises rose behind her, accenting her own imposing style. "Let's talk about your case. You're set for trial on Monday, March fourth. Tell me now if you'll be ready for trial. I don't like last-minute requests for continuances."

"The People will be ready," Ortiz said.

"I'll be ready as well, Your Honor," Mason echoed.

Judge Carter continued. "There's been an awful lot of pretrial publicity. Are you going to ask for a change of venue?" she asked Mason.

"No," Mason answered. "Hopefully, the press coverage will die down and we can get a fair jury." Mason had been pleased with the press coverage so far, and was actually counting on the jury to have read and remembered the stories that cast doubt on the police investigation and Blues's guilt.

"When we get to jury selection, you'll both ask the jurors if they've read anything about the case, if they've made up their minds already, and if they can be fair. The ones who want to serve will answer no, no, and yes. The ones who want to go home or go to work will answer yes, yes, and no."

Judge Carter had recited the truth about jury selection that every lawyer and judge wrestled with in every case.

She said it with more resignation than humor, and the lawyers nodded their own understanding of the dilemma.

"Any other problems lurking out there on either side?" she asked them.

Mason kept silent, waiting for Ortiz to raise the question of bail.

"There is one issue," Ortiz said. "Defense counsel is a suspect in an arson and a homicide that took place last Thursday night. In the event that he's charged with either of those crimes, it could affect the trial date." Ortiz dropped his bombshell with a routine matter-of-factness that underscored the crippling impact of his words.

Mason's stomach nosedived as he stared at Ortiz, unable to contain his utter amazement. Ortiz looked straight ahead at the judge like someone who'd farted in a crowd and pretended not to notice.

Judge Carter continued the exercise in understatement. "I can see how that would be a problem. When does your office expect to make a decision whether to charge Mr. Mason? I'm certain he is as interested in knowing that as I am."

"It's a complicated case, Your Honor. The fire marshal is still investigating the cause and origin of the fire. The autopsy of the victim has been completed, but I don't have the final report. The investigation is ongoing. It's hard to know for sure when we'll be ready to present something to the grand jury. Maybe Mr. Mason will withdraw as counsel and the defendant will hire somebody else so that we can stay on track for trial."

Mason felt as if he were having an out-of-body experience, as if he'd left the room completely and crossed over to the Twilight Zone. Fiora had returned Mason's life-saving favor with his own life-threatening ploy. That was the only thing Mason could conclude. Either that, or Fiora had only had inside information from the prosecutor's office, and not the juice to make Leonard Campbell give up his opposition to bail for Blues. Mason hated that he had compromised himself with Fiora. He hated it even more that his tactic had blown up in his face.

"Mr. Mason," Judge Carter said, "I assume you are aware of the ongoing investigation. Have you discussed with your client the possibility that you may have to withdraw as his attorney?"

Mason breathed deeply, collecting himself. "No, I haven't, Your Honor. I will speak to him today, but I doubt that he will want me to withdraw. I'm confident that I won't be charged with either of those crimes. My client will probably consider the threat to charge me as just another part of the prosecutor's strategy to pressure him into pleading guilty to a crime he didn't commit, and will insist that I remain his counsel. That's how he and I view the prosecutor's opposition to bail and that's how I view these threatened charges."

"What about that, Mr. Ortiz? Why has the state taken such a hard line on bail? I've reviewed the court file on this case. You're relying on circumstantial evidence and one fingerprint for a capital murder case against a man with longstanding ties to the community and the financial ability to post a considerable bond. I've routinely granted bail in such cases. Why shouldn't I do that now?"

Ortiz clenched the sides of his legal pad, plainly frustrated at the change in direction Judge Carter had taken. "The defendant has a history of violent behavior. He's a threat to the community, he's—"

"Getting bail in my court, Mr. Ortiz. Mr. Bluestone has never been convicted of a crime. He served his country in the military. He served this community as a police officer. I hope you are devoting as much time to proving your case against him as you are the one against his lawyer. I'm setting bond at $250,000. That will be all, gentlemen.''

Ortiz exploded out of his seat, nearly running over Judge Carter's secretary on his way out. Mason rose more slowly, making certain that his legs weren't shaking before he stood up. Judge Carter took a pack of cigarettes and a lighter from her desk drawer, leaned deeply into the back of her chair, and lit up. She blew the smoke out her nose, ignoring the NO SMOKING sign that hung on her wall.

"You know something, Mr. Mason?" she said quietly. "You wasted a very expensive favor. I would have granted your client bail anyway."

Mason found the men's room, bent over a sink, and splashed his face with cold water until his skin stung. He wiped his face with paper towels, scrubbing at invisible stains. He challenged his image in the mirror for an explanation, but found no answers in his own bewilderment.

He had wasted more than an expensive favor. He had wasted Judge Carter's career, laid her bare to whatever hold Fiora had on her. If he didn't find a way to unring this bell, he would have wasted his own career as well.

At least, he reasoned, Blues would be out of jail in a few hours and together they could try to find a way out of the wilderness. Mason found a room reserved for lawyers to meet with their witnesses, locked the door, and used his cell phone to call Mickey.

"The judge ordered Blues released on bail," he told Mickey, his voice slightly unsteady.

"You want me to cancel the e-mail to Rachel Firestone?"

"Immediately. Make two copies of the bank records on floppy disks. I've got a safe-deposit box at City Bank. The key is in the top drawer of my desk. Put the disks in the box. I'll call the bank, and tell them that you are coming over to use the box. Then wait for me at the office."

"What are you going to do?"

"Arrange for the bail and wait for them to process Blues' release."

"You don't sound so good, boss. You okay?"

"Yeah, I'm fine. I'm just trying to figure out the part where Jupiter crushes the Titans."

"Don't forget your wingman, boss. You don't have to go it alone."

Mason paused, realizing Mickey was right about that. He didn't have to go it alone, but he didn't want to take anyone else down with him. "I'll talk to you later," he said.

Mason's next call was to Carlos Guiterriz, Mason's favorite bail bondsman. Carlos ran a one-man shop, and took it personally when the prosecutor's office opposed bond for a defendant, claiming they were conspiring against him in his effort to support three ex-wives and five children.

"Guiterriz Bail Bonds," he said when Mason called.

"Carlos, it's Lou Mason. I need a bond for a quarter of million this morning. Can you do that?"

"Who's it for?"

"Wilson Bluestone, Jr., and let's keep it our secret. The press will pick it up soon enough."

"Holy shit, Lou! That is too sweet! How in the hell did you swing that?"

Mason anticipated the question, and knew that Carlos would repeat the answer a hundred times before the day was out. "Judge Carter ordered the bail. She said she'd granted bail to other defendants in cases like Blues and that she wouldn't treat Blues any differently."

"I'll bet that tight-ass Patrick Ortiz shit sideways!"

"It was a thing of wonder," Mason said. Guiterriz's enthusiasm took the rough edge off Mason's mood. "Blues will put up his bar as collateral, and I've got stocks worth fifty thousand bucks if you need more than that. Get the bond to the courthouse right away.''

Guiterriz laughed loudly enough that Mason had to hold his phone away from his ear. ''A thing of wonder,'' he quoted Mason when he stopped laughing. ''I would have put up the bond myself to see Ortiz take it in the shorts like that. Give me an hour.''

Mason wandered downstairs to the first-floor lobby of the courthouse, undecided how to kill time until Guiterriz showed up. He stood at the glass doors that fronted Twelfth Street and watched as pedestrians and drivers fought to keep their balance as a new coating of ice descended on the city.

City Hall was across the street. Mason hadn't heard from Amy White since their meeting in the parking lot of the Hyatt Hotel. If Carl Zimmerman had been keeping her informed about the status of the homicide investigation, she might know something about Zimmerman's whereabouts the night Shirley Parker was killed.

Clutching his topcoat tightly around his collar, Mason made the crossing from the courthouse to City Hall, shook the ice from his shoulders, and rode the elevator to the twenty-ninth floor in the hope that he would catch Amy in her office.

She was waiting for the elevator when it opened on her floor. She stepped into the elevator and pushed the button for the first floor.

''Perfect timing,'' Mason told her as he kept his finger on the button to open the elevator door. ''I hoped that I would catch you in the office.''

''Lousy timing,'' she answered. ''Whatever it is, I don't have time unless you have a hundred thousand tons of salt and a fleet of trucks to spread it. The weather service says we're going to get two inches of ice and ten inches of snow in the next twelve hours.''

''I need to talk with you about something. It's important.''

''What is it?''

''Carl Zimmerman.''

Amy's mouth tightened as if a sudden pain had struck her. ''You've got as long as the elevator takes to get downstairs.''

Mason punched the buttons for all twenty-eight floors. ''This may take a while,'' he told her.

Chapter
Thirty-one

Mason and Amy eyed each other as the ancient elevator lurched to a halt at each of the next three floors. Amy broke off their eye contact with a nervous glance at her watch. The illuminated buttons on the elevator panel promised another twenty-five sea-sickening stops. Mason waited for Amy to speak first and set the course for his questions. The door opened on the twenty-fifth floor. Amy took a step toward the open door when Mason blocked her path.

"I'm getting off," she insisted.

"Nope. A deal is a deal. All the questions I can ask until we hit bottom." Mason pushed the button to close the elevator door.

"Okay, fine," she said without meaning either. "What about Carl Zimmerman?"

"You know him?"

"He's a cop. Good enough?"

"Easy, Amy. How much snow can fall before we finish

stopping at the next twenty-four floors? How do you know that he's a cop?''

''The chief brought him to the mayor's office after Jack Cullan was found dead. He and another detective—I think the other one was named Harry Ryman—were investigating the case and the mayor wanted some answers. The chief told Zimmerman to keep me updated on the case.''

Mason listened, his silence prompting her to continue.

''You know all that already or you wouldn't be asking me,'' she said. ''And you can't be so stupid to think I would lie about something you could so easily prove that I did know. So get to the point. You're running out of floors.''

A barely operable ceiling fan wheezed and sucked warm, greasy air from the elevator shaft into the elevator, filling the car with the metallic taste of friction-heated oil. The odor combined with each ball-bouncing stop, turning their ride into a stomach-churning descent. Amy took off her knee-length navy wool coat and Burberry scarf, and unbuttoned the high-necked collar of her dress. Her face was taking on a pasty, alien hue. Mason couldn't tell if her suddenly green-gilled complexion was due to their rocky ride or his questions.

''When was the last time he checked in with you?''

''I didn't log him into my Palm Pilot. What difference does it make?''

''These are my floors, Amy,'' Mason said, pointing to the glowing buttons. ''I get to use them any way I want. When was the last time you talked to Carl Zimmerman?''

''Last week. I don't remember the day, the time, or what we talked about.''

''The conversation I want to know about is one that I think you'd remember. It was about Jack Cullan's files.''

''That's a conversation I would have remembered and I don't. You've got three floors left. Make them count.''

"Where were you last Thursday night between six and ten o'clock?"

"Probably eating rubber chicken at a civic award dinner with the mayor, or home wishing I was."

"Did Zimmerman call you that night?"

The elevator stopped at the first floor, the doors opened, and they stepped out into the lobby. Amy steadied herself with one hand against a pillar, gulping cleaner air. They could see the snow tumbling from the sky like feathers from a billion ruptured pillows.

"My God!" Amy said. "This is going to be the rush hour from hell." Turning to Mason, she asked, "Do you have any idea how many complaints we will get by noon tomorrow that somebody's street hasn't been plowed?" Mason shook his head. "Everyone but the mayor will call. His street always gets plowed." She touched her forehead with the back of her hand, wiping away sweat she must have imagined. "I'm sorry, Lou. What did you ask me?"

Mason smiled patiently. He'd questioned too many witnesses too many times to be pushed off track. "Did Carl Zimmerman call you last Thursday night?"

Amy drew on her reserves of exasperation. "Yes, no, maybe. I don't remember. Should I?"

"That depends on whether Zimmerman needs an alibi for Shirley Parker's murder."

Amy studied Mason as she tied her scarf around her neck, cinching it securely under her chin, pulled her coat back on, and took her time carefully buttoning each button. She cocked her head to one side in a thoughtful pose and clasped her hands together.

"No," she said at last. "I'm quite certain I didn't talk to Detective Zimmerman at all that night."

* * *

Mason took seriously Patrick Ortiz's announcement that he was a suspect in the arson at Pendergast's office and in the murder of Shirley Parker. While the jailhouse bureaucrats processed Blues's release on bail, he spent the rest of the morning waiting for the police department's records clerk to make him a copy of the investigative reports on both crimes. He nearly pushed the clerk to her maximum tolerance when he asked for two sets of the reports as well as another set of the reports on the Cullan murder. Mason knew that Blues would want his own set of all the reports.

Shortly after one o'clock in the afternoon, Blues emerged from behind the first-floor security doors into the lobby of the jail. Mason was waiting for him beneath a sign that read VISITORS' CHECK-IN. Blues was wearing the same clothes as the day he had been arrested. The suit he'd worn for his preliminary hearing was crammed into a grocery bag.

Mason extended his hand toward Blues, who wrapped his own hand around it with a solid grip that was as much gratitude as it was greeting. They released each other's hand, forming fists they tapped together.

"Do I want to know how you pulled this off?" Blues asked him.

"No," Mason answered. "You hungry?"

"Is a bluebird blue? My tribal ancestors ate better on the reservation than I ate in that jail."

"Let's get out of here," Mason said. "I'm buying lunch."

The snow already had covered the streets and sidewalks, obliterating where one began and the other stopped. The only clues were the cars stacked bumper-to-bumper on every street. Many of the cars were stuck on the sheet of ice that lay beneath the snow, tires spinning in a futile effort to get traction. Drivers of other cars had made the mistake of trying to go around those cars, only to slide into someone else attempting the same maneuver. The result was automotive gridlock accompanied by blaring horns, screaming commuters, and ecstatic tow-truck drivers.

Blues pointed to a bar a block west of the courthouse. "Let's try Rossi's. He never closes."

Rossi's Bar & Grill lived off of the traffic from City Hall, the county courthouse, and police headquarters. Judges, lawyers, and bureaucrats provided the lunch traffic. Cops owned the place after hours. DeWayne Rossi was a retired deputy sheriff who heard everything, repeated nothing, and spent his days and nights parked on a stool behind the cash register chewing cigars. Rossi tipped the scales at slightly over three hundred pounds, limiting his exercise to making change for a twenty. Regular patrons had a secret pool picking the date he would stroke out. Rossi had quietly placed his own bet through one of his buddies, not wanting to let on that he knew about the pool.

Rossi's had eight tables and was decorated in late-twentieth-century dark and dingy. A pair of canned spotlights washed the bar in weak light. Short lamps with green shades barely illuminated each table. A splash of daylight filtered in through dirty windows. A color TV hung from the ceiling above the bar permanently tuned to ESPN Classic. Rossi kept a .357 magnum under the bar in case anyone tried to rob the place or change the channel.

There were two waitresses; Donna worked days and Savannah worked nights. They had both worked the street until they'd had too many johns and too many busts. The cops who used to arrest them now overtipped them to balance the books. A fry cook whose name no one knew hustled burgers and pork tenderloins from a tiny kitchen in the back.

"I haven't been in here since I quit the force," Blues said as he and Mason stamped the snow from their shoes.

"You didn't miss the atmosphere?" Mason asked.

"I didn't miss the company. I'm as welcome in a cops' bar as a whore is in church."

One table was occupied, as was one seat at the bar. Rossi turned away from the TV screen long enough to look at them, giving Blues an imperceptible nod that may just have been his jowls catching up with the rest of his head. Donna, a lanky, washed-out blonde with slack skin and a down-turned mouth, was sitting at one of the tables reading *USA Today* and smoking a cigarette.

Mason and Blues chose a table against the wall that gave them a view out the windows so they could monitor the progress of the traffic jam and the storm.

Donna materialized at their table, setting glasses of water in front of them. She laid her hand on Blues's shoulder.

"Long time, darling. How you been?"

"No complaints that count, Donna," Blues said. "How's life treating you?"

"Same way I treat it. Neither one of us gives a shit about the other. What'll you have on this lovely day?"

"Bring us a couple of burgers, and the coldest beer you've got in a bottle," Blues told her.

Donna wandered back toward the kitchen to turn in their order. Mason unzipped the black satchel he used as a brief-case and handed Blues his copies of the reports.

"I thought you'd want your own set," he explained.

Blues left the reports on the table. "Did Leonard Campbell find religion and decide to let me out?"

Mason shook his head.

"I know Ortiz didn't do it on his own."

"It wasn't the prosecutor's office. It was the judge."

"Judge Carter? You're shitting me!"

Mason shook his head again, watching the replay of Kordell Stewart's Hail Mary miracle pass against Michigan, instead of meeting Blue's head-on.

Blues asked him, "You think that game is going to end differently this time?"

Mason gave up and faced his friend. "No, sorry."

"How much trouble are we in?"

Mason smiled weakly. "It depends on whether we can prove that you didn't kill Jack Cullan and I didn't kill Shirley Parker."

"What about Judge Carter and my bail?"

"Small potatoes compared to capital murder."

Mason filled Blues in on his evening out with Beth Harrell that ended with him saving Ed Fiora's life. He described how Mickey had hacked into Fiora's bank records and been rewarded with a beating by Tony Manzerio. He explained his theory of how Beth could have hiked to Cullan's house, killed him, and returned to her apartment undetected. He detailed his suspicions of Carl Zimmerman and James Toland, making light of his failed surveillance of Zimmerman. He finished with a broad-brush recitation of the scam he'd run on Fiora with the bank records and the favor he'd unnecessarily cashed in to get Blues released on bail.

"You need a keeper, you know that?" Blues told him when Mason had completed his report.

Donna returned with their burgers and beer. They ate in silence.

"Well, at least you're out," Mason said. "Now we can sort this mess out."

Blues picked up the reports and began reading. Mason waited, hoping for the insight that a fresh look often brings.

"Look at this," Blues said.

He placed the initial report on Cullan's murder in front

of Mason. It was dated December 10, the day the house-keeper had diskovered Cullan's body.

"Okay, what am I looking for?" Mason asked.

"The report is routine. It covers all the bases, including forensics. The forensics report identifies the location from which every fingerprint was lifted."

Mason read the index of fingerprints closely. "Damn! There's no record of any fingerprints found on the desk in Mason's office. Terrence Dawson testified at the preliminary hearing that's where he found your fingerprint."

"Now, look at this," Blues said, and handed Mason a supplemental report dated December 12, the day Blues was arrested.

"Dawson went back to the scene for a second look. That's when he found your fingerprint."

"Read the first sentence of Dawson's report on that inspection," Blues instructed.

Mason read it aloud. "At the request of Detective Carl Zimmerman, this examiner returned to the scene to determine if any other identifiable fingerprints were present."

"Zimmerman was a busy boy," Blues said.

"How could Zimmerman have planted your fingerprint?"

"It's not as hard as it sounds," Blues said. "Zimmerman could have made a photocopy of a fingerprint of mine. While the photocopy was still hot, he could have put fingerprint tape down on it and lifted the print. Powdered photocopier toner can be used as fingerprint powder. Then Zimmerman went back to the scene and put the tape down wherever he wanted Dawson to find my fingerprint."

"So where did Zimmerman get your fingerprint?"

"From my personnel file."

"Isn't access to those files restricted? How did Zimmerman get ahold of it?"

"Once Harry started looking at me for the murder, they would have gotten my file without any problem."

"How can we prove your fingerprint was forged?"

"Identification points are the same on all prints from the same finger. That's why fingerprints are so reliable. But no two prints themselves should ever be identical since there's always a difference in position or pressure when the print is put down. If the print Dawson found is identical to the print in my personnel file, Dawson will have to admit it was forged."

"Unless Zimmerman was smart enough to get rid of the original print from your personnel file."

Blues said, "That would have been too risky. If that set of prints turned up missing, there would be a separate investigation of everyone who touched the file. Zimmerman was banking that no one would compare the prints since they had made a new set of my prints when they booked me."

"Which gets us back to the real question," Mason said. "Why would Zimmerman take the risk of framing you?"

"It fits with your theory. Zimmerman and Toland were tired of working for Cullan. They wanted to go into business for themselves, so they killed Cullan. I was a convenient fall guy. Harry already hated me. The mayor wanted a quick arrest. No one wanted Cullan's files to be found. It should have worked."

Mason took the final swallow from his bottle of beer. "I'm going to talk to Harry."

"No way," Blues said. "He'll cover for Zimmerman. That's what cops do."

"Not this time," Mason said. "You find Cullan's files and I'll talk to Harry."

Blues grabbed Mason's wrists with both hands. "You're taking a hell of a risk for both of us. If Harry tips him off,

Zimmerman will come after both of us. He won't have any choice. Are you carrying that gun I gave you?''

''No, and you can't carry one either without violating the conditions of your bail.''

''Small potatoes compared to capital murder,'' Blues said.

Chapter
Thirty-two

Twelfth Street had become a frozen parking lot. Cars on the intersecting streets of Oak and Locust squirmed more than they moved. No one was any closer to home than when Mason and Blues had walked into Rossi's for lunch. The snow poured from the sky in thick, wet flakes heavily enough to reduce vision to a single block. Some drivers surrendered to the storm, abandoning their cars in the middle of the street to take refuge in City Hall or the courthouse.

Mason and Blues waded through the drifting, blowing snow to Mason's Jeep. They waited for the car to warm up and melt the ice on the windows while they considered their options.

"You giving any thought to just waiting this out?" Blues asked.

"Nope."

"You expecting a sudden heat wave to melt this shit and clear up this traffic just so we can go home?"

"Nope," Mason repeated. "And we're not going home. We're going to my office. By the way, how long has Mickey Shanahan been living in his office?"

"Since the day I rented it to him."

"Does he know that you know that?"

"I never asked him. He seems like a good kid."

"He's a con artist, cardsharp, computer hacker who doesn't have a pot to piss in."

"You hired him," Blues answered. "He must fit in. How are you going to get us out of here?"

"Don't try this at home, boys and girls," Mason said.

He engaged the Jeep's four-wheel drive and rolled over the concrete stop that separated the parking lot from the sidewalk on Twelfth Street. He stayed on the sidewalk and turned east, dodging parking meters until he reached Locust. He turned north on Locust, continuing to use the sidewalk as his personal lane until he found a narrow break in the traffic congestion on Locust. He goosed the Jeep across Locust, up onto the sidewalk on the other side of the street. When he made it to Tenth Street, he turned east again, staying on the sidewalk until he was clear of the downtown traffic.

From there, the normally fifteen-minute drive to his office took an hour as he slalomed and cursed his way around one trapped driver after another. The streets were so slick, and the ice and snow so impenetrable that the slightest incline had become an impossible vertical ascent for any car that didn't have four-wheel drive. Mickey was waiting for them when they made it back to Blues on Broadway.

"This is the homecoming crowd?" Blues asked.

"The cook and the bartender called in well," Mickey answered. "They said they were staying home because of sick weather. We're as good as closed anyway in this snow.

The mailman is the only one who has come in through the front door all day.''

Blues picked up a stack of mail that Mickey had left sitting on the bar and leafed through it, tearing open the last envelope.

''Son of a bitch!'' he said, holding up the contents of the envelope. ''The Director of Liquor Control has suspended my liquor license pending the outcome of my case.''

''Who's the Director of Liquor Control?'' Mason asked.

''Howard Trimble. I've got to go see him today.''

''In this storm?'' Mason asked. ''He's probably stuck in traffic somewhere.''

Blues dialed the phone number on the letter and listened as it rang for two minutes. He slammed the phone down, cursing Trimble and his ancestors in a Shawnee Indian dialect Blues reserved for special occasions.

''Cool!'' Mickey said. ''What's that mean?''

''Something about fire ants building a nest in your scrotum,'' Mason told him. ''Trimble will have to wait until tomorrow. If this storm keeps up, everything will have to wait until tomorrow.''

''We may not have that long,'' Blues said. ''Once Zimmerman knows I'm out, he'll bury those files where no one will ever find them.''

Mason and Mickey followed Blues upstairs to his office. Blues opened the floor safe and removed a .45-caliber Baer Stinger pistol and holster. He loaded the pistol, sliding it into the holster he'd attached to his belt, and dumped two extra ammunition clips into his jacket pocket.

''Are you going to talk to Zimmerman or just shoot him?'' Mason asked.

''Depends on my mood,'' Blues said. ''If Toland and Zimmerman stole Cullan's files, they had to have a new hiding place. It's got to be someplace secure that won't attract attention. Zimmerman wouldn't leave it up to Toland, so it's got to be someplace Zimmerman picked. I'm a lot better at watching without being seen than you are," he told Mason.

Mason asked, "Where do you start watching? You don't even know where Zimmerman is. What makes you think he's going to go look at those files in the middle of a blizzard?"

"You," he said to Mason, "are going to find out where Zimmerman is when you call Harry to tell him about my fingerprint. I'd ask where Zimmerman is first, since Harry will probably stop speaking to you after you tell him about the fingerprint. Then I'll go sit on Zimmerman while you go visit Ed Fiora."

Mason asked, "What for?"

"Fiora said he's got videotape to show you. Odds are he has the person who shot at you on that tape. Tell him you think you know who killed Cullan, but you need to see the videotape to be certain."

"You think Zimmerman was the shooter?"

"Probably not. My money is on Beth Harrell, but it doesn't matter. The videotape is just a pretext for your meeting. You'll remind Fiora that you promised to give him his file if you found it. Tell him that Zimmerman has his file. Tell him to call Zimmerman and offer to buy the file and to hire Zimmerman as a security consultant."

"Why can't I just do that over the phone?" Mason asked.

Blues explained patiently. "Because you've got to make certain that Fiora actually calls Zimmerman. You can't take his word for it."

"Why do you think Fiora will be able to flush Zimmerman out on a day like this?" Mason asked.

"Because Fiora will also tell Zimmerman that his offer

expires at midnight. After that, Fiora will put Zimmerman out of business himself.''

Mickey said, ''It's a cross-rough. You figure Fiora won't wait for us to bring him the file. He'll go after Zimmerman. This way, you can take down both of them and get Fiora off of Lou's back.''

''Not me,'' Blues said. ''Harry will take them all down. He'll be the hero. I'll go back to being the bartender. Can you set it up with Harry and Fiora?'' Blues asked Mason.

''Small potatoes,'' Mason said. ''Where will you be while I'm running the snowstorm shuttle?''

Blues smiled. ''Right here, nice and warm. Waiting for your call so I can go out and save our asses! You better take that gun I gave you. I didn't see it in the safe. Where is it?''

''My office,'' Mason said. ''You're probably right.''

Mason's phone rang as he stuck his pistol into his jacket pocket. ''Lou Mason,'' he answered.

Rachel Firestone barked at him. ''How did you do it?''

''How did I do what?''

''Don't give me that crap, Lou! How did you get Judge Carter to order bail for Blues?''

Mason wasn't surprised that Rachel had learned of Blues's release. He couldn't guess at the number of sources she'd cultivated over the years. Her sharp tone carried the unspoken complaint that he hadn't tipped her off.

''Off the record?'' he asked.

''Not a chance.''

''Fine. Judge Carter ordered Patrick Ortiz and me to appear for a status conference at eight o'clock this morning. I mentioned the prosecutor's opposition to bail. She said that she'd routinely granted bail in similar cases and saw no reason to treat Blues any differently."

"Didn't it strike you as odd that there was no formal hearing on bail, no opportunity for Ortiz to object on the record or present evidence?"

It was obvious to Mason that Rachel had already talked with Ortiz and gotten a taste of the prosecutor's fury. "Judges have a lot of discretion," he told her. "You'll have to ask Judge Carter why she handled it that way."

"No can do," Rachel said. "Right after your conference, she turned in her resignation to the presiding judge and left the courthouse. No one answers the phone at her home and no one has seen her. She's disappeared. What's happening?"

Mason dropped into his desk chair and stared out the window at the blizzard. He'd been trying to navigate his way through a storm that had turned into an avalanche, an out-of-control cascading disaster.

"Lou!" Rachel demanded again. "What's going on?"

"I'll call you later," he said, and hung up.

Mason dialed Harry's pager, punched in his own number, and hung up again. Mason's phone rang a minute later.

"Harry?"

The urgency in Mason's voice was unmistakable. "What's the matter?" Harry asked.

"Nothing," Mason lied, gathering himself. "I need to talk to you."

"I thought that's what we were doing."

"No. Not on the phone. Where are you?"

"Same place as the rest of the world. Stuck in traffic behind some moron with rear-wheel drive."

"Where?"

"On Main Street, between Thirty-fifth and Thirty-sixth."

"You alone?"

"Yeah. Lou, what's the matter?"

"Pull over and park. I'll be there in ten minutes."

Main was the next major thoroughfare east of Broadway. Though only four side streets separated them, Mason knew that he would make better time on foot than in his Jeep. Traffic was light on the side streets since most drivers had gotten stuck on the main roads before they could try alternate routes.

As he walked, Mason got a new perspective on the power of the storm. Tree limbs sagged under the heavy weight of ice and snow, some of the heavier ones fracturing and tumbling to the ground. He passed one house where a huge limb had broken and crashed through the roof. Mason gauged the strain on overhead power lines as they too bent in the wind. It wouldn't take much more for them to start snapping, adding another deadly special effect to the storm.

Mason found Harry's car in the middle of Main Street, surrounded by a flotilla of stranded drivers.

"Nice day for a drive," Mason said as he slid into the passenger seat.

"Thanks for dropping by," Harry answered. "We're always open."

"How'd you get stuck on duty? Where's your partner?"

"He got lucky and had some personal stuff to take care of at home. He never made it in today," Harry said as he turned down the radio.

"Any updates on the storm?"

"It's gone past blizzard," Harry said. "It's now officially a whiteout, whatever that is. The expected accumulation is a guess. The real problems are the ice and the wind. A lot of people won't get home tonight. So what's so important?"

"I need a favor."

"So ask."

"I want you to compare Blues's fingerprint that was found

on Cullan's desk to the print for the same finger in his personnel file.''

Harry didn't respond. The wipers squeaked as they brushed back and forth, moving snow from one side of the windshield to the other.

''What would I be looking for if I was to do that?'' Harry asked Mason, still without looking at him.

''To see if the two prints were identical.''

''You mean to see if someone forged the print found at Cullan's house.''

Mason lowered his head and studied his gloved hands. ''Yeah,'' he said.

''You've read the reports?'' Harry asked, still watching the snow fall and the traffic stall.

''I've read them. I know that Carl Zimmerman asked Terrence Dawson to take a second look at the scene and that's when Blues's fingerprint was found.''

''So, you know what you're saying? You know what you're asking me to do?'' Harry turned and met Mason's eyes.

''I know, Harry. It's like you always told me. Knowing the right thing to do is the easy part. I'll see you later.''

Mason stopped at the bar long enough to tell Blues that Zimmerman was probably sitting out the storm at home. They agreed to keep in touch by cell phone, and Mason left again. He had almost finished scraping the newest layer of snow and ice from his car when Mickey opened the passenger door and climbed aboard.

''Damn, this weather blows!'' he said when Mason finished scraping and joined him.

''What are you doing here?'' Mason asked.

''Wingman riding shotgun,'' Mickey answered.

"Any point in telling you to stay here?"

"None."

Mason took his gun from his jacket pocket and put it in his glove compartment. "Did Blues give you a gun too, or are you just glad to see me?"

Mickey reached under his jacket and sheepishly removed a .44-caliber pistol that he added to the glove compartment. "He didn't exactly give it to me," Mickey explained.

"Does he know, exactly, that you took it?"

"Not exactly."

"Then you'll want to return it when we get back and hope Blues doesn't find out, or he'll break both your legs above the knees."

"Exactly," Mickey said.

"If you've got any more toys hidden in your pants or stuck up your ass, get them out now. We'll never get next to Fiora without being searched. If we get to the point that we need weapons, it'll probably be too late to use them."

Mickey put a switchblade knife and a lead sap into the glove compartment and closed it. "Home Shopping Network," he explained.

Mason called the Dream Casino before they pulled out of the parking lot, leaving a message with Fiora's administrative assistant that he was on his way to watch Fiora's home movies. The drive to the casino was an adventure in urban off-road driving. Mason used side streets whenever he could, and sidewalks when he had to. Cops he passed shook their heads and fists at him, but they were too busy with car wrecks and traffic jams to chase him down.

Along the way, Mason couldn't get the image of Judge Carter sitting behind her desk, frazzled and distracted, out of his mind. Now he understood why she had looked frayed at the edges. On the one hand, she had made herself vulnerable to Ed Fiora and paid the price. On the other, Mason had shoved her over the edge. It was another IOU that Mason would have to carry until he could find a way to pay it back.

The clanging, whistling, siren-sounding slot machines were getting a workout in spite of the weather. Once inside, the gamblers were oblivious of the storm that gave them the perfect excuse for getting home late. Tony Manzerio escorted Mason and Mickey to Fiora's office.

"This weather is killing my business!" Fiora complained when Mason walked through the door.

"The storm's like a kidney stone. It'll pass—painfully—but it will pass."

"Is that the kind of legal advice you give, Mason? 'Cause if it is, I'd seriously consider another line of work," Fiora advised.

"I'm close to figuring out who killed Jack Cullan. I need one more piece of the puzzle. It may be in the videotape you told me I should come see after this case ends. I need to see the tape now. If it shows what I think it does, it may help me close the loop on a suspect."

"Mason, you're starting to act like I'm your fairy godmother with all the favors you've been asking. You haven't even thanked me for the last one I did for you."

"As long as I'm asking, I want Judge Carter's account marked paid in full. Take her off your books."

"This is no time to get a conscience, Mason. Everybody's a player at some level. She played, she lost. What's the big deal?"

"If you've got a marker with Judge Carter's name on it, I'd like to see it."

"It doesn't have her name on it. It has her son's name. She keeps him from getting a beating when he comes up short, which happens with some regularity."

"How much does the kid owe?"

"Doesn't matter. He pays up one week, he's down the

next. We send him postcards about Gamblers Anonymous; makes us feel better.''

"Clear the kid's marker and don't let him back in the casino. That's my deal.''

"In return for which I get what?''

"Jack Cullan's file on you.''

"You're squeezing an awful lot of mileage out of that file, Mason.''

"Just show me the videotape and then I'll get you the file. You've probably got me on tape. You can keep that. I want the judge off the books.''

Fiora shrugged. ''That will work. Trade a judge for a lawyer. Too bad you can't throw in a player to be named later.''

Fiora opened a cabinet behind his desk, revealing a television and DVD player. He took a video disk from the shelf beneath the television and popped it into the DVD player. After he pushed a button, the screen came to life.

"Like I told you before,'' Fiora reminded Mason, ''anyone comes into the casino, they are picked up on video before they've lost their first quarter. They move out of range of one camera, another camera picks them up. The videotapes are transferred to disks that are easier to store and that lets us reuse the videotapes. The great thing about disks is that you can edit them to create a video of any one person from the minute they set foot in the parking lot to the minute they leave.''

"So whose video are you going to show me?'' Mason asked.

"Watch,'' Fiora answered. He sat down in his desk chair and aimed a remote control at the DVD player.

Beth Harrell materialized on the screen. The day and date were printed in the bottom right-hand corner of the screen. It was New Year's Eve. Even with the grainy, long-distance perspective of the video cameras, her beauty was obvious. She flowed across the casino floor, drawing stares and envy. The absence of sound added a surreal note to her movements.

"I'll jump ahead to the good part," Fiora said as he punched another button on his remote control.

Mason watched as the camera followed Beth to the rear of the casino, where she had found Mason, then out to the prow of the boat, where they had embraced. Mickey poked Mason in the ribs when the video showed Mason pushing Beth away. Mason winced at the memory of that moment, seeing more clearly the bitterness in Beth's expression that had been captured by the camera as she had walked away.

The video jerked a bit as a different camera picked her up when she returned to the deck. Her face became indistinct as she slipped into shadows that made it impossible to see what she was doing or even to be certain that she was still the person on the video.

Mason recoiled as small flashes erupted from the darkness where the shooter was hidden. Then, Mason saw his own image fill the screen, cowering in the prow and dodging bullets that ricocheted around him, shattering pale blue Christmas lights. He grimaced with sharp memory when he saw a bullet singe his side. Mason touched the healed wound through his clothes and held his breath as his video self vaulted into the river.

Chapter
Thirty-three

"I love happy endings," Fiora said when the screen went blank.

"I want a copy of the disk," Mason said.

He was past understanding or explaining Beth. She had fallen out of first place in the Jack Cullan murder sweepstakes, but she was ahead of the pack in the psycho competition. Mason didn't know what he would do about her, only that he would do something.

"This is strictly pay-per-view," Fiora said. "No more party favors. You get me the file; then we'll talk."

Mason asked, "You know a homicide detective named Carl Zimmerman?"

"Sure. He was one of Cullan's guys. Cullan called him and that other cop, Toland, his golden retrievers. Any time some bigwig or his kid stepped in the bucket, those two guys fetched the bad news to Cullan."

"I think they killed Cullan and went into business for

themselves. They made Shirley Parker tell them where Cullan kept the files and then they stole the files and killed her.''

''They don't call this the land of opportunity for nothing,'' Fiora said. ''Now you're going to go up against two rogue cops and put them out of business while stealing my file back for me. Is that it?''

''I've got help.''

''Must be your client that I sprang from the county jail. That might even be a fair fight from what I understand. Are you keeping the good cops out of this?''

''We've got to until we get the files. After that, the good cops can have the bad cops.''

''Why tell me all of this?'' Fiora asked.

''We don't know where Zimmerman and Toland have hidden the files. I want you to call Zimmerman and offer to buy your file and hire him as a security consultant for the casino. The only catch is that your offer expires at midnight. Tell him if you don't have the file by then, you'll send Tony to get it.''

Fiora said, ''Your partner figures to follow Zimmerman to the files, pop him, and bring me my file. Then you have a come-to-Jesus meeting with the prosecutor, Blues pleads guilty to some bullshit misdemeanor, and the whole thing goes away.''

''Like you said, I love happy endings.''

Fiora thought a minute, drumming his fingers on his desk, calculating the odds for the house. ''You got a phone number for this bum, Zimmerman?''

Mason handed Fiora a slip of paper, and Fiora dialed Zimmerman's number. Mason and Mickey listened to Fiora's side of the conversation. As nearly as they could tell, Zimmerman was going through the stages of grief; denying that he had Cullan's files, angrily accusing Fiora of blackmail, and unsuccessfully negotiating better terms before accepting Fiora's offer.

Fiora hung up the phone and spread his arms wide. "Detective Zimmerman is seriously pissed off and seriously suspicious. He even asked me if you were in on this. The meeting is at nine o'clock tonight."

Mason asked, "Where?"

"Swope Park, at the shelter next to the lagoon."

"Thanks," Mason said. "We're out of here."

"I don't think so," Fiora said. "You and junior will wait right here. We'll all go together."

"Ed, that's not a good idea. This could get ugly. I don't think you want to be anywhere near the park," Mason told him.

"I don't like the odds if I'm sitting here fat and unhappy hoping you keep up your end of the deal. I figure Tony gives us an edge, and I always take the edge. So sit down and sit tight."

"Zimmerman has killed two people already. You don't kill people, remember?"

"I don't kill people. Tony kills people."

Mason looked at Tony, who had planted himself in front of the door to Fiora's office. "I need to make a phone call," Mason said.

"I thought you might," Fiora replied.

Mason used his cell phone to reach Blues. The conversation was brief.

"Nine o'clock at the shelter next to the lagoon in Swope Park," Mason said.

"Good. Meet me at the office. We'll get ready."

"Can't do it."

"Fiora got you on a leash?"

"You got it"

"He and Tony figuring on coming along?"

"All the way."

"Make for a helluva party," Blues said, and hung up.

Mason closed his cell phone. "You got an unmarked deck of cards?" he asked Fiora. "I'm into Mickey for two hundred and fifty bucks. I might as well try and get my money back."

Tony remained at the door, moving only to allow Fiora to go in or out. Mason and Blues had not discussed the possibility that Fiora would hold him and Mickey hostage and insist on coming along. Though unexpected, Fiora's intervention would bring all the bad guys together. The combination would be volatile, unstable, and uncontrollable.

Fiora came back at six o'clock. "Let's get going," he said. "The roads are still a mess and I want to get there ahead of Zimmerman and Toland. What are you driving?"

Mason answered, "I've got my Jeep. It has four-wheel drive."

"Perfect. You drive."

The snow was still falling when they left the casino. Though city crews had been working for seven hours to clear the streets, they were fighting a losing battle. Fresh snow blanketed every plowed surface, erasing tire tracks and hiding the ice beneath like a land mine.

Mason said, "We'll take I-70 east to I-435 south and get off at Gregory Boulevard. Maybe the snow plows have kept one lane on the highways fairly clear."

Tony sat in front next to Mason, leaving Mickey and Fiora in the back. Road conditions were treacherous, even for the Jeep. The wind blew snow across the highway in ground-level clouds, making it nearly impossible to see headlights or taillights.

Salt trucks outfitted with snowplows plodded along Interstate 70, clearing the outside lane while depositing a layer of salt in their wake. In spite of the conditions, eighteen-wheel trucks charged past them, their drivers pushing to deliver their loads. A few had pushed too hard and their tractor-trailer rigs had jackknifed, sliding down embankments along the highway, scattering their cargoes.

Some drivers had been caught too far from home, and had been forced to abandon their cars after they had spun out of control or gotten stuck. The Highway Patrol had spent the day and early evening rescuing stranded motorists.

Mason crept steadily along, occasionally reaching speeds of thirty-five or forty miles per hour when he hit a stretch of clear tire tracks. The exit ramp from I-70 onto I-435 was like a black ski run, forcing Mason to fight for control of the Jeep as it shimmied and fishtailed before straightening out.

Mason took the Gregory Boulevard exit westbound from the interstate. The two-lane road ran ahead of them flanked by snow-laden trees that loomed like ghostly sentinels in the darkness. Irregularly spaced streetlights pointed the way, adding a halo to the falling and blowing snow. A concrete railroad bridge arched overhead as the boulevard funneled them into the park.

Colonel Tom Swope had donated Swope Park to the city in the early 1900s. The largest green space in the city, it was home to the zoo, an outdoor theater, two golf courses, and enough trails for anyone to get lost in. The lagoon was near the center of the park along Gregory Boulevard. Over the years it had been stocked with fish by the city and, occasionally, dead bodies by the less civic-minded.

Mason eased to a stop along the curb where a bike path intersected with the road, and turned off his lights.

"Why are we stopping?" Fiora asked.

"The lagoon is around the next curve. If we go all the way in and Zimmerman is already in place, he'll see us."

"Tony." Fiora spoke his name as a command.

Tony grunted as he opened the door, and disappeared without a backward glance.

"Where's he going?" Mickey asked.

"For a walk, Junior," Fiora answered.

Mason turned onto the bike path, keeping the Jeep at a slow crawl and his headlights off. Driving through the woods with no lights in a blizzard, Mason thought to himself, was the automotive version of blindman's bluff. The bike path emptied onto an unmarked service road that Mason followed another half mile before picking up the bike path again. This time, he backed the Jeep a hundred yards down the bike path and turned off the engine.

If he was lucky, he had made it to his hiding place without being seen. Mason looked at his watch. It was seven-thirty.

"What now?" Mickey asked. "It's cold enough to freeze-dry my nuts."

"Here," Mason said as he handed Mickey the keys. "You can turn the heat on if you have to. Just remember, Zimmerman can find you a lot easier when the engine is running."

"Hey, where are you going?" Fiora demanded.

Mason took his gun from the glove compartment. "For a walk."

"That's not our deal," Fiora said.

"Mickey will keep you company, but don't play gin with him. He cheats."

"Like hell I'm waiting here," Fiora said. "Zimmerman is expecting me and if I don't show, you guys shoot craps."

"Suit yourself," Mason said, knowing there was no way to make Fiora wait in the Jeep.

"Wingman on your flank," Mickey said to Mason as he climbed into the front seat long enough to grab his gun from the glove compartment before joining Mason and Fiora.

"Give me that," Mason said to Mickey, pointing to the gun.

"Are you kidding me?" Mickey asked.

"You don't know how to use a gun. You'll shoot yourself or one of us. Give me the gun."

Mickey held the pistol up with both hands and, before Mason could reach for it, he unloaded it, disassembled it, and put it back together. "Oh, ye of little faith," Mickey said.

"That's pretty good, kid," Fiora said. "Where'd you learn to do that?"

"Video games—the perfect home-schooling curriculum," Mickey answered.

Mason, Fiora, and Mickey hugged the edge of the woods as they briskly walked single file alongside the service road back toward the lagoon, satisfied that the storm made them virtually invisible. Before reaching the lagoon, they stepped into the woods. Mason took off the thick glove on his right hand, put his hand in his pocket, and wrapped his fingers around his gun. The steel was icy and refused to warm against his hand. He found the safety with his thumb and switched it off.

"Let the games begin," Mickey whispered.

If Fiora had insisted on being early, Mason had to assume that Zimmerman and Toland would do the same. Mason knew without asking that Blues would not be the last one to arrive. Tony had gotten out of the Jeep twenty minutes ago. No one was going to be late for this party. It suddenly occurred to Mason that everyone was probably already there, each man fighting off the wind chill, waiting for someone else to make the first move.

"Why in the hell would Zimmerman set the meeting out here?" Fiora asked.

"Look around," Mason answered. "It makes sense. The

interior of the park is isolated but accessible. There's not much chance of other traffic on a night like this. The shelter is out in the open. The nearest woods are far enough away that under these conditions you'd have to be an incredible marksman to shoot someone from the trees."

Fiora wasn't convinced. "You think Zimmerman had that all figured out. How would he know about this place?"

"He's a cop who knows where bodies are dumped. Plus, he's a Cub Scout den leader," Mason explained. "He's probably brought his troop here."

"You're shitting me? This hump is a Cub Scout leader? I oughta pop him myself," Fiora said, "except I don't kill people."

Mason studied the wind-driven waves breaking along the snowpacked shoreline of the lagoon, moving his gaze outward to the road. There were no tire tracks, meaning that everyone else either had walked in or had yet to arrive. Mason bet on the former.

The shelter stood twenty-five feet from the southern edge of the lagoon. There was a streetlight close enough to outline the shelter, but too far away to illuminate what was beneath it. The shelter was little more than a roof supported by four stout poles; a shelter from sun and gentle rain, but no port in a snowstorm. A bright light came on at the center of the shelter's ceiling, startling Mason and the others. Neither Zimmerman nor Toland was camped out beneath the shelter.

The light turned off a few minutes later, only to come on again in an irregular cycle. Mason could make out an electrical line that ran from the roof of the shelter to a utility pole to the west. The line bowed, heavy with ice.

"It's a motion light," Mason said. "It's for security. Any movement near the light turns it on for a preset period. Then it goes off. If the wind blows hard enough, that will turn it on. We'll be able to see Zimmerman and Toland when they get close enough to activate the sensor.''

''Then what do we do, Counselor?'' Fiora asked.

''I don't know,'' Mason confessed.

''In the meantime,'' Fiora complained, ''I'm freezing my ass off. Where the hell is Tony?''

Mason ignored Fiora's complaint and his question. Fiora was used to running the show, and didn't like being a spectator. Though Mason wondered where both Tony and Blues were waiting. Fiora had been standing on Mason's left. Mason turned to his right to talk to Mickey, only to discover that Mickey was gone.

Mason hissed Mickey's name, but the sound died in the wind. Mason remembered Mickey's announcement as he got out of the car. Wingman on your flank, Mickey had said. Mason silently cursed himself for getting Mickey involved. A moment later, he cursed aloud when he saw Mickey emerge from the woods closest to the shelter, being pushed ahead by a tall figure poking Mickey in the back with a shotgun. Mickey stumbled and fell. The gunman prodded him with the barrel of the shotgun until Mickey got to his feet.

As the pair reached the shelter, the light came on again. In the instant before the gunman smashed the light, Mason saw Mickey's panicked face and the block-cut jawline of James Toland.

Fiora started toward the shelter, but Mason grabbed him by the arm. ''Don't,'' Mason told him. ''That's exactly what they want you to do. They'll try to take us one at a time. Mickey can handle himself.''

Mason knew that he was right about everything except Mickey. The kid could deal cards, field-strip a pistol, and hustle a rent-free pad, but Mason knew he was out of his league against Toland. Besides, sending Fiora to bail out

Mickey was like telling the Dutch boy to put a bigger finger in the dike. Without Tony to back him up, Fiora was just a street-wise punk. Toland wouldn't be impressed.

Fiora puffed himself up, as if sensing Mason's dismissive appraisal. "Why not? I'm the guy they're expecting. If I don't go, they'll know they're being set up. I'll tell Toland that the kid is my driver and that he wandered off. You go find Tony and Blues."

Mason couldn't argue with Fiora's reasoning or stop him. Fiora chose a slow, casual walk, raising his right hand in greeting as he neared the shelter. Mickey and Toland were hidden in plain sight under the shelter, swallowed by the dark. When Fiora reached the edge of the shelter, he suddenly collapsed to the ground. Mason couldn't tell whether he'd been shot or struck, but Fiora didn't move as the snow gathered around him.

In the same instant, Mason felt the icy sting of cold steel against his neck. "I had a feeling you were in on this, Mason." Carl Zimmerman pressed the barrel of his gun tightly against the base of Mason's skull. "You should have told your client to take the plea."

Chapter
Thirty-four

Zimmerman jammed his gun hard against Mason's neck. "Hands behind your back," he ordered.

Mason knew that Zimmerman was going to cuff him, taking him out of the game. He had size on Zimmerman, but Zimmerman had a gun on Mason's brain stem. Mason obeyed, and winced when Zimmerman caught his flesh in the cuffs.

"Stand real still," Zimmerman instructed. Keeping his gun in place, Zimmerman patted the pockets on Mason's coat and found his pistol. "Hope you've got a permit for this concealed weapon, Counselor. Otherwise, I'll have to issue you a citation."

"You shouldn't have lied about the body in Swope Park," Mason told him. "Otherwise, you might have gotten away with it."

"I'm getting away with it now," Zimmerman told him.

"You killed Cullan, forged Blues's fingerprint, stole Cullan's secret files, and killed Shirley Parker. That's a lot to get away with.''

"You don't know shit," Zimmerman told him. "And I didn't kill anybody. At least not yet.''

"It doesn't matter what I know. Harry knows you used Blues's fingerprint in his personnel file to forge the one on Cullan's desk. That will be enough for him. He'll hunt you down like a dog. You won't be able to use Cullan's files to wipe your ass.''

Zimmerman spat into the snow. "Ryman's too old and too slow.''

"We'll put that on your tombstone," Mason said.

Zimmerman gave Mason a sharp shove in the small of the back. "Move it," he snapped.

Mason marched toward the shelter, squinting against the snow. There was no sign of Tony or Blues. Fiora was still down. Zimmerman shoved Mason again as they stepped beneath the shelter, knocking him into Mickey, who was handcuffed and sitting cross-legged on the floor of the shelter. It was too dark to see Mickey clearly, but it was enough for Mason to know that he was there and still breathing.

Toland pressed the barrel of his shotgun under Mason's chin, dragging it down to Mason's chest until Mason joined Mickey. Toland crouched down to Mason's eye level, keeping the shotgun flush against Mason. Mason smiled inwardly at the trickle of blood frozen on the side of Toland's face.

"Cut yourself shaving?" he asked Toland.

"That big moose you had chasing us in the woods scratches like a girl. I had to damn near kill him just so I could tie him to a tree. Don't make me tie you to a tree.''

Zimmerman said, "We've got these three. Tony is out of commission, which leaves Bluestone," Zimmerman said to Toland.

The shelter was suddenly flooded with high-beam headlights coming from an approaching vehicle. The lights blinded Mason's view of the vehicle and its driver.

"Who in the hell is that?" Toland yelled.

The vehicle was coming at them from the west on Gregory Boulevard and was aiming directly at them as it picked up speed over the fresh snow. The engine was revving hard as if the driver had floored the accelerator.

"Damn!" Zimmerman shouted. "That's my Suburban."

"It's got to be Bluestone," Toland said. "He's going to ram us. Shoot him!"

Toland fired his shotgun, pumped, and fired three more rounds while Zimmerman emptied his clip into the Suburban. Mason and Mickey jumped to their feet and ran to Fiora. Crouching down with their hands behind their backs, they each grabbed Fiora by the shoulders and dragged him out of the path of the Suburban.

The windshield on the Suburban shattered, but the truck roared on like an enraged beast made angrier by the gunfire, crunching and packing the snow beneath its tires, oblivious of the barrage of firepower. Zimmerman and Toland leaped out of the way at the last moment as the Suburban crashed into one of the poles supporting the shelter, toppling the roof. The car flew past them, becoming airborne before plunging headfirst into the lagoon, sizzling and bubbling as it found the muddy bottom.

Harry and Blues had been following on foot behind the Suburban. Blues ran low and straight at Toland, colliding with him and rolling across the snow. Toland managed to get to his feet first while Blues was on one knee. Toland launched a booted kick at Blues's head. Blues caught Toland's boot and sprang up, sending Toland tumbling onto his back.

The power line had snapped off the roof of the shelter with the impact from the Suburban, its deadly blue current dancing and writhing across the snow, measuring Toland like a cobra as he struggled to get to his feet. Toland slipped in the snow, clawed at the ground on all fours, and screamed as the power line stung him with a lethal jolt. The power line lay across Toland's electrocuted body as the snow sizzled around him.

Zimmerman was in a shooter's crouch, knees bent, arms extended, aiming Mason's gun in a rapid arc, looking for a target. Harry tackled him from behind, flattening him against the pavement and pressing his face into the snow. He planted his knee in the middle of Zimmerman's back and wrapped his hand around Zimmerman's gun hand, forcing the barrel against Zimmerman's ear.

"Pull the trigger, you piece of garbage. Blow your fucking brains out!" Harry screamed. "Pull it, goddammit! Pull it!"

Blues ran to Harry's side, reached down, and covered Harry's hand with his own. "Let it go, Harry. You got him. Let it go," he said.

Harry was heaving. "Okay," he said at last. "Okay." Harry cuffed Zimmerman. "Don't move, partner," Harry told him.

Mason looked at the lagoon, where the back end of the Suburban barely broke above water. He staggered to his feet and made his way over to Blues and Harry.

"How did you do that?" he asked them.

"I'll bet Blues hot-wired the Suburban, put a rock on the gas pedal, and steered with the door open while he ran alongside it," Mickey said.

"Good call, kid," Blues told him. "How'd you know?"

"That's exactly the way I would have done it," Mickey said.

"Next, he'll tell people it was his idea," Mason said.

"That's public relations," Mickey replied. "Get us out of these cuffs."

Harry unlocked their handcuffs and asked, "What's with Fiora? Did Toland clock him or shoot him or did the putz just have a heart attack?"

Fiora was still lying prone in the snow, not moving from the spot where Mason and Mickey had dragged him.

"I think he fainted," Mickey said. "When he walked up to the shelter, he raised his hand as if we were having a reunion. Next thing I knew, he took a dive. Toland didn't touch him."

They walked over to Fiora. Mason nudged him with his shoe. "Looks dead to me," Mason said.

"It's a real shame," Mickey added. "He didn't live to see us kick the crap out of those guys."

"Weather like this," Harry said, "it could be hours before an ambulance gets here. Guess it doesn't matter since he's already gone."

Fiora stirred, groaned, and slowly rolled over on his back. He blinked the snow off his eyelids, and groaned some more. "What happened?" he managed to ask.

"Back from the dead. It's a miracle," Blues said. "I'll go find Tony. We may really need an ambulance for him."

Mason turned to Harry. "So I was right. Zimmerman forged Blues's fingerprint."

"Yeah," Harry said softly. "We took a new set of prints when we arrested Blues. Forensics compared the one found on Cullan's desk to the new prints and got a match. No one ever would have checked Blues's print against the ones in his personnel file if you hadn't asked me."

It was the first time in years that Mason had heard Harry refer to Blues by his nickname. Harry had always insisted on calling him Bluestone, rejecting any closer ties to their days as partners. Harry's face was drawn by more than the cold, and he was shivering from more than the wind.

"Zimmerman counted on that," Mason said. "Don't be too hard on yourself."

Harry shook his head. "Carl counted on me wanting it to be Blues."

"Why'd you come out here with Blues?"

"I figured I owed him that," Harry said. "And I had to see Carl for myself. I had to be sure. If I was wrong, it would stay private."

"What happens now?" Mason asked.

"It's up to the prosecutor. The case against Blues is pretty weak without the fingerprint. Carl has a lot of explaining to do. I guess we're back to square one."

"Zimmerman told me that he didn't kill anybody. You think he's telling the truth?"

Harry thought for a moment. "I'm the wrong one to ask. I was his partner and I didn't see anything that made me think he was dirty."

Mason said, "Toland was killed while he and Zimmerman were committing a felony. Under the felony-murder statute, Zimmerman will be charged with Toland's death. That's a capital-murder charge. Zimmerman is looking at the needle. He'll talk."

"That's not what worries me," Harry said. "It's who's going to be listening."

"Zimmerman will use Cullan's files," Mason replied. "Instead of getting the bum's rush like Blues did, he'll put it all on Toland and offer to keep his mouth shut in return for a citation. He'll probably claim that he was investigating Toland and that we stumbled into his sting operation and screwed it up. Before he's finished, we'll be charged with Toland's death."

"How's he going to explain working a sting operation behind my back?" Harry demanded.

"Simple. You were too close to me. That's why Ortiz

didn't put you on the stand at the preliminary hearing. If there was enough dirt in those files to scare Leonard Campbell into going so hard after Blues, Campbell will make that deal in a heartbeat.''

"You have any suggestions?" Harry asked.

"Just one. My Jeep is parked about a half mile down that service road. I backed it down a bike path. I'd appreciate it if you'd go get it for me." Mason handed Harry the keys. "Take your time. It's real slippery."

Harry nodded as they both looked at the sunken Suburban. "Glad to do it. You be careful not to get wet out here. Your aunt will raise hell if you end up with pneumonia. And don't let my prisoner get away while I'm gone."

Harry ambled away as Blues and Tony appeared from the far side of the lagoon. Tony helped Fiora to his feet, dusted the snow from Fiora's topcoat, and listened impassively as his boss berated him for getting coldcocked by Toland.

"Where's Harry going?" Blues asked Mason.

"To get my Jeep."

"You have to tip him for valet service?"

"That depends on what we find in the Suburban. Let's have a look."

Mason and Blues found Mickey at the edge of the lagoon. The Suburban was twenty feet from shore in water that was at least half as deep. They looked at the truck, the water, and each other, none of them anxious to go for a swim.

"It's too dangerous," Mason said at last. "A man wouldn't last ten minutes in that water without getting hypothermia. We don't know if the files are in the truck, and even if they are, it would be too easy to get stuck inside."

Fiora and Tony joined them. "You think my file is in that truck?" he asked Mason.

"I'd bet the house on it," Mason said. "Trouble is, the odds of us getting it out are a little steep. The cops will have it towed out of there, and we'll never see the files until after the grand jury indictments are handed down.''

Fiora pulled Tony aside. The massive man leaned down to hear Fiora's whispered instructions. Tony straightened up and walked over to Carl Zimmerman, who was still lying facedown in the snow. Tony grabbed Zimmerman by the collar of his coat, yanked him to his feet as if he were dusting off a rug, and spun him once around. Keeping his body between Zimmerman and the others, like a solar eclipse blocking the sun, Tony found Zimmerman's handcuff key and removed the cuffs from Zimmerman's wrist. He clamped his viselike hands on Zimmerman's shoulders and delivered the message Fiora had given him. Tony held on to Zimmerman's left arm as they returned to the edge of the lagoon.

Zimmerman stared at the water, then at each of them. Tony gave him a slight shove toward the water. Zimmerman shook off Tony's hand in a fainthearted protest before stripping down to a T-shirt and boxers. No one spoke as he disrobed or when he dove into the water.

''What'd you tell him, Tony?'' Mickey asked.

''Hey, kid,'' Fiora answered. ''It's like going to a fancy restaurant where they got menus without prices. If you got to ask, you got no business being there.''

Zimmerman climbed onto the back of the truck, opened one side of the split rear door, and disappeared inside the Suburban. He emerged a few minutes later, carrying a hard plastic box under one arm. Bracing himself against the floor of the truck, Zimmerman heaved the box into the water, where it bobbed toward the shore. They all clambered to the water's edge, waiting eagerly for the box to arrive, not noticing as Zimmerman ducked back inside the Suburban.

In the same instant that the box reached Mason, Zimmerman leaned out the rear of the Suburban and opened fire with a pistol he'd hidden in the truck. The first two rounds caught Tony in the neck, spraying the others with warm blood. Tony grasped at his throat before collapsing into the water. Mason snatched the plastic box out of the water, holding it up as a shield against the next volley.

Fiora screamed at Zimmerman and struggled to pull his own gun from beneath his heavy coat. Bullets slapped into the snow at Fiora's feet, then traced a mortal path up his midsection, exploding inside his chest.

Zimmerman had fired his first shots into the clustered target of his five captors, claiming Tony and Fiora with fatal indifference. Mason, Mickey, and Blues had scattered, and Zimmerman's next shots went wide in the dark. Blues dropped and rolled over, coming up on one knee, his gun drawn as Harry skidded to a stop with the Jeep's headlights spotlighted on Zimmerman, drops of water glistening like ice crystals against his dark skin.

Harry swung the door of the Jeep open and dropped to the ground, his own gun extended through the open driver's window.

"Put it down, Carl!" Harry demanded.

Zimmerman held one hand to his eyes, trying to block out the glare of the headlights. "Why, Harry? You got what you came for. I'm out of options, man. Either I kill all of you or you kill me. That's all that's left."

"No! That's not the way this is going to go down. Think about your family."

"Too late for that, Harry. You're gonna have to kill me!" he shouted, opening fire again.

Harry fired at the first flash from Zimmerman's gun, not stopping until Zimmerman fell face-forward out of the Suburban, folded over the open door at his waist, his arms and face dangling lifelessly in the black water.

Chapter
Thirty-five

The blizzard suffocated the city for two days, keeping businesses, schools, and government in suspended animation, an emphatic reminder that nature's power to destroy was a match for man's worst instincts. The difference between nature and man was that nature looked good doing it. The city was draped in a thick white blanket that sparkled brilliantly under the cold rays of the sun. The snow reflected a painfully beautiful glare that polished the ice-blue sky with aching clarity.

Seventeen inches of snow had fallen on top of three inches of ice. One hundred thousand people had been left without power, and hundreds of electrical lines had gone down breaking the fall of limbs that had snapped off from trees like matchsticks under the weight of ice and snow. Property damage had been estimated at close to eighty million dollars.

Nineteen people had been killed in car accidents. Two men had suffered fatal heart attacks while shoveling snow from their walks over the vigorous objections of their wives. Four men—two of them cops and two of them hoods—had been killed at the lagoon in Swope Park.

The story of those last men had led every newscast, filled every front page, and clogged the phone lines of every radio call-in show, shoving the snowstorm of the century to the back page. The people preferred bloodshed to blizzards.

The chief of police personally suspended Harry when he made it to the lagoon. He demanded Harry's gun and badge on the spot, and came within a hairsbreadth of arresting Harry for something, anything. Every cop who shot someone to death was placed on administrative leave while the shooting was investigated. Almost all of them were ultimately welcomed back to duty with more thanks than reprimands.

Not one cop in the department's collective memory had killed his partner, let alone turned over crucial evidence to the FBI before summoning his brother officers to the scene. Not one, that is, until Harry Ryman.

Harry had explained to the chief that the box containing Cullan's files was evidence of a federal crime of political corruption and that the Bureau's jurisdiction was obvious. The chief explained to Harry that he was full of shit and would be lucky not to be fired and convicted of murder. The exchange between the two men had been hot enough to nearly melt the snow at their feet.

"You were right to call the Feds," Mason told Harry later as they sat in the Jeep waiting for the crime-scene techs to finish up. "Nobody does a good job cleaning their own house."

"I know that, but it won't make things any easier if they let me come back. Did you find what you were looking for in Cullan's files?"

Harry had let Mason examine the contents of the plastic box while they waited for the FBI to arrive. Zimmerman and Toland had kept only the best of Cullan's files, limiting themselves to the dirt on the mayor, Beth Harrell, Ed Fiora, the prosecuting attorney, and a handful of influential business people. They could, Mason had concluded, have released the files on a CD titled *Blackmail's Greatest Hits*.

Mason studied the pictures of Beth, this time focusing on her face, searching for, but not finding, a clue that would bring her into focus. True to form, Cullan had given a set of Beth's pictures to Fiora, saving his own copy for another time.

The mayor's file was surprisingly thin, nothing more than a few ledger sheets that may or may not have been a record of payoffs. Though he had only had a few minutes to study Fiora's file, Mason hadn't found proof of any links between Fiora and the mayor.

Mason's calculation of the destruction caused by his search for these files rivaled the storm's devastation. Four men were dead, as many families were ruined. Judge Carter's career was in shambles. Harry had been suspended. Blues was still accused of Cullan's murder, and Mason was still under suspicion for the death of Shirley Parker.

Harry had repeated his question, not certain whether Mason had heard. "Any luck with Cullan's files?"

Mason had shaken his head. "There should have been something more in those files, but it wasn't there. Maybe Zimmerman and Toland were holding back." He hadn't known what else to say.

By Friday morning, the city was crawling back to life. Streets had been cleared, creating mini-canyons paved with asphalt and surrounded by curbside walls made of exhaust-blackened, plow-packed snow. Mason was in his office when he got a call from Patrick Ortiz.

"We're dropping the charges against your client," Ortiz said.

"Thanks," Mason told him. "Was it Zimmerman and Toland?"

"Doubtful," Ortiz answered. "Zimmerman's wife told us all about his deal with Cullan. They've got an autistic kid. She claims he did it because they needed the money to pay for a special school for the kid. Toland just liked the good life—big Harley, women by the hour, booze by the case. Zimmerman's wife and Toland's girlfriend of the week gave both of them alibis for Cullan's murder."

"Any other leads?"

"The truth is we don't have shit on anybody, but tell your client not to get too comfortable. We may refile the charges if we come up with something."

"What about Shirley Parker?"

"She and Cullan are dead-end bookends," Ortiz said.

Mason permitted himself a small sigh of relief and changed subjects. "What do you hear from the Feds?"

"They skipped the investigation and started with the inquisition," Ortiz answered. "Harry Ryman has as much chance of getting his shield back as I have of getting it on with Jennifer Lopez."

Mason said, "I don't know. My guess is that the chief will end up begging Harry to come back."

"Right," Ortiz said. "If Jennifer turns me down, I'll have her call you. See you around."

Mason found Blues in his office, adding up his losses over the last month.

"I'm going to have to hire strippers and give away whiskey just to pay my mortgage," Blues said when Mason walked in.

"Don't give up yet," Mason said. "Patrick Ortiz just called. They dropped the charges against you."

Blues leaned back in his chair and looked at Mason, then swiveled to get a look out the window. He stood up, scanning the view down Broadway, before turning back to Mason. He pursed his lips and nodded. "Good."

"That's it?" Mason asked. "That's not the reaction of a client who's happy enough to pay his lawyer."

Blues said, "I didn't belong in jail. Nighttime was the worst. My pillow felt like quicksand. Makes it hard to get excited when it never should have happened. Makes it harder to forget when I know how easily an innocent man can get put away."

"Man, you are one depressing son of a bitch when you get philosophical," Mason told him.

Blues laughed. "I'll tell you what will cheer me up. Let's go see Howard Trimble at Liquor Control and get my license reinstated so I can pay your bill or buy you lunch, whichever costs less."

Blues had recently bought a Ford F150 and insisted on driving. They parked in front of Rossi's bar and walked to City Hall.

Howard Trimble wore a Patagonia vest that zippered down the middle over a denim shirt tucked into khaki pants a size smaller than the belly that hung over his belt. Trimble's handshake was fleshy and moist when he greeted Mason and Blues as his secretary showed them into his office, a disorderly and disheveled space where coffee cups and donuts competed for desk space with official business. Trimble gestured Mason and Blues to be seated in the two chairs opposite his desk.

Blues led off. "I'm Wilson Bluestone. This is my attorney, Lou Mason. You sent me this notice that my liquor license has been suspended," Blues added as he handed Trimble the notice he had received in the mail.

"That's because you violated our regulations," Trimble said. "From what I've seen in the news, your liquor license is the least of your problems."

Trimble showed no interest in Blues's situation. He was simply reporting the news with the inevitable disinterest of civil servants.

"I haven't violated any of your regulations," Blues said.

Mason heard the edge creeping into Blues's voice. Blues had less patience with regulations and regulators than Mason did.

"Well, now," Trimble said, sensing the rising tension. "Liquor control regulations require that a license holder be of good moral character. That generally excludes murder, don't you think?"

Mason stepped into the conversation between Trimble and Blues. "Mr. Trimble, all charges against my client have been dropped. The city is about to erupt in a major political scandal. You've got a chance to avoid getting caught up in that mess by reinstating my client's license."

Trimble slid the zipper on his vest up and down as he considered Mason's advice. "You don't mind if I check your story, do you, Mr. Mason?"

"By all means," Mason said. "Call Patrick Ortiz at the prosecutor's office."

Trimble dismissed Mason's suggestion. "I don't mess with the middleman, gentlemen. I go right to the top floor of City Hall. The mayor's chief of staff is a personal friend of mine."

Trimble called Amy White while Mason and Blues gazed around his office, examined their cuticles, and generally pretended not to eavesdrop. Trimble's eyebrows dropped and gave him twenty push-ups while he cupped his hand over the receiver and turned his head to muffle his end of the conversation.

"Good news, Mr. Bluestone," he said after hanging up the phone. "I'll reinstate your license just as soon as I can." He spoke as cheerfully as a man could who had just lost the perk of giving bad news.

"What's that supposed to mean?" Blues asked, naturally suspicious of too much good fortune in one day.

Trimble's hands fluttered to his zipper in a failed effort to be casual. "It's just a matter of completing the paperwork. It's all about forms, you know."

"Well, let's get it done right now," Blues said. "I've got to be open tonight and I can't take the chance that some overexcited cop busts me because he didn't get the word."

"Don't worry about it. I'll see to it myself."

Blues wasn't satisfied, and Mason didn't blame him. If Trimble worked his zipper any harder, the friction would start a fire.

"I want to see my file," Blues said.

A red stain began to creep up Trimble's neck as he tugged at his collar. Trimble was devoted to the bureaucratic dodge, but was running out of places to hide.

"I'm afraid that's not possible," Trimble said.

Mason interjected, "I'm afraid *that's* not possible, Howard. Mr. Bluestone's file is a public record and we have an absolute right to see it. My client has been held in jail for a month for a crime he didn't commit. You suspended his license and put him out of business. There's a lawsuit headed your way, Howard, if you don't come up with that file."

Trimble gave up on his zipper and resorted to hitching up his pants to untangle his underwear. "There's no need for threats, Mr. Mason. I'm not refusing to show you Mr. Bluestone's file. I just can't. Not right at this moment."

Blues asked, "And why not?"

Trimble shifted his weight and lifted his butt off his chair, grimacing as if he'd just given himself a wedgie. "Amy— Ms. White—has your file," Trimble confessed.

"Which regulation says it's okay to give my client's file to the mayor's chief of staff but not to my client?" Mason demanded.

Trimble stuffed his hand down his pants, rearranged his balls, and wiped a thin film of sweat from above his lip.

"Listen to me," Trimble pled. "I've known Amy White since she was a young girl. Her father, Donald Ray White, was the director of liquor control when I came to work here. Amy and her sister Cheryl used to come down here to visit their daddy. They took to me like I was some kind of an uncle. Then things turned bad for them."

Trimble paused and poked the inside of his mouth with his tongue, choosing his next words carefully. "Amy had a hard road and has come a long way. I'm real proud of her, and I don't want her to get into any trouble."

Mason's gut tightened as he wondered what Trimble was getting at. "How could she get in any trouble over my client's liquor license? The file is a public record." Mason chose a conciliatory approach, hoping it would keep Trimble talking.

Trimble let out a sigh. "Her having the file isn't a problem. I mean, I know you want it right now, Mr. Bluestone. And I don't blame you."

Mason said, "Mr. Trimble, you sure sound like a man who's trying to tell us something without saying it. Like I told you, the charges against my client have been dropped. If that's what this is all about, you'll help yourself and Amy if you just tell me why she has the file."

Trimble hesitated, struggling with his answer, uncertain whether he should give it up, but not strong enough to hold it in. "I hope you're right. Amy called me at home late one night last month. It was a Friday night."

Blues looked at Mason, silently telling him to take the lead as he got up from his chair and took a slow tour of Trimble's office. "You remember the date?" Mason asked.

"December seventh," Trimble said. "Pearl Harbor Day. I remember because my grandfather was killed at Pearl Harbor." He kept his eyes firmly on the floor.

It was also the night of Blues's confrontation with Cullan at the bar, Mason thought to himself. "Did she tell you why she wanted the file?" he asked Trimble.

Trimble shrugged. "She only told me who wanted it, not why." Mason waited, letting his silence ask the next question. "She said Jack Cullan wanted it. It was late. I asked her why it couldn't wait until Monday morning. She said that Mr. Cullan wanted it right away. So, I met her down here and gave it to her." Trimble kneaded his hands like a kid who'd been caught shoplifting.

"What time was that?" Mason asked.

"Around midnight, a little after."

Amy had told Mason that Cullan had called her that night and demanded that she get him Blues's liquor license file. She had told Mason that she had put Cullan off until the following Monday. Trimble's version could put Amy in Cullan's house the night he was killed if she had picked up Blues's file and taken it to Cullan. Yet that didn't square with Amy still having the file.

"Do you know what she did with the file?"

Trimble shook his head. "I didn't talk to her about it again until today."

Mason asked him, "What did you mean that Amy had a hard road?"

Trimble looked up at Mason, uncomfortable with answering, but more uncomfortable with being pushed. "Amy's father died when she was fifteen. A tough time for a girl to lose her father even if he wasn't much of a father. That's when I took over this job. That was eighteen years ago.''

''How did he die?''

Trimble sighed again. Mason thought Trimble would hyperventilate and pass out if he did it one more time. ''Amy's sister, Cheryl, shot him to death,'' Trimble said softly.

Mason had been trying to keep his interrogation casual. Blues was roaming around Trimble's small office, reading the diplomas and certificates that traced Trimble's career. Both of them came to attention at Trimble's explanation.

''What happened?'' Mason asked.

''Cheryl was three years younger than Amy. Their father was arrested for abusing Cheryl. His lawyer got the charges dismissed and hushed the whole thing up so Donald could keep his job as director of this department.'' Trimble tilted his head back as if trying to expel his memory of Donald Ray White. He continued the story, biting off each word with obvious distaste.

''When Donald Ray was released from jail, he beat Cheryl so severely that she was permanently brain-damaged. Somehow, Cheryl managed to get ahold of Donald Ray's pistol and killed her father. Amy's mother hired the same lawyer who got her husband off to get her daughter off. Cheryl wasn't prosecuted because she was a brain-damaged child. Their mother drank herself to death a few years later, and Amy has taken care of Cheryl ever since.''

''Who was the lawyer?'' Mason asked.

''Jack Cullan,'' Trimble answered, aiming his words at a blank spot on the wall.

Mason put his hand on Trimble's shoulder. He wanted to thank Trimble for telling him the truth, but from the broken expression on Trimble's face, Mason knew that he didn't want any thanks.

Chapter
Thirty-eight

Mason pushed the button for an elevator going up as Blues pushed another button for an elevator going down.

"I'm going to see Amy White," Mason said. "Don't you want to come along?"

"My guess is that she bolted right after Trimble called her. I'll wait in the lobby just in case she decided to clean her desk out first," Blues answered. "I'll follow her if I get the chance. You can call Mickey for a ride back to the bar."

Mason walked off the elevator on the twenty-ninth floor and into the mayor's suite of offices. Though the city was officially open, many people had taken another day off, leaving the mayor's office with a skeleton staff.

The one secretary who had come into work confirmed Blues's guess. Amy White had left without saying when or if she would be back. Mason was composing a lie he hoped would convince the secretary to give him Amy's home address when the mayor opened the door to his office.

"Your car is ready, Mr. Mayor," the secretary told him.

"Thank you, Margaret," the mayor said.

Mason cringed at the sound of the secretary's name, and abandoned any hope that a secretary named Margaret would tell him anything other than to get lost. Mason was convinced that he'd done something in a past life to offend the goddess of bureaucrats, civil servants, and secretaries named Margaret. He was willing to make a sacrificial offering to appease the goddess, but was afraid that the opening bid would be one of his testicles.

Mayor Sunshine was wearing jeans, a Kansas City Chiefs sweatshirt, boots, and a down-filled parka. Mason assumed that Amy had advised him to maintain a workingman's look to identify with everyone else who was still digging out of the storm. Though the mayor was known for his unflappable good humor and insistence on shaking every hand, he walked briskly past Mason, his face cold, his smile buried in a snowdrift, his hands jammed in his coat pockets.

"I don't have time today, Mr. Mason," he said over his shoulder.

Mason caught up with him at the elevator. "Thanks all the same, Mr. Mayor. Actually, I was looking for Amy White, not you."

A panel on the wall with columns for each elevator and numbers for each floor kept track of the vertical routes of the four elevators that serviced City Hall. As each elevator passed a floor, the number for that floor was illuminated so that anyone waiting for an elevator could watch with growing frustration the tortoise-paced progress of the cars. The mayor gave his full attention to the flashing lights, shutting Mason out.

"Amy had asked me to find the file Jack Cullan kept on you," Mason said as if he and the mayor hung out together all the time. "Ah, but she probably didn't bother you with stuff like that."

The mayor chose not to hear Mason until he cleared his throat as if he were about to cough up a lung.

"Sorry about that. It's this damn weather. Makes me drain like a leaky faucet," Mason explained. "Anyway," he continued, "I came by to tell her that I did find your file, but the FBI snagged it before I did. Man, you should have been at the lagoon when that cluster fuck broke out. I'll bet the chief of police, the prosecuting attorney, and Amy tripped all over each other to deliver that piece of good news to you. Luckily, I did get a chance to read your file. So tell Amy to give me a call and I'll tell her what's in it."

The mayor turned to Mason, his mouth and eyes fighting over which could open wider. "You read my file?"

"Cover to cover, Mayor Sunshine. Though I have to tell you, it was a disappointment. I mean, I was expecting more than some lousy ledger sheets that a pencil-necked bean counter will probably weave into a money-laundering and bribery indictment. Still, it was almost like someone had taken the good stuff out of the file and left just enough behind to chap your ass."

The mayor glared at Mason. "What do you want?" he asked.

"Not much," Mason answered. "At this point, I'd settle for Amy's home address."

"Go fuck yourself."

"Is that an apartment or a house?" Mason asked as two elevators arrived at the same moment. Mason stepped into one and waved at the mayor as the doors closed.

Blues wasn't in the lobby, and Mason assumed that he was following Amy White. Blues carried a cell phone, but rarely left it on. If he wanted to be found, he told Mason one day, he'd make it easy. Mason tried his number anyway, and wasn't surprised when a digitized voice announced that the customer Mason had called was either out of the service area or had turned his phone off.

Mason called Harry at home and at his aunt Claire's, finding him at neither place.

"How's Harry doing?" Mason asked Claire.

"Everybody takes their turn in the barrel. This is his turn," she said. "He went to see Carl Zimmerman's wife. She wouldn't let him in. I think he's out roaming. He left his cell phone and pager at home."

"Have him call me on my cell phone as soon as he surfaces. It's important."

"It always is," Claire said with a mix of sarcasm and sadness.

Mason called Mickey, told him where to find a spare key to the Jeep, and promised him lunch in return for a ride. City Hall had an ancient boiler that generated too much heat and an unbalanced ventilation system that created a worldwide array of climates throughout the building. The lobby felt like the tropics cooled with bursts of cold air drawn inside each time the revolving doors spun around. Mason lingered against a cool marble column near the entrance waiting for Mickey. His cell phone rang, rupturing his fantasy of lying on a beach next to a suddenly heterosexual Rachel Firestone.

"You looking for me?" Harry asked.

"Yeah. Do you have any friends left in the department who would do you a favor?"

Harry snorted. "Like what? Box up the stuff in my desk and mail it to me postage-due?"

"That's an option," Mason answered. "Would they do you a favor that might make them unpack your box?"

"Talk to me."

Mason explained to Harry what he wanted. "Is that doable?"

"It's a long shot on a good day, and this ain't a good day. I'll see what I can do, but don't be in a hurry. This may take a while. Leave your cell phone on."

Mason and Mickey stopped at Winsteads, home of the steakburger, and fortified themselves against the cold with double cheeseburgers with everything and grilled onions, crispy french fries, and chocolate shakes. They dipped their last fry into a pool of ketchup, then navigated through traffic back to the office.

Mason tried returning some of the calls from lawyers on other cases he was handling, but gave up when he realized they were using those cases as an excuse to talk about the shoot-out at the lagoon. Instead, he called Rachel and asked her to check the *Star*'s clipping file for stories about the death of Donald Ray White.

"Who was Donald Ray White and why are you interested in that story?" she asked him.

"Because," he answered.

"Because it has something to do with the mayhem epidemic you started, or just because?"

"Donald Ray White was the director of liquor control until he was killed eighteen years ago."

"If I ask you who killed him, will you tell me?"

"According to Howard Trimble, who inherited Donald Ray's job, he was killed by his brain-damaged daughter, Cheryl White."

"Why aren't you convinced? Do you have another suspect in mind?"

"Yeah. Amy White."

"Mayor Billy Sunshine's Amy White? Get out of town! Give it to me!"

"Do your homework first. I'm at the office."

Mason sorted through his mail, the volume of which had doubled. Much of it was from cranks and kooks who wanted to hire him. One writer even asked Mason to sue the planet Zircon for bombarding him with radiation.

His phone rang so often, he let his answering machine screen calls. When Beth Harrell called, he nearly succumbed to the sound of her voice and picked up the phone. She sounded distant, almost as if she were adrift.

"Lou," she said, "it's Beth. I know things are crazy for you right now. They sure are crazy for me. Call me when you can. There's something I have to tell you."

Mason ran down a mental list of what that could possibly be, and didn't come up with anything he was anxious to find out. The sun was making its late afternoon exit, carpeting Broadway with shadows, when Mason's cell phone rang.

"Do you make house calls?" Blues asked.

"Depends on the patient's condition. Is it critical?"

"Could be. I followed Amy from City Hall. She stopped at the Goodwill Industries sheltered workshop and picked up a woman who must be her sister. They went out to lunch, did some shopping, and came home."

"Sounds very suspicious," Mason teased.

"Wait till you hear about the snowman. The two of them came back outside and built a snowman and had a snowball fight. Then they got back in the car and went sledding on Suicide Hill on Brookside Boulevard, which isn't far from her house. Amy acted like she didn't have a care in the world. Her sister was obviously a little slow. Amy had to help her with her mittens and show her how to steer the sled, things like that. They just got home."

"Give me the address," Mason said, jotting it down.

"Keep an eye on them. I'm waiting to hear from Harry on something. As soon as he calls, I'll be there."

Mason stacked and unstacked the papers on his desk, rearranged the pencils in his drawer, and shot baskets with Mickey using wadded-up crank letters as basketballs and his trash can as a hoop. Mickey let him win the first two games, then suggested they play for money. Mason knew he was being set up, but didn't mind. Mickey ran his scams with good humor, even making Mason feel charitable as the money changed hands.

Rachel rocketed into Mason's office at four o'clock with a set of clippings under her arm and high color in her cheeks. Mickey was bent over backward, making the winning basket in a game of HORSE.

"Who's the contortionist?" Rachel asked.

Mickey looked up, sprang forward on one hand, and extended the other. "Mickey Shanahan," he said.

"Beat it, Mickey," Rachel told him in a sharp tone that left no room for argument. "And close the door behind you."

Mickey looked at Mason, who nodded and pointed at the door. "She's usually a lot meaner," Mason told him. "She's having a good day."

After Mickey closed the door, Rachel and Mason had a staring contest. Mason caught a merry glint in her eye and a fragment of a smile that turned the corner of her mouth slightly upward.

"First one to smile is a weenie," Mason said.

"Stand up," she commanded him, "and get over here."

Mason did as he was told, stopping well inside her territorial imperative while he tried to decipher the mixed message that was scrambling his hormonal network. Before he was able to crack Rachel's code, she grasped the back of his neck with both of her hands, pulled his mouth to hers, and crushed him with a kiss that nearly sucked the life out of him. Mason couldn't decide whether to hold on or beg for mercy. He settled for the Issac Newton kissing principle of equal, and opposite reaction.

"Damn it!" she said when she released him and came up for air. "Nothing!"

"What's the matter?" he gasped.

"It's not your fault," she said. "You're just not a woman. What a waste!"

"Could I have a translation here or at least a reverse-angle replay?"

Rachel stroked the side of his face with excruciating tenderness. "I'm sorry, Lou. I told you not to get a crush on me because I'd break your heart. I should have listened to my own advice. You're cute, funny, and you give great tips. Today's was a mega-tip. I guess it all overwhelmed me, and I had to find out if it was you or the tips that were making me wet."

"Shouldn't we at least have sex just to be certain?"

"Further proof that you'll never be a woman," she said. "You'll have to settle for the clippings on Donald Ray White. Why didn't you tell me that Jack Cullan was the family's lawyer?"

Rachel handed Mason the clippings and sat down on his couch as he leafed through them. "And take all the fun out of your job?" he said.

Rachel joined him on the couch. "Okay, give me the rest of it," she said. Mason started to protest, and Rachel interrupted him. "I know. It's all off the record until you tell me otherwise."

"Jack Cullan and Blues had an argument in the bar the Friday night that Cullan was killed."

"I know. That was the key to the prosecutor's case," Rachel said.

"Cullan threatened to shut Blues down. Later than night, he called Amy White and demanded that she bring him Blues' liquor control file."

"That night?"

"Cullan lived for immediate gratification. Amy told me about the call from Cullan, but said that she told him that he'd have to wait until Monday morning. This morning, Howard Trimble told me that Amy called him that night and he met her at his office and gave her Blues's file."

Rachel whistled. "So, you think Amy took the file to Cullan and killed him for making her come out late at night?"

Mason shook his head. "Not exactly. According to Howard Trimble, Donald Ray was a child-abuser. He'd been arrested for abusing Amy's sister Cheryl. Amy was fifteen and Cheryl was twelve. Cullan got him off and kept it quiet and, in the process, added Donald Ray to his stable of indebted city officials. After Donald Ray got out of jail, he took his frustrations out on Cheryl, leaving her brain-damaged. Then Cheryl shot her father with his own gun. Cullan made that case go away too."

"How does a brain-damaged twelve year old kill her father?"

"I don't think Cheryl shot her father. I think Amy did, and Cullan pinned it on Cheryl because nothing would happen to her. He made a long-term investment in Amy, and was collecting—again—when he told her to get Blues's file."

"Maybe Amy decided her account was already paid in full," Rachel said.

"More likely that she decided to cancel the debt."

Rachel said, "The newspaper reported it as an accidental shooting, a tragic accident. The story says that Donald Ray had just cleaned the gun and set it down for a moment. The wife said Cheryl thought it was a toy and was playing with it when the gun went off accidentally. Everybody said how sad, and that was it. What now?''

"Harry Ryman is doing a ballistics check to see if Donald Ray and Cullan were killed with the same gun.''

"Where's Amy?''

"Blues is baby-sitting her—from a distance. As soon as I hear from Harry, I'm going to go see Amy.''

"Why not just send the cops to pick her up?''

Mason shrugged. "They already arrested the wrong person once. I'd like to be sure this time.''

It was Rachel's turn to smile. "You're better than I thought for someone with the wrong chromosomes. Keep me posted,'' she added before kissing him lightly on the cheek in the best tradition of sisters everywhere.

Harry called shortly after six o'clock. "You were right,'' he told Mason. "But there's more there than even you thought.''

Mason listened as Harry outlined what he had found. "How do you want to play this?'' Harry asked him.

"Carefully. She's the last witness.''

Fifteen minutes later, Mason turned onto Amy's street. It was a neighborhood where garages were used for storage or spare bedrooms and people parked on the street. Every car had been plowed in, sandwiched between a three-foot snow wall and the curb. Some people had dug out, and others had simply gone back to bed until spring.

Mason slowly prowled down the block. Amy's house was the third one in from the corner. It was dark. There was no car parked in the driveway or on the street in front of the house. Nor was Blues anywhere in sight. He wasn't parked on the street or around the corner, and he wasn't hiding behind a shrub next to Amy's front porch.

Mason opened his cell phone and realized it was off. He turned it on and saw the digital readout informing him that he'd missed a call. He punched in the code for his voice mail. The message was from Blues. Amy was running.

Chapter
Thirty-seven

Mason banged his fists on the steering wheel, nearly sending the Jeep into a figure eight spin before he pulled it back to the center of Amy's street. He drove out of her neighborhood, parked in front of a Circle K convenience store, and dialed Blues's cell phone certain that this time Blues wanted to be found.

"Where the hell have you been?" Blues demanded.

"Don't turn codependent on me," Mason snapped. "What happened?"

"I lost her."

Mason said, "I hope the story is better than the ending."

"About an hour ago, Amy started turning out the lights in her house. A little while later, she started loading suitcases into the trunk of her car. She drives a black Honda, probably a couple of years old."

"What? You were hiding in the garage?" Mason asked.

"No, boy genius. I was hiding in my car at the back of

a driveway across the street. Amy's house has a detached garage. I had a clear shot.''

''You don't think she noticed you sitting in her neighbor's driveway?''

''It's like this,'' Blues said. ''The driveway had been plowed down to the concrete. That meant the people who lived there used a service. Newspapers from the last three days were lying on the driveway. That meant those people were out of town. The driveway curves around to a side entrance garage that is blocked off by tall evergreens. That meant I could see Amy but she couldn't see me. I waited until it got dark and drove up with my lights off. She never saw me.''

''You are too good for words and you are my hero. So how did you lose her?''

''I was following her from a distance, about half a block, with a few cars in between us. I was in an intersection when one of the cars in front of me stopped suddenly and we had a chain-reaction collision. My new truck got sandwiched, and then I got T-boned by a car coming through the intersection.''

''Are you all right?'' Mason asked.

''I'm all right but we're fucked. Amy's in the wind, man.''

Mason had brought Rachel's newspaper clippings with him. He fanned out the articles on the passenger seat, looking for the one he'd scanned a few hours ago without paying any real attention to it.

''Maybe not,'' he told Blues. ''I'll call you later.''

The Jeep's heater couldn't keep up with the cold, and Mason's breath crystallized and evaporated in quick, gray puffs as he found the article he was looking for. It was a human-interest piece on Memorial Day observances that featured a picture of Amy and Cheryl visiting their parents' graves at Forest Park Cemetery. The accompanying story recounted that Cheryl had suffered brain damage in a fall at home; that their father had been killed in an accidental shooting; and that their mother had passed away a short time later.

Amy had been quoted as saying that they always visited their parents' graves on Memorial Day. She had added that they also visited before going away for a long trip in keeping with a tradition started by Cheryl's guardian, Jack Cullan.

Mason couldn't imagine Cullan as a guardian of anything except a junkyard where he dumped people after he had used them up like rusted-out, stripped-down cars sitting up on blocks, their guts scattered to the four corners. He also couldn't picture Cullan taking the time to honor the dead, with the obvious exception of Tom Pendergast. Mason hoped that Amy had kept alive Cullan's curious tradition of visiting the dead before hitting the road.

A black wrought-iron gate normally barred access to Forest Park Cemetery after dark, according to the sign Mason saw mounted on the gate as it hung open, tapping against a stone wall with each gust of wind. He pulled up to the entrance, his headlights shooting bright streamers into the cemetery that spread out like buckshot before dropping harmlessly in the distant darkness. The entrance into the cemetery was wide enough for two cars. Mason parked the Jeep squarely in the middle, hoping to make it impossible for another car to pass on either side.

He found a padlock hanging from a chain looped through the gate. The lock had been smashed until it had given way. Though the lock was tarnished from years of exposure, it bore fresh scratches and dents, evidence of the pounding it had absorbed before yielding. There were also fresh scrapes on the rails of the gate, as if the assailant hadn't been able to stop after simply breaking the lock.

Mason found a woman's white cotton glove lying in the

snow at the foot of the gate, stained with fresh blood. He got the message. Whoever had opened the gate was out of control, and anyone that got in the way was going to take a beating.

The main road through the cemetery had been scraped, leaving a bottom layer of packed snow and ice harder than the underlying asphalt. Mason stayed on foot, following tire tracks illuminated only by the moon. Snow had drifted against many of the tombstones, all but burying them. Some heirs and mourners had erected taller monuments to the deceased, capped by crosses that reached through the snow toward heaven.

Mason's footsteps slapped against the packed snow, a hollow sound in a silent theater, his shadow a poor accompaniment to a night owl passing overhead, its moonlit silhouette leading Mason deeper into the cemetery. A rasping, grating, fractious noise drew Mason off the main road along a winding path among the dead, until he crested a small rise and looked down on a pair of graves.

Amy White was bent over one of the headstones, her back to Mason, flailing at it with a hammer, cursing the rock, the ground, and the bones beneath. Her car was stuck nose down in the snow on an embankment opposite where Mason stood, its engine running, headlights glowing beneath the snow. A woman he assumed was Cheryl lay nearby on her back, making angel wings in the snow with her arms.

"Amy," Mason called to her.

Amy wheeled around, her face twisted with exhumed rage, her movement revealing Donald Ray White's name engraved on the stone. Her cold skin was paler than the moon, colored only by flecks of blood at the corners of her mouth.

Amy raised the hammer above her head as if to throw it at Mason, then spun back to her mad work, striking another blow against her dead father. The head of the hammer flew off, knifing into the snow as the handle shattered, spearing her hand with a jagged splinter. She clamped the splinter with her teeth, yanked it from her fleshy palm, and spat it out.

"I knew it would be you!" she screamed.

Mason walked down the hill toward Amy, keeping his hands in plain view in an effort to calm her down. "How could you know it would be me?"

Amy gulped air and wiped her bloody hand against her jeans. "That day in the parking garage, when I asked for your help—I knew you wouldn't do it. I knew you thought I was just Billy Sunshine's toady. That I just wanted to protect his precious goddamn career."

"You're right," he told her. "That is what I thought. But I was wrong, wasn't I? You wanted me to find *your* file, not the mayor's."

Amy heaved, gradually catching her breath, forcing her madness back into a genie's bottle. "If you had told me where the mayor's file was, I would have found mine," she said. "Then everything would have been fine, except I knew you wouldn't do it. I knew you wouldn't let it rest until you found out."

"Until I found out that you killed your father, not Cheryl; that you used the same gun to kill Jack Cullan."

Amy threw her head back. "How did you know about the gun?"

"You told me that Cullan had wanted Blues's liquor license brought to him on the Friday night he and Blues had argued at the bar, but that you put him off until Monday. Howard Trimble told me that he gave you the file that same night. Yet you didn't give the file to Cullan, and I couldn't figure out why. Then Trimble told me what your father had done to Cheryl, how your mother had hired Cullan to defend your father and then to defend your sister.''

''My father was a hell-born bastard that deserved to die!''

''That's what a jury would have said, Amy. Especially since the police reports showed that you shot him in self-defense. The cops found a gun in your father's hand. Your mother said that he'd fired a shot and threatened to kill all of you. Her mistake was calling Jack Cullan before she called the police.''

Amy slumped to the ground, her back against her father's tombstone. ''I don't remember very much after I shot him. My mother and I were screaming. We didn't know what to do.''

''Cullan must have convinced your mother that the only way to save you was to blame Cheryl since she would never be prosecuted. Cullan had the juice to make everyone look the other way. Your mother even got to keep the guns. Instead of a fee, Cullan got you, just like a future draft choice.''

''Jack Cullan was as rotten as my father. When he called me that night, I did what he told me, but I couldn't stand it anymore. I couldn't stand that he was going to ruin some-one else. I had found the gun in my mother's things when she died. I took it with me to Jack's house. I was going to make him stop.''

''What did Cullan say?''

Amy pawed the snow at her sides as her face slackened into a dull, exhausted gaze. ''He laughed at me and told me to give him the file. I took the gun out and he kept laughing, so I shot him. Then I turned off the heat, opened the windows, and went home.''

Mason studied her, searched her suddenly detached face for a hint of meaning. She leaned against her father's headstone, reaching idly toward her mother's to dust the snow from the channels of her mother's engraved name.

"What did you do with the gun?"

Amy stood, brushed the snow from her jeans, and gave Mason a sly look. "I threw it into the Missouri River on New Year's Eve. By the way, you're quite the swimmer," she added.

Mason flashed back to New Year's Eve. He remembered seeing Amy in the mayor's entourage just before Beth found him at the back of the Dream Casino. In the video Ed Fiora had shown him, Beth had left him on the prow of the boat. The next thing he'd seen was the flash from a gun. Though the shooter's face was obscured, he and Fiora had assumed that the shooter had been Beth.

"If it makes you feel any better, you didn't miss."

"Actually, that makes me feel worse. I didn't know what to do about you. I just knew I couldn't let you find out about me. I saw you and Beth Harrell go outside and I took a chance. You should have bled to death and drowned."

"Sorry to disappoint you," Mason said.

"That's all right," she answered as she reached into her coat pocket, pulled out a gun. "I get a second chance."

"Your father's other gun," Mason said. "The one you used to kill Shirley Parker. Harry Ryman matched the ballistics reports. I told Carl Zimmerman where Cullan's files were, and he told you. You knew about the tunnel to Pendergast's office from when you worked at the mayor's campaign headquarters on the other side of the alley behind the barbershop."

"Jack even gave me the tour," she said.

"You ran into Shirley in the tunnel and killed her."

"Kind of makes it your fault," Amy said.

"Except I didn't pull the trigger. You did."

"Shirley was hysterical. She came at me with a pair of scissors."

Mason shook his head. "Self-defense would have worked when you were fifteen. That story won't sell. There were no scissors where you left Shirley's body. You got your file and part of the mayor's, but you left enough behind to convict him. Why?"

"I just took the parts about me."

"Carl Zimmerman and James Toland were late to the party. They stole the files they wanted and booby-trapped the rest. Did you know about that?"

"No," she said. "I would have helped them if I had known."

"Blaming all this on dear old Dad won't work anymore, Amy. Killing me won't save you. Your car is stuck in the snow. You'll have to leave my body on your parents' graves. That's a pretty big clue. And your sister is an eyewitness. Are you going to kill her too?"

"Amy, I wanna go home," Cheryl said. "I'm cold."

Cheryl had abandoned her game of making snow angels and was standing only a few feet from Amy's side. She spoke with a thick-tongued child's singsong whine. Though she was nearly thirty, her mind was trapped in those last moments when she'd been an innocent child, before her father had beaten her future out of her. Her labored speech was a lasting reminder.

"In a minute, Cheryl," Amy said, keeping her eyes and gun firmly on Mason.

"Now," Cheryl said. "I wanna go now!" Cheryl stomped her feet and hammered her sides with her fists.

"In a minute, I told you," Amy snapped.

Cheryl began to cry, softly at first, then building to a wail that convulsed her. "Now!" she bawled. "Right now!"

Cheryl ran toward Amy like a child grabbing for her

mother. Mason bolted at Amy in the same instant, knocking the gun from her hand as the three of them collided. Mason and Amy rolled into the headstones, with Amy on top of him howling and scratching his face. He gripped her wrists, and she crashed her forehead into his nose. Mason felt the cartilage crumble and tasted the blood that ran into his mouth. He pulled her toward him, cocked his arms like springs, and threw her off of him.

A shot rang out, stopping Amy for an instant in midflight, before she tumbled to the ground at Mason's side. Cheryl sat on the snow, the gun in her lap.

"I just wanna go home," she said softly.

Chapter
Thirty-eight

Mason always found April a soothing month. Its cool breezes and sun-painted skies made promises the rest of the year could never keep. Though the life cycle continued unaltered, April convinced his soul that life had an edge over death.

Mason thought about that perpetual scorecard as he stood at the foot of Amy White's grave, the sun warming his neck without penetrating to the chilled memories he carried of the past winter.

Patrick Ortiz had ruled that Amy White's death was accidental. It had been his first official act after Leonard Campbell had resigned and he was appointed to serve out Campbell's term as prosecuting attorney. Campbell had gone on the offensive, quitting and denying any wrongdoing before he was indicted.

"What happens to Cheryl White?" Mason had asked Ortiz.

"She's a ward of the state for now, but Howard Trimble has started adoption proceedings. What about you? I hear that Campbell tried to hire you."

Mason had laughed. "I took a pass. He and the mayor have been leaving me messages every day. I hear that Donovan Jenkins made a deal for immunity with the U.S. attorney that will put the mayor away."

"So why not defend one of them?"

"I'm too close to what happened. I'll probably be a witness."

Mason hadn't told Ortiz that he was waiting for his own visit from the Feds. Galaxy Gaming Company had bought the Dream Casino and renamed it the Shooting Star. Mason figured it was just a matter of time before some Galaxy employee found the tape recording he was certain Fiora had made of Mason conspiring to gain Blues's release. He figured that Galaxy would either turn him in or book a favor. He couldn't decide which alternative he dreaded more—the visit from the Feds or the visit from Galaxy.

Beth Harrell had visited him first. He was studying notes he had written on his dry-erase board about his newest case. Mason had agreed to defend a professional wrestler who'd been indicted for involuntary manslaughter when he'd killed his archrival during a match.

"From the ridiculous to the sublime," Beth had said from the open doorway.

Mason had looked up and pointed to the board. "My case or your life?"

"Fair question," Beth had said. "I suppose an explanation is in order."

"No. I'd say it's out of order," Mason had replied. "You don't owe me an explanation. You just need to quit blaming your weaknesses on your past and move on. You may be kinky or just fucked up. I don't know which and it doesn't matter.''

Mason cringed inwardly at his coldness toward Beth, but shook it off with the realization that it was the only way he could break from her. She had a toxic allure that he couldn't risk.

"Meaning you don't care?"

"Meaning it doesn't matter. I can't help you either way."

Mason had picked up the wrestler's file and started reading. When he looked up a moment later, Beth had gone.

That had been a month ago when winter was just releasing its grip. Mason bent down and pulled a dandelion from the sod covering Amy's grave. When he stood up, he saw Harry Ryman walking toward him.

"Blues said I might find you here," Harry told him.

"Yeah," Mason said. "I just thought I'd stop by and pull the weeds. What's up?"

"The chief wants to know if I'm coming back to work." Harry had declined a commendation for solving the murders of Jack Cullan and Shirley Parker, and had been using up his accumulated vacation and sick leave. "There's a lot of outside pressure on him to bring me back, and a lot of inside pressure the other way."

"What are you going to do?"

"Carl was six months shy of a full pension. The department lets you buy out the time so you can retire, and still collect your full pension. I told the chief if he'd let me buy out Carl's time, I'd retire. What do you think?"

"I think we're both pulling weeds," Mason told him. "Maybe that's the best we can do."

Harry looked out over the acres of grave sites. "I suppose so," he said.

"Listen, I'm on my way to a rugby game. You should

come along. I promised Rachel I'd take her to a game. You can keep her company while I get beat up.''

''Sounds great,'' Harry said. ''I'll pick up Claire and meet you at the game.''

Mason thought about Amy's father and his own father, whom he scarcely remembered, as Harry ambled away. Mason had pictures of his father, but little else. Jonathan Mason had been a tall, sturdily built man who his aunt Claire said had an easy laugh.

He couldn't remember the scrape of his father's unshaved cheek against his own. He couldn't summon his father's smell after he'd worked in the yard on a dusty, hot afternoon, nor after he'd slapped cologne on his neck on Saturday night. He couldn't remember the view from atop his father's shoulders. He had never caught a ball his father had thrown, nor measured his own strength against the man who'd given him life. Mason couldn't repeat the stories his father must have read to him. Nor could he conjure the fear he must have felt at his father's raised voice, or the comfort he surely had found in its softer tones. Mason examined his hands, searching without success for the memory of his father's touch.

There were times when Mason would have killed for memories of his father, though he knew the depth of his longing was metaphorical. Amy White's memories of her father had made the metaphor murderous.

Mason bent down to pull another young dandelion. Casting it aside, he placed a small rock on Amy's tombstone in the Jewish tradition of remembering the dead, certain that no one else would remember Amy White.

For a sneak preview
of Joel Goldman's next thriller
Coming from Pinnacle in 2004—
just turn the page

Chapter One

Ted Phillips, the Channel 6 cameraman, watched Earl Luke Fisher sit cross-legged on the sidewalk answering Sherri Thomas's questions. He listened on his headphones, filming Sherri's and Earl Luke's "live from the street" duet on the ten o'clock news.

Earl Luke was a homeless panhandler still prospecting for donations on a hot night in a deserted downtown. Sherri was a Channel 6 television news reporter filling her slot on a slow-news Labor Day. They were both desperate optimists, Phillips thought. Hands outstretched—his for money, hers for ratings.

Locked into his camera and headgear, Phillips didn't hear the window shatter eight stories above or a woman scream as she jackknifed through the glass. Earl Luke saw it happen, and popped his toothless mouth open as if he'd just seen a naked Madonna.

Phillips swung his camera in a quick arc from Earl Luke

to Sherri's raised hemline. Not slowing for an instant as he cleared her breathtaking chest, not pausing at her upturned slack-jawed face, not stopping until he caught the falling woman in his lens, pinwheeling in a fatal tumble. Finally stopping when she pancaked onto the pavement, one side of her head flattened like a splintered melon.

"Hold the shot," Phillips said to himself, keeping the camera on the woman's body. "Take it back," he said, satisfied that he'd preserved the moment of her death.

Phillips aimed his camera at the broken window, lighting the way with its built-in lamp, zooming in until he had a tight shot of the ragged outline left by the remaining glass. A shadow flickered in the window frame, or so he thought. He blinked, uncertain of what he'd seen, but confident that the camera had a steadier eye than he did.

Phillips put his camera down, wiping away flecks of blood that had hung in the air like ruby raindrops before chasing the dead woman to the ground. Earl Luke was gone. Sherri was panting, pounding Phillips on the arm, and shouting.

"Son of a bitch! Tell me you got that, Ted! Son of a fucking bitch! If you got that, we're golden!"

"And live on the air," he reminded her.

Lou Mason rewound the tape of the dead woman's plunge and replayed it for the tenth time, forcing himself to focus on the TV screen sitting next to the dry-erase board in his office.

"Too bad you can't ask Dr. Gina one last question," Micky Shanahan said as he came in and sat down on the sofa across the room from the TV.

"Like who shoved her through that window?" Mason asked.

"For starters. Better yet, tell me how she got such a cushy gig giving advice for the lovelorn and sleep-deprived."

"Sleep-deprived?" Mason asked.

"Yeah. You know, I'm deprived of sleeping with my good-looking neighbor even though my wife doesn't understand me."

"Her cushy gig was the highest-rated radio program in town and one of the biggest in national syndication," Mason said.

Micky picked up a hardcover book on Mason's coffee table—*The Way You Do the Things You Do* by Dr. Gina Davenport. "Best-seller?" he asked.

"*New York Times* best-seller," Mason said. "Twenty-six weeks on the list. Same for the audio version. Psychotherapy the easy way. People loved her."

"Not everybody," Micky said. "Not whoever kicked her ass out the window. You gonna take the case?"

"There's no case yet. Dr. Gina's office and the radio station are both in the Cable Depot Building in the garment district downtown. Arthur and Carol Hackett own the radio station and the building. They want me to represent their daughter if she's charged with the murder."

"Who's the daughter?"

The tape ended with Sherri Thomas covering her mouth, realizing that her ecstatic outburst had been broadcast throughout Channel 6's two-state viewing area. Mason punched rewind on the remote control.

"She was a patient of Dr. Gina's until somebody killed the doctor. Her name is Jordan Hackett. She's a twenty-one-year-old head case. The cops interviewed her, took fingerprints, hair samples, and fiber samples. Her parents waited to call a lawyer until the cops were through. Said they didn't want to treat her like a criminal."

"Good thinking. If she's not a criminal, why are the cops

checking her out and why are her parents scared she'll be charged with murder?''

Mason pulled a bottle of water from the small refrigerator beneath the bay window that looked out on the street from his second-story digs above Blues on Broadway, taking a quick pulse of the traffic as he drank. Broadway hummed with people heading home, back in the groove after a three-day weekend.

Yesterday was Labor Day and most people hadn't worked, but Sherri Thomas and her cameraman put in a full day. Earl Luke Fisher never worked or never stopped, depending on your view of panhandling. Gina Davenport was in her office at 10:00 P.M., probably catching up. Her killer worked overtime. It had been some holiday, Mason thought to himself.

''Don't forget which side we're on, Mickey. She's not a criminal unless she's convicted,'' Mason said.

''Even if she did it?''

It was an argument he and Mickey had been having regularly since Mickey started working for Mason. Mickey claimed that public relations was his true destiny, and that he was only working for Mason until he got the gig he really wanted working on the big political campaigns. Spin was everything for Mickey, who could shape an issue for any audience, except for Mason's criminal-defense clients. Mickey had to know they were innocent. Mason accepted that he only had to make the state prove they were guilty.

''It's not that simple, Mickey, even if she killed Gina Davenport. Jordan Hackett could be guilty of first- or second-degree murder, voluntary or involuntary manslaughter, or innocent by reason of insanity. Or, she may have killed Dr. Gina in self-defense. Our job is to make the state do its job and prove she's a criminal. Otherwise, no one is safe, especially the innocent.''

"I hear you, but working the angles in a PR campaign is a lot cleaner than massaging a murder."

"You need to bring your nothing-is-black-and-white-when-you-spin-it-right morality to criminal-defense work."

Mickey chuckled. "You're the best spinmeister I've seen, boss, but you haven't answered my question. Why do the cops want Jordan Hackett?"

"And you're getting better at cross-examination, Mickey. I met with her parents this afternoon. They said that Joslyn didn't do it. They think the police are checking out all of Dr. Gina's patients. I'll know more after I talk with Joslyn tomorrow."

"How did they get the videotape? Did the cops hand them out as party favors to the suspects?"

"The Hacketts are plugged into the local media. They arranged for me to pick up the tape from Channel 6."

"I read in the paper that Samantha Greer is the lead homicide detective on the case. You guys still dancing between the sheets?"

Mason shook his head, more at Mickey than the question. "Not for a while. She told me she's not a car battery I can jump-start whenever I feel too lonely for another night alone."

"That in Dr. Gina's book?"

"Page 210, under bad analogies used to answer stupid questions," Mason said.

Mason fast-forwarded the videotape to the moment when the cameraman retraced Dr. Gina's flight back to the window. He used the freeze-frame function of his VCR to break down that segment frame by frame so he could study each image.

"You see anything unusual in the window?" Mason asked Mickey.

"What's to see?" Mickey asked. "It's dark, the picture is fuzzy. I can barely tell it's a window."

Mason said, "Maybe you're right. When he gave me the tape, the cameraman told me he thought he saw a shadow, like someone standing close enough to look out the window without being seen."

"The killer?" Mickey asked.

"Or a witness."

"Why was Dr. Gina treating Jordan Hackett?" Mickey asked.

Mason turned off the tape. "Her parents said she had a problem with anger management. When we got past the shrink-speak, they told me that Jordan is too violent to live at home."

"Swell. Where does she live?"

"Safe House. It's a residential facility for teenagers and young adults with emotional problems."

"So there's no case yet, but there's gonna be a case. Are you gonna take it now or when it gets ripe?"

"You want to get paid this week?" Mason asked.

"That I do, boss," Mickey said as he got up from the sofa. "Hey, doesn't Centurion Johnson own Safe House?"

Mason nodded. Centurion gave up a promising career as a drug and thug entrepreneur for the not-for-profit world of social services. Harry busted him a few times and sent him to jail for a long stretch. Soon as he got out, he was back in the game until Blues helped him find religion."

Mickey said, "I'll bet that was a painful conversion."

Mason nodded as he opened the dry-erase board on the wall and began—as he always began—by writing down what he knew and what he had to learn to keep Jordan Hackett off of death row. He wrote Gina Davenport's name, circled it, and labeled her *victim.*

Moving from left to right, Mason drew a line and wrote

Jordan Hackett's name, giving her a casting list of roles: *patient, witness, killer*. In the upper right-hand corner, he drew a circle around Centurion Johnson's name and labeled it *trouble*—then added a capital *T*.

Returning to Gina Davenport, he drew a vertical line straight down, capping it with a horizontal bar, like a family tree. He labeled the next branch *winners and losers*. That's where he would find the killer.

Feel the Seduction of Pinnacle Horror

__**The Vampire Memoirs**
by Mara McCunniff   0-7860-1124-6 $5.99US/$7.99CAN
& Traci Briery

__**The Stake**
by Richard Laymon   0-7860-1095-9 $5.99US/$7.99CAN

__**Blood of My Blood: The Vampire Legacy**
by Karen E. Taylor   0-7860-1153-X $5.99US/$7.99CAN
